Illusion of the Heart

Loretta Heard

PublishAmerica
Baltimore

ISBN: 1-4241-1709-7
PUBLISHED BY PUBLISHAMERICA, LLLP
www.publishamerica.com
Baltimore

Printed in the United States of America

This book is dedicated to the memory of my deceased father,
Deacon Lessie Heard

Dedicated to my deceased friend Bruce
and loving cousin Lovey.
I miss you all very much. Rest in the Lord.

Acknowledgments

First, I want to thank God for being in my life; with Him all things are possible.

Mom, the depths of your love is infinite. Thank you for loving me so much. Your prayers, faith, believing in me, mostly keeping me strong in faith.

Courtney, I thank God for blessing me with a son like you. I love you both very much.

Special thank you to Colleen Wilson. You're the best editor in the world. You've been a ray of sunshine in my life, a blessing from on high. I Thank God for blessing me with a true believer of his word. You're beautiful people and I'm truly blessed to have you as my editor and friend.

Heartfelt gratitude to my family and friends for all your support and inspiration.

God is good all the time! He blesses us with so much. I can do all things through Christ who strengthens me.
Philippians 4:13

Love Me Now

Love me now while I am near
Life is a vapor it vanishes away.
Here today, gone so soon.
Tell me all you want to say
Today is the day.
Love me now while I am near
Tell me that you love me while I'm still here.

Loretta Heard

Beloved—let us love one another for love is of God.   (1 John 4:7)

Set me as a seal upon your heart
As a seal upon your arm
For love is as strong as death.

Song of Solomon 8:6

Part One

I Never Meant to Make You Cry

"Code Blue, Code Blue!" How I remember these words so clearly in my mind. A waiting room full of hope turned into a moment of disbelief. The doctor approached my family with the most shocking words I had ever experienced. "We lost him; he's no longer breathing." I sat there unable to comprehend the words that came through his mouth. I was numb at the words that I heard, and didn't want to believe that my father was dead. Gone, finished, never to speak again. I was devastated. The core, the rock that held our family together was now a missing link.

Robin was the second of five siblings. She knew that the task ahead would be very difficult. How would she mirror all that her father stood for? For she knew she'd be the one to fill his shoes. Robin knew that she had to hide her emotions, bury them deep within to hold the family together. Holding back tears, she embraced her mom who let out a loud scream which could be heard through the closed doors. Robin held her mom tight, felt her trembling body, and knew that there was nothing she could say or do to take away the pain. Robin, tried so hard to keep her faith in God, knowing this was one of the values taught and instilled in her by her parents. She fought a feeling of despair, wondering why? Why would God allow so much pain? Why would he take away the one man whom she loved in the entire world? Why is my Daddy gone, she wondered.

Westchester

September 4th—six years ago to the day. Robin reached over to turn off the alarm clock to start her workday. The anniversary of her dad's death was the first thing on her mind. She held her stomach, feeling the pain as if it were yesterday, so vividly in her mind she could recall that day in the hospital waiting room when she heard those words, "He's gone."

She made her way to the bathroom with tears rolling down her face. *I'm not going to be sad today—this is the day that the Lord has made. I'm to rejoice and be glad in it.* But oh, how she longed to just hear her daddy's voice! She pulled herself together, washed her face, looked at herself in the mirror and decided that this day was going to be a happy not sad day. *I'm going to think on the good times we had with Dad, and rejoice in that.* Off to work she went.

Robin pulled into the parking lot; she arrived at the same time her girl Raine did. Robin, reading the expression on her girlfriend's face, knew how much they both hated their jobs at the factory.

"Twelve long hours," Raine said. "I don't feel like this today."

Robin, feeling it, too, said to herself, *It's 4:00 in the morning; even the birds aren't out of bed. I don't feel like doing this either.*

Raine knew from the expression on Robin's face that there was something wrong, something other than coming to work. Raine was a close friend, one who didn't hold back on what she felt. She was tough on the exterior, but soft on the inside.

"Are you all right, Robin?" Raine asked.

"This is going to be one long day," Robin replied.

Robin had always been good at masking her feelings. Deep down inside she knew that was half the reason why she had married Fred. Thinking back on that mistake, she now realized she had tried to escape her hurt over her Dad's death by seeking love—someone to rescue her from the pain. What a nightmare! All her life, from the time she was a little girl, she had longed for a beautiful wedding. God granted her that wish, but to the wrong man. Robin met Fred soon after her Dad's death.

Fred had none of the qualifications Robin sought in a mate, qualities that her dad had displayed. Robin's belief was that a man was supposed to be the head of his house, the provider, the man in every respect of the word. Fred had a sense of humor and made Robin laugh; often she could forget her hurt, the pain which she had buried inside after her dad's death.

Fred was tall, slim and attractive in his own way. Physically there was no attraction on Robin's part, but she saw great potential in Fred. Fred was a jack-of-all-trades and could fix anything with his hands. It was a God-given talent, which came very naturally to him. Robin looked at the talent he possessed and felt the need to nurture him, bring out the best in this person who seemed lost. She needed a sense of purpose, someone to build up; little did she know this was a road to destruction.

When she first laid eyes on Fred, his appearance was that of a homeless person, someone who didn't believe in himself. Fred seemed to keep up with his hygiene, but the rest of him was torn up. He had an innocence about him that made it possible for Robin to look beyond his outward appearance. He made her laugh. Robin, living at home with her mom, felt a great pressure and responsibility in helping her mother maintain the house. Robin felt overwhelmed at times. She felt responsible for her mom; someone had to be strong for her, after all, she was grieving after thirty-five years of marriage.

Everything that could go wrong with the house after dad's death did go wrong. There was a terrible flood in the basement, and Robin, not knowing who to call, knew that she'd better take on the responsibility and get it fixed. This was her very first encounter with Fred. He had been introduced to Robin by an associate. She called him to see if he could fix the problem, and indeed Fred did save the day. Robin began to see Fred on the regular and because of his sense of humor, she took a liking to him. He was her safety net, her way out of a dark and grieving pain.

Robin encouraged Fred to get his appearance in order, to feel good about himself, to be grateful for the gift that God had given him and allow that gift to bless him. They began seeing each other every day. It was a friendship, each one feeding off the other's weakness for their own strengths.

Fred had his own apartment. He was always a gentleman, never stepping out of place with Robin. She could see the excitement in his face whenever she was in his presence. She began to see that he was beginning to feel good about himself. Since Fred lived within a short distance from her job, every day after work Robin stopped by to see him.

Fred was unemployed but looking for a job. He claimed he made his money by using his handyman skills. Robin kept Fred a secret from her girlfriends because she didn't want anyone to know that she was seeing Fred on the regular. Robin even kept Fred from her best friend Ellen, whom she shared her deepest feelings with. Ellen was spiritual-minded and accepted a person for who they were. Robin and Ellen had a special kind of closeness, like sisters so

Robin knew that she had to give in to her secret about Fred and eventually tell Ellen. Robin and Ellen had always talked about family, that special someone, and how they both wanted that for each other. Robin knew that if anyone would understand the relationship she had with Fred it would be Ellen.

Robin had just finished a long twelve-hour shift and was looking forward to paying a visit to Fred. Fred didn't have a phone, so she always dropped in unexpectedly. He often looked forward to her coming. Fred was hilarious; he'd say the craziest thing just to make Robin laugh, and that was the highlight of her day. Often when she visited they'd sit outside the brick apartment building. She wondered why he'd never invite her in, but it wasn't a big deal; she enjoyed his company. This particular day he wasn't outside waiting for her.

Robin figured he'd gotten busy doing a job so she would stop by tomorrow. Instead she decided to pay a visit to Ellen—now would be a good time to tell Ellen about Fred.

"Ellen, he's not anyone I would romantically involve myself with, but we've been spending a lot of time together. Girl, let me know if you need anything fixed because he's good with his hands."

Ellen was glad that Robin had met a new friend who kept her laughing.

Robin, not looking for anyone in a romantic sense, had just been going along day to day praying that one day she'd stumble into Mr. Right. Besides, her long-lost love was Gerald. How much she adored him! Gerald was tall, dark, and handsome and had a smile that could win any woman over. He was quite a catch; the only problem was he was married. Robin knew that he was off-limits, but her heart ached for him. Gerald ached for her, too.

He had a passion for Robin, but also knew that it was wrong to cross the line. There was no denying that when they were in each other's presence they both felt the chemistry. The attraction drew them like a magnet. Robin would keep her distance, because she knew she would be weak when it came to resisting the temptation of Gerald. He had her spellbound. She loved Gerald with every fiber of her being.

Robin imagined what it would be like waking up to him every morning, spending her life with him, her true love. Robin knew that was one dream or fantasy that would never become a reality. Gerald was loyal in every sense of the word, and this made her adore him more. Robin and Gerald had a special bond with one another, but they knew they couldn't do anything about it. They had been intimate one time long before he was married. That one night of passion had nothing to do with the love she felt for him; it was love at first sight. The one night of desire just opened her heart more. Robin never loved any other man the way she felt for Gerald, but Gerald had unsettling issues with the woman he had married and didn't want to inflict any hurt upon Robin. Gerald explained to Robin that he would always love her in his own way, but they could never be more than friends.

Robin's shattered heart knew that she could never ever love anyone as much. She stopped the clock, put love on hold, promising to love this man until her dying day. Robin would never forget the day they said goodbye to love, but hello to a beautiful friendship.

Robin often remembered the times she'd cry on Sydney's shoulders about Gerald. Sydney was twice her age and the father of her child. He wore many hats, not only as the father of her child, but he was like a father, friend and companion to Robin. She was able to be herself with Sydney. Sydney had a deep love for Robin, but he knew that the age difference between them just didn't work.

Sydney was so thankful for their child. Robin's bearing him a son gave him a new lease on life. He was a great father to Larry. They were inseparable. Robin had no worries when it came to Sydney being a responsible father. Larry never wanted for anything.

Sydney was a character. He was very distinguished for his age. If he liked you, he'd do anything in the world for you; if he didn't care for you, he didn't see the sense in wasting either your time or his. Sydney and Robin both accepted each other for who they were and realized their bond was special. Sydney adored Robin, thought she was the prettiest black woman he had ever laid eyes on, but he knew that he could never fill all of her heart's desires of one day having a husband. Still, he felt a need to always care for her.

Robin never took advantage of Sydney's kindness; she loved him in her own way and always looked after him. Larry never wanted for anything; if Sydney could get it for him, he would. Robin felt very blessed to have had a man of his character for her son's father and to be his best friend.

"Raine," she said now, "we've got six hours more to go. Girl, these twelve-hour days are killing me."

Robin knew she'd be going to visit Fred after work. She drove up in front of his apartment building. Since this time Fred wasn't on the steps, she decided to ring the bell. After she'd rung it several times, he finally came to the door. Robin knew from the look on his face that something was different. He had shaved all the hair off his face, had gotten a clean cut. When she first met him, he had looked like a walking cave man. Robin was impressed.

Although the look was impressive, Fred was acting different. He acted as though he had been drinking. His speech was slurred, and he didn't seem so innocent. Robin thought it would be best if she left.

Fred grabbed her arm as she walked to her car and said to her, "Woman, you're the one for me, the one I prayed for, the one who'll marry me."

Robin got into her car and took off in disbelief. She had never seen that bold side of Fred, but then she realized that she kind of liked it. Driving home gave Robin time to collect her thoughts, and she decided not to drop in on Fred unexpectedly again. Turning into her driveway, she knew what coming home meant. She'd have to face her grieving mom, her face filled with sorrow and hurt.

She went inside to get ready for the next long day. Mom seemed so lost, nothing but grief eating at her. As much as Robin hated her long twelve-hour workdays, she would rather be at work than watch the pain in her mom's face.

Raine had a way of sensing when something was on Robin's mind. The next morning on the job she said, "Robin, what's up with you today? You seem so preoccupied in thought."

Robin had been thinking of the day before, and the difference she had seen in Fred. Wondering when she'd see him again, Robin said she just had some things on her mind, nothing to worry about. Robin felt that she wasn't ready to tell Raine about her new friend. Ellen would understand; Raine would say, "Why waste your time on someone who doesn't have a job?"

Raine was sensitive to certain things, but when it came to a man she had no sympathy at all. Raine had a mate, one she had been with for years, and he was good to and for her. She wanted the best for Robin, and nothing less than that. Anything that appeared to have a flaw she had nothing good to say about.

Another long day was over. When it was time to leave work, the place was like a racetrack, with everyone racing to see who would leave the parking lot first. Raine noticed a note on the windshield of Robin's car. Robin grabbed the note, which read, "I'm sorry about yesterday. Please stop by." It was a note from Fred. Trying to hide it from Raine, Robin stuck it in her bag.

Raine said, "What was that, some secret admirer? Girl, don't involve yourself with no one around here; it's not worth your time."

Robin went straight to Fred's apartment. He was sitting on the steps waiting. As always, he greeted her with his humor and said, "It's a big world out there, and I just happened to have you."

Robin looked surprised, because she then realized Fred had taken a liking to her. Fred had made dinner for Robin, and this was the first time he invited her inside. She didn't want to hurt his feelings by declining the dinner invitation so Robin went inside with hesitation. She was not afraid of Fred in any way, but she felt uncomfortable.

The apartment was shabby, none of the décor was modern or even new. It was a very small studio with a couch bed, table and a small black and white TV. Still, although the apartment didn't have much and had very little décor, it was very clean. Robin realized how blessed she was to have so much. She told Fred she'd take a rain check on the dinner, since she'd had a big lunch.

Fred was shy; he had explained to Robin that he had been married before, but was now divorced. He also told her that in his entire life he had only been intimate with two women. Fred was forty-three years old. Robin couldn't believe her ears. In a lot of ways, Fred acted like a scared little boy, almost as if he'd never grown up, a boy in a man's body. He seemed very naive when it came to the opposite sex.

Fred said he came from a family of eight kids. It was obvious he didn't have fatherly guidance. Fred told Robin he had to work for everything. He had nothing given to him by his parents. He told Robin that he had hurt his back on the last job and, due to permanent injuries, he was on disability compensation. This was his only means of support, which wasn't very much a month. He used his talents to pick up odd jobs and make extra money to survive.

Robin accepted Fred for who he was and didn't look down on him for having less. She was glad he was able to open up to her to talk about the things that had happened in his life.

It was Christmas. Three months had passed since Robin and Fred had met. He was so excited, like a kid in a candy store, with Robin helping him decorate the apartment. Robin couldn't believe she was out in such bad weather. There was a blizzard, and she was worried about getting home. Fred asked her to stay the night, otherwise he'd be worried about her safety. The weather advisory flashed on the TV screen every five minutes. Robin had no choice but to stay; she was snowed in for the night. Fred didn't have a phone, and she was worried about letting her mom know she was safe. She didn't want to upset her mom since she had enough to deal with.

Fred suggested he ask his neighbor if it would be all right to use his phone. Robin called home to tell her mom she was staying over with a friend, and that she'd be home first thing in the morning when the roads cleared. Robin then called Sydney to make sure Larry was okay. Sydney took good care of their son, and she never had to worry when Larry was in his care.

Fred only had the foldout couch, and Robin was wondering where she would sleep. Fred was a bit uneasy, and he explained that he had never had a woman stay overnight before, especially one as pretty as Robin. He reassured her that she'd be safe and that she could sleep in the foldout bed; he'd sleep on the floor.

They hung the Christmas lights in the window and stayed up half the night just talking. Robin fell off to sleep and, before she knew it, the sun was shining on her face. When she awoke, Fred was sitting in one spot just staring at her. Robin asked him if something was wrong. He said "You're just so beautiful."

Robin thought, *What a way to start the day!* She smiled. Fred said he hadn't slept at all.

"I looked at you half the night," he said. "I watched you sleep."

The storm was over. Robin made her way home, all the while thinking about how she had stayed the entire night with Fred and he hadn't made one sexual attempt, not even to kiss her or coach her in bed. She thought that made him an exceptional man. It just made her wonder about him.

Robin had a nice weekend. She spent Saturday with Larry and Sydney in the park. Robin knew that Larry loved her, but she couldn't compete with the bond that he and Sydney shared. Larry spent most of his time with his dad.

Sydney had a gangster mentality and taught Larry at a very young age to shoot a gun. Although he did teach him the safety of a gun, Robin felt that her baby was too young to be experienced with a gun. Sydney bought Larry his first hunting rifle at the age of seven. Robin was beside herself. She couldn't understand how Sydney thought bringing their son to the woods would later prevent him from hanging in the streets. Larry had a passion for hunting, just like his dad. He'd rather sleep in the woods than eat when he was hungry.

Larry had always been in church from the time he was a baby. Robin had been reared in the church, and that was one of the values she instilled in her son, just as her parents did with her.

The Family

Since her dad's death, the family had never seemed able to connect when it came to family gatherings. Now it was Christmas time, a time for love, family and togetherness. The absence of Robin's dad put a distance between family members. Robin knew how much it meant to her mom to have everyone together.

She could remember her childhood Christmas years; she had always been grateful for what Santa left under the tree. Dad, always at the head of the table, had blessed the meal which Mom had prepared days in advance. The family had always been so thankful to God for the blessings that were given. Robin, as the second eldest of five children, had tried to make the spirit live on. She was determined to have the family together for Christmas dinner.

Everyone had his or her own agenda and their own unique personalities. Lamont was the eldest and the only boy. He was spoiled by all the girls and had always considered himself to be the black sheep. Lamont had a drug problem, though he never blamed anyone else for the choices he made or the road he chose in life. Still, he was always looking to his family for help, in and out of jail, always making that his second place of dwelling. Somehow Mom felt secure knowing when he was in jail.

Janet, the middle child, was always busy. A real super mom. Her focus was on her job, kids and mate. She was close but kept a safe distance from the family. You could count on Janet; she'd be there when she had to be.

Karen was next to youngest; she carried a few extra pounds and was always self-conscious about her weight. Karen was very outgoing, always a people person...if she liked you. She had a voice for singing. She could sing like an angel, but she lacked self-esteem because of her size, she always found excuses not to be present at family gatherings.

Tutie was the baby; she was wild, young and crazy. Tutie was the family comedienne. She never took anything seriously.

Janet and Robin were the two best cooks. Tutie couldn't boil water. Being the baby, she had never had to cook. Mom had been working when everyone lived at home; she worked the second shift so she'd taught Janet and Robin to fix the meals when she was too tired. Everyone had a job to do around the house because of Mom's work schedule, Dad made sure the girls kept the house in order.

Robin knew if she was to pull this gathering off successfully she'd better contact Janet. Besides, she didn't want to put the burden on her mom; it was too much. It was time for her mother to relax and let the girls do for her.

Robin called all the sisters. "Janet, we're all meeting at Mom's for Christmas dinner. What can you bring?"

Janet said, "My money is tight; if you buy the food, I'll cook it."

Robin knew that was coming. Janet was always penny-pinching. She'd contribute, but it was like pulling pearls out the sea.

"Okay, Janet," Robin said. "I'll bring the money by there tomorrow; you buy what you need."

She called Karen next. "Hi, Karen, I'm planning Christmas dinner for us at Mom's. What can you bring?"

Karen said, "Robin, you know I'm not cooking."

Robin knew that was out of the question. Karen started naming foods she wanted on the menu. "Yeah, don't forget the yellow rice, turkey, ham and green beans…"

Robin thought *What nerve!* "What the hell are you going to bring, since you've got the menu in order?"

Karen said, "I'll bring paper plates and napkins."

Robin didn't get an attitude, because she knew what to expect from Karen, and she figured anything was better than nothing.

She called Tutie last. "Tutie, Christmas dinner is at Mom's. What are you bringing?"

Tutie said, "I'll pick up the soda and alcoholic beverages."

Robin said, "Tutie, do you think you can at least read the directions on the back of a box of cake and figure out how to make it?"

"Robin, don't play me," Tutie said sharply. "What kind of cake? I don't have a cake pan; what should I bake it in?"

By now Robin's nerves were spent; she hung up the phone.

Robin didn't bother to contact Lamont. His being there alone would be a miracle. This was the first Christmas she'd known him not to be in jail. She told Tutie to get in touch with him, let him know what time and tell him to please show up.

Robin said, "Momma, I've set the table, the Christmas music is playing, and everyone will be here soon. Don't worry, there's more than enough food."

Her mom said, "You know your sister Janet; she won't cook enough food to say grace over."

Robin had been slaving over the stove for days. Now she said "Mom, don't worry, everything will be fine, and we'll all be together."

All Mom's kids were there and all the grandkids. She was happy but still there was sadness. Kevin, the oldest grandchild, had four kids; he was Lamont's only child. Janet had three kids, Niki, Deon and Lenna. Karen's two girls were Tracy and Jasmine. Tutie's three were Jackie, Kim and Mike. Robin's son Larry was there, too. Mom loved when all her grandkids were present. She said it made her feel old, being a great-grandma.

Tracy, Karen's eldest daughter, was always a smart-mouth. She and her mom were always at odds because they were so much alike. Tracy and her Aunt Tutie were always at each other. They'd argue over the stupidest thing, and then they'd laugh and make up as if they'd never had words. Robin thought her family was very dysfunctional, but it all boiled down to them loving one another in their own way.

Mom began the grace. "Bow your heads and let's give thanks to God. Thank You, Lord, for my family being together. Amen!"

Mom was sitting at the head of the table, the place where Dad had always sat. She said grace with a tremor in her voice. It was a tradition for the family to always give honor for the food they were so thankful to have.

Everyone was getting their grub on; it was very quiet at the table. Robin sensed that everybody was feeling the same thing, missing Dad. Tutie started talking in her baby language. She was a clown who rubbed Tracy the wrong way; before you knew it Tracy and her Aunt Tutie were arguing. Things were back to normal. Tracy resembled Robin. She didn't lack anything in the self-esteem department; she'd always say "I look good and so does my family."

Organizing dinner had been tough, but Robin managed it. The family was together, everybody under the same roof, and that pleased her mom.

Robin asked, "Who's doing the dishes?"

"Mom, can I take a sweet potato pie?" Karen said. "I'm sick and ready to go home."

After getting her belly full, she decided to get sick. Robin smiled because everyone was acting like old times. Janet, always the first to exit with half the leftovers, everything except the kitchen sink, never wanting to contribute but never left empty-handed, made her exit first with her family.

Everyone had gone home. Robin did last minute touch-ups and asked, "Ma, did you have a good time?"

Her mom said, "Baby, it was wonderful, all my kids being with me, especially Lamont. Thank You, Lord, all went well."

Robin said, "Good night, Ma."

"Good night, Robin," her mother replied, "and thanks. Your Dad would be proud."

Robin wrapped up a plate for Sydney. He was a part of the family, but didn't like gatherings. He'd rather stay in and watch his baseball game. She also put a plate aside for Fred, figuring she'd bring it to him after work tomorrow.

Robin was exhausted and ready to call it a night; she waited for Sydney to pick up Larry. *Let me make sure the door is locked, then I'm down for the count,* she thought. She said her prayers and to bed she went.

Westchester

Mornings came so quick; the phone rang. Robin wondered who could be calling so early, it was 3:00 a.m. It was her friend Ellen.

"Hello, Robin? I'm sorry to call so early. I hope I didn't wake your Mom. My car won't start. Can you give me a ride to work?"

Robin said, "Sure, Ellen, not a problem. I'll be there in the next thirty minutes."

When she got there, Ellen said, "Hey, girl, thanks for picking me up. How are things with your new friend Fred?"

Robin said, "Ellen, I stayed over the night of that bad blizzard, and he did not make one pass at me."

Ellen said, "Girl, is he gay? Is he a man, or what?"

They both laughed. Robin said, "Not that I wanted him to, but it was nice to be in the presence of a gentleman."

When they arrived in the parking lot, Raine pulled up beside them.

Robin whispered to Ellen, "Promise not to say anything to Raine yet about Fred. I want to be the first to tell her."

"I promise," Ellen said.

"What's up? You all ready to do the long day?" Raine said. "I hate this place; there's got to be a better way. These hours are way too long and it's burning my nerves out."

"Maybe we can get lucky and find a rich guy," Ellen laughed sarcastically.

Raine said, "Stop trippin'. It's too damn early; let's just do this."

Raine was tough, but she was a real sweetheart, too. She was very selective in her choice of friends. She liked Robin a lot and would always tell it like it is.

At the end of their shift, Robin said, "Raine, we'll see you in the morning. I'm going to take Ellen on home. I'll give you a buzz in the morning to wake you." They had a buddy system with the phones just in case they overslept.

Ellen said, "Robin, aren't you going to go by to see your friend Fred?"

Robin said, "I figured I'd drop you off first. Don't worry, Ellen, you'll meet him in time."

Ellen said, "Call me in the morning, girl, to wake me up. Have a good time over Fred's. See you tomorrow."

Robin, running behind schedule, arrived at Fred's later than usual. She hated that he didn't have a phone. She didn't know if he would still be waiting on the steps or not. *I'll just ride by and take my chances. I want him to have this plate of food.*

Robin pulled up in front of the building, and sure enough, he was there. He greeted her with a big smile.

"I thought you had forgotten about me. I've waited for you all my life...I mean...an hour!" Fred joked.

Robin explained to him that her girlfriend's car wasn't working, and she'd had to take her home.

"What's wrong with her car? I fix cars, too. You break it, I fix it," Fred said.

Robin said, "I have no idea what's wrong, but I'll be sure to pass that information on to my friend."

Robin thought it was her imagination at first, but she was sure she smelled alcohol. She said, "Fred, have you been drinking?"

Fred answered, "I drank a beer or two to quench my thirst."

Robin asked, "Do you drink every day?"

"No," he said, "Only when I don't have a job to do."

Robin thought no more of it. She handed him the plate of food. He thanked her for thinking of him. Fred was six feet four, like a giant towering over Robin at five feet three. He looked down at her and kissed her on the cheek.

"What was that for?" Robin asked innocently.

"For being so thoughtful, I get this urge when I'm near you," Fred replied.

"What kind of urge, Fred?"

"You know how a man gets when he's near a woman. Like butterflies in my stomach."

Robin just looked at him with a strange look on her face, wondering what Fred was trying to say.

"You make me nervous, sweet thing. What are you doing to me? Can I be with you, Robin? Can I hold you?"

Robin, not knowing how to react to Fred's forwardness, was nervous because he had caught her off guard. She didn't want to hurt his feelings or destroy the friendship. Robin knew she had to choose her words carefully.

"Fred, you're funny. I like you a lot. But we're not ready for what I think you're trying to say to me. Let's take it slow, okay?"

"If that's what you feel, Robin. It's been five years since I've been with a woman, and I got this burning in my soul for you. I think of you every minute. I hear love songs on the radio, and every one reminds me of you. I can't sleep at night, and when I do I dream of you. I sit waiting for hours for you to come by."

Robin was speechless. She didn't know what to say except, "I'd better get going. It's late, and I have to work in the morning."

"Robin, wait. Can I just hold your hand, please?" Fred begged as if his life depended on it. He held her hand and walked her to the car. "Can I see you tomorrow? Please come."

"I'll be here after work, Fred. See you then." Robin took off, leaving dust behind her.

What am I going to do? SShe was thinking. *I like Fred, but I don't want to be intimate with him. He hasn't been with anyone in five years! He might kill me! I need to go talk to Ellen.*

She called Ellen. "Ellen, girl, wake up. I need to talk to you.

"Is everything okay, Robin? Your mom all right?"

"Yeah, girl. I need to talk to you. Fred came on to me today."

"Say what? It's 10:00 o'clock. You should be in bed."

"I know, but I had to talk to somebody. I might give in to him. Ellen, what should I do?"

"Girl, I can't tell you what to do. Follow your heart. We'll talk tomorrow at work."

Robin's phone was ringing.

"Girl, you up?" Robin could just barely hear Raine on the other end of the phone.

"Girl, what time is it?"

"It's almost 3:30. You better make moves or you'll be late."

"Okay, Raine, thanks. I'm up."

Robin had hardly slept a wink all night. She kept thinking how long it had been since she'd been with a man. *Fred's not my type,* she kept telling herself, *but what is my type?* All night she had battled with her mind.

When she got to work, her friend Weesee said, "Robin, girlfriend, you look tired as hell."

Robin said, "What's going on, Weesee?"

Weesee was off the meter. The girl was a trip. She was real about everything, and you'd have to know Weesee to relate to her. She was hilarious, always kept everyone at work laughing. She'd break real-life issues down to you in a way where you'd be like, "She ain't never lied, and that's so true." The girl was deep.

Weesee said, "Robin, girl, I know you ain't had no dick working these long twelve hours. If I had a man all he could do is look, 'cause I'm so damn tired I can fall down. So tell me something…"

Robin was laughing at her, because Weesee was so animated with different facial expressions you couldn't help but laugh. Robin said, "Weesee, girl, I couldn't sleep last night. I had some things on my mind."

Weesee said, "Things on your mind? Shoot, I got things on my damn mind too, like how the hell I can make me some more money; twelve hours just ain't gettin' it for me. I'll tell you what, Robin. If I had me a man, you better damn well believe I wouldn't be working these long hours."

"It's rough!" Robin agreed.

Weesee said, "See, if I were like you, living at home with my mom, I'd have a little change in my pocket. But I got rent, gas and electric, phone, car note and every damn thing looking me in the face like it's my man. I say it like that, 'cause I got to take care of it. What the hell you got on your mind?"

Raine was on the floor laughing. Weesee had that kind of effect on people. Robin said, "Weesee, girl, I just need some sleep."

Weesee said, "You sure do, 'cause you look worn out, like you been working that thang all night. I tell you what, don't bring your ass in the ladies' room at break time, 'cause I got the chair, and I'm going to sit my tired black behind down. You should take your sleepy ass to sleep at night. I'll check you later, Robin."

"Okay, Wees. Do you know where Ellen is working?"

"No, but I'm sure she's around here somewhere trying to save somebody's soul."

Robin said, "Wees, go take your nap. Girl, you too much!"

Robin had to talk to Ellen. "Ellen, girl," she said, "I had to call you last night. I hardly got any sleep, and I'm feeling it. I think I like Fred, and I don't know what to do."

Ellen said, "Robin, girl, I thought I was dreaming when you called. Did you say to me you were thinking about knocking boots with him?"

"You wasn't that sleepy," Robin said. "You got that part. Ellen, I don't know what to do. It worried me so last night. I came to the realization that I really like this man."

Ellen said, "Well, that don't make you sleep with him. Why don't you get to know him better, see if it builds into something? Maybe date. Robin, I'm your best friend, and you've been through a lot since the death of your dad. Give yourself a chance. Love will find you, and you'll know it when it comes. Robin, you deserve the best."

"Ellen, you're right; maybe I'm reading too much into this. Maybe I'm just lonely and like the attention. You know my heart stopped at Gerald. Fred is nothing like him, but it was cute the way he came on to me. Kinda sweet and innocent."

"Get to know him better," Ellen said, "That's all I got to say about it. Innocence can sometimes be scary, 'cause then you have to teach him. Kinda like a baby in the world knowing nothing about life. Do you want a child or a man? Just take your time."

"Ellen you're right. See, that's why I call on you. That why you're my best girl. Do you think I should avoid him, maybe stay away?" Robin asked.

"Follow your heart, Robin. If he makes you laugh and you enjoy him, then capture every minute."

"Thanks, Ellen, just for being you."

Just then Weesee butted in. "Robin, girl, we only got four hours to go. My damn feet hurt, and I'm ready to get the hell out of here. These hours are kickin' my ass, but the money keeps me hanging. Girl, I got to hit a lottery or something."

Robin said, "Wees, I'm feeling it, too. Straight to bed for me when I get home."

Raine said, "I'll see you tomorrow night, girl. Only two more to go. At least we get to sleep in in the morning. I'll see you tomorrow, Robin. Get some sleep."

Robin said, "Okay, Raine, you get some rest, too."

Everybody was racing out to the parking lot, headed in different directions. Robin let out a sigh of relief after her long work day. Her body was telling her to go home and relax, but she had Fred on her mind. She drove by the apartment, and there he was, waiting outside.

Fred said, "Hi, Robin, you came. Listen, about yesterday...I didn't want to frighten you off. I only wanted to tell you how I was feeling. Get out the car; stay with me a while. I promise I won't bite."

Robin said, "Fred, I really can't stay long. I'm exhausted. I just wanted to check and make sure you were okay."

Fred said, "I'm fine now that I've seen you. Why don't you come inside for a while? Maybe get something to eat. Let me cook for you."

"No thanks, Fred. I really need to get moving. Maybe I'll stop back over after my night shift is over on my way home."

"That will be nice. I'll make breakfast for you," Fred said.

"I'll see you later, Fred," Robin said.

She was thinking, *Why did I tell him I'd be there early in the morning after work, when I know I should go home and get some sleep after working all night?* Deep down she knew she wanted to be with him.

When she walked into the house, Robin said, "Ma, how you feeling today? How was your day?" She was glad her mom kept busy with church activities. That kept her mind occupied, and it was good for her to be around people. Her mom and dad had been dedicated to each other. Having been married for thirty-five years, all they had were each other. After Dad died, Mom had to make a new life for herself. Robin had always admired the commitment in her parent's relationship. They had believed in till death did them part, and that was the way it was. Robin longed for that solid commitment, but how could she have that unless she allowed herself a chance to be involved with someone? Robin was feeling as if now that she was getting older she was ready to settle down, build a foundation, and have a solid relationship. *I've got to give myself a chance*, she thought.

On the night shift, Robin asked, "Weesee, you ready to do this long night? I got plenty of sleep."

Weesee said, "I can tell, girl. Your ass ain't dragging like yesterday. I just want to get this over 'cause my lottery number came out last night and my pocket is empty.

Robin said, "Good for you, Weesee. Maybe one day you'll hit big enough to leave this place for good.

Weesee said, "I hope the hell you're right, 'cause I'm ready to be out; it's been too long."

When the night shift was over, the parking lot was like the racetrack, everybody racing to get home.

Robin went by Fred's. It was 5:30 in the morning, still dark out. Again she hated that he didn't have a phone. She rang the bell, and Fred came to the door.

Robin said, "Good morning, Fred."

Fred said, "Good morning, Robin. Come in. I made you breakfast, and I've got the coffee going. I'm all ready for you."

Robin walked inside. Fred had the little table out. The aroma was kickin'. The kitchen was too small for two people to be in. It would have been a tight fit. Robin was impressed, and she loved the attention. She was so exhausted from the long night. She didn't want to hurt Fred's feelings by not eating.

Fred said, "Sit down, Robin. Make yourself comfortable." He went into the kitchen to prepare the food. Robin turned on the TV to catch the early news. Breakfast was nothing fancy, but Robin could tell Fred had put his heart into it. After they finished eating, they watched TV. Fred was very quiet and just sat staring at Robin.

Finally he said, "Robin, did you enjoy your breakfast?"

Robin said, "Yes, it was delicious. Thank you so much. That was nice of you."

"When you care about someone," Fred said, "You do special things."

He got up from the table and came to sit on the small sofa where Robin was sitting. He pushed her back and kissed her. They both got caught up in the moment. Robin didn't resist the kiss. When the kiss ended, Fred was panting like a dog. He took a deep breath and apologized.

"I'm sorry. I just wanted to know what you taste like. I'm never like this with any woman. Please forgive me. I feel butterflies in my stomach."

Robin was shaking. Fred's aggressiveness had caught her by surprise, but she liked it. She liked the feeling it gave her. She hadn't kissed anyone in a long time. Different sensations were going through her body. She wanted more. Before she knew it she blurted out, "Fred, make love to me!"

She stopped and shook her head. "I'm sorry I said that. I must leave. I just got caught up in this kiss, and it's late, it's too early…I don't know what I'm saying. I need to get home."

Fred grabbed her hand. "I want you, Robin," he said, "Let me have you!"

She sent him to the store for condoms. Shaking in her clothes, she was nervous, but not too nervous to remember that they had to practice safe sex. She was thinking, *Is this the right thing to do? Maybe I'll feel different when he comes back.*

Fred must have run to the store, because it seemed all of five minutes before he was back. He seemed just as nervous as she was. His face was sweating. Robin didn't know if it was because he had run to the store or if it was the anticipation of making love. He drew the drapes in the small room, came closer with trembling hands, kissed her and, before she knew it, they were in the heat of passion.

The aftershock of what had just taken place was obvious to both of them. Her hair was wild and all over the place. Her body was drenched with sweat. The sweat of the body heat between the two of them was heavy. The old couch bed was so small there was no air between them.

Immediately she made her way to the bathroom to clean herself up. Reality slapped her in the face and she thought *what did I just do?* Although the sex had given her good feelings, when it was over she felt it was all wrong. She stayed locked in the bathroom for what felt like an eternity, feeling embarrassed and ashamed because she had had selfish motives. The only reason she had given in to temptation was to be satisfied sexually. She had been unable to resist.

How could she face Fred now? What could she say? Could she act as if nothing had happened between them? How was he going to react to her? What now? Robin's head was full of unresolved questions without answers, without reason for her selfishness. What was she going to do with Fred? She had to get her composure intact.

She opened the door slowly. Fred was lying on the tiny couch bed staring straight at the ceiling, eyes fixed, with a wide grin on his face. Robin's first reaction was, *Is he dead?* He was stiff as a corpse with a death look, but a happy death look. Robin called his name.

"Fred! Fred! Are you okay? Are you all right?"

There was no answer at first. She just knew she had killed him. He was dead. She panicked, her palms were beginning to sweat. *What am I going to do? Should I leave him? Do I call Ellen? Wake up, Fred, say something!*

Fred smiled at her. The first words he said were, "Babe, Robin, you're the best! I feel like I died and came back again. I'm a new man, all because of you."

Robin said, "Fred, we need to talk. This shouldn't have happened."

Fred said, "Robin, do you know how long it's been for me? I feel so good right now I can rebuild every house on this street. Girl, you give me energy; you take my breath away. You put a smile on my face. I've never felt like this before. Never, ever. Please stay with me. Make me brand-new again."

Robin said, "Fred, I've got to go. I'm sorry!"

She ran out of the apartment, leaving Fred in what sounded like Heaven for him. Robin was torn with emotions, overly exhausted from work the night before and the work Fred had just performed on her.

She went straight to Ellen's house. Blinded with emotions, she was frantic. *How and why did I allow this to happen?* Robin tortured herself all the way to Ellen's. She began banging on the door.

"Ellen, wake up, wake up!"

It was 11:00 a.m., and Ellen was knocked out from a long night of work. She dragged to the door, and slowly opened it. She saw Robin and said, "What's wrong? Is it your mom? What's so urgent?"

Robin said, "I'm so sorry to wake you, but I just made love to Fred. Girl, get some coffee in you. Wake up, talk to me. What am I going to do now?"

Ellen's eyes popped wide open like she'd drunk a whole pot of coffee. Her eyes got wider than golf balls. She said, "Girl, you did it. What happened, when and where?"

Robin said, "I should have gone home right after work, but I stopped by Fred's. He cooked breakfast and one thing led to another, and it just happened."

Ellen said, "I hope you used some form of protection."

Robin looked insulted. "Give me some credit, of course I did. Ellen, I was thinking solely of myself, getting my kicks off. I just got caught up in the passion, and I found myself helpless wanting this man. Since Gerald, there's been no one, and when he kissed me, all kinds of signals and alarms woke my body up. I was asleep, then I awakened to a sexual encounter and not love. Ellen, I left the apartment speechless, unable to face him or myself."

"Robin, stop torturing yourself," Ellen said. "You're human. You're not made of stone. Look, it's a done deal now. Don't beat yourself up, especially if you enjoyed the feeling it gave you. Look at all the stress you've been under. Your dad's death, caring for your mom, and work. Don't you deserve to let yourself go?"

Robin said, "Ellen, I lost myself in the moment. I don't love him; he's not my type of guy. Don't get me wrong, he makes me laugh, and he's attentive in his own way, but there's a lot missing. He doesn't give me that feeling Gerald gave me. How could I give myself to him when I can't feel like that for him? He doesn't even have a job."

"Girl, relax, okay? Of course he'll never measure up to Gerald. No other man in this lifetime will. You're going to meet others and fall for them, but believe me, every love will be different. One day you'll even find someone to love greater than Gerald. The man you've waited for, for so long. Live for today. What just happened is past now. Get a hold of yourself and keep moving. Enjoy Fred for Fred," Ellen said.

"Ellen, you're right," Robin agreed. "Thank you, girl, for being my sounding board and a good friend. What would I do without you?" She got up to leave. "I'd better let you get back to sleep. We've got one more night to do. We'll talk at work. Oh, and remember, Ellen—please don't say anything to anyone."

"I promise," Ellen said. "See you tonight, girl."

"Love you and thanks," Robin said.

The drive home seemed endless. Robin's mind was a blur. She was mentally and emotionally exhausted. As she pulled into the driveway, she parked the car, put her head on the steering wheel and cried. Warm tears streamed down her face because she was beat. Beat from the pressures of a lifetime trying to pick up where her dad had left off, working a long twelve-hour shift and keeping her family together. She was on overload. Where did she have room for someone else or even her own pleasures? She laid her head down on the steering wheel and slept.

At work, Weesee said, "Robin, girl, what's up with the scarf on your head? Now, you just got a new hairdo last week. I know it's the night shift and all, but see, you can't fool me. That's the kind of scarf you'd wear soon after you been laying up sweating with a man and your hair-do just gone to the dogs. Don't think you can fool me. I know what I'm talking about. Did the nigga have any money? That's all I got to say."

Robin said, "Weesee, it nothing like that at all. I just slept late and didn't have time to do my hair."

Weesee said, "Girl, you need to stop frontin' with me. Been there, done that. All I got to say is, make sure the nigga has got some loot and you got paid. See, there's a lot of dirty dicks out there wanting something for nothing. You make sure you get yours, 'cause I damn sure is gonna get mine. The nigga better have gas and electric money, phone bill or something or he don't get any honey. Got it? No money, no honey!"

"Got it, Weesee," Robin said.

Weesee said, "See, maybe you don't need no money, but Weesee need plenty of money, honey, 'cause Weesee got bills to pay, and a man can't speak my name let alone get between these legs without the Benjamins. Bring it to Weesee, Daddy. I'll call out his name all night as long as he's paying. Without the money, honey, Weesee get funny. "That's why I got to do these long-ass hours. If I had a man, a rich one at that, I'll be damned if you see me here all night long. Hell, I'm ready to sleep right now and we've got five hours to go. It's a trip."

Robin said, "I know, Weesee, it's long. I got plenty of sleep today. Slept like a baby."

"I bet you did." Weesee's eyebrows were raised, suspicious about the way Robin had been acting lately.

Robin said, "What's going on, Raine? You having a good night? We're busy; that helps. How are the boys doing?"

Raine said, "They're doing good. School will be starting soon. I need to make some overtime to get their school clothes."

Robin said, "I hear you, girl; knock yourself out. Do what you gotta do. I've got enough on my plate. I'm so tired these days I can't work it."

With another long work day completed, Robin looked for Ellen. She had been a no-show for work. Robin, feeling guilty, thought that it was because she woke Ellen out of a sound sleep and maybe she had overslept.

Robin said, "Raine, I'll see you later. Have a nice weekend." Robin reached for her cell phone to call Ellen to make sure she was okay.

Ellen picked up on the second ring. "Hello?"

Robin said, "Hey, girl, what happened to you? You didn't make it to work."

"I overslept," Ellen sighed. "I got dressed and was going to come in late, and then the car gave out on me."

"Ellen, I'm sorry," Robin said apologetically. "I shouldn't have come over disturbing you. Why didn't you call for a ride?"

"Robin, really, it's no big deal; that's what friends are for," Ellen said with a smile. "I'm just tired, girl. I needed the night off. When I decided to come in and do six hours, the car was dead. I couldn't see calling you at work."

Robin said, "Listen, do you need to go anywhere? I'm just going home to sleep. You can use my car if you need it. I can stop by on my way home. I'll stop by Fred's to see if he can fix your car. I'm sure he won't charge me much. That's what friends are for. Plus that gives me an excuse to see how he reacts after our encounter together."

Ellen said, "Robin, that's a good idea. I don't need to go anywhere right now. I'm all set. Call me when you get home, Robin. Just enjoy the moment."

Robin rang the bell to Fred's apartment. It was 6:00 in the morning. Fred wouldn't be sitting out this time of the morning waiting for her. It was still dark out. Fred came to the door. He said something, but his speech was slurred, and Robin couldn't understand him.

"Good morning, Fred. Don't I at least get a 'hello'?" Robin could smell the stench of alcohol on his breath. She was trying to decide if she should stay out or go inside.

"Robin, come in out of the rain. I was just about to make coffee."

"Have you been drinking, Fred?" Robin asked emphatically. "Do you have a drinking problem? Maybe I should come back some other time."

Fred grabbed her arm, pushed her against the wall and said to her, "You're not leaving me now. I stayed up all night waiting for you. You come inside, Robin."

Robin jerked her arm away, shocked by his actions. She knew he was drunk now, because of his temperament. "Let me go, Fred! You're hurting me. Let me go!"

She ran to her car. Fred, following her, picked up a two-by-four and shot it through the windshield of her car. He was screaming at her. "You walked into my life, now you want out? I'm not going to let you go. Stay with me, Robin! Come back!"

All the drama awakened the neighbors. Someone called the police. The windshield was shattered and so was Robin.

What had she done? Fred was a madman, out of control, under the influence of alcohol. All she wanted to do was ask him about fixing Ellen's car. Someone had called the police. Robin was a nervous wreck. And to think she had slept with this man. The police asked Robin if she wanted to press charges for the broken windshield.

She said no. She was hysterical; she just wanted to leave. She got into her car and drove off as fast as she could.

Robin went straight to Ellen's house, the wind and rain blowing through her windshield. *How am I going to explain this? Ellen is the only person I can tell. What was wrong with Fred? Why did he react like a crazy person?* Robin didn't want to upset her mom. She didn't want her mom to think she'd been in an accident, so she made up her mind to stay over at Ellen's and get the windshield fixed as soon as possible. Ellen came to the door. Robin was shaking like a leaf, frightened, nervous and shook up by what had just happened.

Robin said, "Ellen, he was like a crazy drunk person. He didn't want me to leave and he threw a piece of wood through my windshield to stop me from going. He scared me to death. Please, I can't go home like this; my mom will worry herself sick. It all happened so fast, without warning."

"Robin, you can't go back there. Stay away from him. What made him react like that?" Ellen asked worriedly.

"I think he'd been drinking, and my sleeping with him has made him obsessive. I'm afraid. Please don't tell anyone," Robin pleaded. "I have to fix the windshield right away. First I should call my mom to tell her I'm staying over with you for the night and I'll be home tomorrow."

Ellen said, "Good idea; call your mom while I get you something to relax you. Girl, you are a wreck."

Robin called her mother. "Mom, listen I'm over at Ellen's. We're working on a project. I'm going to stay overnight here. Call me if you need anything."

Her mom said, "Robin, are you okay? You don't sound too good. Where's Ellen? Is everything all right over there?"

"Mom, I'm fine, just tired from a long night. Ellen and I are going to go car shopping, and I'm just going to stay over and hang out with the girls. Do you mind?" Robin tried to calm her.

Her mom said, "Robin dear, you're young, you should have fun, but you sound…"

Robin cut in on her mom and assured her that she was fine and to call her if she needed anything.

"Is your mom okay? She knew something was wrong, didn't she?" Ellen asked.

"Ellen, I had to lie. My mom knows me. I just don't want her to worry," Robin confessed.

"Why don't you take a long shower, lie down and rest your nerves, and we'll talk when you're rested. You've been up all night and you just had a traumatic experience. If your mom calls, I'll cover for you," Ellen comforted her.

"My head is pounding. I need to lie down. Thanks for being my friend. I'm going upstairs. We'll talk later."

Robin tossed and turned in bed, wondering what she had done to bring the rage out in Fred. She knew that she had to stay away from him because he could fly off the handle at any moment. With her head pounding and eyes red from crying, she finally fell off to sleep.

It was late in the evening when the phone rang; it was Robin's mom. Ellen answered the phone. "Hello?"

Robin's mom said, "Hi, Ellen, this is Mrs. Jacobs. Is Robin there?"

"Hi, Mrs. Jacobs, how are you doing? Robin went to lie down for a nap. If it's important, I can wake her."

"No, baby, let her rest; just give her a message for me please. Tell her a young man named Fred has called several times looking for her."

"I'll give her the message, Mrs. Jacobs. Are you okay? Are you home alone?" Ellen asked.

Mrs. Jacobs said, "I'm fine, Ellen, and the grandkids are with me. You girls have fun and good luck car shopping."

"Thank you, Mrs. Jacobs. I'll give Robin the message as soon as she wakes up. Take care. Talk to you soon."

Robin was all worn out, and her anxiety showed in her face as she made her way into the kitchen, where Ellen was preparing dinner.

Ellen asked, "How did you sleep, Robin? You've been out for hours. Your mom called earlier to say you had several phone calls from Fred."

"Oh, no! What if he said something to my mom? Why is he calling me?

What could he say or want with me?" Robin worried.

"Calm down, Robin. Your mom sounded fine, no different than she normally does. Stop panicking. We have to think about getting your windshield replaced. I called several places while you were asleep to get estimates. In the morning we'll get it fixed like new."

"I don't know what I'd do without you, Ellen. Was my mom okay? Were the kids with her?"

"She's fine, and yes the kids are there so she's not alone. I want you to get a grip, get yourself together. Don't worry; together we'll get through this, but you need to stay away from Fred until things die down."

"I promise, Ellen. I won't go over there again. I'm afraid to."

Robin and Ellen had a nice quiet evening watching movies. The next morning they got Robin's car fixed like new.

The weekend was over, and it was back to the long work week.

Robin was having a problem staying focused. She kept thinking about what had taken place with Fred. Somehow she knew that wouldn't be the end of him. She had never dealt with anyone who had a drinking problem. She wondered if he realized how out of control he was, how different he was when he was drinking.

All day she isolated herself from Raine and Weesee. She kept a low profile. Her excuse was that she wasn't feeling very well. Ellen knew differently. Ellen was worried about her friend staying away from Fred for good.

After work everyone raced for the parking lot. Robin found her car and noticed several notes sticking out of the door. They were from Fred. She said goodbye to everyone. Waiting for Ellen to come out so she could give her a ride home, Robin opened and read the notes. The first one read, "Robin, I'm sorry. Please let me reimburse you for the damages done." She opened the second note, which read, "I never meant to hurt you. Please forgive me, Fred."

Robin took both notes and crumbled them in her hand. Ellen was on her way to the car. Robin didn't tell her about the notes; she kept them to herself. Robin took Ellen home first, and then she went home herself. Robin just wanted a quiet evening to herself. She wanted to erase Fred from her memory. She was home relaxing in her bedroom when the doorbell rang.

Her mom called up the stairs. "Robin, the young man who fixed the flooded basement is here. I believe his name is Ed. Will you come down?"

Robin's hands began to sweat. She couldn't yell down to tell her mom to send him away; her mom would get suspicious. She got dressed, took her time and strolled down the stairs. There was Fred standing in the foyer.

Fred said, "Hi, Robin. Please let me talk to you. I left several notes on your car."

Before Fred could get another word out, Robin interrupted him by saying, "Let's go outside and talk." Once outside, she said, "Fred, you had no right to come here. What do you want from me? What's wrong with you? I don't want my mom knowing about what's happened. She's been through enough."

Fred said, "Robin, I'm sorry; it won't happen again. I had one too many beers. I lost control of myself. Please forgive me. I'll never do anything to hurt you again. Please let me fix this. Give me a second chance."

Robin said, "Fred, second chances rarely come; they are few and far between."

Still, Robin gave in to him. A few years later they were married. Yes, it was the Cinderella wedding, the one she had dreamed of from the time she was a child, but all to the wrong man. Robin learned that second chances can be a very costly. After the wedding vows were exchanged, the truth about Fred came out. Not only did she not know about the drinking binges, but she later learned about his drug addiction. Fred was arrested three years into the marriage and sent to federal prison for selling drugs. Robin saw that as her way out and didn't look back. She divorced Fred, and tried to put the memories and pain behind her. She had a new lease on life.

Be careful who you give your heart to, she thought. Robin realized after years of recovery that she had tried to hide her grief, pretending to love someone when all she did was compromise love to hide hurt. She had never allowed herself time to cry or feel pain when she lost her dad. She hid her sorrows and tears in the laughter that Fred gave her, only to feel those tears later in their marriage.

Westchester

Three years later...

Robin moved on with life, surrounding herself with family and friends. She even built up the strength to let go of her mom. She knew that her dad's shoes could never be filled, and that her mom had to find life all over again for herself.

During the hardship of her marriage to Fred with all its abuse and pain, Robin lost Sydney to lung cancer. She lost her best friend, but she was so grateful to Sydney for rearing their son on the right path.

Larry was now in college, in his sophomore year, and Robin was gaining the years back that she had wasted on Fred. She was happy about her mom's independence. Everyone had their own agenda and was moving on with life.

Robin continued to work long hours. Living at home alone with Larry away was at times lonely, but when she looked back on all the drama with Fred, she appreciated the peace. Robin spent a lot of time with her girlfriend Ellen taking nice vacations. They both felt they worked hard enough to enjoy some of the finer things in life. She kept in touch with Raine, who relocated to Atlanta and never lost contact with Weesee.

Weesee got lucky, met a suave dude with money, and now lived in Virginia. Robin had friends who were dear and close. Once a week, she babysat for her nieces. She hadn't been in the dating world for four years. After the divorce, she focused on herself. She was afraid to put her heart on her sleeve. She kept to herself until she met Oscar O'Neil.

Robin remembered March twelfth as if it were yesterday. That was the day Oscar James O'Neil, otherwise known as OJ, walked into her life. Winters were very cold in Westchester, New York. Larry, while he was at home for spring break, kept reminding his mother to get the furnace cleaned. Robin was so preoccupied with work and classes she had forgotten about Larry's suggestion. March 12th was a cold, cold winter night, and the furnace died suddenly.

Robin felt that she was a marked target for things dying out on her. She had no other option but to call an emergency heating company. She searched the Yellow Pages to see who serviced twenty-four hours. It was 10:00 p.m. There was no way she could sleep in the house; it was like a refrigerator. She phoned S.O.S. Heating Service, which advertised itself as the "on the spot heating company." They told her someone would be out as soon as possible.

Thirty minutes later, Oscar O'Neil was at her door. He was pecan brown, medium height, with a muscular build, clean-cut hair, a thick black mustache, white pearly teeth, and the most beautiful dark brown eyes she'd ever seen. Robin was immediately attracted to him. No one had captured her attention in this way in years. He was very polite in speaking, with a strong, solid voice. He introduced himself as Oscar O'Neil and gave her his personal business card.

She then escorted him to the basement where the problem was.

He assured her that he'd do all he could to get her heat working properly, quickly and efficiently. He began to make conversation about the weather and how cold it was that night. Robin had a portable heater running in the kitchen, the only part of the house that was warm.

As he worked in the basement, OJ explained to Robin that he couldn't get used to the cold weather. He told her he was from Florida and would be returning home within the next three weeks. He told her that he was on the job training and working towards his degree. Robin was impressed knowing he was a long way from home.

"Mr. O'Neil, please forgive my manners. Can I offer you something to drink?" Robin asked.

"No, thank you," OJ said. "Please call me OJ—everyone does."

"OJ, since you're not used to our cold weather, how did you end up coming to Westchester?" Robin queried.

"Ms. Jacobs, I'm working on my degree, and S.O.S. Company offered an eight-week course with the credits I needed to finish."

"Please call me Robin. So you've been here for five weeks? Have you done much? I mean seen much of our little city?"

"As a matter of fact, I haven't to either question. I keep very long hours; by the time my days end it's too late to do anything. I don't really know anyone here in Westchester."

"Where are you staying?" Robin asked.

"I'm downtown at the Holiday Inn. In fact, all the guys who are from out of town taking the course are staying on the same floor of the hotel."

"So you've met a lot of new associates?" Robin asked.

"Not really; everyone has a different schedule. I never see my roommate. Only three weeks left, and then I'm home," OJ replied politely.

"It'll be nice to get home to some warm weather. I imagine you have a wife waiting?" Robin asked inquisitively.

"I'm not married, never been married. Maybe one day," OJ answered.

"I'm sorry. I didn't mean to be nosey."

"It's not a big deal. Are you married?" OJ inquired.

"Actually, I'm divorced," Robin said.

They both made eye contact.

"Looks like the furnace is up and running again. If you turn the thermostat all the way up, Robin, I can hear it kick in and you'll be back to normal."

OJ checked Robin out as she went up the stairs. He knew that the attraction was too strong to leave there without a phone number.

Meanwhile Robin was thinking, *How can I see this man again?* There was something about him that piqued her curiosity. She didn't want to be aggressive and scare him off, but she knew she wanted to see him again.

OJ yelled from the basement. "It just kicked over. She's up and running again."

As he headed up the stairs, Robin greeted him with gratefulness. "Thank you so much, OJ. How much do I owe you?"

"I'll tell you what. If you'll have dinner with me and show me some of Westchester, we can call it even."

Robin hesitated to accept the offer. But knowing she wanted to see this man again, she said, "It's a deal. But with only one condition—you have something to drink with me right now. "

"It's a deal, then. Coffee would be nice." OJ smiled.

"Coffee it is then. How do you take it?" Robin asked.

"Black and sweet, like I like my women. The sweeter the better."

Robin flirted with him, "Black and sweet, huh?"

With a huge smile on her face, she made the coffee. They were out in the kitchen talking for hours. Both were amazed at how much they had in common. They both loved horror movies and most of the same foods. Robin felt very comfortable in OJ's presence.

OJ looked at his watch. "I think I've overstayed my welcome. I'd better get moving. About that dinner...I have your phone number from when you called the company. I'll call you tomorrow after I look at my schedule. Is that okay with you?"

Robin said, "That's fine, OJ, I work long hours so if I'm not at home leave me a number to reach you."

On the back of his business card, OJ wrote the phone number to his personal cell phone, the hotel number and his pager number. He made sure he covered all bases. He definitely wanted to see her again. Robin, thanking him again, walked him to the door.

"I enjoyed our talk, Robin."

"So did I."

"I'll give you a call tomorrow."

"That sounds good. Take care. Good night," Robin said as she waved goodbye.

"Good night, Robin. Stay warm and lock up. Call me if there are any problems."

Robin liked the idea that he was protective. She listened while he stood behind the door until she put the locks on. She watched him as he brushed the snow off the van. He sat in the driveway until the van heated up, then he drove off. Robin watched until the van was out of sight.

Robin completed another long work day. Things were different at work with Raine and Weesee gone, and Ellen had gotten promoted and moved to another building. Robin was taking business classes to complete her degree, which would open doors for a career change. And since she didn't have class tonight, she thought she'd phone Ellen to see what her plans were. Robin didn't feel like being alone.

Ellen answered on the second ring. "Hello?"

"Hey, girl, how you doing?"

"I'm okay. Looking in this empty fridge of mine for dinner," Ellen said.

"Perfect timing. Why don't we meet for Chinese? I've got something to share with you."

"Sounds good. Give me an hour and I'll meet you at our favorite spot."

"Perfect. Later."

At the Restaurant with Ellen

Robin arrived first. She waited for Ellen to show. Ellen had always been a procrastinator and was never on time for anything. OJ ran across Robin's mind; she wondered if he'd called. She hadn't been home yet to check her messages; maybe good news awaited her.

Ellen arrived.

"It's about time you made it! I'm starving!" Robin teased her.

"Well, let's go get our grub on; I'm ready."

They sat at their table. They both ordered the all-you-can-eat buffet. "Ellen, how's the new job coming?" Robin asked.

"It's challenging, and the hours are just as long, but I'm using my brain now. I like the people; everyone is so nice."

"Ellen, you've always been a people person, and you're very good at what you do. I imagine sales will go up with your marketing skills. So have you met any attractive men?"

"Nope, I haven't met anyone yet, and work is all that I'm good at. I can't seem to find the right man. All the good ones are either married or dead. So I give up. Besides, with my new position I have enough on my plate. Not to change the subject, but have you heard from Raine or Weesee?"

"Weesee called last week. She left a message on the machine saying she was in Aruba with someone tall dark and handsome and he had plenty of money. All she could say was 'Lordy, lordy, lord, I hit the jackpot!' I laughed when I heard that. So she's fine. I spoke with Raine a few days ago; she and the boys are good. They both said to tell you hello."

"How's Larry adjusting to college?" Ellen asked.

"He's doing good. I miss him so much. You know he thinks he's my man. He calls every chance he gets to check on me. I told him to call on the weekends and not to worry about me. I have enough to keep me occupied. Plus the phone bill is outrageous. He's fine, and said he received your package. That was nice of you to send him a gift box."

"Well, he is my godson. I just want him to have all he needs," Ellen said.

"Thanks. Listen, Ellen, the thing I wanted to tell you is, I met a guy. He's so cute."

Ellen looked surprised. "Do tell. When and where?"

"Last night he came out to service my furnace. When I first laid eyes on him, the attraction was there. We talked for hours. He's supposed to call for a dinner date."

Ellen said, "Girl, that's good. You haven't smiled like that in years. Is he available?"

"I suppose so. He said he wasn't married, but he lives in Florida."

"Florida?" Ellen questioned. "What is he doing here in Westchester fixing your furnace?"

Robin said, "He's been here for several weeks on a work-study program for the company he works for, which will enable him to complete his degree. He's only here for three more weeks."

"Sounds like he's got it going on. Where is he staying?" Ellen asked with a wink.

"Downtown, at the Holiday Inn. Ellen, he's got the darkest bedroom eyes I've ever seen, almost piercing. And he's a good conversationalist. We hit it off good."

"So, when are you guys going to dinner?"

"Soon, I hope," Robin responded. "He's got to get back to me on his schedule. I'm looking forward to seeing him again."

"Are you nervous, Robin? I know how hard it is for you to trust anyone after Fred."

"I am, but it's only a dinner date. I'm not looking for anything serious,"

Robin said matter of factly.

Ellen said, "Girl, you never know what could happen. I'm just glad you're giving yourself a chance again. Wear something sexy."

"It'll be nice to be in the company of an intelligent man who's on the rise. He says he wants to start his own business once he completes his degree."

"Interesting. Maybe he'll settle down here in Westchester!" Ellen said.

"You never know." They both laughed!

Robin and Ellen finished their dinner and said their goodbyes.

Robin went home to a warm house. She's walked in, threw her bag on the bed and went straight for her answering machine. The answering machine was blinking. She had two messages.

First she heard Larry's voice. "Hi, Mom. I know it's not the weekend. Just called to say I aced my chemistry test and to tell you I love you. Holla at you soon."

The second voice was OJ's. "Hello, Robin. Thought we could get together on Saturday if your schedule isn't full. Please call me on my cell number at any time day or night to let me know if Saturday is good for you. Hope to hear from you soon."

Robin was smiling from ear to ear. She didn't want to seem too anxious. She figured she'd stall him for a day, and then return the call. She was both nervous and excited to hear from him.

OJ couldn't wait. He called her.

Robin picked up the phone. "Hello?"

OJ said, "Hi, how are you doing?"

"I'm fine OJ. Hey, about Saturday, that's a good time for me."

"I'll pick you up around 7:00 p.m. if that's okay with you," OJ said.

"Seven will be fine," Robin confirmed.

Robin's hands were trembling at the sound of his masculine voice on the other end of the receiver. She felt like a high school girl going out on her very first date. She felt anxious and excited. She thought it was time to go shopping for a new outfit, and decided to bring Ellen along for her opinion. Robin felt that a whole new makeover would do her good, plus she hadn't pampered herself in years.

Robin and Ellen made a day of it. They started with an early breakfast. After breakfast they went to the spa, had a facial, nails and hair done. After the beauty makeover, they were ready to bargain hunt for sales.

Robin held up an outfit on a hanger. "Ellen, what do you think of this black pantsuit?"

"You go, sexy momma; that will knock him dead," Ellen encouraged her.

Robin was a full-figured woman with a tiny waistline, an hourglass shape with the curves in just the right areas. Almost anything she wore stood out.

"Ellen, you don't think this is too much, do you?"

"No. Robin, it's elegant, conservative and sexy. Believe me; your guy will take notice."

"Okay, then this it is. I just have to get the accessories, and I'm all ready for Mr. O'Neil."

At OJ's Hotel

OJ was just as excited about their date. He knew from the moment he laid eyes on Robin that he had to see her again. At that moment he had forgotten that he had a woman and two kids in Florida with whom he shared his life. Although he'd been with this woman for over twenty years and she was the mother of his children, he couldn't bring himself to marry her. He'd been so preoccupied with raising his kids that marriage had never been an issue. OJ vowed that because his father had run off and left his mom to raise him and his siblings alone, he would never do his kids that way.

He knew he stayed with this woman because of the kids and problems from her past. His relationship to her was an obligation. He provided for her and the kids by working two jobs, which meant there was never time for romance. He often wondered if he still loved this woman and how they had grown apart. The relationship was more like a business. He believed whatever it took to give his kids a healthy, stable life with a mom and dad was what mattered to him.

Robin was the first woman who'd captured his attention in a romantic sense. All OJ had in mind up until he met Robin was finishing school and starting his business. Robin was very attractive and easy to talk with. Communication was the biggest problem he had with the woman he lived with. They worked opposite shifts, hadn't done things together as a couple for years. Their conversation was always about the kids or finances.

OJ felt as if they were roommates. He was tired of pretending, putting on airs for other people to think they were the happiest couple alive. He buried himself in his career. He never gave any other woman a chance to know him. He was too busy. Robin was the first woman outside of his relationship that he ever paid any attention to.

He had a secret and didn't want to tell Robin of his relationship at home.

He didn't want to risk knowing her, even in friendship, but OJ couldn't let this opportunity pass. He'd had never felt like this before. He didn't like the idea of not saying anything about his life in Florida, but he only had three weeks left in Westchester. He wanted to know this woman.

OJ felt that a little time was better than no time. Besides, how far could this go? He thought about what his brother used to say to him "All work and no play make OJ a dull boy." He thought, *My brother is right. All these years I've worked my fingers to the bone to make a life for my children; now it's my time. Time for me to enjoy the finer things in life.* He thought Robin was the finest thing he'd ever laid eyes on. *It's time for me to be happy. Let me call my brother for encouragement.*

OJ and his brother Aaron, whom everyone called AJ, were identical twins. As kids growing up they were very close and looked so much alike no one could tell them apart. OJ was the elder by fifteen minutes, but he always looked to A.J for advice when it came to women. As kids growing up with no dad and one sister, they had made a pact to always protect one another.

AJ was smooth with the ladies, always juggled two, sometimes three women at a time. He lived a very flamboyant lifestyle, always traveling on the go making money. AJ was a hustler and loved his women.

When he and OJ were growing up, whenever one of them had a problem they'd always meet on the rooftop of the tall building in Brooklyn where they were raised, look out over the city and together figure out what to do. They'd call it their peace ground. As adults, they kept their peace ground meetings a tradition. OJ thought, *I can't go to AJ so I'll call him.*

"Hello?"

"What's up, man? How's things going?" OJ asked.

"I'm straight, man. What's up with you?" AJ answered.

OJ said, "Man, I'm still in Westchester trying to finish this class. It's cold as hell here."

"Man, you keep that cold weather; I'm under the AC as we speak. I went by to check on the home front for you. Everything is straight," AJ said.

"Thanks, man," OJ said. "I can always depend on my little brother to hold it down. Listen, I met someone, a woman."

AJ was surprised. "You say what? You, Mr. Too Busy to Have a Life?"

OJ laughed. "All right, all right, yes, me. Man, she's beautiful. I made a date with her for tomorrow night. AJ, man, I'm scared. I never told her I had someone at home."

"Man, is she beautiful? If you diggin' her, why does she need to know who you're with? Man, you're too straight for me. Didn't I teach you anything?" AJ chided him.

"Hey, I like to be honest, and this secret is killing me, AJ, but if I tell her, I won't get a chance to know her. I just know that about her. I feel it."

"OJ, listen up. You're only going to be there a short time. Enjoy the moment. Isn't that what I always tell you? Live for the moment. Stop sweatin' yourself about this honesty stuff. Enjoy yourself. Live for once. It's not like you're taking her to the altar. It's only a date. Besides me and you knowing, what are the chances of her finding out the truth with the distance?"

OJ thought about it. "You're right."

"All right, then, get yourself together and do this. You are my twin, so don't be half-steppin' either. Show this woman what you're made of and have a good time," AJ said.

"Thanks, man. Love you."

"Love you too. Bro. Later."

OJ knew that AJ would give him the confidence he lacked. They were identical in looks, but their personalities were like night and day. AJ had always been the brave one, the twin who took risks at any cost. AJ wasn't the type to settle down with one woman.

He'd always say "Why settle for one when you have a variety to chose from?" That was his lifestyle: women and money. OJ was the opposite. He believed in family, settling down and being more laid back and reserved.

OJ wanted this date to be a memorable date. He wanted memories he could take back to Florida with him, memories he could reflect on when loneliness set in. He was starving for affection, for love, and deep inside his soul he knew Robin would be the woman to fill him.

OJ knew nothing about Westchester so he began to research to find the popular spots to take Robin. He wanted to impress her and have a good time in doing so. He called the front desk of the hotel for a tour guide of Westchester. OJ did his homework. He planned ahead for dinner reservations at a four-star restaurant, and then he phoned for a luxury rental car because he couldn't see picking up Robin with his work van. She had too much class for that. He wanted to escort her in style. He thought to himself *What would AJ do if this was his date?* OJ knew his brother's style and taste oh so well and always admired him for those qualities.

The Date

Time was getting close. It was 6 p.m. OJ had showered, shaved and he had to remember to pick up the flowers he had ordered for Robin at the front desk. He was ready; he checked himself out in the full-length mirror. To his amazement, he was shocked at how much he looked like his twin brother. He thought he looked very debonair. For the final touch, a splash of cologne. *I hope she likes the fragrance*, he thought.

OJ stopped at the front desk to pick up the bouquet of flowers. He noticed women's heads turning to watch as he exited the hotel.

All he could think about was his brother AJ, because that's the kind of stares he often received from the ladies. He knew that he had it going on, which boosted his confidence level. He was ready for a night of romance. OJ felt like he was on top of the world, and that he had deprived himself of feeling like a man for too long.

The air was brisk, but the night didn't seem cold to OJ—maybe because his heart had opened up to this beautiful woman. Overcoat across his arm, he rang the bell.

Robin opened the door. Knees shaking, she invited him in for a cocktail.

Robin smiled at him. "Good evening, Mr. O'Neil."

"Good evening, Ms. Jacobs. You look lovely."

"Thank you. You're looking suave yourself. Help yourself to a drink while I get my things." Robin pointed to the bar.

"These flowers are for you."

Robin reached for the flowers. "Thank you, OJ. They are absolutely beautiful. I'll put them in water."

"Beautiful flowers for a beautiful lady," OJ eyed her.

Robin blushed and excused herself, went upstairs to get her purse and coat. She went to her bedroom, took a deep breath and let out a sigh. She was thinking, *What a handsome man! He looks so good in that black suit, and those eyes! He smells so good, too. I've got to get my composure together. Okay, Robin, you can do this. Calm down, relax and act normal.*

Robin came down the stairs. OJ was sipping a Coke; he never had been much of an alcohol drinker. He helped Robin with her coat and off they went. The night air was cold and snowy. OJ reached for Robin's hand and opened the car door. On the drive to the restaurant, they smiled like two kids with a crush on each other.

When OJ told her where they were going, Robin broke her silence.

"So we're dining at the Plaza Crown Royal tonight?"

"Nothing but the best for such a beautiful lady as yourself, Robin."

"Thank you, OJ, That's very sweet of you. In all my years in Westchester, I've never been to the Plaza Crown. I guess there's a first time for everything."

"Yes, indeed, first time for everything," OJ said. "I can't remember how long it's been since I've dressed up in a suit or gone dancing or been in the presence of a beautiful woman like you."

Robin said, "Come now, OJ, I know better. A man as attractive as you has got to have women flying around him like flies."

OJ blushed. "I've been so preoccupied with work, school and providing for my kids, there was never time for anyone or anything else."

Robin paused. "How many kids do you have?"

"Two. Nichole is ten, and Oscar Jr. is twelve. I'll show you pictures when we get to the restaurant."

"What about their mom? Are the two of you still involved?" Robin asked.

OJ was sweating bullets. He wanted to tell the truth, that he lived with the kid's mom, but that they had grown apart years ago. He wanted to be honest, but couldn't bring himself to tell her because he didn't want to ruin his chances of seeing her again.

"No, we're not involved, Robin," he said. "We grew apart years ago. We interact; keep in touch when it concerns the kids. I've been by myself for a long time. My kids have been my life."

Robin said, "I didn't mean to pry; it's just that you never know about people. It's hard for me to open up since my divorce, if you know what I mean."

"Robin, believe me I do understand, so let's just enjoy our evening, dance a little and have some fun. I hope you're hungry."

Robin said, "As a matter a fact, I am." She was thinking, *Not the kind of hunger you're thinking of!*

They arrived at the restaurant. The lobby was like a grand ballroom with a huge fireplace. The atmosphere in the room was classy. The music playing was a soft jazz. The setting was very romantic. They were escorted to their table. A beautiful spray of flowers was arranged on the table, with candles surrounding it. OJ comfortably pulled out Robin's chair and waited for her to be seated.

His piercing dark brown eyes reflected the candlelight. Robin felt like a princess dining with her prince charming.

The waiter came over to start them off with drinks. Robin ordered a glass of wine to relax her. OJ ordered a glass of tonic water with a twist of lemon. They gazed into each other's eyes. OJ asked, "May I have this dance?"

The dance floor was crowded, but OJ and Robin danced close, as if the room was theirs alone. Robin laid her head safely upon his broad chest. She felt a sense of security. OJ held his arms around her tiny waist as if he had found a precious jewel. They were locked together in a feeling that they both longed for, the feeling that they were inseparable. They danced through song after song, forgetting about hunger. Their hunger was fulfilled with the affection they shared for each other.

"You're a wonderful dancer, Robin. And you smell delicious," OJ cooed.

"Thank you. So do you."

They separated long enough to smile at each other. Luther Van Dross' tune "Let Me Hold You Tight, if Only for One Night" was playing. O. J. began to hold Robin close, serenading her in her ear.

Robin got weak as a wet noodle. She was so relaxed against his chest it was as if she was sleeping on a pillow. OJ lifted her head, stared into her eyes with those dark brown eyes, and thanked her for going out with him. "Robin, I really appreciate your being here with me. This is the best time I've had since I've been in Westchester. I'm so thankful to have met you."

Robin whispered, "I'm having a great time too, Lightfoot."

They both laughed. "Shall we order dinner, Ms. Jacobs? No one is dancing but us."

Robin said, "Yes, we shall, Mr. O'Neil. Time flies when you're having fun."

OJ led her back to their table. They dined on a fine meal and talked until closing time. Everyone had left except for the kitchen staff, and they were still talking.

OJ said, "Robin, I think we'd better be making moves; looks like we're the last to leave. I'm going to take care of the check and get the car warm. You wait in the lobby by the fireplace. I'll come back for you."

OJ made his exit to the car. Robin sat mesmerized by the glowing fire. She kept thinking, *Where has this man been all my life? He's a perfect gentleman, and an excellent entertainer and dancer.* She was deep in thought when OJ whispered her name. "Robin, honey, the car is ready."

Robin didn't want what felt like a perfect night to end. She decided she would suggest they drive to Highland Falls, a park with high mountains which overlooked the city. She thought it would be a nice sight to show him, the night scenery of Westchester.

As they drove, Robin said, "OJ, dinner was lovely. Thank you."

"You're very welcome."

"I have an idea," Robin said. "Why don't I show you the night scenery? We can drive to Highland Falls. It's beautiful at night."

"Just lead the way. The night is still young," OJ said.

They arrived at Highland Falls; the view of the city was breathtaking. The moon was bright.

"Robin, this is unbelievable; how beautiful! It's like we're up in an airplane, the lights look so tiny. I had no idea that Westchester was this big."

Robin said, "I used to ride up here all the time after my dad died to collect my thoughts."

"I'm sorry you lost your dad. Mine left us when we were kids. My mom raised us kids alone. Now she's passed away."

"How sad! OJ, I'm sorry."

"I was only thirteen when my mom passed. My grandmother took us in and cared for us. I loved Big Momma, but she was nothing like mom. My mom worked so hard it killed her. She had a heart attack; my dad leaving her with three kids was rough on her. That's why I vowed to always be there for my kids. I don't want to do to them what my dad did to us. He didn't want us."

Robin said, "I'm sorry." She felt his pain. She reached for his hand to let him know, *I feel you're hurt. I know your loss. I recognize those feelings.*

OJ apologized for the emotions he displayed. "Robin, forgive me; it all seems like yesterday. You just never get over it."

"Don't apologize," Robin said. "I understand. I haven't cried a tear since the day my dad was pronounced dead. I can't remember a single tear on that very day, and I've buried the rest along with him. It just builds up on the inside. One day I'll break; one day it will come out. But I had to be strong, OJ, I had to keep my family together."

"Robin, you're a strong woman. I'm a man, but even I cried when my mother died, and I still cry. Come here let me hold you. Please let me hold you. It's okay. You're safe with me. You're safe to cry, you're safe to scream, but let it go, baby, let go. Let me hold you."

OJ couldn't believe the emotion in his own voice. It wasn't an emotion of a romantic gesture, but that of empathy and caring. He felt Robin's pain. He wanted her to let all those bottled up feelings go. He wanted to be the one to open her heart.

Robin, feeling very secure with him, laid her head on his shoulder, and before she knew it the tears began to flow like a river. She was crying uncontrollably.

OJ held her so tight; he rocked her like a baby. Soothing her, caressing her. *It's okay; I'm here for you Robin, it's okay.* He took his handkerchief from his jacket pocket and wiped the tears from her face. From out of the glove compartment, he took a small pamphlet. He placed it in Robin's hands. It was a Biblical scripture which read; "Weeping may endure for a night, but Joy comes in the morning." Psalm 30:5

Robin looked at the words, and OJ recited them to her with hope in his eyes.

"It's okay, Robin. Take this scripture and believe in your heart that your dad and my mom are resting in the Lord. It's okay to cry; even Jesus wept. Please keep these words, and know that life will bring you sorrow, but it also brings great joy."

Robin looked at him with amazement. No one had ever given her such comforting words. She knew then that there was something special about him. "OJ, you're so kind and thoughtful for a guy. I needed to hear those words, and I'll always remember you for such encouraging advice. You're something else. Thank you." She kissed him on the cheek.

"Robin, keep those words with you whenever you feel like shedding a tear. Know that God is in control and joy does follow sadness. After all, I met you."

Robin looked into his eyes; she saw the seriousness on his face. She said, "I'm glad I met you, too, OJ"

They caressed each other, hugged and looked out into the moonlit night. The moon was bright, the snow sparkled, and love was in the air.

Finally OJ said, "I'd better get you home. I don't want to overextend my welcome. It's been an interesting night for us both. Robin, I hope you enjoyed yourself and we can see each other again."

"OJ. I haven't ever laughed and cried so much in one night. Thank you so much for a lovely date. Yes, I'd love to see you again."

On the drive home, Robin was very relaxed. She laid her head to rest on his shoulder as her prince escorted her home safely. OJ walked her to the door. They kissed so passionately they forgot about the cold. The kiss was warm, gentle, and lingered until they both let go. Staring into each other's eyes, they both said at the same time, "Good night." OJ took the keys from her hand, unlocked the door and waited until she was inside.

"Thank you, Robin, for such a memorable night. Please see me tomorrow."

"I will. I'll call you."

"Okay, goodnight. Now lock up until tomorrow." He blew a kiss.

"Good night, Mr. O'Neil," Robin said as she closed the door.

OJ stood there with a grin on his face until he heard the lock and saw the upstairs light go on. He wanted to be sure she was safely inside. He walked back to the car with a burst of energy, nothing but Robin on his mind and the scent of her perfume on his jacket. He felt like a new man, like he had won the lottery. OJ realized that he had been missing out on feelings. He knew from their date that he could care for someone again. What he shared with the woman at home was dead, but Robin gave him a feeling of life. As he drove to his hotel room, he kept thinking about seeing her tomorrow. How he couldn't wait to see her lovely face again, her smile, and hold her in his arms once more.

Robin dressed for bed. As she hung up her attire, she got a sniff of OJ's cologne. She sniffed her blouse just to reflect on how close he had held her when they danced. Robin hung up her outfit, got on her knees and began to pray. *God, thank you for a beautiful date, thank you for allowing me to meet OJ Thank you for such inspirational words. Lord, I'm scared to love. Help me, guide me, Lord. Amen.*

Robin felt the need to confess her feelings before her Creator. It was OJ who had steered her back in the direction in which she was raised. It was his comforting scripture that led her back to her Heavenly Father.

Robin couldn't wait to see OJ again. He made her feel special. She realized, *With this man I can be me and show my emotions.* That's what she had always wanted in a mate. Not only did he have good looks, he had emotion. Robin knew she had to see him again.

Until tomorrow.

The Next Day

She was sound asleep when the phone rang. The answering machine picked it up before she could. It was Ellen. "Robin, if you're there, pick up. I want to know what happened last night. Girl, wake up. Or maybe you have company, and I should leave you alone. Wake up!"

Robin picked up the phone. It was 6:00 a.m. "Ellen, do you know what time it is?"

Ellen said, "Yes, I do. It's time for you to wake up and tell me how the date went. I'm at work, and I can't get started until you tell me."

Robin, wiping the sleep from her eyes, sat up in the bed. Just speaking OJ's name gave her a burst of energy.

"Ellen, girl, let me tell you, I've never met anyone like him. We dined in style. He picked me up on time, looking handsome as ever and smelling real good. He brought flowers, girl. He took me to the Crown Royal. We danced half the night. The food was excellent. We left there and went to Highland Falls. Ellen, it was so romantic. He's a perfect gentleman. I really had a good time."

"Robin, that's good. Did he kiss you good night?"

"Girl, did he. I was elevated above Heaven, if there's any such place. He's a fantastic kisser. He's special."

Ellen said, "Girl, I can hear it all in your voice. Are you guys going out again?"

Robin said, "I would hope so. I'm going to call him today."

Ellen said, "Robin, you need this. I'm so excited for you. Just take it slow. Listen, I better start my day. I've got a 7:00 a.m. meeting. I'll buzz you later. If Mr. O'Neil doesn't make plans with you, maybe we can take in a movie."

Robin said, "Sounds good. Talk to you later."

The phone rang again. Robin said, "Hello?"

It was Larry. "Hi, Mom. How you doing?"

"I'm fine, son. How are you?"

Larry said, "I'm good. Listen, Mom, I won't be coming home for spring break. I met a girl, and she invited me for dinner to meet her folks. Mom, please understand."

"Larry, you know how important it is for the family to be together. I planned a dinner for you. What would the party be without you? Honey, I understand meeting someone and wanting to spend time with that person, but nothing or no one takes the place of family."

Larry said, "Mom, I'm sorry. You're right. I didn't mean to upset you. I'll be home for spring break. Maybe Angela can arrange for me to meet her parents some other time. Mom, I know how much it means to you, the family being together. How is Grandmother?"

"Honey, she's fine. Listen, tell me about Angela. It sounds a little serious—your meeting her folks and all," Robin said.

"Mom, she's smart and pretty. I wouldn't say it's serious, but we are seeing each other on the regular. We study together. Mom, she's a bio major. She knows her stuff. I'd like for her to one day meet you. I tell her all the time, my mom is the rock in my life. I tell Angela you keep me on the straight and narrow, and that I want to make you proud of me."

"Honey, you've made me the proudest and happiest mom on this earth. I love you and want what's best for you. For now, it's an education. I'd love to meet Angela one day; she sounds like a nice young lady."

"Mom, I believe you'd like her. So it's settled; I'm home for spring break. Oh, and Mom, say hello to Ellen for me, and tell her the goodies were right on time."

"I'll do that baby. Do you have enough winter gear?" Robin asked.

"Mom, I'm fine. I miss you."

"I miss you too, sweetheart."

"Have you been keeping yourself busy? How are your classes coming along?" Larry asked.

"Honey, I've got a lot on my plate these days. Classes are hectic. I'm trying to maintain my 3.0 average. Gonna be tough this quarter, but I'm determined."

"That's my mom! Guess what?"

"What, honey?"

"I'm a chip off the old block; my average is running high this quarter. I've aced every test so far."

"See, Larry, how can I not be proud? I love you so much."

"I love you too, Mom. I'd better get to class. Listen, don't worry; I'll be home for spring break. I'll call you next weekend. Love you, Mom. Later."

"Love you too, son. Be good."

The phone rang a third time. It was OJ. "Good morning, Ms. Jacobs. How are you?"

"Good morning, Mr. O'Neil. I'm fine, thank you. How are you?"

"I'm good, Robin. I really enjoyed myself last night. How about meeting me for lunch?"

"OJ, that's really sweet of you, but you don't have to do that."

OJ cut in. "I don't have to, but I want to see you today—soon!"

Robin admired his persistence. She also wanted to see him. "How's 12:30?" she asked.

OJ said, "That's fine. I'm on call. Hope you don't mind if we're interrupted."

"Believe me, it's not a problem. I do understand when duty calls."

"Robin, would you mind if we met at the restaurant? I'm all over the city today. It would be easier if you decide on a place, page me with your decision, and I'll meet you there."

Robin said, "Not a problem at all, OJ I understand."

"Thank you. Oh, and Robin, I'm in uniform today, so please excuse my attire. It won't be anything like last night."

Robin laughed. "OJ, it's cool. I understand. You're working. It's 9:00 a.m. now so let's say I page you within the hour with the details."

"Sounds like a plan. Until then."

"Later, Mr. O'Neil," Robin said and hung up the phone.

A Picnic at the Pier

She looked through her wardrobe to see what she could wear. She wanted to look radiant for OJ. She decided on her tight purple sweater with the low neck-line and a pair of fitted jeans. She wanted to be comfortable and not overdressed, since he was dressed in work attire.

Robin couldn't decide where to meet for lunch. *I know the best food joint in Westchester,* she thought to herself. *Robin's kitchen. I'll fix a basket lunch for us, and we can picnic in the van.* Robin decided what she should prepare. She made herself very busy in the kitchen. She made her family's secret chicken salad recipe on rye bread, and filled the thermos with hot vegetable soup. She cut fresh fruit for dessert. She made a thermos full of coffee just the way OJ liked it. She packed the basket with her fine tablecloth, silverware and a freshly cut rose.

There, lunch is ready to be served. Time flew; she hadn't paged OJ since she'd gotten so caught up in preparing the meal she had let time slip by. *I'd better page him; he's probably thinking the worst.*

She paged him. Within minutes he phoned back.

"Robin, I thought you had forgotten me. I figured something came up."

Robin said, "As a matter of fact, it did."

OJ was silent. She wondered if he was disappointed. She said, "OJ, are you there?"

"I'm here, Robin. I wanted so badly to see you today, but if you've got other plans, believe me, it's okay."

Robin laughed. "I'm not letting you off the hook that easy. Yes, I do have other plans and they include you."

She imagined OJ smiling, just from the way his voice changed. "Oh, is that a fact, Ms. Jacobs?"

Robin said, "Yes, it is, Mr. O'Neil. We're having lunch in your work van."

"In my van?" OJ repeated. "You mean stop and go at some fast food place?"

Robin laughed. "No, silly. I've prepared lunch, and we're having a picnic in the dead of winter. In the back of your van. How's that for style?"

Now it was OJ's turn to laugh. "Woman, you're incredible. I'm flattered. Where shall we meet?"

Robin said, "Are you familiar with the Lake Street Pier? It's north of the hotel you're staying in downtown."

"Yes, I know the spot. Call the time and I'll be there."

"Let's keep it at 12:30," Robin said.

"12:30 it is. I'll be there and, Robin, drive safely. You might want to wear an extra sweater since it's really cold today."

"OJ, you're just not used to this Westchester cold. Florida has thinned your blood."

"Okay, okay you're right. I can't adjust to the cold, but I want you safe and warm."

Robin said, "Okay, Mr. O'Neil, let me get dressed so that I can meet on time."

"See you soon, Robin."

"Later."

OJ was stuck in traffic on the other side of town; quite a distance from the pier. It was 11 a.m., and the dispatcher had just called him to go on a job. OJ looked at the time and the traffic. He was trying to figure out how he could turn down this next job so it wouldn't interfere with his plans to meet Robin. He got off the highway at the next exit, pulled over and put the van in park.

He phoned his roommate Sam. Sam had the day off, but he wanted to make some extra money. OJ felt that Sam was qualified to do the job; besides, the dispatcher wouldn't know as long as someone showed up at the residence. He phoned Sam back at the hotel.

"Hello, Sam. It's OJ."

"Hey, man, busy day or what?"

OJ said, "Yes, it is, as a matter of fact—that's why I'm calling. I've got more runs today than I can handle. Can you help me out?"

Sam said, "Sure can, man. I need the hours."

OJ said, "Great! Dispatcher says the hot water tank at this residence isn't working properly. The call came in about fifteen minutes ago. The address is 131 Oakland Drive. They're expecting someone within the hour."

Sam jotted the information down. "I'm on it. 131 Oakland Drive?"

"That's it. Thanks, man," OJ said.

Sam said, "Thank you, OJ. Oh, and by the way, your brother left a message. He said for you to contact him. Nothing urgent."

OJ said, "Okay, thanks. Later."

He let out a sigh of relief. The only thing he had to deal with now was the traffic. He wanted to get there before Robin, so that he could clean out the back of the van, make it presentable for her and give them sit-down room. OJ made his way through the traffic. The roads were slippery, covered with snow, and the cars were bumper to bumper. He couldn't get used to driving in the snow. Everything was slow motion, especially making his way to the woman who made him feel so alive. OJ felt as if he was in a funeral procession. Steadily blowing his horn for cars to move along helped to relieve some frustration. He didn't want anything to hinder him from getting to Robin.

It was 11:30 and he was closer to the pier. OJ wanted to stop at a florist to get Robin a flower. Downtown Westchester was busy for a Sunday. Seemed like the whole town had one thing in mind today—shopping. Circling the area for a parking spot, he located a floral shop. OJ quickly drove into the parking space, the van slipping and sliding from side to side. He accelerated the gas too hard, which caused the van to glide.

At last he found a space, put the van in park, added coins to the parking meter and went inside to see what flower he'd buy for his rose, Robin. He thought he'd phone Robin again to tell her to drive slowly and safely. He wanted to suggest maybe he should come to her place. He was thinking of her safety, and he knew how bad the traffic was. He didn't want to ruin her idea of a picnic; besides, he was looking forward to it. It sounded so romantic to him. He gave her a buzz from his cell phone, and found himself listening to her answering machine. "Hello, you've reached the Jacobs' residence. Please leave a message, thank you."

OJ hung up when he heard the machine. He was feeling anxious and nervous; he wanted so badly to see Robin, but he wanted her safe. He proceeded inside the flower shop. His pager beeped. It was the dispatcher calling. He had to phone in.

"Hello," he said. "This is badge #234. Oscar O'Neil returning the call."

The dispatcher said, "O'Neil, there's been an emergency call concerning the residence at 131 Oakland Drive. Apparently there's a gas leak in the house. The fire department called to tell us not to report there for our own safety. If you're en route to the location, cancel your run. The family had to evacuate the premises, and I'm instructed to tell you not to go there. The fire department is at the scene. They're avoiding a possible explosion."

OJ was sweating and nervous. "I was en route to the location. I'll stand by for further instructions. Thanks."

"Very good," the dispatcher said. "Thank God I stopped you, and you're safe."

OJ, in a panic, hurried and got the dispatcher off the phone. He had to contact Sam right away. Putting his thoughts of Robin on hold, he realized he had to act quickly. He phoned Sam at the hotel; there was no answer. Panicked, he searched through his wallet for a list of pager numbers which included Sam's. Dropping his wallet to the floor, he picked up the contents. Out of his wallet fell a picture of his kids. All OJ could think of at that moment was Sam and his family.

What would his family do if something terrible happened? It would be his fault. How could he explain his asking Sam to cover for him?

OJ was petrified. Where had he put those pager numbers?

The Blizzard

He realized that he'd put the pager numbers in the glove compartment of the van, so he rushed to the van. Within those few minutes the weather took a turn for the worse. Visibility was terrible due to the high wind. OJ had met his first blizzard. He couldn't see his way to the van. Finally he located it, and it was completely covered with snow. His mind was shifting back and forth, worrying about Robin traveling in the blizzard. Once inside the van, he tore open the glove compartment and pushed everything to the floor. He scrambled through the mess and found the list of numbers. Immediately he paged Sam from his cell phone. He entered 911 emergency code for Sam to return the call. OJ sat anxiously waiting; after a few minutes of waiting there was no response. OJ didn't feel the temperature of the cold weather. Instead he was sweating, hot and nervous. He paged Sam a second time. *Please, Sam,* he thought, *answer the page.*

Please Lord help me. Finally his cell phone rang.

OJ thought, *Sam, please let this be you.*

It was. "OJ, man, it's me, I'm stuck in traffic on the expressway. Visibility is so bad I can barely see. I'm trying to make it to Oakland Drive. The reception is bad due to the weather; my cell phone was dead for a while."

OJ said, "Man, thank God you're safe! Listen, don't go to Oakland Drive. Dispatch called; there's an emergency gas leak, which could cause an explosion. The fire department is there now. Thank God for bad weather."

Sam said, "I know. God saved me between the blizzard and the traffic. If this blizzard hadn't started, I would have been there by now. Thanks for calling me. I'm going to make my way back to the hotel."

OJ said, "Man, that was a close call. My heart was racing. I'm so glad you're safe. Drive safe, okay? I'll see you later tonight. Sam, thanks for being there for me."

"Yeah, OJ, you drive safe. The wind is getting worse out, so be careful. Talk at you later."

OJ, wiping the sweat away, thanked God that Sam was safe. He had no way of contacting Robin. He didn't have a cell number for her so he hurried to get to the pier. In the vicinity of the pier, he noticed cars pulled over on the side of the road due to the hazardous driving. He could barely make out the sign "Lake Street Pier." OJ turned into the parking lot. The pier was deserted, neither a person in sight nor a single boat.

He left the van running and got out to brush the snow off. It was so cold that when he opened the back of the van, the doors were frozen stiff. He glanced at his watch. It was 12:45. OJ began to pace back and forth. He didn't see or hear a car approaching the lot. His mind began to wander. Maybe Robin got into an accident, maybe she was stuck on the side of the road somewhere, or maybe she was stranded in the freezing cold.

OJ stood outside the van, looking in every direction. He noticed a car coming his way. He heaved a sigh of relief. It was Robin. She was driving about five miles per hour. OJ ran to her car, waving both hands for her to stop.

"Robin, are you okay?" He squeezed her tightly. He was so relieved to see her.

Robin said, "I'm fine, OJ. I didn't realize how bad the weather was. I traveled too far to turn back. I took my time."

"Get back in the car. I'll drive you to the van, and from there I'm taking you home. We can pick your car up later after the blizzard dies down. Better yet, I'll get one of the guys to trail me, and I'll drive your car home safely. I'm not taking 'no' for an answer."

Robin realized she couldn't argue with a protective man. She followed OJ to the van. He carried the basket lunch. OJ had had enough excitement for one day. He wanted to be sure Robin was home safe, so he drove her himself. On the drive to Robin's house, they passed many cars pulled over to the side of the road, and still the snow fell steadily.

OJ drove very slowly; it gave him time to talk with Robin. It took them two hours to get to her house. In normal driving conditions, it would have only been an hour. OJ pulled into Robin's snow-covered driveway. He escorted her to the door and then told her to go inside and warm up while he shoveled the driveway.

Robin didn't argue with him; she went inside and made a fresh pot of coffee. Next she spread the tablecloth on the living room floor. Robin was persistent; she was determined to have their picnic. She heated the vegetable soup and unpacked the basket. OJ made his way into the house. He was drenched in snow, and his clothes were soaking wet.

"OJ, you're soaking wet," Robin said. "Get out of those clothes, and let me dry them for you. You'll catch your death of cold. I'll get you something of my son's to wear until your clothes are dry."

"Thank you, Robin. I am chilled to the bone."

Robin went upstairs to Larry's room. She found a pair of jeans and a sweatshirt. They would do for now. She came back downstairs, gave them to OJ, and showed him to the bathroom where he could get cleaned up and then they would eat. OJ went upstairs to change clothes. Robin sat in the living room waiting for him to bring the wet clothes down.

OJ came downstairs. "I feel better now. Thank you, Robin."

Robin said, "You're welcome. Are those clothes comfortable for you? I can give you a bathrobe."

"I'm fine, Robin. Here are my wet clothes."

"Do you mind if I wash them?"

OJ didn't care; that would give him more time to spend with her. "No, not at all," he said. "How about I start a fire in the fireplace while you're working on the clothes?"

"Great! Let me make you a cup of coffee. You've got to be cold, and I know how you like your coffee. Black and sweet."

OJ laughed. "Yeah, just like you." They both smiled.

Robin made her way to the kitchen. She couldn't get over how masculine and fit OJ looked in Larry's jeans. His protectiveness and his physique turned her on. He was well formed. She gave him the coffee. As he was placing the logs on the fire, she couldn't help but notice his nice, round proportioned ass. He was built. Robin hurried to the laundry room to keep her composure together.

When she came back to the living room, OJ was lying in front of the fireplace, his body stretched, showing his masculine curves.

Robin said, "The fire looks cozy, OJ. Your clothes are in the wash."

"Robin," he said, "come sit with me."

Robin moved to his side. She gazed into the firelight in OJ's eyes. He reached for her hand and took her to the tablecloth where she had neatly arranged the food.

"Let me serve you, my dear," OJ said. "Everything looks delicious."

Robin had a spread fit for a king. The setting was romantic. OJ dimmed the lights. The reflection from the fireplace lit the room. They sat on the floor, comfortable, gazing at each other; neither of them had food on their mind. OJ brought the chicken salad to Robin's mouth, and then he took a bite from the same side of the sandwich. He began feeding her like she was his sweet baby.

Robin, speechless, mouth full, adored the attention. Gazing into his eyes, she wanted to kiss him at that very moment. OJ moved closer to her. Without a word said, he lifted her chin and slowly kissed her. It was as if he had read her mind. Robin, overcome with emotion, let herself go into the arms of her protector. She immediately pushed back, wanting to maintain control.

"I'd better go check on the laundry," she said.

She was running away from the feeling. She was afraid to give in to what she felt for OJ, OJ was feeling it too; he'd forgotten about his situation in Florida. He wanted Robin in every way. He felt life had been brought back into his dead soul. OJ sat thinking, *should he tell her his secret and risk not seeing her again?* Robin came back into the room and noticed the look on his face.

"OJ, is there something you want to say? The look on your face is so serious. A penny for your thoughts."

"Robin, listen to what I'm about to say, and please don't take it the wrong way…"

Robin sat very quietly wondering what was on his mind.

"Robin, before I met you, life was dull. I made my children my life. I filled my life with work. I had forgotten what it was like to hold a woman, care for her, and want her. You restored those feelings again. Never have I felt this way for any woman. I wish we had met at a different time in our lives. Forgive me for my forwardness, but this is how I feel about you. I want to continue seeing you until I go back to Florida."

Robin sat in amazement, not knowing what to say. She felt the same way about him. Their feelings were mutual. After the divorce, she had buried herself in work and school. Oscar O'Neil was the best thing that had happened to her in years.

Now she said, "OJ, I've been hurt. Please understand I'm afraid to let my feelings go, afraid to love. My heart can't bear another heartache."

OJ reached for her hand to hold. "Robin, I would never hurt you. I care about you. Trust me, please. Just let me show you. Let's take it day by day."

"My ex-husband was the last man who told me to trust him, and it almost destroyed me."

"I'm not your ex. Robin, look me in the eye and tell me you don't feel what I feel, and I'll walk out of this house never to bother you again."

Robin turned away; she couldn't avoid the feeling. OJ took her in his arms and held her close. He caressed her long black shoulder-length hair. He reassured her that her feelings were safe with him. In the back of his mind he knew he had to keep his secret if he wanted to keep her.

They kissed passionately. OJ unbuttoned her sweater; he succulently kissed her breast. Robin was in ecstasy; too weak to resist, she gave in to the passion. They moved in slow motion as if they were waltzing, each stroke penetrating, fire slowly burning. They made love until they both lay in exhaustion, their naked bodies in sweat-drenched closeness.

They lay in front of the fire, exposed in their nakedness, OJ holding Robin tight in his arms as if he never wanted to let her go. They had forgotten about eating; the food was secondary. OJ was steadily kissing Robin as if she was something delectable to eat. The lovemaking was sensual, and they played most of the night, finally drifting off to sleep in each other's arms.

OJ awakened in the middle of the night. The fire was still smoldering, but it was a bit drafty in the room. He stared down at his princess, worrying about his secret. Then he tiptoed out of the room so as not to wake Robin. He searched for a blanket to cover her.

He gently placed the blanket over her and then he restarted the fire, putting more logs on to burn. He went to the window to check the weather. Gazing into the night, all he could see was snow covering everything. The van was completely covered. They were snowed in.

Silently he made his way to the kitchen to put the food away. Careful not to wake Robin, he turned on the TV in the kitchen to listen to the weather report. The TV flashed a weather advisory telling people not to travel in the blizzard. It was expected to last twenty-four hours. OJ couldn't think of anywhere else he'd rather be. He peeked in on Robin. She was sleeping like a baby. He thought he'd check his cell phone messages. There were three messages on his phone.

Message # 1: "Hi, Dad, Oscar Jr. We heard the weather is really bad up that way. Mom and Nichole wanted to talk. Hope you're okay. Please call us back when you get this message. We're all doing fine. Love you, Dad."

Message # 2: "Hey, OJ, man, it's AJ Just checking to make sure everything went okay with your date. I'm leaving for Los Angeles this afternoon, got business there. I'll be gone a few days. Checked in on the family; everybody is good. Call me on my cell, man, when you stop romancing. Keepin' it real with you, bro. Have a good time; you deserve it. Holla back at me, man."

Message #3: OJ, it's Samone. You should have called by now. The kids and I are worried sick. The blizzard has caused a state of emergency. It's all over the news here. Nichole is crying for her daddy. Call us as soon as you can. I hear a lot of the phone lines are dead. We love you."

OJ panicked when he heard Samone's voice. He had to call home to ease their worries, and let them know he was safe. He didn't want to chance Robin's waking up and hearing him talk to Samone. He peeked in on Robin, she was still asleep. It was breaking daylight, and the snow was still falling. OJ went to the laundry room and put his clothes in the dryer. He thought he better check on Sam, so he called the hotel. The phone line was dead. He couldn't even get a signal on his cell phone.

He picked up the phone in Robin's laundry room; it was dead, too. He made his way back upstairs and thought he'd make fresh coffee. OJ worried about calling home. He had to reach Sam to let him know he was safe and to relay the message to his family if they called the hotel. He was going to tell Sam he had been dispatched to a residence, and the family was nice enough to care for him during the blizzard.

He kept trying the hotel. Still no outgoing dial tone. He didn't like the idea of putting Sam in the middle of his confusion, but he had to make sure he covered all bases, plus he wanted to make sure his family didn't worry.

OJ finally got through to the hotel from the cell phone.

"Holiday Inn, may I help you?"

OJ said, "Room #1101, please. Thank you."

"Hello?"

"Sam, hey it's OJ"

"Man, are you all right? Where you been? Are you stranded?"

OJ said, "Sam, I'm fine. I got dispatched to a residence right after we talked. The blizzard was so bad the family was nice enough to let me camp out until the weather eases up."

Sam said, "I know, man. People are stuck everywhere. A state of emergency has been called. I'm glad you're okay. That was decent of that family. Speaking of family, yours called several times. I told your son I'm sure he had nothing to worry about."

OJ said, "Sam, you're a lifesaver. I owe you big-time, man. Listen, if my family calls back, pass on the information I gave you. Let them know my cell phone is down. I'm fine, and I'll contact them as soon as I can."

Sam said, "Will do. OJ, don't worry, I'll make sure to ease their worries. Call me if you need me for anything."

"Thanks, Sam. Once the weather breaks in a few days I may need you to help trail a friend's car that got stuck in the blizzard."

Sam said, "Not a problem. Take care, OJ"

OJ went back into the living room to check on Robin; she was still sleeping. He sat in front of the burning fire. OJ's thoughts were in Florida, wondering how he could have remained in a dead relationship for so long. Being with Robin made him feel so alive. OJ knew in his heart he felt very deeply for Robin. He also knew that the time would come when he'd have to tell her about Samone. He slowly approached Robin and kissed her on the forehead.

Robin opened her eyes. "Good morning, Mr. O'Neil," she said smiling up at him.

"Good morning, sweetheart. How did you sleep?"

"Very well. Thanks to you."

OJ took Robin in his arms, held her very tight and whispered in her ear, "I think I'm falling in love with you. You're the most beautiful woman I've ever had in my life. You give me a new reason for living. You've brought happiness into my heart. How can I leave Westchester without you, Robin?"

"OJ, I think you're wonderful, too. Kiss me, take me."

They began to make love again, both expressing heartfelt feelings. OJ blocked out all thoughts of never seeing Robin again. They lay in each other's arms in front of the fire.

After a long time, Robin said, "Do you realize we're snowed in?"

"I can't think of anywhere in the world I'd rather be right now but in your arms. In fact, when I leave to go back to Florida, if I send for you, will you come?"

Robin sighed. "Yes, OJ, I'll come." She hugged him very close. "Now, how about something to eat?"

"That sounds good, but I'm doing the cooking. I make a serious omelet. You relax, and I'll make breakfast."

"You cook?" She smiled.

"Yes, I cook. I'm going to take care of you today, Ms. Jacobs. Your every wish is my command."

Robin said, "Then kiss me."

OJ kissed her. They both were like wild animals craving each other.

"I'm going to shower while you're in the kitchen cooking."

"Take your time," he told her. "I got this. I'll freshen up in the downstairs powder room, than I'll get started on breakfast."

Robin made her way upstairs. OJ went downstairs, than made his way to the kitchen. He wanted a moment alone so he could try calling Florida again. Using his cell phone, the number was ringing. He peeked his head around the kitchen door to listen for the shower running.

Samone picked up. "Hello?"

OJ said, "Hi, Samone. It's me. Where are the kids?"

"OJ, are you all right? We've been worried sick."

"I'm fine, Samone. The weather is really bad here. A customer was nice enough to put me up. We got snowed in."

Samone said. "That was very nice of them. We called the hotel several times. Sam told us you were safe. The kids and I have been watching the Weather Channel all day. Nichole was so worried."

"Samone, I'm sorry. I'd have called sooner if I could. I was just missing the kids. Are they okay?

"Oh, so you don't miss me?"

"Samone, look, I didn't call to argue. Please let me speak to the kids."

After OJ talked to the kids, he felt relieved. He got off the phone before Robin came down. He felt so torn. Things were happening so fast. He had finally met the woman of his dreams. He had a family in Florida, and he'd soon have to leave his soul mate behind with miles of distance between them. OJ's head began to ache. Too much to think about for right now. This situation was definitely a peace ground discussion; he felt the need to talk to his brother. OJ listened for Robin and heard her singing in the shower. Wow, she had a nice voice—she sang like an angel, his angel. She sounded very happy.

OJ called his brother. He needed to hear his voice and get some reassurance.

He got the answering machine. "Yes, you dialed right. This is AJ, and apparently I'm busy. So please leave a message and I'll fit you in. If this is an emergency, hit me on my pager #720-9197."

OJ left a message on A.J's voice mail. "Hey, man, so you're in L.A.? Man, things are good. I think I love this woman. AJ, she's everything I ever dreamed of. I'm stuck in a blizzard at her house and loving every minute of it. Man, I got a situation. Need to talk with you, bro. Listen, you be safe in L.A. Hit me back on my cell when you get this message. AJ, man, she's the one. Peace."

OJ began preparing breakfast. He set the table, complete with candles burning. He was a good cook and loved to do it. He couldn't remember the last time he'd prepared breakfast for Samone. He and Samone had grown up together, they were kids when they met. Samone had gotten pregnant, and he remained in the relationship to do the honorable thing, to be a man.

He felt obligated to Samone and the kids. Never had he loved her in the way he felt for Robin in such a short period of time. OJ realized that he had just settled for less, and thought about how much happiness he had missed out on. He knew he wanted to see Robin again once he left Westchester. What was he to do? How could he keep his secret? He didn't want to keep Robin in the dark, but he didn't want to lose her either. He only had a few weeks left in Westchester, and he wanted to spend as much time as he could with Robin. It was as if his heart had opened up to her.

Breakfast was ready and smelled delicious. OJ cooked a stuffed omelet with all kinds of fresh veggies Robin had in the fridge. He waited for her to come downstairs and placed a towel over his arm like a waiter.

"Baby, it smells so good! And look at this table! I'm impressed; a girl could get used to this treatment."

Pulling out her chair, OJ announced, "Ms. Jacobs, I'll be your server. Please be seated. May I start you off with coffee?"

Robin was smiling, loving the attention. "Coffee would be nice. I'm going to have to give you a big tip."

OJ served her with pleasure. Then he sat across from her, watching her eat. "Robin," he said, "you're beautiful early in the morning. I hope you know how much I enjoyed you last night." He reached for her hand.

"OJ, you're incredible, and a good cook, too. You know, I could get used to this. You'll be leaving in a few weeks. I'm going to miss you."

"Babe, I'll be a call away, and I'm going to send for you. Robin, I need you in my life. You've given me happiness. I know it's premature to be talking this way, but do you believe in love at first sight?"

"Yes, I do, OJ, and I'm feelin' you, too. The distance between us is so far but, like you said, we can call each other. See one another when we have time."

OJ said, "Honey, I promise not to let you go. You're here now." He patted his heart. "Let's not worry about tomorrow; let's enjoy the time we have left. Eat your food before it gets cold."

Neither of them was concerned with the blizzard; all that mattered to them was that they were together. They finished breakfast, and then cleaned up the kitchen. Robin pulled out her photo album and showed OJ pictures of her family.

"Maybe one day you'll get a chance to meet my family," she said.

OJ said, "Yes, I believe that will happen, and you'll have a chance to meet mine."

The remainder of the day they talked, getting to know each other. OJ was snowed in with Robin for two whole days. They both blocked out the world and enjoyed one another.

The after-effects from the blizzard slowed everything down. Even though the blizzard had started on a Saturday, businesses and schools were closed for two more days. Neither of them had to go to work. They were as excited as the kids were, having that time to be with each other. They exhausted each other with lovemaking.

Finally Robin said, "Since you've only got a few weeks left in Westchester, why don't you stay with me until you leave? I'll make your life nice and cozy here at my house. You're more than welcome and I'd love to have you."

"Thank you, Robin, I appreciate the offer, but I don't want to impose. But if you will allow me to, I'd like to see you every chance I get before I have to go."

"You've got a date, Mr. O'Neil."

A Few Weeks Later

Ellen called after OJ left. "Robin, girl, I don't hear much from you these days. Dating hot and heavy?"

"Ellen, forgive me. OJ and I have built something strong within these past few weeks. My honey leaves me tomorrow. Tonight we're celebrating, going back to the Crown Plaza where we had our first date. Ellen, how do I say goodbye to the man I love?"

"Robin, maybe it's not goodbye, but hello. Somebody has got to relocate. How are the two of you going to handle the distance?"

"For now we'll commute, visit one another whenever we can. I'll visit Florida soon."

"Robin, you know you can lean on me if you need to talk. I'm sure you guys will work through the distance."

"You're right. Neither of us can let this go," Robin assured herself.

"Just look your best tonight. Enjoy your last evening together. Will you be taking him to the airport?"

"Yes. His flight is at 6:00 a.m., so we'll have dinner and turn in early. He's going to bring his things with him when he picks me up tonight for dinner."

"Girl, stop worrying. You know that man is not going to leave here with you all down and depressed. Cheer up, enjoy him. Look forward to the next time."

"I know, Ellen. Let me get dressed. I may need you tomorrow, girl, so listen for me."

"You know I got your back, Robin. Have a good time and don't worry."

"Thanks, Ellen. Love you."

"Love you too, girl; chin up. Talk at you soon."

Dinner at the Crown Royal

OJ wiped the tears from Robin's face. "Robin, look at me. Please don't cry. Once I get to Florida, I promise you in a few weeks I'll be sending for you."

Luther Van dross' song "Here and Now" played in the background.

OJ immediately took Robin's hand, led her to the dance floor where they had their first dance. They held each other so close, as if they were one.

"Robin, how can something so right be so wrong?"

Robin almost stopped dancing. "What do you mean?"

"I mean the timing, the distance, us. I leave you in the morning, carrying with me a heart full of love for the woman I've waited for all my life."

"Honey," Robin said, "this is the beginning for us. I promise you this much, I will make a way to see you every chance I get."

They danced until the restaurant closed. For the remainder of the night, they held each other as they lay in bed. No lovemaking, just holding on to the short time they had to be together. Then it was daybreak, time to go to the airport.

Robin said, "I've packed everything and soon you'll be in sunny warm Florida."

With a sad expression on his face, OJ said, "Yes, I will be in Florida, but my heart will remain in Westchester. Let's do this. Let's get to the airport."

The ride to the airport seemed endless. Both were very silent.

As they drove, OJ said, "Once we're at the airport, please just let me out in front. I want you to head back home and be careful driving. You know how I worry about you in this weather. Call me on my cell phone; leave me a message to let me know you made it safely. Promise me you'll do that for me, honey."

"I promise, OJ."

"I hate farewells," he said. "So once you drop me off, let's just kiss, and I'll walk straight until I see you next time. Goodbyes are so final. This is the beginning for us, 'cause I'll be sending for you in a few weeks."

They were at the airport. Robin parked the car in front, tears falling from her eyes, she was trying so hard not to be an emotional wreck. OJ took a hankie from his jacket, wiped the tears, placed it in her hand and said, "I love you with every breath I take, and I promise to see you in a few weeks." He kissed her with all his might. Then he removed his bags from the car and started walking toward the door.

Robin immediately unbuckled her seat belt and ran toward OJ yelling, "I love you! See you soon!"

"Baby, please don't make this harder than it is. Please go, and drive safely, and don't forget to call."

They departed, both broken-hearted, OJ on a plane to Florida and Robin on her way home.

Robin called OJ on his cell phone.

"OJ, I'm missing you already. Let me just say these past few weeks have been wonderful. I never thought I'd meet anyone like you. Thank you for being you. Please call me when you land in Florida. I love you."

OJ was riding in a daze. The pilot announced they'd be landing in Daytona Beach in fifteen minutes. For the first time, OJ dreaded hearing the name of the place in which he lived. His mind and heart were left in Westchester, New York, where he wanted to be.

OJ called Robin as soon as he got off the plane.

"Hi, baby. I made it safely. I heard your message, and the feeling is mutual. I'm missing you, too. Robin, listen, if you need to call me, I've given you all accessible numbers to reach me. I'll be sending for you in two weeks, and we'll decide on a date tomorrow. Just wanted to tell you 'I love you and thank you for making my stay lovely'."

"I love you too, OJ I'm sure the kids are dying to see you. Did you have a good flight?"

"To be honest with you, no, I didn't. I left a part of me there with you. I'm feeling a little sad on the inside," OJ admitted.

Robin said, "Honey, I understand; so am I, but we'll get through this. Listen, I want you to focus on us being together again soon, not our distance. We'll see each other real soon. I'll call you tomorrow."

"I love you, Robin. Lock up, until tomorrow."

"I love you, too. Later."

OJ spotted his son waiting to bring him home. He realized at that moment that his son was growing into a young man, how much they both had grown in those weeks. He wondered how the kids would react if he left their mom.

His daughter Nichole was running toward him. "Daddy, Daddy!"

OJ picked Nichole up and gave her a big hug. "I've missed Daddy's favorite girl," he said. "Have you been a good girl?"

Nichole said, "Yes, Dad. I'm glad you're home."

The kids were there to greet OJ, but Samone wasn't. Samone had dropped the kids off to greet their Dad. OJ expected no less of her. He was relieved that she didn't wait along with the kids. Besides, he'd parked his car in long-term parking.

OJ asked his son, "Junior, is your uncle AJ back from L.A?"

"Yes, Dad, he was by the house this morning. He says for you to call him when you get in."

OJ was glad to see his kids, but he also longed for Robin. He and the kids went home, and OJ called his brother.

"AJ speaking."

"Hey, bro. I'm home in lovely Daytona Beach."

AJ said, "What's up, little bro? Aren't you glad to be home?"

"AJ, man, we need to meet at peace ground. I've got some things on my mind I need to talk to you about."

"Call it. Your time is mine."

"How's 10:00 p.m. tonight? I'll bring some beer?"

AJ said, "Fine by me. See you then, bro. Peace."

Samone came in from shopping. "Hello, OJ. How was the training?"

"Hi, Samone, everything went well. I passed my certification."

Samone kissed him on the cheek. "We missed you around here. The kids seem so happy you're home now and things can get back to normal."

OJ said, "Normal? What do you mean?"

Samone said, "I mean with the kids, and maybe we can work on us too, OJ. I know things haven't been right between us in a while. Your being gone has made me realize a lot. I'm willing to work at it if you are."

This was the last thing OJ needed to hear. "Samone, please, can we talk about this some other time? I'm really exhausted from the trip."

"Fine, OJ!" Samone said with an attitude. "Did you at least miss me?"

OJ said, "Yeah, Samone, I missed you. I'm going to take a nap. We'll talk later."

OJ was avoiding Samone. He couldn't look her in the eye. Guilt was eating him alive. Samone was a good mother to the kids and a hard worker, but the love he once felt for her was gone. OJ couldn't wait to talk to his brother. He was overwhelmed with thoughts of Robin and guilt from Samone. His head began to throb so he lay down until it was time to meet with AJ.

Samone came into the bedroom, undressed and showered. OJ had his back turned as if he were asleep. Samone lay beside OJ, trying to fumble with his ears to wake him. OJ knew exactly what she wanted. He had been away for six weeks, and he knew he'd have to face her wanting to be with him sexually. OJ turned over, told her he had a headache from the flight, and suggested they pick this up some other time. Samone felt slighted—something wasn't right.

"OJ, you've been gone six weeks, and you're brushing me off," she said. "I know you. What's the problem?"

"Samone, listen, I don't feel well. I'm tired. I've been working double shifts. Please let me rest."

"Fine. I'm not going to push myself on you or anything. I'm going to start dinner."

OJ knew he couldn't keep this charade up; he'd have to face Samone. His guilt was growing by the minute. He got dressed to go out. He needed to hear Robin's voice.

"OJ, where are you going? I thought you weren't feeling well."

"I'm going to the drugstore to pick up something for this headache, and I'm going to see AJ while I'm out."

Samone gave him a look. "Your brother means more to you than I do."

OJ sighed. "Samone, please don't start. I've only been back a few hours and already you want to start."

He grabbed his car keys and headed for the door. He didn't want to argue with Samone. He knew that the argument was because of his not paying any attention to her. In his heart, he knew Samone was right; he had been gone six weeks, and any man in love with his woman would want to spend time with her after so many weeks. But his mind was on Robin. He realized how much Robin meant to him. He began to lie to Samone to make room for Robin.

OJ called Robin.

"Hello?"

"Hi, baby. How you doing?"

He could hear the smile in Robin's voice. "Thinking of you. Missing you, OJ."

"The feeling is mutual."

"How are the kids?" Robin asked. "Were they glad to see you?"

"Yes, they were. They're fine. Thanks for asking."

"Honey, what's wrong? Something sounds different in your voice."

OJ said, "I'm fine. I think it's the weather change. It's eighty degrees here—from the snow to heat. I'm feeling a little sick. I'm on my way to the drugstore to pick up some cold medicine."

Robin said, "I'm sitting here looking out the window watching the snow fall. Honey, please take care of yourself. I'll worry about you."

"I promise I'll do that for you. Hey, Robin, listen, I want to see you soon. Check your schedule for the weekend of the fifth, which is the week after next. I want to send for you. I need to see you. Just missing you, that's all."

"I can do that, OJ. I'm missing you too, and some warm weather would be nice. OJ, are you sure you're all right?"

"Baby, really I'm fine. Just called to say I love you. I need to see you soon."

"Honey, I love you too, and I'll be there," Robin promised.

"Sounds good. My time is running out. I'll call you tomorrow. You lock up and be safe. I care for you, Robin. I'm in love with you. I'll call you tomorrow evening. Have a good night."

"Take care of that cold. Love you."

OJ felt better just hearing her voice. He sure had a situation on his hands to deal with. He knew he wanted Robin in his life. He was on his way to peace ground to meet AJ He could express his deepest feelings with his brother. They were very close.

Peace Ground

OJ arrived before AJ, which was usual. AJ had never been a punctual person. OJ popped open a beer and looked out over the city. Daytona was beautiful at night, with the houses all lit up along the beach. Their peace ground building was an old abandoned building AJ had purchased to renovate as part of his real estate ventures. He had a lot of business ventures and wasn't hurting for money.

AJ finally arrived. "Hey, man, what's up? You looking out over the city like you wanna jump. Things can't be that bad."

OJ turned to greet his brother and hugged him. "Man, it's good to see you, AJ. Thanks for watching the family while I was away. So how was L.A.?"

AJ popped a beer. "L.A. was good to me. I closed a deal for a half million.

Property I've bid on for a condo complex. Life is good. Hey, you all right, man?"

OJ came right to the point. "I got a situation on my hands. I met the woman of my dreams. Man, she's everything I ever wanted. I had a wonderful time these past few weeks in Westchester. I love this woman."

"Hey, bro, hold up. That's too strong of a word for my vocabulary. Is she really all that, O.J?"

"She's all that and more," OJ said. "She makes me feel alive on the inside, man. Believe me she's all that."

AJ shook his head. "Damn, what did this woman do to my brother?"

"Man, she loved me the way a man is supposed to be loved. A. J., you know things are dead with me and Samone."

AJ said, "I don't see how you tied yourself down all these years, living a lie, settling for less."

"I did it for the kids," OJ said. "I didn't want to walk out on them like Dad did to us. I wanted my family complete. Even if that meant giving up my happiness."

AJ had a sad expression on his face. He struggled with his feelings concerning their father. "OJ, man, I respect that. Our dad wasn't a man. I don't acknowledge him as my father. Not the way he did Mom and us. I hate that man. If I saw him in the streets I'd treat him like a stranger."

OJ knew this was a difficult subject for AJ. OJ felt that the feelings AJ harbored for their father had hindered him over the years from getting close to anyone.

Finally AJ said, "OJ, look you've got a situation that's really not complicated at all."

OJ frowned. "What do you mean? Haven't you heard a word I said?"

AJ said, "Yes, I've heard every word, and you're missing the point."

"And what might that be? Talk to me," OJ demanded.

"Man, it's simple. I do it all the time. You just keep them both. Samone is in Daytona, and Robin is in Westchester. You make ways to visit Robin without Samone finding out and everybody is happy."

"AJ, that's where you miss the point. I love Robin and I can't do her like that. She and Samone both deserve fairness."

AJ said, "Well, my brother, you've solved your own dilemma. Leave Samone for Robin."

"You and I both know it's not that simple. Look, I need you to do something for me?" questioned OJ.

AJ said, "Name it. Whatever I can do to help my bro."

"I promised Robin I'd send for her in a few weeks. AJ, can you make all the arrangement for me?"

AJ grinned. "Not a problem. I know all the hideaway spots. Maybe a suite on the beach would be nice. She'd like that. I'll have all the arrangements complete by tomorrow. I'll just call my travel agent. OJ, stop worrying. Haven't I always come through for you?"

"Yes, you have AJ. It's just that I've never been in a situation like this before."

"Man, listen to me; I won't lead you wrong," AJ said. "I do it all the time, juggle my women. If one don't do then I go to the next."

"Yeah, I know, A. J., but that's not my style. I've been with Samone for over twenty years, and there's nothing left to the relationship. We're just barely civil to each other and that's because of the kids."

"All the more reason to keep Robin on the side," AJ said.

OJ shook his head. "AJ, she's better than that. We click. Man, I love her."

AJ said, "Yeah, I hear you. Have another beer, relax, things will be all right. Samone is a good woman, OJ, I mean, she's done well for my niece and nephew."

OJ nodded. "I know, AJ; I can't take that from her. She's a good mother. But, man, we've grown apart. So many times I wanted to leave, but I stayed for the kids."

AJ patted his brother on the back for being twice the man their father wasn't. "I say it's your time now, bro. God has smiled on you. So reap the benefits and be happy. If Robin makes you happy, enjoy whatever time you have to be with her."

OJ said, "There's one more thing."

"Put it on me, bro."

"Why am I feeling so guilty? I couldn't even look at Samone."

"My brother, lesson number one in the game is never give yourself away. Act normal, OJ. Women can sniff these things out. Samone is a very intelligent woman. So be cool. You've been gone over a month. Tonight of all nights you should be loving Samone, whether you feel like it or not. Lesson number two: never leave any clues."

"AJ, this isn't a game."

"Like hell it isn't! You've got three players and you're the number one player. If you listen to me you can master this game."

"AJ, you don't understand."

"OJ, I understand more than you know. I may not be in a committed

73

relationship like you and Samone. There are women out there who put their claims on me; each of them thinks they are the one, and I keep them all thinking that way. You know I always had a couple of spares in the trunk. That's where you got to get. It's all about you," AJ boasted.

"Man, just make the arrangements for me, okay, AJ? I need to head on back to the house."

They hugged and parted to go their separate ways. AJ felt his brother's uneasiness, and he was worried about him. Before he pulled off in his car, AJ rolled the window down.

"Listen, man, I never told you this, but I'd give anything to be in your shoes. Man, you've done the right things by your kids, and if Robin is who you want, then it's your time to be happy. I'll do all I can to help. Just keep your head straight."

OJ said, "Thanks, AJ. Just take care of the arrangements for me."

"I got this, man. Go on home and relax. I'll call you tomorrow with the details."

OJ drove off feeling a little better, knowing that he would see Robin in a few weeks. He headed on home to deal with Samone. He pulled up in the driveway and their bedroom light was on. He knew Samone had waited up for him. He sat in the car collecting his thoughts. He thought about what A. J. had said about not giving himself away. He knew he had to make love to Samone to keep her suspicions down. He went into the house. Samone was dressed in her red see-through negligee. OJ knew exactly what she wanted.

"Are you feeling any better after seeing your brother?" Samone asked.

"Yeah, I just wanted to thank him for looking after you all while I was away."

"How's your headache?"

"I'm feeling better. Maybe the night air helped."

"Come lie with me, OJ"

OJ knew that was his lead. He lay next to Samone thinking about Robin. He looked at Samone, but only saw Robin. He made love to Samone, but felt Robin. Samone, completely satisfied, fell asleep. OJ, feeling guilty, got up and went to the living room and fell asleep on the couch until the next morning. He awoke to the smell of food cooking in the kitchen.

Samone said, "Good morning, OJ."

"Good morning. The kids still asleep?"

"Yes, they're still sleeping. OJ, about last night…you were great. Maybe you should go away more often."

OJ couldn't look Samone in the face, knowing it was because he was thinking about Robin.

"I guess I missed you, Samone," he managed to say.

Samone said, "OJ, listen, I know things haven't been what they should be with us, but I'd like to try to make things better. I may get lucky tonight again," she said with a smile. "Breakfast is ready and lunch is in the fridge. I'll be home early tonight."

"Have a good day, Samone."

"You do the same."

OJ couldn't remember the last time Samone got up early to make breakfast before work. He knew then that he must have performed really well. He also knew he couldn't go on fantasizing about Robin while making love to Samone. *I have to tell Samone the truth* he thought. *Or Robin.*

OJ ate and left for work. While he drove, he listened to his cell phone messages. Robin had left an early message for him before she went to work. OJ had turned off his cell phone last night, but what if he hadn't and Samone had picked up the phone? He knew he had to find a way to keep the phone out of Samone's sight. OJ thought he could have all his calls transferred to AJ's voice mail. OJ figured he'd call Robin later and get in touch with AJ to make sure he didn't have a problem with him transferring the calls.

He called AJ. "Hey, man, come by the house this evening. Have dinner with us. I need another favor."

"I can't. I've got a business engagement tonight, OJ. By the way, all the arrangements are set. I've got Robin booked on a flight on the sixth, returning to Westchester on Monday the ninth. Hotel arrangements are set, too."

"Hey man, thanks. You're the greatest, AJ I can't wait to call and tell Robin. Now I need your help getting me out of the house that weekend."

"Not a problem. Just leave that up to me. I'll take care of Samone. I'll just tell her I need you to drive me on one of my business ventures."

OJ said, "Good idea. I'm definitely going to need your help pulling this off."

"OJ, stop worrying. I got your back. Just relax. What else do you need, bro?"

OJ remembered the reason why he'd called. "Never mind; I think I can take care of the phone."

"What about the phone?"

OJ said, "Well, I gave Robin my cell number and I didn't want to chance Samone picking it up at night."

AJ said, "Man, all you do is leave the phone in the car, turn it off, and check all messages from the phone in the house. That way if you have to call Robin back, you go out and make the call."

"You're sly, man. What would I do without you, AJ?"

AJ laughed. "Like I told you, be master of the game."

"Okay, AJ. Look, thanks, I'll talk at you soon."

OJ phoned Robin to tell her about the arrangements for her to come to Florida. He got her voice mail. "Hi, this is Robin, I'm unavailable. Please leave a message."

OJ said, "Hi, baby. Hope you're having a good day. I've got good news. All the arrangements have been made for the trip. I'll call you later with details. I love you. Later."

OJ was feeling on top of the world, knowing he was going to see Robin soon. He felt that nothing could spoil his day.

Back in Westchester

Robin was on the phone with Ellen. "Robin, girl, how you holding up? I know you miss your man."

"I miss him so much. He's made arrangements for me to fly to Florida. I'm going for sure. I haven't spoken to him yet about the details, but I'm excited about it."

"See, Robin? I told you that you guys would work through the distance. We'll have to go shopping. It's warm in Florida this time of the year. How long you staying for?"

"Maybe just the weekend."

"What matters most is, you get to see each other. Speaking of seeing each other, how about a movie this weekend?" Ellen asked.

"Sounds good. I've got finals coming up soon and work is keeping me busy, too. It will be nice to get out. Take my mind off of things."

Ellen said, "Okay, it's a date. I'll give you a call back later. I've got a 3:00 p.m. with someone T.D.H."

Robin asked. "T.D.H.? What's that?"

Ellen laughed. "Tall, dark and handsome. Robin, not only is he available, but I think he's not only just interested in my work. This is the third meeting he's called with me in less than a week."

"Knock him dead, girl! I'm glad you're taking notice. You've got so much to offer, Ellen. Give me a call later."

"Will do. Talk at you later."

Samone was at work and on the phone with a travel agent.

"Ms. Henderson," the travel agent said, "I've booked two flights for the sixth of February, and a package at the luxury Sky Hotel. Would you like to reserve this with a credit card?"

Samone said, "Yes. I'm surprising my husband with a weekend getaway. Sort of a second honeymoon in Jamaica."

"We offer the Honeymoon Suite with this package on a special," the travel agent said. "Are you interested?"

Samone said, "Why not? Please reserve that, and I'll pick up the tickets because I want to surprise him."

"Everything is confirmed, then. Thank you, Ms. Henderson."

OJ was in for a shock because Samone had planned a getaway trip for the very same weekend he'd planned for himself and Robin. Samone thought the idea of the two of them getting away would enhance their relationship. Samone wanted to tell him the news after he made passionate love to her. She had realized, with OJ being away, how important it was to save their relationship from dying. She and OJ had gotten too comfortable with the way things were, and if one of them didn't do something about it it was going to fade away.

She figured she'd start the evening off by sending the kids to her sisters for the night since it was Friday. She'd get off work early, fix a nice dinner with all of OJ's favorite food, and they'd have the house to themselves.

They were both in very good moods but for different reasons.

OJ had ended his workday. He figured he'd stop at a pay phone to call Robin before going home, to give her the details of the trip. "Hi, sweetheart. How was your day?"

"Just grand," Robin said. "It's even better when I heard your message. So tell me, honey, when will I be seeing you?"

"Baby, you've got an early flight, 7:00 a.m. on February 6, putting you in Florida at 11:30 a.m. and in my arms as soon as you land."

Robin said, "OJ, thank you. I can't wait to see you. What should I bring? Will I meet the kids? Where will we stay?"

"Baby, slow down," OJ said. "One question at a time. Bring summer wear; it's warm here. I've arranged a suite for us on the beach. As for the kids, it's a little early in the relationship. I want to tell them about you first. Do you understand?"

Robin said, "Yes, of course I understand, OJ, I'm sorry, I'm just so excited. In less than a week and a half we'll be in each other's arms again."

"Yes, baby, and I can't wait to see you in a swimsuit. In fact, I'll pick one up for you, if that's okay?"

"That's fine, OJ, How's your cold? Are you feeling better?"

"I'm fine, Robin, I just can't wait to see you. Listen, baby. I'm on a pay phone 'cause my cell is on a charge. Let me call you tomorrow. You know I love you, don't you?"

Robin said, "Yes, I do, and I love you too, honey. By the way, OJ, thank you."

"The pleasure is all mine. Now you be sure to lock the doors. Sleep tight, my love. Call you tomorrow."

"Love you, OJ. Later."

He hung the phone up with a smile on his face and went home to unwind from a long workday.

He walked into the house to smell the aroma of collard greens, fried chicken and peach cobbler. *What was the occasion?* he wondered.

Samone came from the kitchen with a glass of wine in her hand. "Hi, OJ. You're home early. I'm not finished cooking yet."

"Hi, Samone. Where are the kids?"

Samone said, "They're over at my sisters for the night. I've cooked you a nice dinner, rented a few movies. I figured we could enjoy ourselves tonight, just the two of us."

OJ looked at Samone like he smelled a rat, but he wasn't going to let anything spoil his secret happiness over Robin's visit.

"That's nice, Samone," he said. "I'm going to shower before dinner."

"O.J, would you like a glass of wine or a beer?"

OJ said, "Nothing, thank you. I'll just take my shower for now."

OJ knew he couldn't avoid the evening. Samone had gone out of her way to be rid of the kids, and she'd cooked all his favorites. He knew he had to go along with her. OJ was beginning to feel guilty again, then he thought about what AJ had said to him—master the game, play along.

OJ couldn't remember the last time he and Samone had had an intimate dinner together. His mind kept returning to Robin. He and Samone were at the dinner table. Samone was so eager to tell him of her plans, her surprise trip.

"OJ, how's the dinner?"

"Dinner is delicious, Samone. You haven't cooked like this in a long time."

Samone said, "I have another surprise for you later. Why don't you relax and put in a movie while I clear the table?"

OJ went into the living room to put a movie in. Samone came out of the bedroom in a black teddy. OJ couldn't believe his eyes. Samone had never been so aggressive. He was thinking that she must somehow know about Robin. Samone lured OJ to the bedroom and they made love. OJ thinking about Robin, once again gave an Oscar-winning performance. He rolled over, feeling the guilt. Samone lay in total satisfaction.

Samone smiled. "OJ, that was good. Listen, I have a surprise for you."

OJ, really feeling the guilt, turned around to look at Samone. "What is it?"

"I've planned and paid for a trip for the two of us to Jamaica. Honey, I told you I wanted to try, so I've scheduled a weekend getaway for February the sixth, returning the eighth."

OJ jumped out of bed in total surprise and anger. "You did what? And why didn't you check with me first?"

"That's why it's called a surprise, OJ. What seems to be the problem? Why are you getting so loud and overreacting?"

OJ was trying not to give himself away. "Samone, the thought is nice, but I'm scheduled to work that weekend. You should have checked with me first."

Samone began to cry. "The one time I do something to make this relationship better and all you think about is work? What about us, OJ?"

Feeling bad about his outburst, OJ knew that she had gone through a lot of money and heartache to plan the trip. "Samone, the thought is nice and I appreciate it. Stop crying. I didn't mean to upset you. I'm going to take a shower. We'll watch one of those movies you picked up. I'm just surprised about the trip, that's all. Don't worry, we'll go."

OJ excused himself and went into the bathroom. He was so angry Samone had scheduled the trip for the very same weekend Robin was coming to town. All he could think about was disappointing Robin. His mind raced to AJ. What was he going to do? OJ knew he had to contact AJ—this was definitely a peace ground conversation. After he finished with his shower, Samone took hers. OJ waited until she was in the shower to phone AJ.

The answering machine picked up. "AJ, man, this is very important. I need to talk to you. Call me back at home as soon as you get this message."

Samone went to bed after she took her shower. OJ stayed in the living room. The phone rang—it was AJ. "OJ, man, what's up? You said it was important."

"Yeah, AJ, man, look, I can't talk now," he said, whispering so as not to wake Samone. "Can you meet me at the peace ground at 8:00 a.m. tomorrow morning? It's important."

"Man, what's going on? Are the kids all right, Samone?"

"Yeah, AJ, everybody is fine. It's concerning the matter we talked about the other day. I've got problems."

"Okay, brother. I'll be there, and I'll bring the coffee."

OJ said, "Thanks, man. I'll see you then."

OJ didn't sleep a wink all night. He lay in the living room on the couch. Samone was knocked out. OJ was an emotional wreck. What was he going to do? It was breaking day and still no sleep. He went into the kitchen to make coffee. Soon it would be time to meet with AJ. OJ tiptoed into the bedroom so as not to wake Samone. He wanted to be dressed and gone before she awoke. He figured he'd drive around to clear his thoughts.

While driving, OJ realized that he didn't want to go away with Samone, but if he backed out of it she'd get suspicious. It would break her heart. After all these years he couldn't believe his going away would make Samone see what was missing in their relationship. Now that he'd met the woman of his dreams, Samone wanted to put forth the effort to try to make the relationship work. OJ wasn't interested in trying. He was in love with Robin, and he knew he had to be with her.

He took a long drive by the beach. He looked on, watching couples holding hands, taking early morning walks. There was a time when he wanted outings like that with Samone, but neither of them made time for the other. Just a few weeks in Westchester spending time with Robin made up for all the things he and Samone lacked. In just a short period of time Robin had opened up a whole new meaning of life to him. OJ looked at the clock; it was 7:45 a.m. He headed for peace ground to meet AJ.

Peace Ground

"OJ, man, this better be good," AJ said. "I don't get up this early on a Saturday for nobody."

"Thanks for coming," OJ said. "You're never gonna believe it. Samone has planned a weekend getaway trip for the very same weekend Robin is scheduled to be here."

"Damn, OJ, you've got to be kidding me."

"I'm serious. What am I gonna do?"

"Cool your brain, my brother. Let me think." AJ paced back and forth, looking out over the building into the water. "OJ, man, I've got it. I figured it out. I'm brilliant."

"What? Tell me, AJ," OJ said with excitement in his voice.

"I'll just pretend I'm you with Robin the whole weekend. We are identical twins, and most people can't tell us apart."

OJ looked at AJ with a funny look on his face. "AJ, now I know you've lost it. How do you expect to pull it off? Besides, we may look alike, but we don't act alike. I don't want you getting that close to Robin."

"Excuse me, my brother, you got a better idea?" AJ interjected. "Don't worry, man. I'll avoid sleeping with her. I'll think of some excuse to avoid the intimacy for a few days."

OJ was shaking his head. "It won't work, AJ. We'll never be able to pull this off. Man, she's not just any woman I'd pass off to just anyone."

"OJ, I'm your brother. Do I look like just anyone? Tell me, how long is the trip Samone planned?"

"Only for two days," OJ said. "Leaving on the sixth of February, coming back on the eighth.

AJ thought about it. "Okay, Robin is leaving on Monday, the ninth. That gives you one night to spend with her; then you can perform sexually, making up for lost time. You and I can make the switch just as soon as you get back in town."

"AJ, man, I don't know. I think she'll know the difference. Robin is very intelligent, and she's really into me. I need to think this over."

AJ said, "It can be done. Remember the tricks we played in high school? No one could tell us apart. Remember those days?"

"Yeah, AJ, I do, but we're not in school anymore. We're grown men now. How are you going to get away with not sleeping with Robin? The thought of any other man loving her makes me angry, but especially my own twin brother."

"OJ, man, I promise you I won't lay a finger on her. I'll tell her I'm on medication for a few days, which prohibits me from sexual relations. By then you'll be back in town."

"This is crazy, AJ. Only you would think of such a thing."

AJ laughed. "Master of the Game, my brother. Master of the Game. It can be done. Samone only knows the difference between us two because she's been around us both all these years. But I'll even bet if we had to pull it off with her we'd get away with it. Looking at you, OJ, is like looking at myself. Sometimes the resemblance frightens even me."

"AJ, I know we look a lot alike, but Robin will know the difference. Trust me; I know. She'll know the difference. It won't work."

"OJ, with the right clothing I could be you. You know how I am with the ladies. No offense to you, but you know I'm smooth."

"That's what worries me, AJ. Let me think this over real hard. Robin is important to me. I'd hate to lose her over the same kind of B.S. we used to pull off when we were kids."

"Look, I'm only suggesting an option for you I think can be successfully pulled off. It's all up to you, my brother. You think it over; give me the word and I'll be master of this game. I'll show you, OJ. It can be done. Robin will never know the difference. You're happy, Robin's happy, Samone's happy, and me, I will have done a good deed for my little brother."

OJ took a good look at his brother and the resemblance was uncanny. They looked just alike. OJ just shook his head at AJ. OJ said, "AJ, man, you're crazy. How can you pose as me?"

"Remember how we used to take turns going to each other's classes, taking each other's exams? We scored then and got away with it. It's no different now. All you have to do is clue me in on things Robin shared with you. Tell me all the things the two of you talked about and things you did. Once I've done my homework, then the game begins."

"Let me think this over. I'll meet you back here tonight around 7:00 p.m. Remember, AJ, this isn't a game."

"OJ, my brother, don't think too hard. I know how deep in thought you can get. That's why God made us so opposite; I'm the carefree one who takes risks. I'll be here at 7:00. And, one more piece of advice, OJ, get yourself together before Samone catches on."

"Am I that transparent?"

"Yes, you look deep in thought, OJ. Think about the L-word. Remember that?"

OJ said, "The L-word?"

"Yeah, the L-word…love which is not in my vocabulary. You said you love this woman, then take a chance on love, OJ. It can be done. If I can entertain Robin for two days, you can have one glorious memorable night with her, then she's back on a plane to Westchester and it's over."

"AJ, I do love her and she's not a pawn to be tossed around. Maybe we can get away with the looks, but how can you occupy her for two days without intimacy? Robin is very affectionate."

"Man, you set the stage before she gets here, OJ. Give her some excuse, like you're being monitored by your doctor for heart blockage. You have to wear heart patches for a few days. You hate the timing of the doctor's testing, but it has to be done on the day she's scheduled to come. You've made all the arrangements and want so desperately to see her, if she can bear with you for a few days. You'll make it all up to her once you remove the patches. You also tell her that if she could sort of help you by not arousing you that would be a lot of undue stress off you. You know, man, who knows? Once you tell her that, she may change her mind about coming. If she loves you it won't matter if there's intimacy or not. Her concern would be just being with you."

OJ shook his head. "You're a sick person. Where are we supposed to get heart patches from, and is there even such a test?"

"I don't know if there is, but how would she know if there wasn't? Robin may be intelligent, but she's not a heart specialist. We can use those smoker patches, or get something similar to that without a drug. I have a friend who's a nurse, and with a little charm I can get her to get me something from the hospital like a non-drug patch. Think about it, OJ. I'm brilliant; that's why I'm the number one tycoon real estate broker in the country. I know how to mastermind. It can work. Trust me."

Back in Westchester

Robin's phone rang. "Hello?"

It was Weesee. "Hello, girl, how the hell you doing?"

"Hey, Weesee, I'm fine. How are you doing?"

"Girl, I'm fantastic. You know I struck gold. I'm lying in the sun on the deck of a yacht. Girl, I struck a gold mine, you know? He's not only loaded, but the dick is good, too.

Robin said, "Yeah, Weesee, I heard. Good for you. Thanks for the postcard."

Weesee said, "You're welcome. So, Robin, I hear you got a man. Ellen was telling me he stole your heart."

Robin said, "Yeah, girl, I think this is it."

Weesee said, "Robin, I'm happy for you, girl. Ellen said his last name is O'Neil. He wouldn't happen to be related to that rich real estate guy Aaron O'Neil, would he?"

Robin said, "Weesee, I don't believe so. He never mentioned it to me."

Weesee said, "Girl, that's why I was calling. I figured if he was, you could hook me up. He's worth millions. I met Aaron at a social event last year and, girl, the man is a sight to see. He looks like new money."

Robin said, "Weesee, what about Melvin? I thought you struck gold with him."

Weesee said, "Robin, let me tell you something. You know me. Melvin was my ticket to ride, but now it's time for my ship to come in, if you know what I mean. It's getting old with Melvin. I've spent enough of his money and time. It's time to move on to bigger and better fish."

"I think I know what you mean, Weesee. Aren't you ready to settle down and fall in love?"

Weesee laughed. "Yeah, Robin. I can fall real hard on the dollars. Anyway, girl, just wanted to know how you were doing. How's your family? Say hello to everybody, and, Robin, let me know if your man and Aaron O'Neil are related. Maybe we girls can get together real soon. I hear you're going to Florida soon."

Robin said, "Yeah, soon, Weesee. My man is sending for me."

Weesee said, "Now that's what I'm talking about. Make him pay. Listen, girl, gotta run. My massage therapist is here. You take care and keep in touch."

Robin said, "Bye, Weesee. I'll be in touch."

Peace Ground

"AJ, I'm going to think this over real hard. I'll call Robin, sort of set the stage for the patches. If she buys that and sounds just as excited about coming, I'll consider the plan."

"That's what I wanted to hear. Listen, my brother, I've got to run. Got someone keeping my bed warm and I shouldn't keep her waiting. Let's meet back here at 7:00 p.m. and I'll bring the liquor, 'cause you look like you need a strong drink."

"Peace, AJ, I'll see you later."

OJ sat on the roof of the building wondering if he and AJ could get away with their scheme. He wanted to see Robin so desperately he'd do anything just to spend one night with her. One thing he was sure of, he couldn't get out of his trip with Samone. OJ was feeling like he'd gotten in too deep, but it wasn't time for him to reveal the truth. He sat there for three hours just looking out over the water, wondering what to do.

Finally he figured he'd better call Robin, explain to her that something came up and maybe they could change their plans for later in the month. He didn't want to disappoint her, so he figured he'd lie to her about the heart testing and leave the decision up to her about coming. He called her on his cell from peace ground.

"Hello?"

"Robin?"

"Hi, baby. What's wrong? I can hear something in your voice. Are you all right?"

OJ said, "Yes and no. I mean, I've got good news and some bad news."

Robin said, "Honey, what is it? Tell me what's wrong."

OJ was silent, feeling bad about lying to her. "Robin, remember I told you I wasn't feeling well?"

"Tell me, OJ, are you okay?"

"Honey, I'm okay. There are just a few precautions the doctor wants me to take. He's scheduled me for a heart monitor testing the weekend you're scheduled to come."

Robin said, "Honey, please don't tell me your heart is bad. I've got to be there for you. I've got to make sure you're relaxed. Nothing could stop me, OJ. I love you, and the thought of you going through this alone would make me sick."

"Baby, I know, and I appreciate that. It's just I had a lovely romantic weekend planned for us, and now I won't be able to perform sexually because of the test. The doctor says any sexual encounters would read rapid heartbeats, and that would falsify the test results."

Robin said, "Honey, it's okay. We'll make up for that later; all I care about is being with you, 'cause I love you. I want to go through this with you. I'm still coming."

"Robin, you'd do that for me? Sacrifice your own need for mine?"

"Yes, OJ, I want all of you in one piece, not half of you. Baby, we'll get through this together."

"Baby, that's why I love you. Listen, I only have to wear the patches for two days, and the third day I'm home free. If you can bear with me, I promise you I'll make up for lost time."

Robin said, "OJ, really, it's okay. I love you. Please let me be there for you. Honey, do you want me to come before then? Tell me what I can do."

"Baby, you've done enough just loving me. Listen, promise me you won't worry about this. It's just standard procedure, and the doctor is not saying I have a heart problem; he just wants to cover all bases. I can't seem to shake this tightness in my chest, and he wants to run these tests. Baby, please promise me you won't worry."

Robin said, "I promise, OJ. Are you taking care of yourself? I'm not there to do it for you. Promise me that you'll eat and rest regularly."

"I promise and, Robin, please believe that I love you and would never do anything to hurt you."

"OJ, I trust you. Where is this coming from? Is there more I should know?"

"No, honey. It's just that you've had your share of hurt and heartaches. I want you to know that everything I do is because I love you and would never, ever hurt you. Please believe that, Robin, please."

Robin said, "Honey, I believe you. Let's just pray that all is well with you."

"Robin, I'll be fine. How can anything go wrong with you in my life? You've blessed me to feel, and God blessed me with you. I love you."

"I love you too, OJ, and it's settled. Our plans remain the same."

"Yes, they do, and I can't wait to see you, hold you and kiss you."

Robin said, "Mr. O'Neil, there will be none of that until your testing is over. Are we both clear on that?"

"Yes, Ms. Jacobs. I'm still going to pick up that swimsuit. We'll have the last night to make up."

"OJ, relax. We'll be fine. Don't you worry about that, now promise me."

"I promise, Robin. You know it's a man thang, and I feel bad about it."

"Honey, look, I know what you're capable of doing. I know exactly what you're made of and how good you make me feel. This is only temporary. We both will survive and get through this together. No more talk of it. You're going to follow the doctor's instructions. Have I made myself clear?"

"Yes, Ms. Jacobs. I love you."

"I love you, too."

"Honey, I'm going to go home, get some rest. I'll call you later."

OJ hung up the phone, hearing the concern in Robin's voice. He didn't want to worry her, but he wanted so desperately to see her. His mind was made up to follow through with the plan even if he had to lie to make it happen.

Later at Peace Ground

"AJ, I'm not much of a drinker, but I need a strong one now. Did you bring anything?"

"Yep, right here. So what's the verdict?"

"I've decided to go through with the plan. AJ, man, I called Robin, and she was worried and wouldn't think of changing her mind about coming. AJ, she loves me. How can I abuse that love?"

"OJ, you're not abusing her. You're doing this because you love her. Now get yourself together and let's discuss the plans in detail."

"Fix me up with one of those drinks and maybe it will all sink in better."

"You got it, my brother. Listen, you've got to relax; you can't slip and let Samone catch on or you'll develop real heart problems."

"I know, you're right."

"Do you have any pictures of Robin?" AJ asked.

OJ said, "Yes, I do, in my locker at work," OJ answered.

"Good. Get them to me so I'll know what she looks like when I meet her at the airport. Now, let's go over every detail from day one until you left Westchester. OJ, I'm recording this; I brought along this mini recorder so I can memorize the details."

"I have one question for you."

AJ sipped his drink. "Talk to me, my brother."

"How can you detach yourself emotionally from all the women you've encountered, AJ? You've had some beautiful women in your path, and you don't seem to involve yourself for long with any of them."

"Man, it's simple, just like a business deal. Everybody is looking to profit from something. I've attained a successful life for myself. There's no time to settle down. I have to keep it movin'."

"I know your success has earned you much financially, but what do you do when loneliness sets in? Do you ever think about kids and a wife?"

"Now you're getting deep on me, OJ. If kids were in the plan that would be great, but I have my nieces and nephews. As for a wife, I wouldn't want to settle down with all the traveling I do. I'm on the go too much to limit myself or anyone else. I don't have time to get lonely, and everywhere I go I know and meet people. There's just too many beautiful women in this big world for me to just pick one."

"Sometimes I admire your lifestyle, and as your brother I'm often mistaken for you, which earns me privileges, but other times I worry about you, AJ"

"You worry about me? Why?"

"AJ, I know you've never gotten over what Dad did to us, and I know family life is something you run from because you're afraid of losing."

"So you think you got me all figured out, Dr. Psychology? You're far from the truth, OJ. I spent three lovely days with our sister Diane and she had the same assumption. Why are the two of you on my case so much? I like my life."

"AJ, maybe it's because Diane and I both love you. How are Diane and the kids?"

"They're fine," AJ said. "I love the two of you as well, but this is my life, okay? I've done my share of spoiling our sister. I can't resist her whenever she needs something. She looks at me with those light brown eyes of hers and I see Momma all in her. OJ, she turned out to be a fine woman."

"She does look a lot like Mom. I appreciate you looking after both Diane and me. Mom would be so proud of you."

"Okay, OJ, let's get back to the plan. Tell me about how and when you met Robin."

OJ began to talk about his relationship with Robin as if it had happened just yesterday. AJ was recording every word.

Finally OJ said, "That's everything, AJ That's the story of our romance. I love her so much."

"She sounds like a special lady. I noticed how your face lights up just giving me the details. Are you going to eventually tell her the truth?"

"Yes. I will even if it means losing her. She's had her share of headaches, and I hate to add to the list. One thing I'm sure of and that's my love for her. She gives a new meaning to my life."

"OJ, man, that's deep. I didn't realize things were that bad with you and Samone."

"We're only together for the kids. Before my trip to Westchester, there were months without any intimacy. We were like roommates and business partners. We both went our own ways unless it involved activities with the kids. I had forgotten what it was like to have that closeness with a woman. We lost that long ago."

AJ shook his head, "Man, the two of you grew up together as sweethearts and now the flavor is gone after all those years. Well, I can say that she's a good mother to my niece and nephew. I'll give her that. OJ, whatever you decide to do, I'm in your corner and you know I got your back."

OJ said, "Thanks, man. How about a refresher on the drink?"

"You got it, brother. Listen, I have to prepare Samone for the trip you'll be taking with me the day you all get back. I'll set the stage for that so she doesn't suspect anything, and that will give you all night with Robin. I'll stop by the house tomorrow and drop a few hints so she'll know."

"I can't thank you enough, AJ. You know I'd do the same for you if I could." They toasted each other with their drinks.

"I know, my brother, 'cause we're blood. Look, I'm leaving for Chicago day after tomorrow, so I'll stop by the house tomorrow evening. We'll get this thing started."

OJ said, "Sounds good, and I'll give you Robin's picture then. When you get her from the airport, let her freshen up, then take her around sightseeing or something."

"OJ, stop worrying; leave that up to me. You're talking to Mr. Entertainment, remember?"

"Please don't overdo it. I mean, you're used to high-class places, AJ and she knows I don't have it going on like that to afford such places. Just keep it kinda low-key."

"Let me handle this. I know exactly what's affordable to you. I'll show her a good time. Don't worry about that. I'll play the role. Who knows you any better than I do?"

"Okay. I'm leaving it all in your hands, AJ."

"She'll be in good hands. I won't let either of you down. Listen, man, I got to get movin'. I've got something lined up for tonight. Are you relaxed about this?"

"Yes, let's do it."

AJ said, "Deal. Then you keep it straight on the home front. I'll be over there tomorrow night. Keep your head together, OJ, and you'll see the love of your life soon."

OJ hugged his brother before parting. Feeling buzzed from the drink, he was also feeling comfortable about his decision. He sat at peace ground for hours contemplating what could go wrong in the switch. He convinced himself that if he and AJ got away with it in school without anyone catching on, why couldn't they get away with it now? It was settled in his mind.

Back in Westchester

Ellen called. "Robin, I have a date with Mr. T.D.H. His name is Dameon. I'm so excited."

"That's terrific! You've got to look sexy. Wear something tight and slinky to show off that big butt of yours."

"I don't know," Ellen said. "It's sort of like a business dinner to go over contracts. We've been spending a lot of time together. He's definitely single and available. You should see how the women flock around him. Like bees on honey."

"Girl, he sounds like he's got it going on. Ellen, you deserve that. What can I do to help you prepare?"

Ellen said, "Funny you should ask. I need to borrow your pearl necklace."

Robin said, "Fine, stop by after work. Bring your outfit along so I can give you my opinion."

"Okay, Robin. He's tall, dark like chocolate and he's very smart."

Robin said, "You're very intelligent too, Ellen, so he's got himself a prize. Oh, I meant to tell you, Weesee called the other day."

"How's she doing?"

Robin laughed, "You know Weesee; crazy as ever. She was asking me if OJ was any relation to some rich real estate tycoon named Aaron. You know Weesee, always sniffing out new prospects with money."

Ellen asked, "Is there any relation? Is OJ loaded, too?"

Robin said, "I really don't believe so. OJ never said anything to me about a brother named Aaron. He mentioned his sister Diane. I haven't asked, 'cause of the plans for the trip and now his health."

"His health? Is something wrong?" Ellen asked.

"I'm praying there isn't. As a precaution, the doctor is monitoring his heart the weekend I'm scheduled to see him. Ellen, I'm worried about him."

"Girl, I know you got to be and knowing you, wild horses wouldn't keep you from him now."

Robin said, "You're right. I got to see him, be with him, and make sure all is well. Hopefully the test will be good."

"Girl, it's always something. Listen, I've got another call coming in—I'll stop by after work. Try not to worry, Robin. I know you."

"Okay, Ellen, see you later."

She had barely hung up the phone when it rang again. It was Raine. "Hey, Robin, what's up?"

"Raine, how you doing? It's so good to hear from you. How are the boys?"

"I'm fine, everybody is good. Just had you on my mind. I get homesick sometimes. Atlanta has been a big adjustment for me."

"Raine, it's all new to you. Once you learn your way around you'll be okay," Robin tried to comfort her.

"Yeah, I guess you're right. How's Ellen? I spoke to Weesee last week with her crazy self. As always, she had me dying laughing, in stitches."

Robin said, "Ellen is good. She's successful with her new job, and she met someone. I know I spoke with Weesee a few days ago, too. She sounds good," Robin replied.

Raine said, "Yeah, Weesee was telling me you met someone in Florida. Is he nice, Robin? Are you happy?"

"Yes, to both questions. Raine, he's perfect for me. You'd like him. I'm going to Florida next week. When I get back I'm going to plan a big dinner party and I want you to come. I'll invite you, Weesee, Ellen and my family; then everybody can meet my man. Will you come, Raine?"

"Robin, I wouldn't miss it for the world. You're my girl. Just let me know in advance so I can make arrangements for the boys. I hate to take them out of school."

"Don't you dare think of leaving my godsons. I'll make it on a weekend so that way you can bring them along. I'd love to see them—I bet they've grown. If money is tight, I'll pay for the boys."

"It's a deal, Robin. I'd love to see everybody. You sound very happy, and I hope this guy is right, 'cause you deserve someone to love."

"Thanks, Raine. I think he's the one."

"Well, we will all get to meet him one day. Listen, you enjoy Florida and be safe. Send us a postcard."

"I'll do that. Give my boys a kiss and tell them I love them and will see them soon."

"Take care." Raine hung up.

Back in Florida

Samone opened the door. "Hi, AJ! Come in. OJ is in the family room watching basketball."

AJ said, "Samone, I hear you guys are going to Jamaica for a few days?"

"Yeah. You know your brother and I work so much we hardly have time for each other. I thought a mini vacation would do us both some good."

AJ said, "That was thoughtful of you. I came by to ask a favor of my brother if it's no bother to you. The day you all get back, I'm going to need OJ to travel with me and drive my spare car to Atlanta. I'm auctioning off both cars, and we'll fly back the next day. Do you think that'll be a problem, Samone?"

Samone said, "Not a problem for me, AJ, I'm not driving. Talk that over with your brother."

AJ knew Samone's answer that she didn't care that would excuse OJ for the night to be with Robin.

"Let me go in there and distract him from his game. Where are the kids, Samone? I've got something for them."

Samone said, "Junior is in his room. Nichole is at her piano lesson. AJ, you have got to stop spoiling these kids. Have some children of your own."

AJ never did like Samone's sarcastic attitude. She always said what was on her mind. He excused himself and went to the family room.

"Hey, man, it's a go. I dropped the seed for you being with me. I told Samone you'd be driving my spare car to Atlanta with me to an auction. So it's set. She didn't have a problem with it."

"That sounds good. Hey, AJ, by the way, how do you come up with all these ideas?"

"Easy," AJ said, "mind over matter. Did you bring the picture?"

"Yes, it's in the car. I'll walk you out when you leave and give it to you."

"Okay, listen, on our way out, mention the drive to Atlanta so Samone will let it sink in."

OJ said, "Got it."

AJ said, "Okay, let's make moves. I did what I had to do, now I got to get movin'."

The two brothers walked through the kitchen where Samone was washing the dishes.

"AJ, how long of a drive is it? We'll fly back?"

AJ said, "It's not that long. We'll sleep over and get an afternoon flight out the next day."

Samone was taking in every word. OJ and AJ went outside to get the picture from the car. AJ was grinning. "Man, she bought it. You're in there now. We'll make the switch just as soon as you get back. All you have to do is page me. Put 911 in and I'll meet you at my place. I'll tell Robin it's work paging me, I'll have to leave her for a short time and I'll be right back. Then you'll come back instead. We'll switch clothes. She'll never know."

"AJ, you certainly don't mind taking risks. I hope this doesn't backfire on me. The picture is inside this envelope. Look at it when you leave and call me later."

"Will do, and, OJ, keep it straight. Stop worrying. Things will fly. I'll call you later."

Back in Westchester
Ellen's Date

"Ellen, you look very lovely tonight."

"Thank you, Dameon."

"Why don't we start with a cocktail before we get down to business?" He ordered his preference of drink for them both. Ellen didn't like the thought of him not allowing her to order what she liked to drink for herself. After dinner, Dameon and Ellen discussed contracts.

"Ellen, for the fall casual wear line, I'd like to incorporate a six-month agreement. The styles for fall will be very marketable in France. Have you seen the designer sweaters?"

"No, Dameon, I haven't seen the new line, but I propose we extend the contract for a year. Give the sales a chance to fly, make our profits, then expand if needed."

"That's all well and good, Ellen, but six months is ample enough time." He reached for her hand. "You must see the sweaters. After our deal is closed with Mr. Sinclair—whom I may add, will be meeting us at 8:00 p.m. to sign the deal—I'd like to bring you to my place and present to you our new fall sweater line. Do you have any remarks?"

"No, nothing at all, Dameon. Six months it is."

"Good! Now I want you to excuse yourself and freshen up your makeup before Mr. Sinclair arrives. We want to make a lasting impression. This is a million-dollar contract and, believe me, if we land it, you'll be compensated personally by me. Now run along and make yourself pretty."

Ellen excused herself. She didn't know if she liked his arrogance or not, but he was so cute. She couldn't believe he was taking her to his house after the first date. Was she reading too much into it?

Later, over dinner, Mr. Sinclair said, "Dameon, I must say that I'm very impressed with what you and Ellen have put together here. I'll be happy to sign off on your proposal."

The deal was sealed, and they all shook hands. Ellen had just landed her first million-dollar contract. She was excited. She couldn't wait to give Robin the news.

After Sinclair left, Dameon said, "Ellen, I'd say this calls for champagne, which I just happen to have chilling on ice at my place. Shall we—"

"Yes, we shall."

Ellen was feeling on top of the world, thinking to herself that Dameon must have had a celebration planned. Certainly he was interested in her, and she couldn't refuse his offer. Besides, a celebration was in order.

They arrived at Dameon's place. His house was huge; more like a mansion. The foyer alone was as big as Ellen's whole apartment. He welcomed her into the living room while he went to get the champagne. Ellen was very impressed with the décor. Dameon was very immaculate and had an artistic flair.

"Ellen, would you care for something to eat? The maid has left for the evening, but I'm sure I can prepare a snack."

"No, thank you Dameon. Champagne is just fine."

She was in awe at the house and couldn't believe her eyes. He was definitely Weesee's type. Dameon poured their drinks, and they toasted each other.

"Here's to a job well done, Ellen. I couldn't have done it without you."

Ellen was blushing. "Thank you, Dameon."

"Let me bring you upstairs, Ellen, and show you the fall casual line."

Ellen followed him upstairs. She couldn't believe the size and number of rooms. The room they went into was nothing but a huge walk-in closet with all kinds of women's clothing, designer name clothes from sweaters to coats, all nicely arranged. Ellen couldn't believe Dameon collected every single line he had ever contracted. She was speechless.

"Ellen, what size are you? I'd like to have a sweater designed especially for you."

"Dameon, that won't be necessary. But I appreciate the offer. Everything is so expensive."

"I won't take no for an answer." He selected a beautiful cashmere sweater from one of the racks. "I believe this will fit you. I'd like for you to try it on. Make yourself comfortable in the dressing room, and I'll bring it in."

Ellen made her way into the dressing room, a room with mirrors all around and lights around every mirror. She had never seen anything like it. There was a door inside the room; she was curious to know what was beyond the door. She reached for the doorknob, but it was locked. Oh well, she didn't want to be nosey and ask.

Dameon knocked on the door to give her the sweater. It was beautiful. Nothing she owned was that costly. The tag read $850, just for one sweater.

Ellen was thinking her entire wardrobe wouldn't add up to that much. She put the sweater on, and it fit like her skin. What a difference money can buy. Dameon was waiting outside the room for her.

"You look so elegant, Ellen. It fits you perfectly. It's yours, and it's my pleasure. I'll have another made for you."

"Thank you, Dameon," Ellen beamed.

"Now get dressed and let me bring you home. We both have an early morning. I'll give you a garment bag for your sweater. I'll be in the foyer downstairs waiting for you."

Ellen appreciated the sweater, but she felt Dameon was too forward for her. She was attracted to him, but he was very arrogant. She removed the sweater, got dressed and went down to the foyer. Dameon was waiting with a bottle of champagne to give to Ellen to take with her. They went out a different door of the house which led to the garage. He drove his sports car to take her home. Ellen wasn't sure if he was trying to show off or impress her, but impressed she was. He was a gentleman; he opened the car door for her and took her home safely.

Outside her apartment, Ellen said, "Dameon, I had a wonderful evening. Thank you so much for the sweater. Your house was very welcoming and nice."

"Thank you, Ellen, for a job well done. Let me escort you to your door." He walked her to the door and said, "Good night. See you in the morning."

"Good night, Dameon."

She'd had a nice evening and had made a huge commission, but she was slightly disappointed that he didn't make a pass, or at least kiss her good night.

Meanwhile, Dameon, excited about the deal he just closed, wanted to share his news with his close friend and love, Aaron John O'Neil.

He called and got AJ's answering machine. "AJ, It's Dameon. Just called to say my million-dollar account is signed, sealed and will be delivered to the bank tomorrow. Listen, I'd say a celebration is in order. Check your calendar; see if you can meet me in Seattle next Tuesday. I'd love to see you. Call me when you get this message."

Florida

AJ had arrived home after visiting with his brother. He hung up his coat and out fell the envelope with Robin's picture. With all the business deals on his mind, he had forgotten it. He hung up his coat and opened the envelope.

AJ thought Robin was attractive; she had a beautiful smile. She was very plain compared to all the beautiful models who had crossed his path. Still, he thought Robin was perfect for his brother. He studied the picture carefully, placed it on his night stand so that once he awakened, Robin would be the first face he saw. He was going to study the tape of all the details OJ had given him, but he wanted to listen to his phone messages first. He was happy to hear Dameon's voice. He returned his call.

Westchester

"Dameon speaking."

"Congratulations, Dameon. I knew you could do it. I had confidence in you all along."

"Thank you, AJ. I need to see you. I'm missing you. Can you make the Seattle trip? Of course, I'll spring for the trip. We'll stay at our favorite spot."

AJ said, "I'll have to check my calendar. That would be relaxing. I've got a lot on my plate, and a few days of relaxation would be nice. I'll get back to you tomorrow. Is that all right? Hey…by the way, what are you wearing, Dameon?"

"A hot deep-purple number. Your favorite color. If you make the Seattle trip, I'll come full of surprises," Dameon coaxed.

"That sounds very enticing. I'll call you tomorrow night. Congratulations again, Dameon. Talk to you soon."

AJ had a serious thing for Dameon. They had been off and on in their relationship for five years. No one else knew of AJ's desires for men, and he kept that a secret, especially from his family. Dameon understood him, the rush he got from business, the pressures of keeping his image intact. Dameon was his close friend and lover. They'd often meet in secret places like Seattle, or Paris, whenever Dameon had business in France.

AJ had desires for women, too, but what he shared with Daemon could not compare. AJ would get attitudes when his brother OJ and sister Diane would talk to him about marriage and children. He had a bisexual lifestyle which he enjoyed. Neither kids nor a wife fit into that lifestyle. Dameon had a way of easing his tired soul, making him feel very relaxed. AJ fell asleep listening to his brother's voice on the tape, detailing his relationship with Robin.

Westchester

"Ellen, you never called last night. How did the date go with Dameon?" Robin asked inquisitively.

"We closed the deal! I made a lot of money last night. I also went to Dameon's house, which by the way, is a mansion."

Robin said, "No wonder I didn't hear from you. You went to his house? Do tell!"

"Robin, it's not what you're thinking. We went there to have a glass of champagne to celebrate the deal. He didn't make one pass at me, but he did give me a sweater worth $850.00."

"Did you say $850.00 for one sweater? You've got to be kidding."

"Robin, I kid you not. He was very generous. I don't mean to sound so ungrateful, 'cause I've never owned any item of clothing worth that much, and he was the perfect gentleman. When he invited me over, I guess I was expecting a come-on. He's so attractive."

Robin said, "Girl, give it time. He'll come around. Just be yourself. So, his house is nice?"

Ellen said, "Robin it's like a celebrity's house. He has a maid, and let me tell you about the dressing room. His dressing room is a walk-in room full of designer clothing. There are mirrors all over the room. I've never seen anything like it in my life."

"Are you serious, Ellen? Those must be all the lines of clothing he's sold."

"Yes, they are. Girl, expensive clothes, too. There was a door inside the room, but it was locked. I'm curious to know what was behind that door."

Robin laughed. "Well, if you hang in there long enough I'm sure you'll find out. Did he ask you out again?"

"No, not officially, that is."

Robin said, "What do you mean?"

"It's always business with him. We're meeting today for lunch. We're working on a new project."

"He keeps coming back to you, Ellen, so that's got to mean something. Give it some time; he'll come around. He's cute, hmmmm?"

"Very. Girl, I've got to have this man. I'm crazy over him," Ellen confided.

"You watch, he'll make a move when you least expect it. You just throw your bait out so he can bite. Be patient, my friend, things will work out."

"Maybe you're right. Thanks, Robin. I'm always giving you advice; it's good to hear my own words."

"That's what friends are for."

"You started packing yet Robin?"

"Yes. I'll be seeing my man in a few days. I'm soooo excited."

"Don't forget the tanning lotion."

Robin laughed. "That was the first thing I bought. Ellen, I got another call coming in, buzz me later."

"Will do. Talk at you later."

Florida

"OJ, you got to meet me at peace ground to go over the details. I'm leaving for Seattle on business on Tuesday. I'll be gone a few days, arriving back before you leave for Jamaica."

"Okay, AJ, I'll come straight there after work. Let's make it 6:00 p.m. Is that good for you?"

"I'll be there. Why don't we get a bite to eat after we talk? Like old times."

"I'd like that. See you soon."

AJ phoned Dameon's private number. The answering machine picked up: "This is Dameon Davenport; I'm either away on business or engaged in something important. Please leave a message."

AJ said, "Dameon, hi, AJ. Listen, I've freed my calendar for Seattle. I'll meet you at our spot on Tuesday evening 7:00 p.m. Dameon, bring all those surprises you've got me fantasizing about. See you soon, my love."

Peace Ground

"What's in the bag?" OJ asked.

"I went shopping and picked up a few clothes I thought you'd wear, so I brought them along for you to look at."

OJ looked at what AJ had bought. "This is definitely my style. I guess you're right; no one knows me like you. I can't remember the last time you wore a pair of jeans."

"Yeah, you're right; it's been a while. It will be nice to dress down for a few days. You know suits are my style. To play the part I have to dress the part."

"Good thinking, AJ. You've got everything under control. I guess that's why you're so good at what you do. You're on top of it all."

"Yes, I've got to be. Okay, let's go over everything in detail."

"Okay, I'm to page you once I bring Samone home from our trip. Then I'll meet you at your place, change into the clothing you had on, and then go back to the hotel to meet Robin."

"Correct. Remember to put 911 into the page so that I'll know it's you. I've also got some fake patches which you are to place on your chest. Once you're back at the hotel with Robin, after a few hours you tell her your forty-eight hours of testing is over; then you're home free to do your thang."

OJ smiled. "It sounds like it could work."

"It's gonna work, my brother. Remember, master of the game. I have a keen memory. I've memorized everything you told me. Just ask a question."

"Okay, how did I meet Robin and where was our first date?"

"You were dispatched to her house on a job, and the first date was at the Crown Royal, where the two of you danced until sunset," AJ finished, throwing in a little humor.

"Good, AJ, you did your homework. I think we can do this."

AJ said, "Consider it complete. We'll go over the plan one last time when I get back from Seattle. Now let's go eat."

"AJ, thanks. Why don't you let me treat you to dinner? I appreciate all that you're doing for me."

"Okay my, brother. You know I've got an expensive appetite."

"Okay, I'll dig deep in my pockets. I may have to get a loan, though." OJ laughed.

They both laughed and then went to dinner.

Westchester

Dameon called Ellen. "I'm leaving for Seattle for a few days. I'll need for you to cover the McDonald account while I'm away. Please come by the house around 7:00 p.m. and we'll go over the details."

Ellen said, "Seven it is, Dameon."

Robin's phone rang. It was Larry. "Hi, Mom, how you doing?"

"I'm fine, son. How's the new apartment? Have you been eating okay?"

"Mom, I'm just fine. I'm not a baby anymore. So, you leave for Florida soon. Are you excited?"

"Yes, baby. I'm long overdue for a vacation." Larry could sense her smiling as she spoke.

"Mom I need to meet this OJ guy, and he better treat you right while you're there. You've got all the phone numbers to call if things aren't right, don't you?"

Robin laughed. "Yes, I do, son. Anything else?"

"No, Mom, except have a great time and be safe. I love you. You're my Mom and I want you to be careful, okay?"

"Yes, dear. I love you too, and I'll call you before I leave. You need any money or anything?"

"Mom, I'm fine. Gotta get ready for work. Love you, Mom, talk at you soon."

"Love you, too, son. Be good."

Robin hung up the phone, smiling over her son's protectiveness. She realized that Larry was growing up, feeling like he was the man in her life.

Dameon's Place

"Please come in, Ellen and make yourself comfortable in the den."

"Thank you, Dameon."

"I've made some tea; please excuse me while I fix it."

Dameon went off to the kitchen. Ellen took work out of her briefcase and reviewed the McDonald account. She heard the phone ring.

"Ellen, help yourself to some tea. I just received an urgent phone call. Would you excuse me for about an hour? I have an important errand to run that can't wait. I'll return as soon as possible. Help yourself to the kitchen, and the rest-room is off the foyer down to your left. I'll make it quick so we can get down to business."

"Not a problem, Dameon. I have enough with the McDonald account to keep me occupied," Ellen reassured him.

"Fine. Make yourself comfortable, I'll return soon."

Dameon went out the front door, leaving Ellen alone in the huge mansion. Ellen felt a little frightened at first. She began to look over the accounts. When she became restless, she put the work aside to find her way to the restroom. While she was walking down the foyer, she thought of the closed door off the dressing room she had seen on her last visit. Ellen thought this would be the perfect time to see what was behind the door while Dameon was away. She looked out the window to make sure he wasn't home yet, and made her way up the stairs.

There were so many rooms at the top of the stairs, she had to remember which room was the dressing room. The first door she opened was a bedroom, so was the second door. Finally she tried one more door before giving up. It was the dressing room with the secret doorway. She went inside and turned on the lights. She saw the secret door. Hoping it would not be locked, she reached for the doorknob, and it opened! The door opened to a second walk-in closet.

On the inside was a shelf full of wigs on dummy heads, perfectly arranged from blonde to brunette, in different styles as well as lengths. On one side of the wall were huge posters of the most beautiful woman Ellen had ever laid eyes on. The woman looked a lot like Dameon. Could this be Dameon's sister? Or maybe his mom in her younger days? She was trying to figure out what all the wigs were for and for whom when she heard a car pull in the driveway. She hurried out of the room, turned off the lights, shut the doors and quickly made her way back down to the den. She ran as if she were in a marathon race, took her seat, breathless and panting. She took a sip of tea to compose herself.

Dameon strolled in. "Ellen, thank you for waiting. Did you make yourself comfortable?"

Ellen, catching her breath, said, "Yes, very, Dameon."

Dameon settled in a chair across from her. "Well then, let's go over the documents."

Ellen's mind was distracted by what she had seen in that room. She needed to find out if Dameon had once sold a line of wigs and possibly collected them as he did his clothing lines. Maybe Dameon lived with a woman, and no one knew of his secret affair; maybe those things were his mom's or his sister's. Ellen's mind was working overtime. She was so attracted to Dameon, she needed to know who the other woman was in his life.

"Ellen, are you okay? You seem a bit preoccupied. I just asked you the same question twice."

"I'm okay, Dameon. It's been a long day."

"I understand. We'll be wrapping this up soon. Let's go over the figures once more, then we'll call it a night."

"Sounds good. I'm a bit tired."

"Ellen, you've outdone yourself once again. Everything looks excellent. I'm confident that while I'm in Seattle you'll represent me very well. I'd like to make you a gift of a bottle of very rare red wine from my cellar."

"Thank you, Dameon, that's very kind and thoughtful of you."

Dameon went to the wine cellar. Ellen's mind was in a frenzy trying to figure out who this mystery woman could be. No one she knew had ever seen Dameon out in public with a woman. He always attended social functions alone. In the society papers he was known to be the most available bachelor. All the women flocked around him like flies. Ellen knew she had her detective work cut out for her.

Dameon came back from the wine cellar and offered Ellen the bottle of wine. "This should relax you," he said, "1976 was a good year. Go home, take a nice bubble bath, and tomorrow I'll schedule you for a full body massage with my therapist, my treat."

"Thank you. Dameon, you're so generous."

Dameon returned her smile. "You're welcome, Ellen. I'm only generous to those I care about."

Ellen tried not to show emotion or read too much into those words. "Well, I better go take that bubble bath."

"Let me escort you to your car."

Dameon walked Ellen to her car, and they said their good nights.

Florida: One Week Later

Samone said, "OJ, thank you so much. I was so worried about the trip. You didn't seem too excited about it at first."

OJ looked puzzled. "What are you thanking me for, Samone?"

"Silly me, I've ruined the surprise. The bikini you bought for me. I'm sorry, but I had to try it on. It's a perfect fit. She threw her arms around OJ and hugged him.

OJ had a sour look on his face. "That was a surprise, Samone. You weren't supposed to see it."

He'd been preoccupied with the plans, worried about something going wrong, and forgot to put away the swimsuit he had purchased for Robin. Samone had found it and thought it was for her. Tomorrow morning they would leave for Jamaica, and Robin would be in Florida. He hadn't heard from AJ, and he was nervous.

"Samone, has AJ called?"

Samone said, "Oh yeah, I forgot to tell you; he said his flight was delayed in Seattle. He said he'd call just as soon as he made it in."

"I just wanted him to watch the house while we're away, check on the kids, that sort of stuff," OJ said.

"Honey, we'll only be gone for two days."

OJ thought *Honey?* He looked at Samone, wondering what in the hell had gotten into her. "I forgot to pick up shaving lotion," he said, going for his car keys, "do you need anything while I'm out?"

"No, thank you, OJ. Don't be too long. I'd like to close the suitcases."

OJ had to go out to call Robin one last time and make sure all was well with her. He was worried about AJ hooking up with him one last time.

Robin answered right away. "Hello?"

"Hi, baby, you all packed?"

"Packed and ready to fly. OJ, I can't wait to see you. My stomach is in knots. I guess it's the anticipation."

"I know, sweetheart. I'm feeling the same way. Especially about depriving you intimately."

Robin said, "Honey, please stop worrying. As long as I'm with you, that's all I care about. You know what time the flight arrives?"

"Yes, I'll be there on time. Robin, I love you."

"I love you, too, OJ. Until tomorrow, my love. Sleep tight. Get some rest."

"Until tomorrow, love. Good night."

"Good night."

OJ hung up the phone feeling as if the pit of his stomach was falling out. His hands were sweaty, and he felt sick. Where was AJ? He was getting more anxious by the minute. He tried to contact him. on his cell phone with no luck.

Westchester

"Robin, you've got to wake up. Please pick up. It's important. Thinking about it all is driving me crazy," Ellen complained.

Robin, waking from a sound sleep, said, "Hello, what's wrong? Ellen, are you all right?"

"Robin, are you wide awake? I'm sorry. I know you have an early flight."

"Girl, it's all right. What's going on?"

Ellen sounded hysterical. "Robin, I went into Dameon's secret room a few days ago. I snuck in and there was a shelf full of women's wigs, and on the wall was this huge poster of this beautiful model. Do you think she's his woman? Why would all the wigs be there and locked behind that door?"

"Ellen, calm down. Don't let your imagination get the best of you. Number one, if there was another woman, would he bring you home with him twice? Number two, maybe the wigs are a line of products he sold before he met you. Don't do this to yourself."

Ellen said, "What should I do? Maybe hire a private detective to find out who this mystery woman is?"

"Don't waste your money on an investigator. Trust me, you're getting uptight about nothing. The man is an entrepreneur and a fashion expert. Why wouldn't he have different lines of products, including wigs?"

"Robin, maybe you're right, I'm sorry for disturbing you. It's just been bugging me these last few days, and I wanted your take on it before you left me for Florida. I'm obsessed with it."

"Girl, don't be sorry. I'm your friend. Ellen, give it some time. I don't want you worrying yourself over nothing. Besides, you're in there with him. You've been to his home twice."

"I guess you're right. I apologize for waking you. Listen, you have a good time in Florida. Send me a postcard."

"I'll do better than that. I'll call you as soon as I get there. I want to make sure you're okay, and please try not to worry. Promise me you won't go doing any detective work."

"Okay, Robin, I promise. Now go back to sleep. Talk at you soon."

Ellen had been restless since snooping at Dameon's. Dameon was embedded in her mind. She went to the kitchen to pour a glass of the wine Dameon had given her. The phone rang—she thought it was Robin calling her back. "Hello?"

"Ellen, I'm sorry to disturb you so late." It was Dameon.

"Oh, Dameon, it's never too late for you. Is everything all right?" Ellen asked.

"No, as a matter of fact, it isn't. I was calling to ask a favor. I'm stranded in Chicago, and my luggage got put on a different flight. No one else is free to retrieve it for me. Would it be a problem if I asked you to pick up my luggage at the airport tomorrow?"

"Not a problem at all, Dameon. How terrible. How was Seattle?"

"Breathtaking. It was a pleasurable trip. Ellen, you're a dear; thank you so very much. The flight number is 268 and it will be arriving at 10:00 a.m. If you would take my bags to your place, I will pick them up as soon as I arrive."

"It's my pleasure, Dameon. You've been so generous. It's not a problem at all."

"Thanks. And by the way, how have you been sleeping the past few nights,

Ellen? I've found that wine is a great relaxer."

"I'm pouring a glass as we speak. I've been sleeping much better, thank you."

"Again, I appreciate your helping me out, and I apologize for the late call. I'll see you the day after tomorrow, Ellen. Good night."

Ellen hung up the phone, shivering pleasantly at the sound of Dameon's voice. She couldn't believe he had called her long distance. She poured a glass of wine to relax her nerves, then another and another. Before she realized it, she had drunk half the bottle. *What was this man doing to her?* she wondered, feeling buzzed from the wine and fell asleep on the living room sofa. She was a wreck.

Florida 1 a.m.

OJ's phone was ringing. He ran for it so as not to wake Samone. "Hello?"

"What's going on, my brother?"

"AJ, where the hell are you? I've been pacing the floor, worried out of my mind!"

"I'm in your driveway in my limo."

"Limo? I'm getting dressed. I'll be out there in a few seconds," OJ said angrily.

He opened the door to the limo and noticed his brother in a state of intoxication. A. J. was sloppy drunk. There was an empty cognac bottle on the floor.

"AJ, man, what's going on? You drank that whole bottle of cognac? Man, talk to me."

In a slurred voice, AJ said, "See, my brother, I made it. How could I let you down? You're the only one who cares for me."

"Man, what are you talking about?"

"OJ, man, I blew it. I lost my good friend. He/she is gone and doesn't want to see me again."

OJ said, "'He/she'? Man, you're tore up. What are you saying to me? Did someone die while you were in Seattle?"

"No, no, I mean he, we fell out over a business deal, ending a long-term relationship that I'll never recapture."

OJ looked at him with a blank look on his face. "AJ, man, you're coming inside. I'm putting on some coffee; then we'll talk when you're sober." OJ knocked on the window of the limo to get Bentley's attention. He let the glass down.

Bentley said, "Yes, Mr.O'Neil? May I help you with something?"

"Please help me get my brother inside, Bentley."

"Yes, sir. Mr. O'Neil insisted I bring him to your house."

"Not a problem, Bentley. Thank you. Please help me with him."

OJ and Bentley held AJ up between them as they escorted him to the basement.

"Will that be all, Mr. O'Neil?"

"Yes, Bentley, you're done for the night. Thank you. I'll see my brother home."

OJ had to get some sense into his brother. He was worried about AJ. He hadn't seen him this drunk in years. OJ made a pot of coffee first. Then he ran the shower. He figured if he ran some water on AJ, it would wake him; then he'd fill him with coffee.

"Okay, AJ, in the shower you go."

Still slurring, AJ said, "Get Bentley to take me home. Nothing matters anymore."

Really angry, OJ snapped, "Bentley is gone. I sent him home, and everything does matter. AJ you're going to put on this bathrobe and drink this coffee. Then you're going to talk to me straight."

By 4:00 a.m. A. J. was full of coffee and ashamed of his actions. He wondered how much he had said to OJ about his relationship with Dameon. He had to think quickly and cover up whatever had slipped out. OJ, sitting in the chair on the other side of the room, was waiting for AJ to come alive. He said, "Man, you all right?"

"Yeah. I'm ashamed of myself more than anything. I apologize for coming to the house like this."

"All right, now talk to me about this friendship you lost and what got you sipping on the booze like that."

"My business associate, my close partner, we argued, and he ended our partnership."

"AJ, you never said you had a partner. I always thought you were an independent broker."

"I kept it silent because he wasn't one for the limelight. OJ, he's helped me get to where I am today. When I lost him, I lost a part of myself. We were that in tune with each other on business matters."

OJ asked, "You said it was over business? You split up over money? AJ, you're worth millions, and from what you're telling me you're partner can't be too far behind you. So why split over money?"

AJ couldn't tell OJ the truth about his relationship with Dameon; that the real split was because Dameon had found a new lover in France. Dameon had wanted to meet with AJ one last time before he committed himself to his new relationship. AJ didn't dare tell OJ the truth. He realized that his brother wasn't as naive as he thought, but still the time was not right. He needed to keep his life private. AJ changed the subject. "OJ, listen, this is my problem. I'll deal with it, okay? Don't worry about me."

"I'm very worried about you. Let me talk to your business partner, reassure him that whatever differences the two of you have, you can still preserve the friendship. Let me make him realize just how good a friend you are."

"No!" AJ said in a harsh tone. "It's my problem, and I don't care to discuss it any more. Please, now, let's go over our plans. We don't have much time."

OJ threw up his hands as if to say, *OK, have it your way.* "All right, AJ, I'm on your side; you gotta know that."

"I know, and thanks for taking care of me."

Westchester, 9 a.m.

Ellen had overslept. She reached for the clock, saw the time and jumped out of bed. Chains couldn't hold her from picking up Dameon's luggage. What a hangover she had from the wine! She ran to the shower, rushing to make the 10:00 a.m. arrival time. She wanted to be at the baggage gate when the luggage came down the belt. There was no way she could make it to work today. She would call in sick; she was feeling ill. Ellen called work, and then threw on a sweatshirt and jeans. Her intention was to pick up the luggage, return home and sleep through the day so she could be fresh and alert when Dameon arrived to pick up his luggage. She thought about preparing a nice dinner and inviting him to stay. She was on a mission.

Traffic was so heavy. Ellen arrived at the airport exactly five minutes early. She parked in short-term parking and made her way to baggage claim. Dameon always flew first class, and his luggage was personalized so there was no way for her to miss it. Ellen checked the flight schedule to be sure there were no delays. The flight was on time. She was the first person at baggage claim for Flight #268. Her head was pounding from the hangover. The baggage belt began to move. She stood up close so she could grab the luggage as it came out.

Ellen waited ten minutes before the first piece of luggage appeared, but it wasn't Dameon's. The belt turned steadily. Eventually she spotted his luggage, designer bags with his initials engraved in gold. She knew Dameon had expensive taste. Ellen removed three pieces of luggage from the belt. She couldn't believe Dameon took so much luggage for a short stay. Ellen had the valet attendant put the bags in her car. On her drive home, she kept wondering why Dameon had brought so much luggage. Ellen was curious to know what was inside. She wanted to know if she could smell Dameon's scent from the cologne he wore.

Ellen arrived home. She carried the luggage in piece by piece, and by the time she brought the last piece in, she was out of breath. She flopped down in a chair to catch her breath—meanwhile she kept looking at the luggage. A crazy thought came to her mind. What about breaking into the luggage to see what it contained? But how would she explain to Dameon about the locks being broken? She had to think quickly. Why pay money for a P.I. when she could snoop around to find things out on her own?

She looked for something to pry open the large bag. She thought she'd open the biggest one and leave the others—this way her explanation would be justifiable. She'd tell Dameon it was damaged at the airport. Why wouldn't he believe that, the way luggage is handled? Ellen went to the kitchen to look for a screwdriver. She made her way back into the living room, and then she began to pick the lock. After two hours of picking, she finally got the lock undone.

Ellen was ashamed of what she had done, but curiosity was eating her alive. She took a deep breath before opening the bag. To her surprise, on the inside was ladies lingerie, sexier than anything she'd ever wear, perfume, wigs, dresses and makeup, all the belongings of a woman with expensive taste.

Ellen sat back down in the chair, shaking from what she had found. She wanted to know who this mystery woman was whom Dameon was keeping out of sight. Ellen thought it must be serious for him to take her on a trip using his luggage. Ellen began to cry. Tears rolled down her cheeks. First sadness then anger set in. She thought about all the long hours she had invested in trying to impress this man, and how she rushed to pick up his bags.

She felt like a big fool, a fool for love. If only he knew how she felt about him! Ellen made up her mind to take a stand. She was going to fight to unveil the truth, find out why this woman was such a well-kept secret. She looked through the bag again for more clues.

She found two pairs of size twelve women's shoes. She didn't even know women's shoes came that large. *She must be a really big woman with large feet,*

Ellen thought. Why would Dameon want someone that over-sized? Dameon was six foot three, tall and very handsome. Why would he settle for that? *Maybe she's the model on the poster. She's gorgeous; maybe she just has big feet.*

Her imagination took her to places she didn't want to go, and she became very depressed. What was she to do? She couldn't tell Robin, because she'd promised her she wouldn't do anything stupid. Ellen went straight to the kitchen to pour a glass of wine. She drank and cried. Torturing her mind, she imagined Dameon in Seattle with his mystery woman. Ellen was so pissed off! *The nerve of him, calling me to pick up their luggage! I'm not one of his servants.* Ellen was furious with anger and jealousy. She drank what was left of the wine; then she lay on the sofa and cried herself to sleep.

Florida

"OJ, why are you dragging your feet? We have a plane to catch in three hours."

"I'm just feeling a little nervous about the flight, Samone. I've been up all night. I couldn't sleep."

"Ever since I told you about this trip, it's been one excuse after another. If you didn't want to go, all you had to do was say so. You've flown many times before."

"Samone, please don't start. I'm not making excuses. I'm just feeling a little sick, that's all."

Samone said sharply, "Well, take something and get over it, 'cause we are going to enjoy ourselves."

OJ just looked at her with disgust. He was thinking about Robin arriving today, and something possibly going wrong. His mind was certainly not on Jamaica. His nerves were making him ill. Samone was making him ill. OJ had to pull himself together. He went in the bathroom and snuck on his cell phone to call AJ

"AJ, man, today is the day."

"Relax, bro, it's going to be fine. In a few days you'll be with Robin. Get yourself together before Samone figures out something is wrong."

"Man, I should just forget Jamaica. Tell Samone I'm leaving her. AJ, my mind won't be there."

AJ said sarcastically, "Okay, do it then. Walk out just like that. Man, keep your head cool. You're not thinking clearly. Take a deep breath. Now, I want you to think about the kids. If you walk, Samone will never let you see your kids again. Man, that's no way to do it. Go along with her plan. Pretend to have fun in Jamaica, then when you get back, your prize will be waiting for you. OJ, it will work, but you have to play your role and keep it straight with Samone."

"You're right AJ, I lost my head. Listen, I'll have my cell phone with me. Call me if anything goes wrong. Call me, please! I love this woman. Please take good care of her. Our flight leaves in two hours. Are you ready?"

"Ready as can be. Now let me get dressed so I can be on time. OJ, I got this. Don't worry. Now go so you can get back. Remember to page me with the 911 code as soon as you arrive in town, then we'll make the switch. Now go."

OJ started to say, "But AJ–" but he was left with a dial tone. AJ had hung up.

AJ took one final look at himself in the mirror. He was the spitting image of his brother. He was on his way to the airport to pick up Robin.

Westchester

Ellen lay on the couch like a corpse. She reached for the bottle of wine Dameon had given her, but there wasn't a drop left. She wanted to drown her thoughts in a bottle. She figured she'd just go to the liquor store to buy another bottle, thinking that would help her forget about Dameon. Ellen didn't realize she was developing a drinking problem. She arrived at the liquor store, rushed in to buy her bottle and headed back home. Once she entered her apartment and took another look at the luggage, she lost her cool. Ellen took the luggage and slung it across the room. She sat in the middle of the floor and poured a glass of wine. She had cared for Dameon from the day she laid eyes on him. No man had ever made her feel the way he did. Maybe no man ever would again.

Daytona Airport

AJ stood at the arrival gate waiting for Robin to get off the plane. He took the wallet-size photo of Robin from his coat pocket to get one last peek. AJ was very relaxed, he set his mind in focus to play his role. Robin was approaching in his direction with the biggest smile on her face.

"Hi, baby!" AJ/OJ said, reaching out to hug Robin. "How was the flight?"

Robin said, "Hi, sweetheart. I made it! I'm here! The flight was good."

AJ/OJ said, "Stand back and let me take a good look at you. Honey, you look good enough to drive a crazy man wild. Let me kiss you."

Robin, still smiling from ear to ear, said, "OJ, you're looking good yourself. I can't help but notice something is different, though. Maybe it's been so long since we've seen each other. No kissing just yet. Remember, I'm here to help you. I don't want to get your heart rate going too fast."

AJ/OJ said, "Robin, I know it's been too long. I'm wearing the patches now, but in a few days I'll make all this up to you. Let me at least hold your hand. What harm can that do?"

Robin said, "Okay, Mr. O'Neil, just hand holding. How have you been?"

AJ/OJ said, "Missing you more than you know. I'm fine now. Listen, are you hungry?"

"I could eat a bite."

"Good, I've got a day planned for us. We'll bring the luggage to our hotel, get something to eat, and then I'll show you off around town."

Robin laughed. "Show me off, huh?"

"Yes, show you off. You're the most beautiful woman in Florida, and I want the men to stare at my woman. Take a look, 'cause she's all mine."

AJ and Robin picked up her luggage and headed for the hotel. He couldn't believe how gorgeous Robin was in person. The picture he had didn't do her justice. He played his role very well; she had bought it, and she couldn't tell the difference. AJ was ready to show her some of his charm. Not only was Robin very attractive, but she smelled fantastic. He could see what his brother saw in her. AJ sensed she had a warm personality and was very affectionate.

They held hands on the drive to the hotel. AJ had flowers delivered to the room in an assortment of colors and styles to welcome Robin. He had selected a beach-front resort. He wanted to leave a lasting impression with Robin and wanted to make OJ shine. AJ had a line of women's summer wear delivered to the room, waiting for Robin. His connections with Dameon, the world-famous designer, allowed him to have access to the latest women's clothing, free of charge. He wanted OJ to be impressed with what he'd done when he returned from Jamaica.

AJ had a full day scheduled—lunch overlooking the ocean, a full day at the spa, then a lovely evening dancing. He had even arranged a boat tour of the Florida shore for the next day.

These were some of his personal preferences being displayed. AJ had money, and he believed in the finer things in life. Entertaining was his specialty, and cost was never an issue. He tried to keep it simple so as not to make Robin think he had used all of OJ's life savings. She'd wonder how a man of OJ's stature could afford such luxuries. AJ was ready to answer any questions she had. All he wanted to do was to show her a memorable time. They arrived at the beach house.

Robin said, "OJ, this is lovely and right on the beach."

AJ/OJ said, "I'm glad you like it. You take the key and go inside while I get our bags."

Robin opened the door to a room full of beautiful floral arrangements. She'd never seen so many flowers at once except in a garden. She stood there for a second in disbelief. AJ entered with the bags, and Robin ran to embrace him with a huge hug.

"OJ, honey, thank you. They're beautiful. How thoughtful of you." She began to cry, tears rolling down her cheeks.

"Robin, did I do something wrong? Why are you crying?"

Robin wiped her tears. "No, honey, it's just that no one has ever welcomed me in this manner. Never have I had so many flowers at one time."

Robin walked toward AJ and gave him a kiss. AJ, not resisting the moment, for a second forgot why he was there. The kiss was so touching he couldn't help but respond. AJ pulled himself away from Robin very quickly.

"Honey, remember the testing. I can't get too excited, but I must say that kiss was well worth the flowers and more."

"OJ, I'm sorry. I forgot for a moment about the testing. All the flowers excited me."

"Baby, I understand. Why don't you freshen up, and then we'll get a bite to eat and do a little sightseeing?"

"That sounds good. I'm going to change into something cooler."

"Speaking of cooler, sweetheart, in the closet you'll find a few summer outfits I've selected for you. I'd like to see you in them while you're here."

"OJ, you didn't! All this must have cost you a fortune." Robin gave him another hug.

"All right, baby, enough of that." He put her hands down to her side. "You deserve all of it and more. Now, you freshen up while I go gas up the car."

"OJ, you're the best! I love you."

AJ just looked at her. He had a hard time dealing with those words.

AJ/OJ said, "The feeling is mutual. Now freshen up; I'll be back in a few."

AJ went to the car, which had a full tank of gas. He realized that his plan would be harder than he imagined. Robin was very affectionate and sexy on top of it; how was he going to keep his emotions intact? AJ was attracted to her. He had a problem. He had two days and nights to be with Robin. AJ had never allowed any woman other than his sister Diane to affect him emotionally. He wouldn't allow any woman so close. AJ sat in the car to collect his thoughts. He remembered the words he had said to his brother OJ in a moment of weakness. Master of the Game…in other words, mind control over matter. AJ had to keep his mind focused on his purpose of playing the role of his brother. AJ started the car and took a drive around the block. He gave Robin enough time to freshen up, and himself enough time to get his head straight.

Jamaica

"OJ isn't it beautiful? Aren't you glad we came? Jamaica is a lovely honeymoon spot."

"Yes, Samone, just happy to be here."

"Do you ever think about marriage, OJ?"

"Marriage, Samone? Where is that coming from?"

"Well, OJ, maybe it's the atmosphere. We have been together long enough to finalize it. Make it right before God. Surprise the kids."

"Samone, this is supposed to be a vacation. We didn't come all the way to Jamaica to be married."

"You're right, OJ. If you put it that way, I can make wedding plans when we get back home. A nice intimate wedding with both families."

"Samone, don't go putting words into my mouth. I said nothing about a wedding, be it here in Jamaica or back home. Let me be the one to ask you. Don't back me into a corner. Where in the world is all this coming from, and why now?"

"OJ, we've spent all these years together. You gave me an engagement ring years ago, and it stopped there. I think we both need to think about our future."

"Samone, I can't deal with this right now. I'm going for a walk."

"Fine, OJ, but when will you deal with it? I got us the honeymoon suite; why not deal with it now?" As he walked away, Samone was screaming at the top of her lungs.

OJ walked out on her, slamming the door behind him. He was furious. The last thing he wanted to hear from Samone was talk of marriage. OJ's mind was in Florida, wondering how things were going with Robin and AJ This Jamaica thing was turning into a nightmare.

Westchester

Dameon looked at his limo driver. "Raymond, would you phone Ms. Ellen? I need to go by her place to retrieve my luggage."

"Yes, Mr. Davenport."

Ellen picked up the phone. "Hello?"

Raymond said, "Phone call from Mr. Davenport, ma'am, please hold."

Dameon said, "Hi, Ellen, I just arrived at the airport, and I'm en route to your house. Is this a good time for you?"

"Dameon, I'm afraid not. May I please bring the luggage to you later this evening? I'm a bit under the weather, and I need to shower, dress, and bring myself to life."

"Ellen, I'm sorry to hear you're not feeling well. Is there anything I can get for you? Your voice sounds terribly weak. Don't worry about delivering the bags this evening. I'll have Raymond pick them up tomorrow."

"That will be fine, Dameon. I'm just not feeling up to company. Please don't take it personally."

"Ellen, are you sure I can't do anything? Are you going to be all right alone?"

"I'm fine, Dameon!" Ellen said very curtly.

"Thank you for picking up the luggage, Ellen. If you need anything, anything at all, please don't hesitate to call and that's an order. I'll let you go. I'll call you later."

"Good bye, Dameon."

Ellen was hung-over and angry with Dameon. His voice didn't excite her. She had to come up with an explanation for the broken luggage. She wasn't ready to face him. Ellen dragged herself to the bathroom to turn on the shower. She walked past the door-length mirror; the way she looked frightened her. Her makeup was smeared from falling asleep on the sofa, and her hair was a mess. She needed a complete body makeover. Then there was the super-size headache she had from the wine.

She took a good look in the mirror, talking to herself. "I am not going to let Dameon emotionally badger my mind. He's got to know how I feel about him after I explain the broken luggage. He's just so cute, and he should be mine, not belong to some big-foot Amazon freak. I'm going to fight for my man!"

Somehow Ellen knew she had to muster up the strength to fight this mystery woman. "May the best woman win!" she said. Then into the shower she went.

Florida

AJ/OJ and Robin had arrived back at the beach house. Robin ordered a bottle of champagne from the front desk.

"OJ, honey, I felt a toast was in order in honor of our finally being together. I'll drink for both of us. It's not a good idea for you to drink until your tests are complete."

AJ/OJ said, "Robin, honey, I'm sure a little won't hurt."

Robin poured a small glass for him. "OJ, thank you so much for the beautiful clothes. They're lovely, and I know they're very expensive. Everything fits perfectly. Let me model for you. You sit and relax and let me do my thing."

AJ sat comfortably in a lounge chair. Robin turned on the radio to smooth jazz. A.J was wondering how OJ was doing in Jamaica. He wanted OJ to know he had everything under control so that he could relax and not show Samone how tense he was.

Robin came out of the bathroom in a canary red two-piece swimsuit which showed off every inch of her well-proportioned body. AJ couldn't help but stare at her. It was almost as if she were tempting his sexuality. AJ got to his feet.

AJ/OJ said, "Baby, you're wearing that. It looks really nice on you. The color becomes you."

Robin began turning around in circles. "Honey, for your eyes only. Thank you. I love it."

AJ/O.J said, "Good. Now get dressed so I can feed you. This is too tempting for me, Robin."

"OJ, I'm so sorry. I didn't mean it in that way. I just wanted you to see how well everything fits. Let me put something else on. I'm so sorry."

AJ/OJ said, "I'm going to wait out by the water and get a bit of fresh air."

"Okay, OJ, I'll be right out."

AJ needed to slip away out of Robin's sight for a second. He wanted to leave a message on OJ's phone to assure him everything was going well. He walked away from the beach house along the shore.

OJ's voice mail answered. "Hi, I can't take your call; please leave a message."

"OJ, man, this is AJ I got to make this quick. Everything is fine. She doesn't suspect a thing. She's very happy, and pretty, too. Man, I got everything under control. So relax and try to enjoy Jamaica. Later."

AJ worried about his brother's happiness; he wanted OJ to rest his mind.

When he came back to the beach house, Robin asked, "Is this more like it?" She was dressed in a sheer two-piece skirt set.

"Robin, you look lovely, and you smell so good. I've picked a great place for us to dine. Hope you're hungry."

"Starving is more like it!" She took his arm and they walked to the car.

AJ had taken a serious liking to Robin. She was warm, and her smile did something to him. It reminded him of his mother.

Jamaica

OJ checked his phone messages. He listened to the message his brother had left and was relieved everything was going smoothly. He headed back to the hotel to deal with Samone.

"Samone, look," he said. "I'm sorry I stormed out on you. It's just that all this is happening so fast."

"All of what, OJ?"

"First the trip, and now this talk of marriage."

"OJ, we've been together all these years. Don't you think it's time to legalize our living arrangements? God forbid something happens to you. What would become of me and the kids?"

"Samone, if that's what you're worried about, you need not be. I've made provisions if something should happen. You all will be well taken care of."

"Do you love me, OJ?"

OJ looked away for a second. "Yes, Samone. How could I not feel something for you? You're the mother of my children."

"OJ, I realize we haven't been as close as a couple should be over the years. When you were away, it made me realize just how much you really mean to me. I missed you so." She walked closer to OJ.

"I missed you and the kids, too."

"So let's try to mend what was lost. That's why I planned this trip for us, OJ. Can we both work together on this?"

"Samone, I'll try, but don't back me into a corner. Marriage is so final, and I'm not ready to discuss that now."

"Final? What do you mean by that, OJ? You've spent half your life with me. Are you having second thoughts about the rest?"

"Samone, let's not argue. Let's try to work together, not against each other. How about a swim in the pool?" he suggested, changing the subject.

Westchester

Ellen took one last look at herself in the full-length mirror. She was gorgeous. She was ready to pay Dameon a surprise visit. She'd spent half the afternoon at the beauty salon getting a full makeover. The dress she chose was so tight it showed every curve. She wanted Dameon to see what he was missing. For her finishing touch, she sprayed her favorite perfume. Ellen thought she'd take an aggressive approach; boldness was her friend. She strode out the door, ready to catch her man.

On the drive to Dameon's, she took a few sips of wine. With the top down on her convertible, Will Downey playing on the CD player, she was a woman on the move and with a mission. Ellen was turning the heads of men passing her on the expressway. She looked straight ahead with one thing in mind, getting to Dameon.

Ellen arrived at Dameon's house. She boldly walked to the door and rang the bell.

Dameon opened it himself. "Why, Ellen, what a surprise! Please come in."

"Hello, Dameon. I was in the neighborhood, and I wanted to explain something to you about the luggage."

She took one look at Dameon dressed in his silk robe, and all of her boldness went out the window. This man mesmerized her with his penetrating eyes.

"Ellen, you look stunning for someone who was ill. Do you have a date?"

"As a matter of fact, I do, Dameon. We're meeting for cocktails."

"Lucky fella. You're a sight for sore eyes, and I like that perfume. What's the name of it?"

"It's Chameleon, by Dave Pier."

"Smells great, Ellen. Now about the luggage——"

"I forgot to make mention to you that one of the locks had been damaged. Apparently it was damaged en route. I filed a claim with the airport. It slipped my mind, and I forgot to tell you earlier when you called."

"It's no big concern, as long as there isn't anything missing. I've got plenty of luggage. But I appreciate your taking care of the problem. In fact, did you happen to bring the luggage with you?"

Ellen said, "No, I was just passing through the neighborhood on my way to meet my friend, and I wanted to tell you about the accident. I apologize for dropping in."

"That was very thoughtful of you, Ellen. I'll send Raymond to fetch my bags tomorrow, if that's not a problem. No apology needed; you're always welcome."

"That will be fine, Dameon." She was staring at his masculine body.

"Ellen, may I offer you a drink before you meet your date?"

"Yes, I'd like that, Dameon."

Dameon brought Ellen into the den. Ellen wanted so desperately to kiss him. Dameon turned his back to prepare the drinks. Ellen studied him from behind, her imagination getting the best of her.

"Ellen, might I make a suggestion without your being offended?"

"Why sure, Dameon."

"That is a lovely after-five dress, but it would look more elegant if you wore your hair up."

Ellen couldn't believe he took that much of an interest in her. "May I use a mirror to put it up?" she asked.

"We can do better than that. Bring your drink, follow me to the dressing room, and I'll do that for you. I don't want you to unravel yourself. You're way too pretty for that tonight."

Dameon took Ellen by the hand and escorted her to the dressing room. He put a smock over her dress, and he went to work. Ellen was like butter in her chair. Dameon ran his long fingers through her hair. Ellen put her head back, closed her eyes and imagined him caressing the rest of her body. She was completely relaxed. Dameon pinned her hair in a French twist with dainty curls hanging on the side. She was breathtaking by the time he finished. Little did he know it was all for him. There was no date.

"Ellen, open your eyes; look in the mirror."

"It's gorgeous, Dameon. Where did you learn to do hair?"

"I have my secrets, and you have yours. I'll never tell. Your date will be impressed."

Ellen turned to Dameon and, looking him straight in the eyes, boldly kissed him on the cheek. "Thank you so much, Dameon."

"You're so welcome. Now you'd better get going. No man likes to be kept waiting too long."

"Yeah, you're right," she said with hesitation in her voice. She wasn't ready to leave him. She headed for the door, only to turn around as if she'd forgotten something.

"Dameon, I wanted to tell you something else before I leave."

"Yes, Ellen, what is it?" he asked, his dark eyes gazing at her.

She looked into his dark penetrating eyes and froze. Boldness had died. She said, "Don't forget we have a 7:00 a.m. meeting in the morning."

Dameon smiled. "Don't you forget. You're the one with the date. Now go knock him dead. Have a lovely evening, Ellen."

"Thanks, Dameon. I plan on it, and thanks for the hairdo. Good night."

Dameon said, "Good night. Be safe."

Ellen got into her car and drove a few blocks, but was forced to pull over because her tears and sobbing were uncontrollable.

Florida

"OJ, Florida is beautiful. I could get used to this weather. I'm so glad I came."

AJ/OJ said, "I'm glad you came, too. We're having dinner at the Oceanfront Grill."

"Do you recall the first time we met, how we danced? I feel like dancing tonight OJ."

"Oh yes, I sure do remember our first dance. How we held each other close. We'll go dancing after dinner." AJ was glad he remembered everything OJ had shared with him.

"I love you, OJ"

"Me, too. I feel the same."

Robin looked at him funny. That was the first time he hadn't said he loved her in return. It made her feel a little awkward. "Are you all right?"

"I'm fine, Robin. Is there something wrong?"

"It's okay. It's just probably me. Let's go inside to order dinner."

They went inside the restaurant. This was one of AJ's regular hangouts, and he was well known at this restaurant. He had a table reserved especially for him overlooking the ocean.

The hostess said, "Good evening, Mr. O'Neil. Would you like your usual table?"

"Yes, thank you." He and Robin sat at the table.

"Do you come here quite often?"

"On occasion, with my brother, the other O'Neil."

Robin looked surprised. "You never mentioned you had a brother."

"We're not that close."

"He wouldn't happen to be that rich tycoon real estate broker, would he?" Robin asked.

"The one and only. How would you know of him, Robin?"

"I don't. But one of my girlfriends was inquiring about him when she found out I was seeing you. She put the two last names together, associating you both with Florida. She said she met your brother at a social function."

AJ/OJ said, "That would be my brother. Always in the spotlight, a regular social butterfly."

Robin asked, "What happened to your relationship? You said you weren't close."

"Robin, honey, please, I really don't care to talk about it."

"I understand."

"How are your son and your girlfriend Ellen?"

"Oh my, I forgot to call Ellen. Honey, remind me to call her tonight. They can't wait to meet you. In fact, I was thinking of giving a party in the next few months, and you'll be my guest of honor. I want to show you off."

AJ/OJ said, "I wouldn't miss it for the world."

Robin reached for OJ's hand. "That's what I love about you most; you want to see me happy."

AJ looked deep into Robin's eyes. He saw in her something he hadn't seen in years. A woman truly loving her man. He realized why OJ was in a dilemma. He had spent all of those years with Samone and the kids, and now there was this beautiful, warm intelligent woman who loved the hell out of him. OJ had a mess on his hands. AJ just stared at Robin.

"Honey, are you feeling okay? You're looking at me so strange."

AJ/OJ said, "I'm just so glad you're here. I just can't believe it."

"OJ, I want so badly for you to kiss me, to make love to me. This is harder than I thought. I know it's not easy for you, either."

"I'm trying not to think about it. Why don't we order our food?" he suggested, quickly changing the subject.

"Where are your kids?"

"They're spending the weekend with their mom."

"I hope someday I'll get to meet them."

"Sure, honey, that will all come with time."

"I know, OJ. You do love me, don't you?"

"Why of course I do, Robin, without a doubt."

"It's just that you haven't said it once since I've been here."

"Haven't I?"

"No, you haven't. I first noticed when I said it to you. Has anything changed?" Robin asked innocently.

"Of course not!" He reached for her hand. "I love you! I love you! I love you, Robin. See, I can't stop repeating it!"

AJ couldn't believe those words had rolled so easily off his lips. He had vowed never to say those three words again after losing his mother. Robin was the only person who was able to bring it out of him. He had a different look in his eye towards her. Suddenly she meant more to him than someone he could play games with. AJ began to feel ashamed of himself. Now he realized what his brother meant by "She's not just anyone." In a matter of hours of being with this woman, he had opened up his heart to feelings. AJ got up from the table and excused himself.

"Robin, please excuse me while I go to the men's room. I'm feeling ill all of a sudden. Just give me a minute. I'm sorry."

Robin sat at the table puzzled by OJ's sudden illness and wondering if he'd been ill all along, and he'd just been putting on a good show for her. She felt something wasn't right. She sat alone for twenty minutes.

Meanwhile AJ was in the lounge drinking a shot of cognac. He couldn't believe after all these years the last woman he'd said those words to was his mom. AJ was puzzled, wondering what made Robin so different. He felt it was something about her smile. AJ for the first time in a long time lost control of his emotions. He downed another shot and then went back to the table.

Robin wasn't there. He assumed she was in the ladies room. He asked the hostess if she'd seen the woman he was with. The hostess told him she had left in a cab.

AJ panicked. Twice in one night, within minutes, his emotions had been torn down by this woman. He paid for the meal and ran to the car. He assumed Robin was headed back to the beach house. *Where else could she have gone?* He wondered, *She knows nothing about Florida.* Worried that something might happen to her, AJ raced for time, running red lights. How could he explain to

OJ, after he had left Robin in his care, if something happened to her? *Why did I leave her?* he asked himself.

Robin didn't know the city, but she remembered the name of the beachfront hotel and told the cab driver to take her there. She was upset with OJ. Their communication was apparently stronger at a distance. If he wasn't feeling well, why would he have hidden it from her? She needed to be alone, to think about what to do. She thought she'd check into a different hotel and leave OJ a note. Maybe she was over-reacting. Just as the cab driver pulled up to the door of the beach house, AJ's car pulled up behind them. Honking his horn, he jumped out of the car, grabbed Robin and hugged her tight.

"Robin, are you all right? Why did you leave like that? You scared me. My heart can't take this."

"OJ, I'm sorry. I forgot about the testing. I was upset. I thought you were making a mockery of your love for me, the way you repeatedly said it. I thought you were making fun of it, taking it lightly." Tears ran down her face.

"No, no! I didn't mean it that way at all." Hands trembling, he reached for his handkerchief to wipe her face. "Robin, I am so sorry. I love you. Please know that, please forgive me. I never meant to make you cry." AJ, not pretending at this point, meant every word he said to her.

Robin said, "Let me pay the cab driver and send him on his way. We'll go inside and talk this out."

AJ forgot about his role-playing, forgot about OJ and let his guard down. He was getting attached to her.

Jamaica

"That was a good swim. Would you like to have dinner out or would you like for me to call room service, OJ?"

"Whatever you want to do is fine with me." He was preoccupied with thoughts of Robin and not paying attention to what Samone was talking about.

Samone ordered dinner in. She figured they'd have a romantic dinner on the terrace of their room; she had a lovely evening planned for the two of them. Why not enjoy the honeymoon suite? Noticing OJ was quiet, she asked, "A penny for your thoughts."

"Did you just say something, Samone?"

"Yeah, I did. Where are you, OJ? You're certainly not here with me. I've ordered dinner, and we'll be eating on the terrace."

"Anything you want, Samone." He was looking off into the distance from the terrace.

"Yes—there is something I want, OJ. I want for you to act more enthused about being here. Kiss me."

"Samone, I should call home and have AJ check in on the kids," he said, still avoiding her.

"OJ, the kids are fine. Kiss me."

OJ heard her the first time. He didn't feel romantic.

"Samone, listen, can we think about the romance later, like after dinner? We just got here. Give me time to adjust to Jamaica."

"OJ, I didn't bring you here to stare out into the sunset or stay locked up in the room. What seems to be the problem? Is this about us or is it someone else?"

OJ looked guilty. "Samone, there's no problem. We have no problems, and there's no one else. Why would you ever think such a thing?"

"It's your actions, OJ. You seem so distant."

O J. had made up his mind. He'd better do whatever Samone wanted him to do; she was starting to suspect something.

"Samone," he suggested, "why don't you change into something sexy? You want me to be romantic, then help me out."

Samone went into the bathroom to freshen up. OJ snuck out his cell phone while she was in the shower. He called AJ and left a message on his voice mail.

"AJ, I received your message. Man, I'm so restless. I can't get into this. Samone is getting on my nerves. She's starting to suspect something. She asked if there was someone else. I have to get the situation here under control. I'm relieved to know you've got it all handled there. Isn't Robin a sight for sore eyes? Be good, man. I'll see you soon. Thanks. Later."

Samone came out of the bathroom wearing a bright orange thong and matching bra. OJ had his back turned, standing on the terrace.

"OJ, come here, baby."

OJ turned to face her. He couldn't believe his eyes. Samone had never been so provocative in all their years together. She would always wear his shirts to bed, nothing so revealing. OJ couldn't believe what he was seeing. Two kids and twenty plus years later, she still had a shape out of this world. She had just kept it hidden from him until recently.

OJ said, "Wow, Samone! You look—"

Samone covered his mouth with her hand. "Don't say it, OJ, Just show me."

Westchester

Ellen sat in her car, head on the steering wheel, makeup running down her cheeks from her tears. She had lost all track of time. Suddenly there was a knock on the car window; it was Dameon.

"Ellen, are you all right? I noticed your car parked on the side of the rode as I was driving by."

Ellen's heart was pounding. Caught off guard, she began to wipe the tears away so Dameon couldn't see them "Oh, Dameon, I'm fine. I was just reaching for my cell phone. My date had an emergency, so we'll have to take a rain-check."

"Thank God! You scared the heck out of me. I spotted your car so I backed up. I wanted to make sure you were all right. Sorry about your date. You look so lovely; it's his loss," Dameon consoled her.

"I'm okay. Thanks, Dameon."

"No, you're not. You're too pretty to let this evening go to waste. I was on my way to Lamarage for dinner. Would you care to join me? I'd love to have a beautiful woman like you with me."

Ellen looked up at Dameon; her eyes lit up. "Yes, I'd like that, Dameon, very much."

"Ellen, your makeup is smeared. Have you been crying, dear?"

Ellen, put on the spot, couldn't tell Dameon she was crying over him. "Oh, no, it's my allergies, driving with my convertible top down and all the pollen in the air. You know how allergies can be."

Dameon played it off. He knew she had been crying. He knew how matters of the heart and broken dates can make a girl teary-eyed. He'd had plenty of disappointments in his day, most of them from Aaron O'Neil. For a moment he reflected back to all the broken dates with AJ, and he knew exactly how Ellen felt.

"Yeah, Ellen, I know. Allergies can mess a girl up. Let's take your car back to the house, get your makeup freshened up, and then we can be on our way."

Ellen was on cloud nine. A real date with Dameon, without work. She was sure glad she had stopped on the side of the road. Dameon followed her back to his house. Like a gentleman, he got out of his car, opened her door, took her hand and escorted her into the house. She couldn't help noticing what a sharp dresser Dameon was with his Stacy Adams shoes on. He took Ellen to the dressing room to fix her makeup, and he re-did her hair.

Dameon said, "Ellen, now you look like new money. Shall we?" he asked, holding his arm out for hers.

Ellen thought she'd died and gone to Heaven. The man she adored was on her arm. She was all smiles. She wondered where his mystery woman was tonight. She certainly wasn't on his arm. Off they went in his Bentley to Lamarage.

Florida

"Robin, I'm so sorry I left you like that. Please forgive me."

"Is everything all right with us, OJ? Are you feeling all right?"

"Honey, I'm fine, really. Everything is fine. Look, you've had a long day, and I know you're hungry. Let me make this up to you, please. I'll order delivery service from the best restaurant I know. You just lie down and relax."

"I'm okay with that, but are you sure we're all right?"

AJ/OJ looked her in the eye. "Yes, Robin. I love you. If it means anything, I wasn't making a mockery of our love."

Robin walked toward AJ, put her arms around him and romantically kissed him. They both got caught up in the kiss. AJ, not letting go of her, lost himself in Robin's arms. Her kiss was so sexual, warm, and heartfelt, he forgot his role playing. Quickly he jumped back.

"Robin, forgive me. I lost myself for a minute," AJ said, literally meaning every word.

"OJ, you kissed me as if it was our first kiss. Are you sure everything is okay?"

"Yes, Robin, everything is fine. Now let me get some food in you. I'm going to order the biggest lobster dinner you've ever had. Why don't you get comfortable while I go to the front desk to get the number to call? I'll be back in a few."

"Okay, but please don't be long."

"I promise I'll be right back."

He got beyond their room door and leaned his head against it. He couldn't believe how caught up in that kiss he had gotten. He was feeling sexually attracted to Robin, and it frightened him. He was feeling something for his brother's woman. AJ wanted Robin sexually. The game had turned out to be a trick on him. He never thought his feelings would be drawn to Robin. AJ was no longer role-playing; he was falling in love with Robin, and he didn't know what to do about it.

He walked to the front office to clear his head. He knew the restaurant number by heart, but he needed time away from Robin to resist the temptation. He wanted her just as much as his brother did, and there was nothing he could do but play his role.

Jamaica

OJ and Samone lay in bed after making love.

"OJ, you are awesome—that was great. Hey, by the way, there's something I've been meaning to tell you."

"Yes, Samone, what might that be?"

"I stopped taking the pill. I figure a baby would be good for us. Then we could be married before the baby is born," Samone said innocently.

OJ jumped out of bed. "Samone, we don't need any more children. How dare you stop taking the pill without discussing it with me! I don't want any more kids. I don't want to get married! I didn't want this trip!"

OJ blew up. He'd had enough of Samone and her wild plans.

"I'm afraid it's no longer what you want, OJ. If you don't decide to make a legal woman out of me, you can forget about me and the kids. If I get pregnant, we'll just be starting over."

"Samone, what's gotten into you? You can't force me, nor will I let you use the kids against me. Why are you doing this?"

"I've been with you all these years, OJ, and I know you better than you know yourself. Ever since you've come back from Westchester, you've been acting differently. I don't know what happened there, but I do know one thing: we are going to be married or I'm out, me and the kids, for good."

OJ didn't argue with her; instead he got up and left the room. He was furious. He knew Samone suspected something. He had just blown it big time. What if she is pregnant? He felt as though his life was out of control. Trying to smooth things over to get back in Samone's good graces, he went to the front desk of the hotel to order flowers and champagne to be sent to their room. He needed that one night with Robin once he returned to figure everything out.

OJ was angry, but he had to role-play just like his brother. He figured if he gave Samone a romantic evening, she'd forget all the things he had said to her. He thought about what his brother had said to him about being master of the game.

Westchester

"Ellen, it's too bad your date cancelled out. You look absolutely stunning tonight."

"Thank you, Dameon. Lamarage is so cozy. Do you often dine here?"

"Yes, as a matter of fact, I do. You know, Ellen, I just realized we've always talked business. I can't say that I know anything on a personal level about you. Tell me, have you lived in Westchester all your life?"

Ellen, her hands sweating, thought Dameon was taking a serious interest in her. "Yes, Dameon, I was born and raised right here in Westchester."

"And the young man you were meeting for cocktails, is he your man?"

"Oh no, by no means, Dameon. He is just a friend."

"I ask because everyone desires to have that special someone in their lives." He was gazing at her with his deep black eyes.

"Yes, you're right. What about you? Is there a special someone in your life?"

"There was, but we've decided to keep it on a friendship level. My schedule demands so much of my time. There's really no one, nor a solid relationship."

"Dameon, could it be you haven't found that special someone yet? Sometimes things can be right at our feet and we miss them." She was trying to tell Dameon how she felt.

"You're absolutely right, Ellen. I believe in exploring my options. For now I feel I'm where I should be in my life. I have a successful business, health, money in the bank. What more can a person ask for?"

"Do you ever get lonely, Dameon?"

"Why, certainly not. I have enough on my plate to keep me occupied."

"How was Seattle? Did you travel alone or did you meet with friends?" Ellen inquired.

"Seattle was lovely, and of course I have plenty of friends there. The flight was long, but the stay was well worth it. I purchased some property while I was there. A good friend is into real estate and talked me into buying a house there."

"Oh, a good friend? So I imagine you'll be spending a lot of time in Seattle." She was thinking that the mystery woman lived in Seattle.

"It's a possibility. Ellen, I can't help but notice that the two gentlemen at the table across from us keep looking over at us. Would you care to send them a drink over? You may get lucky and meet that someone special."

"Dameon, I'd rather not leave the door open. I'm sort of feeling my way out on someone I admire."

Dameon said, "Is that a fact? Do tell—who's the lucky guy?"

Ellen eyes were as big as tea cups from being put on the spot. She couldn't tell him. She was speechless.

"Dameon, I have my secrets, and you have yours," she said finally. They both laughed.

Florida

"Robin, dinner will be delivered within the hour. How about a game of chess?"

"I'd like that. OJ, that handkerchief you gave me outside had 'Dameon' written on it. Is that a new brand name?"

AJ looked nervous; he'd forgotten where he'd gotten the hanky. Dameon must have slipped it in his jacket pocket for a keepsake, as a remembrance of him and Seattle.

"No, it's not a name brand. Dameon is a good friend. I borrowed the hanky from him. In fact, he's the designer I purchased your summer wear from. He's a very dear friend. Robin, have you ever met someone for the first time in your life and felt as if you've known that person forever?"

"Yes, OJ. That's exactly how I felt when we met."

"Well, that's how it was when I met Dameon."

Robin said, "Some people have that effect on you. How about that game of chess?"

Jamaica

"The flowers are so pretty. Thank you, OJ." Samone seemed to be softening.

"Samone, listen, I apologize for the things I said to you. Let's just try to have a good time while we're here."

"OJ, were you really serious about not wanting any more kids? What if I get pregnant?"

OJ kept his voice even, trying not to display his anger. "Samone, we'll deal with it if it happens. I just want to enjoy our time together without stressing over things that have yet to occur."

"You're right, OJ." She walked towards him to kiss him.

The two days in Jamaica flew by. Samone was very happy. OJ tried to make it a memorable trip for her, although his mind was in Florida. Finally it was time to go home—OJ couldn't wait to see Robin. He gently reminded Samone of the trip he was to take with AJ to Atlanta.

"Samone, honey, let's pick up the kids on our way home. But remember, I've gotta leave with AJ this afternoon to bring the cars to the auction."

"We just got back in town. What's the hurry? Don't you at least want to spend time with the kids, OJ?"

"You knew about this trip with AJ. Please let's not argue over it. Didn't you enjoy yourself in Jamaica?"

"Yes, I did. Very much."

"So what's the problem now? AJ and I are only going to be gone overnight. He already booked an afternoon flight, and I'll be back before you realize I'm gone."

OJ was rushing to get to Robin. He took Samone and the kids home and headed straight to AJ's place to await the switch.

Beach House

"Robin, these past two days with you have been Heaven," AJ/OJ said, expressing his true feelings towards her.

"OJ, kiss me just once. It's so hard to hold back," Robin pleaded.

AJ took her in his arms and held her as close as he could. He kissed her with passion. His last few minutes with Robin were soon to end once he received the page from OJ AJ looked deeply into her eyes.

"Robin, I'm in love with you. I love you." From the depth of his soul, he was able to tell Robin he loved her, because it was true. He really had fallen in love with her.

"OJ, now I know you do. I feel your love. I love you, too."

"Just let me hold you close in my arms. I want to savor this moment and keep it fresh in my heart forever, Robin." He held onto her as if he would never see her again. And then his pager went off with the 911 code.

Westchester

"Ellen, would you care to dance?"

Ellen was getting nervous. She was finally getting a chance to be close to him. "Yes, I'd like that, Dameon."

As they walked towards the dance floor, the two men who had been sitting across the room were staring at Dameon. One gentleman came up behind Dameon and introduced himself.

"Please excuse me. I don't mean to interrupt you all, but haven't we met?" he asked Dameon.

Dameon said, "It's a possibility. I remember faces but lose track of names."

"My name is Mark," the stranger said. "We met at a club in Seattle. Do you remember?"

Dameon tried to brush him off so Ellen wouldn't pick up on the conversation. He had met Mark in a gay bar in Seattle.

Dameon said, "I'm sorry, I'm afraid you have me mixed up with someone else. But please, let me give you my business card if you're ever in the need of designer clothing." Dameon handed Mark the card with his private phone numbers on it. On the back of the card it read: "Call me later; we'll get together."

Mark read the card and played it off. "I'm terribly sorry, sir. Thank you for your card."

Dameon said, "My pleasure."

"Dameon, you are so popular. Are you frequently mistaken for someone else?"

He smiled. "People always seem to come up to me for some reason. They use that same old tired line. 'Haven't we met before?' Knowing they never knew me. That's one of the oldest lines in the book."

Out on the dance floor a slow melody was playing, and Dameon pulled Ellen close to him. She laid her head on his broad chest, closed her eyes and got a good sniff of his expensive cologne. She thought she'd died and came back to life. She was in Dameon's arms at last.

Dameon was thinking about AJ. This very song was their theme song. Oh how he longed to hear AJ's voice. Dameon realized the break-up was causing him a lot of stress. Maybe he had done the wrong thing— breaking it off with AJ in the hopes of forcing his hand into committing to him.

AJ had a variety of people he saw on the regular, and Dameon had wanted him all to himself. To get even, Dameon led AJ to believe he had gotten involved with someone in France. Dameon was playing hard to get, but hurting himself in the process. The longer the song played, the more he needed to hear AJ's voice.

"Please, let's stop, Ellen. I have to make an important phone call."

Back at the table, Ellen was looking sad, wondering why he stopped in the middle of the song. Her imagination was getting the best of her. Maybe he had to call his mystery woman.

Florida Beach House

"Robin, honey, my pager just went off. Remember I told you I was on call for work? Well, I just received a page. I have to report in and make sure everything is running smoothly, and then I'll be right back. Trust me—I don't want to leave you. Just let me hold you close before I go."

"OJ, what's wrong? You're holding me as if you're not coming back. I understand duty calls, but I'll be here when you return."

"I know, Robin. I've got to get going. How about one more kiss for the road?" AJ liked the way she kissed him and the warm feeling it gave him.

Robin laughed. "Okay, honey, now get going before you lose your job. I promise you I'll be here when you return."

AJ didn't want to leave her. He was in love with her, but he knew he had to get to OJ.

"All right, Robin, I'm out of here. Give me that smile before I go."

Robin looked at him strangely with a smirk on her face, as if to say, 'What is going on?'

"Robin, I love you. Hold onto that until I come back."

"I will."

AJ walked out, closing the door behind him. He drove around the corner and parked. He had to get his composure together before he met with OJ. He had to deal with his feelings. He wiped the lipstick off his lips and then phoned his house where he knew OJ would be waiting.

"OJ, man, it's me. Pick up the phone."

There was excitement in OJ's voice. "What's wrong, AJ?"

"Everything is fine. I'm on my way. I told Robin work was paging me."

"AJ, man, thank you—I owe you so much."

"I'll be there soon," AJ assured him.

He was torn between his love for OJ and his love for Robin. *How am I to explain to my brother that I'm in love with his girl? How can I hide this from him?* AJ's cell phone rang. He picked it up, thinking it was OJ calling him back. "Hello?"

It was Dameon. "Aaron John O'Neil, I can't stop thinking of you. I want to see you."

"Dameon, I can't talk to you now. Please not now. I'll phone you later." He hung up the phone.

Robin had helped him to overcome his feelings for Dameon. Now Dameon wanted him back, but he was in love with Robin not Dameon. He felt like his emotions were on a rollercoaster. AJ wanted a drink.

Westchester

Dameon went back to the table where Ellen was waiting. His attitude very curt after AJ had hung up on him. Hurt and angry, he didn't care to be with anyone.

"Ellen, gather your things. We're leaving."

"Dameon, is there something wrong? Did I do something? Did something happen?"

Dameon was very short with her. "It's not you, it's me. Now let me take you to your car. I had a lovely time tonight."

Ellen was quiet on the drive back to Dameon's place. She figured he must have called his mystery woman, and they had a spat because he had a completely different attitude after making his phone call. Ellen was furious.

How dare she interrupt my evening with him? I'm going to find out who this big bitch is and confront her.

They arrived at Dameon's. He didn't invite her in. Ellen was upset. She had thought the evening was hers.

"Ellen, I apologize for my demeanor, but suddenly I'd like to spend the evening alone. Don't take it personally. I have a few problems I need to attend to."

"I understand, Dameon."

"Thanks for the date. Drive safely."

Ellen was frantic. She had to know who this person was who had so much power over the man she wanted. She made up her mind to hire a private detective, even though she had given Robin her word that she wouldn't. Dameon meant too much to her not to know who was getting all of his attention.

Florida

"AJ, tell me, how did it go? Did she believe you? Or should I say 'us'?"

"Yes, OJ, she bought it. I passed for you." AJ was not happy about what he had done.

"Is there anything I should know, anything you need to fill me in on?" OJ asked.

"No. She's a fine woman, and she loves the hell out of you."

OJ grinned. "Man, I told you she's special."

"Let's change clothes. You don't want to keep her waiting."

They exchanged clothes. OJ was nervous; the moment he had been waiting for had finally arrived. Once again he was going to see the woman who gave him life.

"AJ, I just want to tell you how much I appreciate what you've done for me." He hugged his brother and told him he loved him. "I love you, man. You're the greatest. I gotta go now, but I'll get in touch with you when she leaves."

"Okay, OJ, now go."

OJ left as if he was going to a fire. AJ poured a drink to calm his nerves. He was so saddened in spirit. He had let his guard down and allowed love to fill his heart. Emotions were running deep. Robin was everything he had dreamed a mate could be. How was he to deal with it? He didn't want to hurt his brother, but he didn't want to say goodbye to Robin either.

OJ pulled up to the door of the beach house. Both his hands and knees were trembling because he was so nervous. He got out of the car, approached the door and fumbled to put the key in to open the door to the woman he loved. OJ ran to Robin and picked her up off her feet. He held her tight in his arms and kissed her before he said a word to her.

"Robin, Robin, oh how I missed you so! I love you so much!" OJ was kissing her on her neck and in the places that aroused them both.

Robin was confused. "OJ, what's wrong? You're acting like you're seeing me for the first time. I'm not complaining, but what's going on?"

OJ said, "Baby, everything is fine." He picked her up, carried her to the bedroom, laid her across the bed and began to kiss her all over. They both got caught up in the heat of love.

"OJ, the test, what about the test?"

"It's over now. I want you. I need you. I got to have you!"

"Take me, OJ, I'm yours."

OJ made love to her as if he hadn't been with a woman in years, gently stroking her with every ounce of love he had to give. There were no words spoken; their bodies did the talking. They both were in ecstasy as they made love for hours.

Westchester

Meanwhile, Dameon was an emotional wreck from AJ's putting him off. He thought his scheme of making AJ think there was someone else would make him run back to him. Instead, it was backfiring. Dameon had tried to fight the feelings he had for AJ He had tried to move forward, but love stopped him. He was angry, yet saddened by their breakup. Dameon poured a glass of scotch, sat in his recliner and reflected back on his trip to Seattle.

Dameon knew AJ couldn't go for long without him. They both shared a common denominator. The secret love affair they had shared for years. Dameon awaited AJ's call. Emotions spiraling downward, he needed to feel confident about himself. The only time he felt sure about himself was when he was dressed in elegance; the way AJ adored seeing him. He went upstairs to the dressing room and pulled a shoulder-length blonde wig off the shelf. He began to put his makeup on, preparing his face as if he were in a beauty contest. Face beautifully made up, he slipped on his wig and looked at himself in the mirror.

He was ready to call AJ again. Dameon had the confidence he needed. This time he was not going to be rejected. He was ready to tell AJ how he felt, ready to express his love. Feeling very feminine gave him boldness, a power to conquer all roadblocks. Adoring himself in the mirror, he needed the appropriate outfit to complete his look.

He went to the closet and pulled out a purple and silver sequined dress, AJ's favorite. Dameon got dressed. Looking in the mirrors that surrounded the room, he was able to take a full look at himself. He was gorgeous.

Suddenly Dameon snapped. He hated what he saw in the mirror. He hated who he'd become. He took the glass of scotch and threw it at the mirror. The glass shattered everywhere. Dameon fell to his knees and broke down. AJ had crushed his manhood, stolen his heart. Dameon lay weeping for hours.

Florida

"I'd like to inquire about two tickets previously purchased from Atlanta to Daytona tomorrow afternoon. Can you please help me?"

"Ma'am, I'm very sorry, but we cannot give out that information unless you were the one who purchased the tickets," the airport attendant said.

"Lady, look, my husband is flying in from Atlanta with a relative on your airline, and I need to know his flight number and time."

The attendant said, "If you will give me your husband's name, I can tell you his itinerary."

"Oscar James O'Neil is the name, and his brother's name is Aaron John O'Neil."

The attendant said, "Please hold, ma'am, while I look up the information."

Not only was Samone pissed off with the attendant, but she was feeling suspicious and wanted to check on OJ.

The attendant came back on the line. "I'm sorry, ma'am. We have no one by those names on our passenger list."

Samone said, "Thank you."

She was furious. She'd had a gut feeling that something wasn't right when OJ was in such a hurry to get to AJ. She tried calling AJ's house to see if he answered the phone, but she got his answering machine. She knew the two of them were up to something. What it was she couldn't put her finger on.

Beach House

"Robin, I'm so glad you're here. Marry me. Be my wife."

"Are you serious, OJ?"

"Yes, sweet Robin, I've never been so serious about anything in my life. I love you, and I'm sure I want to spend the rest of my life with you."

"Honey, of course I want to marry you. But let's not rush it. Shouldn't we spend more time together? Get to know each other's kids and families? OJ, I've never felt this way for anyone; it's almost frightening. Almost too good to be true. I guess I'm scared of losing what we have. I love you so much."

OJ held Robin's face and looked her straight in the eyes and said, "Robin, as long as there's breath in my body, and I'm able to function, you'll never have to worry about losing what we share. I want you in my future. I need you in my life. My days and nights are incomplete without you. I've found my happiness in you. I'm sure I want to make you my wife."

"Honey, I'm honored to be the future Mrs. O'Neil, but can we slow the pace down a little? At least get in one state? We both have our careers, the kids and the houses. We need to take it day by day and give it some time. I'm not going anywhere. We can travel back and forth until we finalize everything."

"Sweetheart, you're absolutely right. I realize things take time. It's just that

I want you here with me all the time. Kiss me, Robin. How I've longed to be with you!"

They embraced each other in a long passionate kiss, both wrapped in a moment of love. OJ forgot about Samone; all he wanted was Robin.

Westchester

"Hello, this is Got To Know Investigation Services. How may I direct your call?"

"Hello, my name is Ellen Berk. I'm in need of your service. I need your best P.I. available."

"Yes, Ms. Berk, that would be Drake Kimble. He's our top man, very expensive, but very good at what he does."

"Cost is not an issue. Is Mr. Kimble available?"

"Ms. Berk, I'm sorry, but he's currently out working on a case. If you would please give me a number where you can be reached, I'll have him contact you just as soon as possible."

Dameon's Place

Dameon was passed out, lying on the floor when he heard the phone ringing in the distance. His voice was low and emotionally broken when he answered. "This is Dameon speaking."

It was Mark, the man who'd spoken to him at the restaurant. "Dameon, hi, it's Mark. We spoke at Lamarage. Are you busy tonight?"

Dameon pulled himself together, wiping off the makeup he had ruined with his tears. "Why, Mark, you're timing is impeccable. I'd love to meet with you. Shall we say 11:00 p.m. at the Grand Hotel?"

Mark said, "Great, I'll see you there."

Dameon was finished weeping over AJ. He needed to go on with his life. Maybe a date with Mark would help him overcome his feelings for AJ. *It's time to move on*, he thought. He got dressed to meet Mark.

Florida at AJ's Place

AJ heard Samone's voice on the answering machine. He wanted so desperately to contact OJ to let him know Samone was checking on him. He sat gazing at Robin's picture, imagining making love to her. He wanted so desperately to be in his brother's shoes. He needed to see her again before she left Florida. But how? By now, AJ was intoxicated. He drank his troubles away. With Robin's picture in his hand, he drifted off to sleep.

OJ and Robin made love most of the night, but the day had arrived for them to part. Robin had to return home, and her flight was scheduled to leave at noon.

"Thank you, OJ, for three lovely days. I'm going to miss you so much."

"Robin, you know I was very serious about making you my wife."

"Yes, honey. I'm serious too. I can't wait for you to meet my family. I'll plan a dinner party for next month so you can meet everyone."

"Perfect. We can get engaged and tell everyone the news. Robin, you mean so much to me. I love you very much."

"I love you too, OJ, and I'd be honored to be your wife."

AJ awoke with Robin's picture in his hand. He looked at his watch; it was 10:45. He had time to freshen up and get to the airport to see her off. AJ planned to hide in the distance to see Robin one last time. He had to see the woman who had opened his heart to love. Half the night he had battled with the idea of confronting his brother with his feelings for Robin.

AJ didn't want to hurt his brother, but for the first time in years, he was sure of what he wanted. He knew he had to have Robin. He wanted to tell OJ everything about his past relationships, including the long affair he'd had with Dameon. He wanted the truth to be known about why he had never married, why he had all those beautiful models on his arm as a cover-up for the lifestyle he was living. Finally he was ready to give up all the masquerading for Robin. He felt that this was a peace ground discussion.

Robin and OJ were saying their goodbyes at the airport. AJ, disguised in a trench coat off in the distance, looked on as his brother kissed the woman who had stolen his heart. AJ walked away, head hung down, feeling crushed and heartbroken. He had to confront OJ tonight before they compared details of spending time with Robin. AJ walked away and drove off to peace ground.

"Sweetheart, call me as soon as you walk in the door."

Teary-eyed, Robin said, "I promise to call, OJ. Thanks for loving me."

OJ removed a hankie from his jacket pocket to wipe her tears. "Robin," he said, "now there will be no tears. I promise you I'll see you very soon, and once you become my wife, we'll never have to worry about parting again, until death do us part."

They kissed and said their good-byes. Robin walked toward her plane, not once looking back. OJ stood there looking as if he lost everything he ever had in the world.

OJ headed for his car. He opened the door, and on the seat lay a white rose Robin had left with a note. The note read: "My love for you will stand. I'll let nothing separate me from your love until we're together again. Always and forever loving you. Remember someone on the opposite side loves, cares and thinks of you. Thank you for a lovely weekend, Robin."

AJ looked at his watch. Robin's plane was in the air. She was gone, on her way home. *I let the love of my life get away*, he thought. He called OJ on his cell phone to arrange for him to meet with him at peace ground. OJ's voice mail picked up.

"OJ, it's very urgent that you meet me at peace ground at two o'clock. I need to talk to you. I'll be waiting."

OJ hadn't checked his calls. He was feeling rather lonely and down— missing Robin so much already. He thought he'd go to peace ground to sort out his feelings, not even aware that AJ was there as well.

Peace Ground

AJ was sitting on the railing of the building overlooking the view, contemplating how to explain to his brother his love for Robin. Thinking about how close he and OJ had been all their lives, he didn't want to lose the closeness. They were bonded at birth, yet AJ had kept part of his life hidden. Now he was ready to come clean, tell OJ everything, including what he felt for Robin. AJ's back was turned towards the city; he didn't see his brother approaching.

"AJ, hey what's up? What brings you to peace ground this time of day? Did we have a meeting?"

"I guess it's ironic we both end up here to sort out our thoughts. In fact, I did call and left a message for you to meet me here at 2:00 p.m."

"Man, AJ, what's going on? You looked deep in thought as I came up."

"Guess we both have something on our minds. OJ, you know you're the closet person to me, and we've always been able to discuss everything."

OJ said, "I know that, bro. I want to thank you for helping me work this out. There's something I need to tell you before I tell anyone else."

"OJ, before you say anything, I've got something to tell you, too."

"Speak to me, AJ. Tell me what's on your mind."

"For years I've kept part of my life from you and the world. I'm not the person you think I am. Sure, we're brothers, but there are things about me you don't know about," AJ tested the waters.

"What are you talking about, AJ?"

"Well, you've often questioned me about marriage and kids, and as you know, that was a subject I always avoided. Do you want to know why? (pause) Because I dated both men and women. OJ, I was searching for my sexuality."

"What are you saying, AJ? You were bisexual? What about all those beautiful women?"

"They were friends, some of them—really coverups for me. For years I've been seriously involved with a man named Dameon."

OJ looked at his brother with amazement. "AJ, listen, you're my brother, and your personal life is your business. I love you unconditionally. Whatever makes you happy, makes me happy. I'd never think any less of you. Why would you keep this from me?"

AJ said, "For years I wanted to share this with you, but up until today, I saw no reason to."

"AJ, why are you dropping this on me now?" OJ interrupted but wouldn't let AJ answer the question.

"No matter what you're doing, AJ, I love you, bro. (Pause) Hey, wait, and now let me share my news. It's almost as big a bombshell as yours! I asked Robin to be my wife, and I owe it all to you. You made me realize how much of my own life I've lost out on."

AJ's face grew angry. He said, "OJ, you asked me why I am sharing my bisexuality with you now—today? I'll tell you. Because of Robin. I've fallen in love with her."

Both of them were face to face.

"Now wait a minute, AJ, she's my girl. I'm in love with Robin. She's going to be my wife. I'm sorry, my brother, but I was there first," OJ said adamantly.

AJ didn't say a word. Before he knew it, he had taken a swing at OJ. They began to fight. Tossing hits back and forth, they forgot they were on the roof of the building. Suddenly one of them lost his balance, slipped and fell over the rail.

Part Two

Mirage of Affection

Peace Ground

OJ lay unconscious on the ground, blood flowing from his mouth and head. AJ frantically called 911 from his cell phone. He rushed down from the building rooftop to help his brother.

"Oh Lord, please my sweet Jesus! Help him. Please, oh, help him, Heavenly Father," AJ cried out in prayer as he stumbled over to OJ. Blood was everywhere. AJ grabbed a hold of OJ and propped him up, blood was gushing all over both of them.

"Please, somebody do something! He's bleeding really badly! Please don't die! Help me, please somebody! Help!" AJ screamed in a panic to anyone who might hear.

The ambulance arrived within seconds; paramedics immediately rushed to revive OJ.

"Please, sir, you'll have to let us do our job. Please let go of him," one of the medics insisted as he struggled to pull AJ away from his brother.

OJ was taken immediately placed on a stretcher and zoomed into the ambulance, destined for the intensive care unit. As AJ rode along in the ambulance praying, the paramedics tried to calm him.

"Is my brother going to die?" AJ pleaded.

"Sir, please calm down. We're doing all we can to save him. We'll be at the hospital soon."

St. Michael's Hospital

OJ was taken directly into the intensive care unit while AJ was in a daze, pacing back and forth. He was covered in blood and in a state of shock. AJ looked through the windows of the closed doors to see what looked like an army of doctors surrounding his brother.

A police officer promptly appeared out of nowhere to summon AJ for questioning. AJ was escorted to a waiting room.

"Mr. O'Neil, I understand that your brother is Oscar O'Neil. Please tell me what happened on the roof. How did he fall?" the first officer asked.

In a faint voice AJ answered, "He slipped and fell. Oh Lord, it happened so fast."

"So your brother slipped? May I ask what the two of you were doing on top of the building?" the officer probed.

Angry at what the officer was trying to imply, AJ answered bluntly, "Look, sir, are you saying I caused this to happen to my brother? For your information, I own the building. I took my brother, whom I'm very close with, to show him the property. He slipped and fell. Period. Please leave me the hell alone."

"I apologize, Mr. O'Neil, but these are merely routine questions. It's the law; I'm required to ask them since I must file an accident report. I understand this is a difficult time for you with this tragedy. Is there anyone you'd like for us to contact for you?"

"Oh, my God, Samone! Someone has to call her and my sister Diane," AJ bellowed.

"Sir, we'll take care of that for you. If you'll please give us their phone numbers." The officer's tone had now changed.

AJ reached inside his jacket for his address book and gave the officer the phone numbers.

"By the way, Mr. O'Neil, I suggest you change into a clean shirt. The hospital will provide you with something. We will do all we can to contact your family. If we have any further questions, how may we contact you?"

"Here's my business card. Am I done with your questions, now? I've gotta go see my brother," AJ demanded.

"Yes, sir. We'll contact your family and be in touch. We're sorry for your tragedy."

The police officer left AJ alone in the waiting room. With his head hung low, all he could think about was OJ dying. His mind reflected on his mother, and the pain he endured after losing her. It had been years since he had prayed. Remembering the advice given to him and his brother as she lay on her deathbed, he recalled the words his mother had spoken ever so clearly in his mind. It was as if she were whispering them in his ears, "Son, when difficult times in life beat you down, and there's no where else to turn, no one to help you, always remember to call on your Heavenly Father."

AJ heard his mother speaking, "Pray, son. Go somewhere and PRAY!" AJ knew this was his only hope. It had worked for his mother, but for years he had turned away from his belief in God out of anger and rebellion. Anger that God had taken his mother away from him. He didn't want to chance losing OJ, the other closest person to him. If prayer meant saving his brother, he was willing to put all bitterness aside and humble himself before his Savior. AJ immediately looked for the chapel. His trembling body in bloody clothes saw the light.

Inside the chapel, AJ fell to the floor and looked up toward Heaven and cried, "God, please if you're real, please forgive me. Please don't take my brother. Please save him. Please, God, I need him in my life. Please God, help us; I need you."

AJ lay on the floor calling on his creator from the depths of his soul. Suddenly he felt a calming peace. A peace that passes all understanding. AJ felt within his spirit OJ was going to be all right. He felt a presence of warmth, assurance, peace. He felt the presence of God. As AJ reached for his handkerchief inside his jacket pocket, out fell the picture of Robin.

He reached to the floor to pick up the picture, recalling how he and OJ had been fighting over Robin on the roof.

"God! I'm so sorry, how could I let a woman come between my brother and me? Please forgive me."

Somehow AJ had forgotten about Robin. His main concern was his brother's life. He felt the right thing to do would be to contact Robin since he knew all too well how OJ felt about her. Deep within his gut, he wondered if he could put his own feelings aside for Robin and call her as himself. Could he bear to listen to her heartache as she cried over OJ? How was he to comfort the woman they both loved without giving himself away? AJ wiped his face and made his way back to the intensive care unit. He went seeking answers from the doctors about OJ's condition. AJ ran into Samone getting off the elevator.

"AJ, what's going on? I received a call from the police about an accident. What happened to OJ? Where did all that blood come from?" Samone was hysterical. "Is OJ dead?"

As Samone screamed and carried on, AJ realized she was in shock. He had to slap her to get her back to reality. (He had always wanted to do that). Once she calmed down, he embraced her with a hug and took her to the waiting room.

"Samone, listen to me. OJ isn't dead. Please try to stay calm. There's been an accident. He's in intensive care. He slipped and fell from a building, and the doctor's are working on him as we speak."

"AJ, what the hell was he doing on top of a building?" Samone asked, beginning to cry uncontrollably. "I thought the two of you were in Atlanta? Damn it, AJ, what the hell is going on?"

AJ looked away quickly, trying to collect his thoughts. He realized the plan was blowing up in his face. He had to think fast and tell Samone something to keep her from finding out they had never even gone to Atlanta. He didn't want to expose their secret.

"Listen, Samone, we did fly in from Atlanta. We took a private charter plane and landed on the building which I own. I wanted to show OJ the property so he got out of the plane to walk around the rooftop. That's when he slipped and fell. It's my fault, Samone. If I hadn't suggested we go there, none of this would have happened."

Too upset to think clearly, Samone simply looked at AJ in a daze. AJ tried his best to console her, but he needed plenty of consoling and quick answers himself.

"My brother is in there fighting for his life, and I take full responsibility for it. I'm so sorry, Samone. If there's anything you or the kids need, I'll take care of it. OJ would want it this way. Please, Samone, please forgive me."

Looking at AJ with anger in her eyes, Samone pushed AJ away. "You've always stood in the way of me and your brother, AJ. Do you realize we were going to get married? It's all your fault. OJ can't go a day without you and look at him now. What could you do for him now, AJ? I don't need you; the kids don't need you. What if OJ dies? What will we do? " Samone was punishing AJ with her words, going off on him like he had killed his own brother.

Just then Diane walked in. She overheard Samone in the hallway yelling at AJ.

"Samone…wait just a damned minute! How dare you talk to my brother in that tone," Diane screamed defensively. "Whatever problem you have, you and I can take it outside. AJ don't need your lip service. I'll be damned if I let you insult my brother."

AJ had a fight on his hands. Diane had never cared for Samone. She loved her brothers and wasn't going to let anyone abuse them in her presence. Diane was a very arrogant woman, spoiled by her brothers. Her disposition was nasty, as if the world owed her something.

AJ interceded between the two of them. "Ladies, please! Now is not the time for bickering."

With that, Samone stormed out of the room.

Turning to Diane, AJ said, "Please, sis, please be sympathetic. Samone is in shock. Let her outburst go—she's upset. Put the shoe on the other foot."

Diane walked over and gave AJ a hug. "You're right, AJ. We've got to forget about her. I'm sorry. What is going on here? What happened to OJ?"

"Diane, baby girl, there's been an accident. OJ fell from a building, and he's in intensive care. I need for you to be civil to Samone because OJ needs all of our support. Please try to get along with Samone. Will you do this for OJ, sis?"

"I got angry when I heard her talking to you with her attitude—you know, blaming you, accusing you and all that. Are you okay, AJ?"

"I'm all right, Diane. We all have to come together and get through this. OJ's gotta be okay."

"I'll try real hard not to make matters worse. No more outbursts," Diane promised, looking at him with her big brown eyes.

Diane hadn't noticed AJ's blood-soaked shirt. "You're covered in blood, AJ!"

Diane began to cry and sobbed, "Is OJ going to die?"

AJ tried to comfort his sister, re-assuring her the doctors were doing all they could to save OJ.

"Baby girl, please don't cry. Hold yourself together and pray. OJ will be okay," AJ said as he pulled Diane close and consoled her until her cries softened to sobs.

"Diane, will you be all right alone if I go and look for Samone?"

"I'm fine, AJ," Diane said, wiping her tears.

As AJ stood to leave the waiting room, the O'Neil family was paged to report to the intensive care unit. AJ escorted his sister by the hand. Samone was already at the desk checking with the nurse by the time they arrived.

"If you are the O'Neil family, Dr. Casey will be right out to speak with you soon," a pleasant looking nurse informed them.

"Nurse, is everything okay?" Samone pleaded with desperation.

"I'm sorry. I don't have any answers for you. Dr. Casey will be out shortly."

Just then, Dr. Casey walked through the automatic doors. Blood covered his uniform. His face looked tentative. "Are you all the O'Neil family?"

Speaking boldly Samone answered, "Yes, I'm Samone—h-h-his wife. (She lied) This is his brother, Aaron and his sister, Diane. What's going on with him? Is he going to be all right? May I please see him?"

"Samone please let me introduce myself. I'm Dr. Casey, and I'd like for us all to move to the conference room so I can answer all of your questions."

They followed closely behind Dr. Casey in a solemn stride. Diane held AJ's hand, quivering. AJ was secretly praying to himself for a good report. Once everyone was seated at the long board table, Dr. Casey shut the door as he readied to reveal the verdict of OJ's condition.

"It's standard procedure to give families a private room to discuss critical conditions. Mr. O'Neil has suffered internal bleeding to the head from the fall. He's in a coma. The good news is he hasn't lost oxygen from his brain; he could recover with all of his mobility. The next forty-eight hours are going to be very crucial for him. We've got our top neurologist keeping a very close eye on him. If there's any loss of oxygen within the next forty-eight hours, he may not regain consciousness. If oxygen is lost and consciousness is regained, the end result could leave OJ in a vegetative state for the remainder of his life."

"May we see him, doctor?" AJ asked sheepishly, trying to keep his emotions intact.

"Yes, you may all visit with him. Two at a time, please. Visitations are very limited in the ICU, and please don't be alarmed by all the machinery. Mr. O'Neil is receiving the best of care. Are there any more questions before I make my rounds?"

"Doctor, could he die? Will my husband die?" Samone shrieked in excruciating pain.

"The next few days are very critical. We will do all we can to save OJ. I promise."

"Is he in any pain?" Diane asked between sobs.

"I'm certain he's in no pain whatsoever. We have him heavily sedated. He took a pretty hard hit to the head, but we're doing everything humanly possible to keep him comfortable," Dr. Casey assured.

"We want your top notch specialist caring for my brother. No matter the cost, Dr. Casey. Please do whatever is necessary to guarantee a successful recovery. He's got a family—kids. Please do whatever you can to make it right," AJ said authoritatively.

"Let me assure you, Mr. O'Neil, we have the best professional staff here at St. Michael's. We'll do our best. The outcome depends on your brother's will. My advice to you is to pray. These next forty-eight hours are critical."

"How soon may we see him, Dr. Casey?" AJ was purposely blocking out the negative verdict since he knew in his spirit all would be well.

"You all may go in now two at a time. Since he is in a coma, he can only hear you. He is not coherent of his surroundings. Please don't be alarmed by the machinery. His life depends on it," Dr. Casey said.

"Here is a list of my numbers, Mr. O'Neil. You can contact me if any of you have additional questions or concerns. I will be the attending physician looking after Mr. O'Neil, so please don't hesitate to page me," Dr. Casey handed AJ the list as he walked out of the room.

"Thank you, doctor," AJ, Diane and Samone replied in unison.

You could hear a pin drop when Dr. Casey left the room. Finally Diane broke the silence, "Please AJ, I need to see OJ now."

"Okay, baby girl. Why don't I go in with Samone first. Then I'll come back and get you, Diane," offered AJ.

"Yes, AJ, please come in with me. Look, I'm sorry for what I said in the waiting room," Samone said, her eyes searching for forgiveness.

"Samone, believe me. I understand. Let me get a clean shirt from my car, and then we'll go in. Can I trust you two alone for a few minutes?"

"I'm cool, AJ," Diane said nonchalantly.

"I'm straight. But hurry back, I need to see OJ," Samone said.

"Be civil, ladies. It'll just take ten minutes to run to my car and change," AJ assured them.

AJ left the two ladies sitting across the table from one another. Diane broke the silence first. "Samone, how are the kids?"

"The kids are fine now, but I can't imagine how they are going to take this about OJ. How am I going to tell them, Diane? Maybe AJ will come with me to give them the news..." her voice trailed off, and Samone immediately broke into tears. Diane rushed to her side to comfort her.

"I'm so sorry I yelled at you, Samone. I can't imagine how difficult this is for you...especially the thought of telling the kids. Listen. We're in this together. I love my brothers," Diane began to cry. "What are we to do?" They embraced one another, pondering what the future might bring.

Just then, AJ entered the room and found Diane and Samone consoling one another. He knew he had to be strong for them. He had to hold himself together. He reached for his hankie and out fell Robin's picture to the floor. He hadn't noticed, but Samone had begun to walk over to him.

As she picked up the photo she said, "Here, AJ, I believe this fell from your pocket."

Quickly taking the picture from Samone, AJ said, "Thank you," and added nervously, "Are you ready to go see OJ?"

"Yes. I'm ready."

Diane stayed in the waiting room while AJ and Samone went inside.

Back in Westchester

Ellen was at the airport to greet Robin. She couldn't wait to hear all the details about Robin's trip. The plane had landed, and Robin was getting off. As Ellen waited at the arrival gate, she was thinking about her appointment with the P.I. Allen Kimble.

"Hey, Ellen! I missed you!"

"I missed you, too, Robin. Did you have a good time?"

"Fantastic! Wonderful! It was an awfully rough flight back, though. I'm terribly exhausted. I'll have to fill you in on all the details...I do have some very exciting news to share..."

"Girl, say no more. I understand. I'll take you home, and we can talk later when you're rested. Besides, I have an appointment I need to get to."

"Oh, with Mr. T.D.H. Dameon?"

They both laughed.

St. Michael's Intensive Care Unit

Samone fainted at the sight of all the machinery hooked up to OJ. She had to be escorted out by a nurse.

AJ looked down on his brother's face; he reached for OJ's hand as tears rolled down his face.

"OJ, I'm so sorry, man. I love you. You gotta know I never meant for this to happen." AJ held onto his hand very tightly. He noticed the tubing in OJ's mouth, his eyes were sealed closed, and his hands were rock hard. He knelt down beside the bed and prayed. "God, please don't let him die. Please. OJ, if you can hear me, give me a sign. Please show me that you can hear me. We love you, OJ. Diane and Samone are here."

Immediately one of the alarms from the machine went off. A nurse rushed in and excused AJ from the room.

Westchester
Dameon's Date with Mark at the Grand Hotel

"Dameon, it's good seeing you. Please excuse my forwardness at Lamarge. I didn't mean to intrude."

"That was quite all right, Mark. That was a business associate. Tell me what brings you to Westchester? What a pleasant surprise!"

"There's a three-day surgical seminar at the Crown Royale. I'm officially here on business. Remembering this was your city, I couldn't leave town without speaking to you."

"Why, Mark, I'm very flattered. It's delightful seeing you again. I've been meaning to call, but as always, business keeps me very busy. Are you staying at the Crown Royale? Did you travel alone?"

"Yes to both of your questions."

Dameon reached for Mark's hand.

"You're not alone any more, Mark. I'll make your stay in Westchester very comfortable."

"Sweet words to my ears, Dameon," Mark flirted.

"Keep talking like that, Mark, and we'll never make it back to my place. We may have to get a room here." They looked at each other and smiled.

Meanwhile, Ellen and Robin had arrived at Robin's place from the airport.

"Have things changed with Dameon, Ellen?" Robin asked as she and Ellen pulled in her luggage.

"Girl, we went on a date!"

"You don't say! Wow! We got lots to talk about Ellen. Come in and have some coffee."

"Gotta run, Robin. Let's catch up later. I've got an appointment I must be on time for."

"You on time? That's a first. It must be with someone T.D.H.—Dameon maybe?"

"You mean Tall, Dark and Handsome!" Ellen giggled.

Ellen helped Robin with her bags and then they said their goodbyes. Ellen sped off to her meeting with Drake Kimble, the private investigator.

Drake Kimble was noted for his remarkable detective work. He had been a private investigator for over thirty years. Judging by the looks of him, old Kimble should've been enjoying retirement years. He was quite the opposite. Silverish gray hair, bursting with energy and very intelligent. He cut no corners in speaking; he was straight to the point. Detective Kimble sat waiting for Ellen at a downtown coffee shop.

While he waited patiently, Ellen circled the area for a parking spot. This was one appointment she wanted to be on time for. All she could think of was conquering her mission to find out about the mystery woman Dameon was seeing.

Robin's Place

Robin was so exhausted she left her luggage in the foyer and plopped down on her bed. She had OJ on her mind. How much she enjoyed her time with him. She smiled, knowing one day she'd be Mrs. Oscar O'Neil—never having to leave him again. Robin began to daydream about the day they'd wed. For a few seconds she lost herself in her future with the man she had waited for all her life. She couldn't wait to share her news with Ellen. Before she did anything else, she phoned OJ on his cell phone to let him know she had made it home safely.

OJ's voicemail picked up, so Robin left a message.

"Hi, honey. I made it back safely. Missing you already. Please call me…"

St. Michael's Hospital

"What's going on, nurse? Why is his machine alarming like that?"

"I'm sorry, sir. You're brother has gone into shock. I'm afraid there will be no more visitors until Dr. Casey gives him clearance. We have to increase his medication."

With that news, AJ lost control. He slammed his fists against the wall and cried out, "It's all my fault. I'm the cause of my brother lying in there fighting for his life."

Diane, in the next room, overheard AJ yelling. She rushed to his side to calm him down.

"AJ, honey, it's all right. I'm here for you. Everything is going to be okay. Be strong for OJ. Come on, brother."

Out of anger, exhaustion and shame, AJ pushed Diane aside and stormed out of the hospital.

He was pissed off—feeling like if he hadn't met Robin, none of this would have happened. The sad part about the whole thing was there was no one he could tell. No one to talk to except OJ.

AJ was wrecked with emotion. He sat on the bench outside the hospital trying to figure out what he could do to change things. He reached inside his jacket for Robin's picture. In anger, he tore it into small pieces.

"It's you who came between us. You're the reason my brother is lying in there unconscious. Our love for you has separated us. How could I have allowed this to happen?"

Westchester Coffee Shop

"Hello Ms. Berk, you're five minutes late. My time is money. Please have a seat."

Ellen reached out her hand to introduce herself, shocked at Mr. Kimble's forwardness.

"Mr. Kimble, I apologize for my delay. I had to wait for a parking space. It's only five minutes after three, sir."

"Very well, Ms. Berk. I'm a very expensive man. I charge by the hour. A flat rate of $100. All expenses are to be paid by the client plus my down payment of $2500 before I accept a job. Can you afford me?"

Mr. Kimble made Ellen feel very nervous with his deep, baritone voice and abrupt demeanor.

"Yes, Mr. Kimble, I can afford you. Money is no issue," Ellen said, her voice trembling.

"Very well. Now that we've got that part out of the way. Tell me what your problem is, my dear. Could it be a cheating husband or lost relative? Let me put your mind to rest. Whatever the case being, I'm the best."

Ellen couldn't help but notice his arrogance. How he answered his own question before giving her a chance to say anything.

"Well, Mr. Kimble, it's not a cheating husband or a lost relative. Actually, all I can say to you is that I love this person. I need to know if there's anyone else he is seeing. He's not officially mine yet—if you know what I mean."

"Ms. Berk, say no more. You want to know who the other woman is? Am I correct in saying so?"

"Yes, that's correct, Mr. Kimble."

"Love is blissful my dear! Well worth an investment. Would you happen to have a picture of your man?"

"No, Mr. Kimble, not on me. But you won't have a hard time finding one. He's always in the newspaper."

"Your guy is popular, is he?"

"Yes, I guess you could say that. He's Dameon Davenport the fashion expert."

"Oh yeah, Mr. Pretty Boy. He's always in the society section. He's worth millions, my dear."

"Please, Mr. Kimble, it's not about the money! I love him. If only he knew. If I could just find out who's getting all of his attention, then I could take it from there…" said Ellen, as a tear slipped out from the corner of her eye.

Mr. Kimble patted her on the hand for comfort.

"Now, now, dear. Please don't cry. I'll do the best I can to help you out. Look at you! You're beautiful! You can have any man you go after!"

"Thank you, Mr. Kimble," Ellen said in between sobs, "but I want Dameon. I love him so much!"

"Very well then. What I need from you is a photo, address and any other information you think will be helpful."

"Dameon and I work very closely together, and I know where he lives. But the real question is, are you certain you can help me, Mr. Kimble?"

"Ellen, my dear, rest your mind. I guarantee if your guy is seeing someone else, I will find out. Now my question to you is this. Will you able to handle whoever this mystery person is?"

"Why of course, Mr. Kimble," Ellen tried to keep her voice from trembling. "To ease my own mind, I have to know who she is. I need to know who I'm against—my competition so to speak. Yes, I can handle it."

"Very well. Let's get to work. I'll meet you back here tomorrow at 3:00 p.m. Bring with you my retainer fee, a photo and any additional helpful information. By the way, Ms. Berk, just so you are fully aware, the outcome is not always what you think. My job is to get the information you are seeking."

"Believe me, Mr. Kimble. I understand. I'm a big girl. I can handle it. I just need answers," Ellen responded emphatically.

"Tomorrow at three on the dot. See you then."

They shook hands and parted.

Ellen sat in her car wondering how she was going to deal with the outcome. She wanted so desperately to share her secret with Robin. She knew she had made a promise to her, but Ellen knew she had to keep everything about Mr. Kimble to herself. The secrecy was killing her inside. She headed home to relax her tired, weary mind.

St. Michael's Hospital

OJ was in shock. The sound of AJ's voice had aroused him. OJ could hear his brother speaking to him, and in his mind, OJ wanted to respond, and this was the only way he knew how. In his mind he was dreaming, unaware of what had happened or where he was. His eyes were sealed shut; his body was so sedated, he was unable to move. OJ's mind was a flutter with childhood memories streaming to and fro. He saw himself and AJ in their old house they grew up in. They were in the bedroom. OJ vividly saw their bunk beds, and he heard his mother's voice waking them up for school. OJ was having flashbacks of his life.

Throughout all his visions, he and AJ were inseparable. The visions played fast forward in his mind. OJ heard his mother's voice once again. He was looking for her in his mind, but he couldn't see her face. He's reaching for her, calling out to her from his mind. "Momma, where are you? Mom, I'm here. I've missed you!"

Feeling all the emotions of sadness and joy, OJ was overwhelmed when he heard his mother answer, "I'm here. You're not alone. Hold on, OJ, it's going to be all right. Hold on, my baby. Go back. You can't come to me now. You're needed. God isn't ready for you yet. Go back away from the light. Go back, OJ. Your brother needs you. Reach for AJ. Go back. Listen to AJ's voice…"

OJ's body was responding to what's going on in his mind. Machines alarmed as he got excited. Tears rolled down his face; he was unaware of what was happening to him. Hearing his mother's voice excited him.

He mumbled under his breath, "AJ, AJ." OJ had awakened long enough from the coma to call out AJ's name.

The intensive care nurse immediately rushed to attend to the machines. As she was about to administer the shot to relax him, she heard OJ mumbling "AJ" or something like that.

Excitedly she went to find Diane and Samone in the waiting room. "Mr. O'Neil has been sedated with medication that will relax him. He became very restless and irritable a few minutes ago and was calling out for someone by the name of AJ."

"Is he going to be all right? Has he taken a turn for the worse?" Samone asked in a panic.

"He's stable now and resting comfortably. Do you know an AJ?"

"Yes, AJ is his twin brother. The man who just left his room."

"Well, you may resume your visit with him once the doctor has examined him. I just wanted to pass on the information that he was calling for someone."

"Thank you, nurse. I'm going to find my brother and tell him the good news," Diane said.

Diane made her way to the front of the hospital where she saw AJ sitting in despair with his head in his hands.

"Hey big brother, may I join you?"

"Baby girl, I'm sorry. Please come and sit. I lost my temper in there. For once in my life I've encountered a situation I cannot fix. It makes me scared, Diane."

"It's all right, AJ. It's not your fault. We're all in this together." Diane hugged her brother tightly.

Grand Hotel

"Mark, what kind of medical field did you say you were in?"

"I'm a plastic surgeon, Dameon. I specialize in cosmetic surgery. The seminar I'm attending is hosting this conference for the world's greatest surgeons. A few of my colleagues are flying in from various countries to attend. It's going to be rather interesting covering a broad range of topics on body transformation."

"Sounds really interesting. Tell me, Mark, a man with your prestige, credentials and experience must have a steady love to call his own?"

"Why do you ask, Dameon? Out of curiosity or your own interest?" Mark smiled.

"Well, I just got out of a heart rendering ordeal. I'm not completely over it, and well…"

Mark gently cut him off. "As a matter of fact, Dameon, I am very much involved with someone back home. Unfortunately, he couldn't attend the conference with me. I figured while I was here in Westchester, I'd get to know you better. Seeing you at the bar in Seattle with your lover—I could tell you were very much into him. I'd like to be your friend, Dameon. You know, spend some time to get to know one another."

"I'll do all I can to make your stay here in Westchester welcoming, Mark. But my heart belongs to someone else, too."

"Aaron O'Neil, I presume?"

"Yes, Mark. That's my love. We're going through a dry spell at the moment. I suspect he'll come to his senses sooner or later. Hopefully before it's too late."

Reaching for Dameon's hand Mark said, "Is it too late, Dameon? Is it too soon for us?"

"I have to be real about it, Mark. Aaron is my one and only soul mate. I love him." With that, Dameon broke down.

"It's all right, Dameon. Believe me, I understand. He's a great guy, your Aaron."

"You know him?"

"Yep. He sold us our condo in LA. He's a great businessman."

"Yes, he's the best at what he does. You know, Mark, I've never confessed this to anyone, and I don't know why I'm opening up to you. It's just that I need to air out my feelings."

"What do you mean, Dameon?"

"Well, I'll do anything to be with Aaron. I love him so much. Maybe I'm not what he wants. Maybe he wants a woman. Sometimes I wish I was a woman."

"Dameon, are you serious? Would you risk your manhood for love?" Mark said, looking very seriously.

"I'll do whatever it takes to make Aaron love me, want me, marry me, and be with me."

"If that's what you think Aaron really wants, and you're really serious about it, I can make it happen. I can change you into a woman."

"What do you mean you can make it happen? And how?" Dameon looked intently at Mark.

"I'm a plastic surgeon, Dameon, and my colleagues specialize in the field of transformation. If you want to be a woman, we can hook you up from your head to your toes. We can make you the next Tyra Banks," Mark said encouragingly.

"Wow! Are you serious, Mark? You and your team of surgical associates can actually change someone from head to toe?"

"Yes, Dameon. The technology and expertise is right here at your fingertips. Clear your schedule for tomorrow and come along with me to the seminar. I'll prove it to you."

"How are you going to prove it to me, Mark?"

"You'll get a perfect example—a live version of a nude man changed into a gorgeous woman. Dameon, she's so fine I forgot she was a man to begin with. I'll introduce her to you, and then show you before and after pictures. She's a real transvestite. Her name was Alex before the surgery and now it's Alexis."

Dameon sat in a state of shock listening to Mark. It was as if his innermost desires were being answered. He couldn't believe it.

"This is absolutely incredible. I've got so many questions to ask. This is awesome. I can't wait until tomorrow. I'd love to speak to Alexis if it's at all possible."

"Not a problem, Dameon. I'll arrange for you to meet and speak with her tomorrow. You need to seriously think this over. This will be a life changing experience that will last forever, Dameon. Is Aaron O'Neil worth all of that to you?"

"If you knew him like I know him, you'd probably want to do the same thing. Aaron and I are one in the same. He loves me just as much as I love him, but he just doesn't realize it. I know in my heart I'm the one for him."

Robin's Place

Robin woke from her nap and went in to check her messages.

She heard Larry, "Hi mom. Just calling to see if you made it back safely. I missed you. Call me and let me know how your trip was. Love you, Mom."

Robin listened to Larry's message. She was glad to hear her son's voice. No message from OJ, though. Robin wondered why he hadn't called back yet. *Not like him,* she thought. Instead of calling him again, Robin dialed Ellen's number.

St. Michael's Hospital

"AJ, I know you're scared of losing OJ. None of us have gotten over the loss of Mom, but now this?" Diane began to cry.

"Baby girl, don't cry. It's gonna be just fine. Dry your tears and believe, have faith. OJ will pull through this. He's a fighter."

"You're right, AJ. We cannot give up hope. When you were gone, the nurse came out to tell us that OJ had come out of the coma long enough to call your name," Diane's eyes opened wide and bright.

"I wish I was in there lying in that bed instead of him. I've traveled the world, and made a successful name for myself. Life doesn't owe me anything."

"Stop it, AJ. I won't hear of you talking like that. OJ wouldn't want that. I know how you feel, AJ but stop feeling guilty about taking him there. It's not your fault. It was an accident!"

"If you only knew, Diane. This is all wrong, and there ain't a damn thing I can do to correct it," AJ confided.

At that moment AJ began to think about Robin. He thought about the first conversation he and OJ had about her. How OJ's face lit up when he talked about her. How the mention of her name brought happiness to his soul. AJ knew he had to contact Robin, if for no other reason but to keep his brother's happiness alive. He knew he had to take his own feelings for Robin and put them aside. He'd have to bottle them up and seal them shut. He had to keep the scheme going for OJ.

"Let's go back inside and see what's going on. I need to bring Samone home to explain to the kids. Then I need to make a very important phone call," AJ said, walking arm in arm with his sister back into the hospital's waiting room.

"AJ—Diane, good you're back. The doctor said OJ can't have any more visitors until tomorrow. They said he must rest. It must be quiet. There is no change in his condition," Samone reported solemnly.

"I'm going to take you and Diane home so you both can get some rest. We'll talk to the kids and then I'll come back and stay right here with OJ."

Samone and Diane agreed since they were exhausted.

Dudley Correctional Facility

Fred Dukes, Robin's ex-husband, was up for parole in one week. It had been five years since he last laid eyes on Robin. He sat in his jail cell thinking back on the time when they were together. Over the years he thought of nothing else except making up to Robin for all the wrong he'd done to her.

He'd made several attempts to write and even call, but he was unsuccessful. Fred had a mission that once he became a free man, he would search for Robin. He had an obsession with her that he couldn't shake. He still loved her. Being incarcerated made him realize how badly he had messed up a good marriage. Robin didn't deserve the hand dealt to her. He felt he must make it up to her for lost time. No matter the cost; no matter what. He wondered how she had changed or if she was remarried. It didn't matter. He just had to see her.

Westchester

"Hello?" Ellen answered the phone on the third ring.

"Hey, girl, what you up to?" Robin chimed cheerfully.

"Nothing much. I was going to call you to apologize for having to run out for my meeting, but thought I'd better wait a bit and let you rest up. So, tell me all about your trip! How's OJ doing?"

"I had a wonderful time. OJ is fine. Life is great!"

"You sound like you're on cloud nine, Robin! What happened in Florida? Is it the sun or what's gotten into you?" Ellen giggled.

"Are you sitting or standing right now?"

"Robin, don't do this to me. Go on and tell me, girl."

"All right then. OJ asked me to marry him. I'm going to be Mrs. Oscar James O'Neil!" Robin screamed with enthusiasm.

"You go, girl! I'm so happy for you. So when are we going to meet Mr. O'Neil in person?" Ellen wondered.

"I'm planning a dinner party for next month. We'll share the news with everyone, and then make the announcement. Of course I had to tell you, my best friend. Ellen, will you be my maid of honor?"

"If not me, than who else? With all we've been through together. I'm so happy for you, Robin. You deserve this special blessing. This calls for a celebration! I'd be honored!"

"A celebration it will be! I'm so happy. Everything is happening so fast. Of course, we won't rush the marriage. There's a lot of things we need to work out. But OJ is the man I want to spend the rest of my life with, so whatever I have to do, I will."

"I'm in awe! I just knew you guys would build something permanent. But be sure to take your time. God willing, everything will fall into place."

"Thank you for your blessing, Ellen. It means a lot. You're my best friend in the whole wide world, and there is no way I could have kept this from you until next month when Larry comes home, and OJ comes up to meet him."

"Won't that be wonderful! You know I'll do everything I can to help. Your trip really paid off, I guess! You must've been wiped out from all the emotion because you could've fooled me you had this kind of news when I picked you up at the airport. You know how to keep a secret, girl."

"Well, I hope you do, too. At least for now, Ellen. Now what about you? What's happening with Dameon? Are you guys seeing each other or what?"

"We went on our first date which was not business related while you were gone. I had a great time. He's everything I ever dreamed of in a man even though he hasn't made any passes at me yet. Hopefully he'll come around soon."

"Don't worry, Ellen. Some men take longer than others. Maybe he's a gentleman, that's all. There aren't so many of those left nowadays. At least you've progressed to the next level from business. It'll all fall into place if it's meant to be."

"Yep. I'm ready, willing and able," Ellen said with a smile.

"Maybe I'll invite Dameon to the party as your guest, and I'll get a chance to meet Mr. T.D.H.!"

"Great idea, Robin!"

"Hey, Ellen, my call waiting just clicked in, and I'm expecting OJ to call any minute. Let me get back to you."

Robin clicked off for a second, but then came right back.

"Nope. Wrong number."

"You sound worried, Robin. What's up?"

"I guess I'm just exhausted, weary from love—you know! OJ is so good about calling, and I guess I'm just missing him already!"

"Rest up from all that romance, Robin! Go take a hot bath!"

"You're right. He'll call. Hey, when can we get together for some fun?"

"How about tomorrow for dinner? We can celebrate your good news and start making a few plans."

"Sounds good. Talk to you tomorrow to set up the time," Robin replied.

Dudley Correctional Facility

Fred was busy thinking once again about how he was going to contact Robin once he was free. Less than a week to go. He had no forwarding address for her, and she wasn't listed in the phone book. He knew he had to make a new life for himself and had saved some good money while in prison. He thought about hiring a private detective to help find Robin. If that's what he had to do to find her, he would. Gazing across his cell, Fred stared into the eyes of their faded wedding picture. He gently took the picture off the wall and kissed his long, lost bride. "Miss you, baby. Soon we'll be together!" he sighed to himself.

Florida

AJ had just left OJ's house; he and Samone had told the kids the devastating news of their father's accident. In his entire life, he had never been faced with such a difficult task. Breaking the news to the kids was gut wrenching. They wanted to be alone with their mom and grieve. AJ respected their wishes so he was on his way home to break the news to Robin. He had settled in his mind that it was time for her to know the truth.

Westchester

Robin paced back and forth, trying not to focus on the clock as each minute ticked by. She got more and more anxious since by now she'd left several messages on OJ's voice mail. Something was wrong; she could feel it. When the phone rang, she jumped with trepidation and grabbed it on the second ring.

"Hello?" Robin said.

"Hello, Robin."

"OJ, honey. I'm so glad to hear from you! I've been worried sick out of my mind, and I called several times. I kept getting your voice mail. I came directly home from the airport and phoned you as soon as I walked in the door..." (She kept talking without giving AJ a chance to explain)

"I called Ellen and told her I thought something was up because you always are so good about returning my calls. Anyway, honey, I'm so relieved to hear your voice!"

Still there was no break for AJ to interject anything. Robin kept rambling on in nervousness.

"Sweetheart, I told Ellen that we're going to be married! She's so excited and can't wait to meet you. She wants to help me plan the wedding, but of course, there will be no plans without consulting you first. Oh, but before we even get into wedding plans, I have the dinner party, and you're my guest of honor, Mr. O'Neil! Baby, sweetheart, are you there? I'm sorry I've been chattering non-stop! I'm just so excited about everything—especially to hear your voice! I'm so happy I met you. Thank you for coming into my life. You've made these past months the happiest time in my life."

"I feel the same way, baby. Listen, I'm exhausted. Would you mind if we talked about the plans tomorrow? It's been a long, tiring day for me?" AJ said, trying to stall and get his mind clear about what his original plan was. It was as if the minute he heard Robin's voice his ability to tell the truth just faded away.

"I'm sorry, sweetheart. Go and rest. But please don't ever scare me like that again. I was so worried. Four hours without hearing from you is way too long!"

"I love you, Robin. I'll call you tomorrow."

"I love you, too, sweetness. Until tomorrow," Robin cooed and blew AJ a kiss through the phone.

AJ hung up the phone realizing how much Robin meant to him. He couldn't stand the thought of hurting her. He had to pretend to be OJ not only for the sake of his brother because he loved her, too. AJ needed to calm his nerves and think about what he should do. For Robin. For OJ. For himself. He made himself a drink before going back to the hospital for the night.

The Seminar at Crown Royale

"I've arranged for you to meet Alexis privately after the meeting. This will give you a chance to ask her your questions in private," Mark informed Dameon.

"Thank you very much. I've given a lot of thought about transformation, and spent most of last night in deep thought about it all. Maybe after speaking to Alexis, I'll be able to settle it in my mind."

Just then an announcement was made to have all guests be seated so the presentation could begin. Dameon's eyes were ablaze with interest and awe.

Westchester Coffee Shop

"Thank you my dear for being on time today. Time is money, and money is time!"

"You're welcome, Mr. Kimble. I want you to get right to work. I cancelled all of my afternoon appointments to meet you. Here's the photo of Dameon."

"Very good. What other helpful information can you share?"

"Well, I've got his home address, private home number, cell number. Oh, and he recently purchased property in Seattle."

"Very good, Ellen. I'll start with the local address here in Westchester. I'll get my associate to scout out the house and see who comes and goes. Then I'll research the property in Seattle, check to see how frequent he's there. Is that the envelope with his photo?" Mr. Kimble asked.

"Yes, everything you need is inside."

"My dear, he looks like millions. Does he always dress so flashy?" Mr. Kimble said as he opened the envelope.

"Yes, he does. I've never seen him any other way. Dameon has very expensive taste, and he works closely with the top fashion designers in the world."

"I bet he does. Now it's time for me to go to work, Ellen. I'll contact you in a few days and give you an update."

"Thanks, Mr. Kimble. You've put my mind at ease. I love him so very much; your work is very, very important to me."

"I understand, my dear. There's nothing like being young and in love. I tell you if I were years younger I'd give your guy Dameon a run for his money. A pretty lady such as yourself worried over being with a man?"

"Thanks for the compliment, Mr. Kimble, but it's Dameon I desire."

"And I can tell you sure do. Now let me excuse myself. Time is money, and right now it's your dollar. Talk to you in a few days, Ellen."

Mr. Kimble left Ellen sitting alone in the coffee shop pondering her predicament. Her mind kept going back to the luggage she had picked up for Dameon. Who could the woman be with the expensive taste? She wanted so badly to share her secret with Robin, but she vowed not to hire a private investigator. Ellen thought friendship was one thing, but loving a man was something altogether different. She knew from the day she laid eyes on Dameon that she had to have him. Ellen had never been intimate with a man. She was saving herself for someone special, someone she was in love with and would live with forever. She knew in her heart that someone was Dameon. She wasn't about to give up on having him and making love to him. She had to have him if her life depended on it.

Florida

Samone was on the phone with her boss, Sterling Powers, explaining OJ's condition and her need to get some time off work to be with the kids. Sterling was the owner of the radio station Samone worked for. He owned several local stations throughout Florida. Sterling was very distinguished for his age; he was in his early fifties with salt and pepper hair, dark-skinned with hazel eyes. He was very attractive and had always been attracted to Samone. Most of the women at the radio station wanted him, but no one knew he had his eyes on Samone for years.

Sterling had a deep attraction for Samone. He had made many advances to be with her, but she had only one thing in mind—advancing her career as a broadcaster. She accomplished this and more when she moved through the ranks from broadcasting to production. Sterling promoted her because of her ability and his attraction. Deep down, Samone knew he had a thing for her; she adored the attention she got from Sterling since her man at home had been ignoring her for too long. Samone had a youthful lilt to her voice and a bright smile as she talked to Sterling. She was attracted to him whether she realized it or not.

"Sterling, listen. I'm going to need some time off. OJ has been in a terrible accident. The kids need me. It doesn't look good…" her voice trailed off as she began to cry.

"I'm so sorry, Samone. You take all the time you need. Is there anything I can do?" Sterling replied.

"I'm afraid not. There's nothing anyone can do at this point but pray, Sterling. He's in a coma. I just need some time to be with him, to be with the kids."

"Believe me, Samone. I understand. Do what you have to do. I'll keep you all in my prayers—you in my thoughts. What hospital is he in?"

"St. Michael's intensive care unit. Sterling, it was just one of those freak accidents…" again Samone began to sob.

"Baby, it's all right. I'm here for you if you need anything. And I do mean anything. You just let me know. I'll visit with you later today at the hospital if you don't mind. And listen, Samone, don't worry about anything. Everything is just fine here at the station."

"Thank you, Sterling. I'll talk to you soon."

Just as they were finishing their conversation, the receptionist buzzed Sterling to let him know he had another call.

"WBLK Radio, Sterling Power's office, May I help you?"

"I'd like to speak to the head honcho!"

"Excuse me?"

"You're excused. I'm calling for Sterling Powers. He'd be very angry if you didn't put me through. It might even cost you your job. Now excuse yourself and put him on."

"I'm sorry, who did you say was calling?"

"I didn't! But if you need to know, this is Elouise Renee Prescott, the one and only!"

"Please hold while I get Mr. Powers."

"Mr. Powers, some woman on the phone by the name of Elouise Prescott; she's very direct and has demanded to speak with you immediately."

"Oh, Amber, that's Weesee. Please put her through. She hates to be put on hold."

"Mr. Powers will take your call immediately!" Amber said, trying to sound as pleasant as she could under the circumstances.

"I knew he would! Could have saved both of us some time, dear. Now excuse me!"

Sterling smiled as he picked up line two.

"Wees, what a pleasant surprise! How have you been?"

"You know me, living the life…bling…bling…Weesee's my name and money is my game. I'm FANTASTIC! Listen, I'll be in Florida later in the week, and I thought maybe we could hook up?"

"For sure, Wees. I wouldn't miss seeing you. It's been a while. Last time I saw you, you wanted to tie me to the bed post," Sterling laughed. "You're too wild for me! I don't know if this old man can handle you!"

"Baby, you better mix you up one of those power drinks—in fact, double up on the vitamins because I want to wrap these thick thighs around you, cellulite and all! Just don't die on me 'cause if you do, I'm leaving your ass right where you are. Just keepin' it real with you, baby!"

"Well now, since you put it like that, I'd better get myself pumped up for some Weesee love. I'll clear my calendar. Give me a call when you arrive in town, okay?"

"No doubt, Sterling. Listen, I've been keeping up with the ratings at WBLK, and I'm very impressed with your producer Samone. Ratings have tripled since she's taken on the position. That's what I like to see—my stocks skyrocketing. Bling! Bling! Money! Money!"

"Yeah, Wees, Samone is good at what she does. Being that you're on the board of directors, I make sure you get a monthly report. Thanks for the vote of confidence."

"I like that, Sterling. I like to see my money on paper. Okay then, we'll hook up later in the week. I can use a good workout. Can't nobody work it like you, baby!"

"I don't know, Wees. You'll try to kill a brother." (They both laugh)

"Just be ready. I'll holla at you when I arrive."

Weesee hung up the phone thinking back on the day she had first met Sterling. She had won tickets from a promotional offer on the radio station in Westchester, and Sterling Powers was the guest of honor who awarded the winning tickets. Weesee laid eyes on him, and all she saw was dollar bills.

She put on her charm, hooked up with him and went on a date. Before she knew it, she made the contact needed to leave the factory and Westchester. Sterling opened the door for her to invest her money in the radio business. As the stations expanded, Weesee was on her way to a lifestyle she had only imagined possible. She felt so grateful to Sterling for bringing her out of a crunch. Never mind that she had fallen for him big time. After all these years, she'd never confessed her secret love for Sterling; she kept up her tough act of not letting any man steal her heart. But deep down, she was in love. Big passionate, love.

St. Michael's Hospital

AJ sat in the waiting room. Waiting for what? Waiting for something to happen. For OJ to wake up and be okay. He camped out in the lounge since no one was allowed into OJ's room yet. Not until morning, the nurses told him.

AJ put all of his business engagements out of his mind; all he could focus on was OJ. He tossed and turned through the night, wondering what he was going to do about Robin. Her beautiful smile was so vivid in all of his dreams.

AJ felt the weight of the world on his shoulders. The only person he was able to confide in concerning personal issues was Dameon. As close as he and OJ were, there were certain areas of his life he had kept secret from him. AJ felt the need to talk to someone; anyone to release the stress. He reached for his cell phone to call Dameon. Just as he dialed the number, he was paged to the ICU over the intercom system.

"Aaron O'Neil, please come to the intensive care unit immediately. Aaron O'Neil."

AJ rushed back to the nurse's station to see what could be so urgent. His heart felt like it was beating out of his chest.

Dr. Casey reached to shake AJ's hand with a greeting. "Mr. O'Neil, I had you paged because the nurse said you were staying the night in the waiting room. I wanted to update you on your brother's condition."

Catching his breath, AJ said, "Is everything all right, Dr. Casey? Has anything changed? How is he?"

"Mr. O'Neil gave us quite a scare yesterday. I ordered his medication to be increased after he went into shock. He's been resting very comfortably since. There's no change in his vital signs, and since he lost a lot of blood we have given him a blood transfusion. His blood count is extremely low. Would you consider donating blood to your brother? Being identical twins, I'm assuming the two of you have the same blood type. Are you willing and able?"

"Yes, of course, doctor. Anything at all to help my brother. And yes, we both have the same blood type."

"Very well then. I'll have the nurse draw your blood. Once the transfusion has been made, it will help OJ tremendously and stabilize his vital signs. Even though he's still in a coma, the best news is that he hasn't lost any oxygen from his brain."

"Thank you, Lord! Does that mean he can come out of the coma unscathed? I mean, he won't be a vegetable?"

"Yes, Mr. O'Neil, but only time will tell. These things sometimes happen overnight. I've seen miracles, but I've also seen months go by. There is no limit as to how long a person can stay in this state." Dr. Casey patted AJ on the back. "Let's just pray for the best! Medically speaking, he's out of critical danger. He will remain in the ICU until his vital signs are up. His brain is functioning well even though he had a very hard fall. God was with him for sure!"

"Thank you God for good news! I do believe in miracles, Dr. Casey. I'm ready to give my brother my blood," and with that, AJ let out a sigh of relief.

The Seminar

"Alexis, you're beautiful. Were you really a man before the surgery? I mean you look absolutely stunning!" Dameon asked.

"Yes, Dameon. My name was Alex, and I was a miserable man. Masking who I really was and who I wanted to be. This was the best thing I could've done for myself. I'm a new person. My emotions are intact—I'm actually a very happy person. I got tired of pretending to be what I knew I was on the inside—a beautiful woman."

Dameon gazed at her in amazement. He couldn't believe she was once a man. No way, no how. It was truly remarkable.

"Was it a painful procedure, Alexis? I mean, did you have to undergo extensive multiple surgeries and long term recovery?"

"Becoming a transgender is a long process because you completely change gender. Any transsexual procedure is painful physically as well as mentally. Everybody is not going to accept your decision. I lost a lot of family and friends, but in the end, I've gained so much more. I'm on the top of the world! I have a beautiful man in my life who loves me for me. I feel good inside and out. You have to make up your mind definitively that this is what you want. There's absolutely no looking back. You have to want this for yourself, Dameon. You and only you."

Alexis' comment struck Dameon; he had to do it for himself and not anyone else. "I have another question, Alexis. You said you were tired of pretending, but was there someone meaningful in your life before the change?"

"Are you asking me if I did this to please someone in my life? If you are, the answer is NO. If you're thinking about doing this for someone else—that's the wrong reason!"

Dameon's uncertainty was apparent on his face, but he answered, "Oh no, no. I'm not doing it for someone else. No way. Now tell me, Alexis, are you really happy, deep down in your gut happy?"

Alexis backed away from Dameon just enough for him to see her full body and then says, "Look at me, Dameon, I'm beautiful! Do I look unhappy?"

"If I were straight, I'd certainly take a big interest in you. You're gorgeous, girlfriend, but I'm going to have to hook you up with a whole new wardrobe," Dameon smiled coyly as he gave her a once over from head to toe.

"You're going to buy me clothes, Dameon?"

"Uh, huh. Honey, you must not know who I am! I'm Dameon Davenport, the fashion expert. I have a line of women's fashion from New York to Paris."

"Wow! You'd do that for me? You're generous and handsome, too!" Alexis winked at him.

"Well, there's a small price to pay..." Dameon said blushing.

"Name your price, Dameon."

"Well, I was thinking while you're here in Westchester, you could spend time with me and fill me in on all the details of a transformation. In fact, why don't you be my guest at my home? I'll make your stay very comfortable."

"You've got a deal!" Then she kissed him on the cheek.

"Very well. I'll have my chauffeur Raymond pick you up here at 7:00 p.m. Okay?"

"I'd be delighted, Dameon. I'll tell you anything and everything you need to know for this wonderful life-changing event. But just remember, my number one advice is you have to do it for you and only you."

"I'll keep that in mind, Alexis. I appreciate your honesty; I feel like I can trust you. I must leave now; I have an engagement I must attend to. Please excuse me, and we'll catch up later at my house."

Alexis winked her eye at Dameon and said, "The pleasure is all mine."

Dudley Correctional

"Hey Dukes, what's the first thing you gonna do when you get out of this hell hole?" a prison inmate yelled across from his cell to Fred.

"Find my woman. What do you think? It's time for us to reunite," Fred said, looking at Robin's picture. "Yeah, it's time to make up for lost time."

"You got a woman waiting for you?"

"Yeah, man. She's some woman, too. Smooth skin, soft like a baby. Dark brown like the sweetest candy bar you ever tasted. Fine as they come," Fred said, smacking his lips.

"A few more days, and you're free, man!"

"Yeah, free to be with my Robin again."

Westchester

Robin and Ellen were on the phone.

"Ellen, girl, everything is okay. Apparently OJ had an emergency he had to attend to, but he finally called. I was so relieved to hear his voice," Robin said.

"I know how you worry, girl! I'm glad everything is just fine."

"What are your plans for tonight, Ellen? Hot date with Dameon?"

"I only wish. What do you have in mind?"

"How about dinner? I'll fill you in on my trip to Florida, and you can tell me about your date with Dameon. We have lots of catching up to do!"

"Great. How's 6:30? I'll swing by and pick you up," Ellen said. Her voice was distant, as though she were in a faraway land.

"I'm straight with that, Ellen. Are you sure you want to drive? You sound like you're unsettled or coming down with something."

"Just burned out a bit from the long hours, Robin. That's all."

"Are you sure that's it? Ellen, I know you girl, and something isn't setting right with me. You sure you're up for dinner?"

"Yeah, girl. There you go worrying again! If it's not OJ, it's me. I'm fine and starving so rest your mind I'll be there at 6:30 on time."

"You on time? You've got to be kidding! I'll see you at seven!"

They both laughed.

St. Michael's Hospital

"Any news about OJ?" Diane asked, bustling into the waiting room.

"YES! I've got good news, baby girl! OJ hasn't lost any oxygen from his brain, and I just gave him blood. Dr. Casey thinks fresh blood will bring up his vital signs. Dr. Casey also said OJ's brain is functioning just fine. It's a miracle, Diane!"

"Thank you, Lord! I'm glad to hear some good news. We needed it. Did Dr. Casey say how long OJ might stay in the coma?"

"That's the bad news. Indefinitely. There's no set time frame, baby girl. We need to keep praying that he comes back to us soon."

As Diane came over to hug, AJ she said, "You look beat, brother. Have you been here all night?"

"Yep. I slept in the waiting room. There's no way I can leave him alone like this."

"Honey, I understand, but what will I do if both of you are out of commission?" Diane caressed AJ's back. "I want you to go home and get some sleep in your own bed. Shower, eat, and change into some clean clothes. Samone is on her way; I just spoke with her. Now go, AJ!"

"You look just like mom right now, Diane. Telling me what to do! I don't want to leave you all alone, and besides, I won't rest well. I can't stop worrying about OJ."

"Come on, AJ, I have my cell phone, and I'll call you if anything changes. Please do this for me. Go home and get some rest," Diane's big brown eyes were sad but had a look of determination. AJ could tell she wasn't going to take no for an answer.

"Oh, all right. You win. But you better promise to call me if anything happens. And I mean anything. If a machine sounds, I want to know about it. You hear me, baby girl?"

"Yes, sir. I love you, now go," Diane pushed him out the door.

As AJ left the building, he ran into Samone and her boss, Sterling Powers who were walking in together. AJ had always disliked Sterling. He could see right through him and knew Sterling had a thing for Samone. He was a real socialite, and AJ heard his name around town plenty. Especially his reputation with the ladies. The way he treated women was disgusting to AJ. It left a nasty taste in his mouth just speaking his name. AJ didn't like the idea that Samone even worked for the guy.

"Hey, AJ, you're leaving? Is everything all right?"

"Yes, Samone. Diane will fill you in on OJ's condition. Powers, what brings you here?"

"AJ man, I'm terribly sorry about what happened. I saw no need for Samone to be alone."

"Yeah, I bet you didn't," AJ said with a look of disdain on his face. "If you all will excuse me." AJ started to walk away but added, "How are the kids doing, Samone?"

"The kids are going to be all right. I just wish they could see OJ. You know, AJ, it's not what you're thinking. Sterling was kind enough to bring me to the hospital..." she said, her tone a bit huffy.

"Whatever, Samone. I'm out of here," AJ said, rather disgustedly.

Samone stood in disbelief as though she had been slapped in the face.

Sterling interjected his two cents. "Don't take it personally, Samone. AJ has never cared for me, but now is not the time to deal with that. I'll handle it. Let's go inside."

AJ sped off in his Jaguar so fast he left tire marks on the pavement. He was dealing with so many different emotions. Samone was parading around town with Sterling when his brother lay dying in a coma. The nerve of her!

Just then OJ's cell phone rang.

"Hello sweetie," Robin's voice cooed.

Caught off guard by the sound of Robin's voice, AJ answered, "Oh, hi, baby. What's going on?"

"OJ, are you okay? You sound different."

"Sweetness, I'm fine. I'm fighting this Florida highway traffic. Is everything okay with you?"

"I just called to say I love you, OJ! Everything's great here except I miss you! Will you please clear your calendar for the first week in May? That's when I'm planning our dinner party—maybe our engagement party by then..." she said.

"Yes, dear. We should get engaged before then. My schedule will be clear for you any time, any day, forever," AJ replied without thinking. *What in the world was he saying? What twisted lie was he concocting?*

"You're awesome, OJ! I'm yours forever!"

"Come on now, Robin, you've got to let me help on the details of the party or something. How about if I wire you some money to help defray the up front costs?" AJ said, trying to continue to make her think he was OJ.

"You'd do that for me, I mean for us?" Robin replied.

"Of course, Robin, but right now I gotta run, my pager is beeping. Love you, honey."

"Bye, OJ. Love you too."

Westchester
Dameon's Place

Mr. Kimble had been waiting patiently across the street from Dameon's gated mansion with his zoom camera. For hours, there had been no activity except the milkman and mailman making their deliveries. Kimble waited patiently. This was the game. This was what he got big bucks for. The waiting game.

Suddenly a silver Mustang approached the gate. As the female got out of the car, made her way to the door, Kimble zoomed in with his camera. Through his lens he saw a tall, slim, gorgeous, very attractive black woman. Kimble noticed the woman looking through her purse, and then she pulled out a key. Immediately he took another photo as she opened the door to Dameon's house.

Well, this ain't no maid, Kimble thought to himself. *This broad must be the mystery woman. Why else would someone have keys to Dameon's home?* Tempted to leave now that he'd accomplished his mission, his wallet got the better of him. I'd better stick around a little longer to be sure my assumptions are correct. I need photographs of Dameon and this lady together for my client. Just a little more time ought to do it.

St. Michael's Hospital

Diane was in the waiting room reading a magazine. Her back was turned toward the door, unable to see Samone and Sterling approach. Samone was still ticked off thinking about AJ, and she was so preoccupied she passed by Diane on the sofa without even noticing her. Suddenly Diane looked up from her magazine and caught a glimpse of Samone and Sterling sitting together smiling on the bench.

"Samone!"

Samone turned to look in Diane's direction, and as she did, she saw Diane flying off the sofa and throwing down her magazine in disgust.

"Don't act like you didn't see me sitting here, Samone!" Diane screamed.

"Honestly speaking, Diane, I didn't! What's the problem? What's up with your attitude?" Samone said nonchalantly.

"My problem? My problem is with you and who's behind you. How dare you bring Sterling Powers here while my brother AND YOUR CHILDREN'S FATHER is lying in there fighting for his life!"

"Diane, I didn't come here to cause any trouble. I'm only here for support..."

Sterling interjected but was cut off by Diane.

"Hold up, Mr. Powers. As I recall, I don't remember talking to you!" Diane was hot now.

Sterling didn't have to get knocked down twice to take a hint. "I'm sorry if I caused you any problems, Samone. I should be leaving."

"For the first time in your life you said something right. See ya!" Diane quipped.

"You are so obnoxious, Diane. You're a spoiled brat and rude as hell."

"WHAT?" Diane screamed at the top of her lungs. Their commotion was causing a scene.

"You and your brother just humiliated my boss, my friend!"

"Oh, so you're admitting you care about him now, Samone?"

Samone started to stutter. "I-I n-never said anything like that. There you go putting words in my mouth once again!"

"Well, if the shoe fits, girl, wear it! My brother's in there in a coma, and you have the audacity to bring Sterling in here knowing how OJ feels about that man?"

A nurse marched into the room. Both Samone and Diane turn in her direction at the same time, "Is there something wrong?" they chimed in unison.

"Yeah. Keep the noise down. This is a hospital," she said sternly.

Dudley Correctional

Fred Dukes was sitting in his cell daydreaming of his woman, the love of his life, Robin. Ironically across the room in a nearby cell was O'Dell O'Neil, father of AJ, OJ and Diane.

"Dukes, when you get outta here I need a big favor of you. I need you to look someone up for me, man. Okay?"

"You got a woman on the outside you wanna send a message to, O'Neil?"

"No, Dukes, my wife died years ago, but I have three grown children. Twin boys, Aaron and Oscar. My baby girl is Diane."

"You're kidding me, O'Neil. How long since you last seen them?"

"My kids were babies when I was convicted. They were too young to understand my not being around them all these years. Working for the FBI as an agent, I had to stay undercover. I had to be separated from my family in order to protect them. I took care of them, of course. Sending them money and all, but now I realize money can't replace relationships. Their mom died without telling them the truth about me."

"That's heavy, man. Tell me more."

"Their mother and I vowed never to tell the kids what my line of work was as an FBI spy," O'Dell confessed.

"How'd you land here?"

"I got in too deep. Got set up."

"Tough break all right."

"Yeah. Well, their mom died knowing the truth; she knew I was innocent and knew how much I loved her and the kids. So my kids went to live with their grandmother. She covered for me for years, too. I've got a lot of scars on my heart. Y'know?" O'Dell's voice quivered.

He continued, "Not being able to say goodbye to the only woman I ever loved and not being there for my kids has made me cry many tears all these years."

"It's a sad tale. I feel for you, man. Whatever you want me to do, I'm your man. Just say the word, and I'll do it."

"Dukes, I'll never see the outside of this place. I'm sentenced here for life and will spend my last breathing moments until I die in this joint. I'd like to somehow reconnect with my kids. See them, talk to them; explain everything to them. My one boy is very rich——he went into real estate. I've read about him in the newspapers and have followed his career. His name is Aaron O'Neil. Maybe you could get a phone number for me, Dukes."

"Sure, man. I'll give it a try."

"Hey, maybe they won't want to have anything to do with me. I don't know. But I can't rot in jail without trying to make peace and asking their forgiveness," O'Dell said visibly shaken by this point.

"I'll do the best I can, Mr. O'Neil. Any ideas where to start? Maybe I can locate him, tell him you're in jail, and he'll come around," Fred replied.

"NO! Dukes don't do that. No jail, no details. Just a phone number, buddy. I believe Aaron's in Daytona. I'll give you a news clipping I tore out. You could call his business and get a personal number or something. I'd be happy just to hear his voice."

"Yes, sir. No problem. I'm slick, man. I'll get a number for you old man, don't you worry about it for one second more. Hey, I'm on your side. I think it's about time your kids know the truth."

"You know, Fred, I'd give anything to go back in time. I've sat in this cell all these years just thinking and praying about my wife, my kids. My boys are identical twins. Just ten years old when I was convicted. My baby Diane was just eight. I know they must think the worst of me all these years not knowing the truth. They're probably going to hate me," O'Dell moaned on.

"Sometimes in love, Dukes, you just gotta walk away to save the other person—even if it means hurting yourself. I did what I had to do to protect my family. I took the fall for that big mob of gangsters. You know, if I hadn't taken the fall for their racketeering, they would've killed my entire family, no doubt. Money was planted in a Swiss bank account under my name. I'm talking billions, Dukes. That and all the evidence to convict me for life. When I attempted to shut them down and prove my innocence, they threatened to kill my family. I just did what I had to do to keep them alive," O'Dell continued.

"Tough break. You were protecting them. Don't be so hard on yourself, old man," Fred tried to encourage him.

"Yeah, well. I did what I thought was right at the time, but my family suffered because of it. Maybe my name means nothing, but I'm still their father, and I love them deeply. Sometimes love brings pain. Lots of it."

"I got the picture, O'Neil, and you can count on me. Three kids. One girl and twin boys. One's loaded, you say."

"Yep."

"All right then. I promise not to say anything about you, and I'll try to locate the rich boy for you first. Aaron O'Neil. Name kinda rings a bell the more I think about it," Fred's voice was upbeat, and he had a strange smirk on his face.

O'Dell saw Fred's expression and said, "Don't do anything stupid, Dukes. I'm just asking for a phone number. I swear I'll make your life miserable if you get any ideas and screw this up, Dukes. I still have connections on the outside you know. Big ones. Don't go making matters worse. I trust you, man. That's why I've confided in you. I need you to play me right. Just get Aaron's number, okay? Do we have an understanding?"

"Yeah, O'Neil. I got you. Cool your nerves, ole man'. I won't blow your cover, word. I believe in what you're doing. Maybe your boy can help you get out. Get a real good attorney. You're an old man with a lot of wisdom. You've served your time. You gotta make peace with your kids," Fred tried to reassure him.

"Me, on the other hand, I don't have nobody, Mr. O'Neil. I messed up my marriage to a beautiful girl. Trapped in this hole, I've learned my lesson. Life is passing me by. There's nothing like having someone in your corner— someone to love, man. I messed up big time, and it's my own fault. But you, you had good reason to protect your family and do what you did. I'd hope I'd be as good a man if I had the choice," Fred replied.

"Listen, Dukes. I'm in here by choice. I had covered the mob operation for three years, and I became part of the Carilini family's biggest hierarchy of criminals in the U.S. They took me in, believed in me. I did my job well. Damn good spy. The first black man ever to be adopted into their world. I sold them. Sold myself and made them trust me until I got careless. I slipped up big time by letting love blind me," O'Dell confessed, feeling more at ease.

"Love of what, man? The love of your family got you in here, Mr. O'Neil."

"Oh no, sir. The love of money got me, Dukes. I had to change my identity; I lived a new lifestyle, liven large and I loved it. Sure I missed my wife and kids something bad, but the love of money overshadowed it all back then." O'Dell continued, "Illusions are deceptive. Being what you aren't, feeling things you don't want to feel, living a lie. Total illusions of the heart." By this point with his true confession verbalized, O'Dell broke into tears of repentance.

"Damn. That's heavy. Tears in the name of love. If I have something to do with it, you'll be able to make your amends and end it all on a good note. No more illusions. No more having to hide the love you have for your kids."

"Yeah, Dukes. The heart rules when it comes down to love. That's the way it's supposed to be. One day it will all come out, and the truth will be known. I've held onto this promise every single day I've rotted in this cell. I'm no dumb man, Dukes. I speak five languages, had to hide away in Germany with the gang for years before the bust. I was so close to getting them, too," O'Dell recollect.

"But I ain't 100 percent innocent, Dukes. No way, no how. I gotta be honest. Maybe the FBI didn't back me; they set me up, too. But I outsmarted them all in the end. I may be rotting away in this cell, but I got a stash from way back when I skimmed some off the top. Just for my babies. One day I'll get the chance to tell them my plan to repay their loss. You're the man, Dukes."

With the talk of money, once again Fred's eyes glazed over, and he said, "Hey Mr. O'Neil, can I ask you just one more question?"

"Shoot."

"Why'd you wait all these years?"

"Because my kids were too young to understand, Dukes. After losing their mom they went to live with their grandmother, Mrs. Mary. Bless her soul, she's gone on now. My mother-in-law was a sweet woman. She took my babies and cared for them; kept my secret to protect them. I owe that woman so much. Never got a chance to tell her how thankful I was for rearing my kids. From the inside of this cell I had to get someone on the outside to make all the arrangements for her funeral. My babies were too young…" O'Dell had a glazed look in his eye.

He continued, "Dukes, I took care of my responsibilities as a man. A real man will do what he has to do. You say, 'Why now?' I did what I had to do for everyone's safety. The majority of the big gang leaders are dead now. I'm safe and so are my kids. That's all that matters."

"Man, I understand," Dukes said with tears in his eyes. "Good thing you out-slicked them and tucked some loot aside. That was slick, man."

"Yeah, I may be old, Dukes, but I'm nobody's fool. I take care of mine. Now tell me one more time. You gonna work with me on this or what? Be straight, Dukes," O'Dell looked him directly in the eye, man-to-man.

"Yes, sir. I got your back. I've got two days left in here. Just tell me what to do and I'm on it."

Smiling, O'Dell says, "Thanks. Believe me, son. You'll be compensated for it. We'll talk at the mess hall over dinner, okay? I'll give you the newspaper clipping and a possible phone number to contact my boy Aaron and tell you what to say."

"I'm on it, O'Neil. I'm there. Hey, maybe if I do this favor for you, you can put your contacts at work to find the address or phone number of my girl Robin Jacobs?"

Florida

AJ walked into his house and threw his keys on the coffee table. He was mentally exhausted. Tired and burned out. All he could think about was OJ and Robin. How he regretted playing this scheme on Robin; how everything had backfired.

AJ went to the bar to make himself a drink before listening to his messages on the phone. He poured a glass of cognac, drew the drapes in the living room and sat down on the leather recliner to collect his thoughts. He desperately wanted to be able to talk to OJ again and take back every word he had said on top of the roof. His mind kept reflecting back to the day OJ first told him about Robin.

AJ recalled the glow in OJ's eyes and the happiness in his voice. He remembered OJ kept saying how much he loved this woman; how she made him feel so alive on the inside. AJ was so sorry he had confessed his feelings to OJ about Robin.

What is it about her that makes me feel this way on the inside? Is it because she's someone my brother wants? Or do I really love her? AJ continued to battle dozens of unresolved questions in his mind...

She does have a pleasing personality. I feel very comfortable with her and much loved by her. Maybe I've fallen in love with the idea of love. Maybe it took Robin coming along to show me that I could love; that love is something you feel on the inside not just something you outwardly speak.

His mind reflected on how the tears flowed from her eyes when she thought he was making a mockery of their love. AJ's mind was tortured by feelings for Robin. What made her so different? Deep in thought, he began to drift off to sleep. Suddenly the phone rang. He rushed to answer it, thinking it might be Diane or the hospital.

"Hello."

"AJ, listen. Don't say anything. Just listen to what I have to say," Dameon coaxed.

AJ held the phone still.

"I never thought I'd see the day. I never thought our love would fade away. After all these years, I can't believe it's gone. Where did our love go wrong, AJ? I can't go on like this. I need you. Please can we meet? Can we talk this out? I was wrong. I know I hurt you. Please, AJ, I beg of you. Give me one more chance..."

"Now is not the time," AJ said firmly, but he broke down and began to cry. "Look, there's been a crisis in my family. My brother has been in a terrible accident. I'm to blame for all of it; it's my fault. I did this to him, Dameon."

"Damn it. Damn, AJ I had no idea. I can be there this afternoon on a charter. You need me now," Dameon tried to comfort him.

"No, Dameon. This is my problem. Please give me some time to get my head on straight. I can't deal with the situation concerning us right now. Please understand. I'll call you as soon as things get better, okay?"

"Come on, man. There's gotta be something I can do to help you. Anything."

"Just pray, Dameon. OJ is in such a bad state. Please forgive me. I'd rather not talk about it any more right now. I gotta go…" AJ's voice trailed off.

Westchester

Dameon sat in his office, numb, still holding the phone. The sound of AJ's voice convinced him that he needed to do something to console him. AJ sounded so stressed; Dameon was worried about him. He figured he'd surprise AJ and go to Florida for support. There was no way he was going to let AJ deal with this alone he told himself while flipping through his Rolodex for the phone number to his private jet charter.

If anyone knew how much his brother meant to him, it was Dameon. AJ would always tell Dameon how much he admired his brother, and how he stuck by his family. Although he had never had the privilege of meeting OJ, Dameon felt he knew him just by all that AJ had said about him over the years.

After setting up his immediate flight, Dameon phoned Ellen at home.

"Listen, Ellen. I'm glad I caught you at home. I've got to go out of town for a few days. Urgent business. I need for you to cover all the accounts until I return. Okay?"

"Oh, Dameon, is everything all right? You sound terribly upset."

"I'll be fine. Thanks for asking. A bit of shocking news is all. I'll be heading out this afternoon so if anything important comes up, I'll give you my red alert phone number for emergency calls only. Gotta pen?"

"Go ahead, Dameon."

"It's 317-220-0777, and Ellen, only use this number if it's an emergency, okay?"

"Sure enough, Dameon. I got you covered. Is there anything I can do to help you prepare for your flight? Seattle can be a very long flight."

"I'm not flying to Seattle. I'm on my way to the house to pack a few things. I'll phone you from the airport to give you the schedule of tomorrow's meetings. Thank you, Ellen, for stepping up to the plate on this."

"No problem. I'm happy to help." Ellen hung up the phone and couldn't wait to give this number to Kimble. Where was he going so suddenly—and with whom?

Meanwhile, Alexis was making herself very comfortable at Dameon's house. She was very impressed by the home's luxurious décor. She picked up her phone to call Dameon.

"Hello, Dameon? I phoned your chauffeur and told him there was no need to pick me up. He came to the Grand Hotel to bring me the house keys at your request. Right now I'm sitting here in style in your den, totally in awe of your artwork."

"Thank you, Alexis! I must apologize for not phoning to be sure you had made it. It's been a very hectic afternoon. I just received some very upsetting news. I'll be leaving this evening for Florida to handle an urgent matter. Please feel free to stay until I return in a few days so we can discuss our business. My maid Hilda will take care of your every need."

"You sound upset, Dameon. Is there anything I can do to help you? I mean it's so kind of you to offer your home to me and all."

"It's just something I have to do, Alexis. I'll be home within the hour to pack my bags. I do have one favor, however. Would you kindly bring me back to the airport? I gave Raymond the afternoon off after you said you'd drive yourself to the house."

"No problem. I'll be happy to help; it's the least I can do."

Robin's Place

The doorbell rang. It was Ellen picking her up for dinner.

"Hey, girl. I knew you'd be late with a smile on your face!"

"Robin, I was trying to make it on time, but I got a distressed call from Dameon."

"Say no more. I understand. Let's go get our grub on. "

Meanwhile, Kimble sat outside Dameon's place like a sitting duck, waiting to take pictures of anything that looked suspicious.

Florida
St. Michael's Hospital Waiting Room

"Diane, I'm not your enemy. I love your brother. Sure we've had our problems over the years, but that's between us. Why can't you accept me? You might as well get used to me being around because I'm here to stay!" Samone spoke with conviction.

"Look, Samone, you don't love my brother any more than I do. What goes on between the two of you is your business. My brother deserves to be happy.

181

All you've ever cared about was advancing your career. It don't take a blind man to see you've lacked paying attention to your man. My brother worked his fingers to the bone, put you in a nice house, paid your way through school, and all you ever did was hold your greedy hands out sucking the life out of him. Don't you realize that every man needs attention from his woman?! I'd be damned if I let you shame him while he lays there helpless. How dare you insult him by bringing Sterling Powers in this hospital!"

Samone, at a loss for words after Diane's tirade, response, "Yes, your brother has been a damn good provider for me and the kids. Don't you think I've appreciated everything he's done for us?" She didn't give Diane a chance to answer but continued, "Now you listen, and you listen well. It takes two to make any relationship work. Just like your brother has needs, so do I! Hell, he never was home with us. All he did was work, work, work. Don't you think for a moment that I needed more than just what he could do for me, the kids? " Samone began to cry. "Hell, when Nicole was born he was working a double shift. So don't talk to me about needs. Sterling is my friend. If he paid more attention to me than OJ did, it's because he's earned the right to because he's been there for me."

Diane slapped Samone across the face. "You selfish bitch. All that OJ's done for you, and you have the nerve to talk about someone else earning rights? My brother deserves better!" With that, Diane walked out of the room, leaving Samone standing there looking stupid.

Meanwhile AJ drifted off to sleep peacefully after hearing Dameon's voice.

Dudley Correctional Dining Hall

"Hey, Dukes. Here's the article about my son. Pack it away with your things. The phone number to his office is in the article," O'Dell said while handing over the newspaper.

"I want you to call the office and ask for him specifically—set up an appointment with him directly. Once you've set up the appointment, inquire about purchasing a condo. Tell him you're from out of town, and a business associate referred him to you. Then tell him your stay in Florida will only be two days, and you'd like to purchase the property as soon as possible. Tell him you can't remember the name of the hotel where you're staying so ask him for all his contact numbers to stay in touch with him. Okay?"

"Yes, sir," Dukes replied.

"It's very simple. Very businesslike. You get the phone numbers, mail them back to me, along with how to contact you. All I want to do is hear his voice for now until I come face to face with all of them."

"Sounds easy enough, O'Dell. I can do this man, no problem. Do you think you can help me out in finding my Robin?"

"No problem, Dukes. I've got connections on the outside, and if you need me to hook you up with a place to live, I can make a few calls. It's the least I can do for you since I appreciate your help. You have no idea how much this means to me."

"Man, I'd appreciate that! Try not to worry. I won't let you down. I promise not to tell a soul."

O'Dell patted Dukes on the back. "Thanks, son. I knew I took to you for a reason. Don't get lost in your woman and forget about me now."

"Put your mind to rest, old man. I got you. You just look forward to receiving my mail. It's a done deal!"

Westchester

Mr. Kimble sat patiently in the car outside Dameon's place. He had his brown bag lunch and coffee in his thermos. Kimble was prepared to camp out for as long as necessary even though he'd been experiencing some tightness in his chest. Thank goodness for his nitroglycerin pills. He just had to get some answers today on this case. It had already been about three hours and no more action than the beautiful woman who had arrived earlier.

Kimble peeked at his watch; it was 6:00 p.m. Time to take his heart medication. As he reached into his pocket for his pill, he noticed Dameon drive up to the gate. Unknowingly Kimble dropped the pill while reaching to the floor to grab his camera. Dameon drove the car around back to the garage.

An hour passed. More pain. Just as Kimble popped another pill, Dameon pulled the silver Mustang around front. As he got out of the car to load up two pieces of luggage, the beautiful woman opened the front door and proceeded to get in on the passenger side. Kimble's hands were trembling as he zoomed in on the couple with his camera.

Kimble trailed behind them very slowly to see where they were going. Dameon got on the expressway; traffic was backed up for miles. Keeping a close eye on his target, Kimble was careful not to lose him. Dameon exited at the airport and drove to the front. Kimble followed close behind. The gorgeous woman got out of the car and moved to the driver's side. Kimble continued snapping photos. By this point, he had used up a whole roll of film. Dameon grabbed both bags and went over to the car door to speak with the woman. Kimble noticed they didn't kiss goodbye. But still, what did this all mean? Who was this woman?

Knowing he couldn't be in two places at once, Kimble decided it was more important to see what airline Dameon was flying on. Where was he heading? His first thought was Seattle so Kimble phoned his partner on the west coast to tell him to keep an eye out for any activity at Dameon's Seattle home.

Restaurant

While Kimble was playing detective, Robin and Ellen were catching up over dinner.

"I can't believe you and OJ are talking marriage already, Robin! Your Florida trip must have been hot and heavy! I can see the glow on your face, girl. It's so good to see you so happy. You deserve it after all you've been through."

"Thanks, Ellen. It's nice to be able to share the good times together. Enough about me. What's your good news? Tell me about your date with Dameon."

"Well, there's not much to tell. We just went out for a few drinks is all. We danced close so I got a whiff of his cologne. Girl, he smelled so good!"

"Yeah…and…" Robin teased.

"I'm in love with him, Robin. He's so cute. But our evening was interrupted by a business call. Had we not been interrupted, I think it would have been a long night for both of us, with me camping out at his place."

"Sounds like you've made progress, Ellen. I told you he'd come around. Hang in there, girl. Things never work when we want them to. I never thought in my wildest imagination I'd meet OJ! So it sounds like you guys have taken the relationship beyond business…" Robin asked hesitantly.

"I wouldn't go that far, Robin, but I've gotten to know him better on a more personal level. He doesn't drink coffee, indulge in sweets, no red meats, works out at the gym three times a week and gets a manicure, haircut and shave every week. He's an immaculate man. Oh yeah, and he has a sister," Ellen added, trying to sound casual.

"WOW! You are tuned in with your man, Ellen!" Robin winked.

"I love the man, Robin. What can I say? I notice every little thing about him. You should see him eat. He takes these small tiny little bites," Ellen cooed.

Robin laughed, "You don't miss a beat, do you?"

"No ma'am. Hopefully I'll have lots more intimate details to share with you when I get to know him the way I hope to real soon. We haven't even kissed yet! Girl, when he does kiss me, I probably won't live to tell about it!"

"You are too much, Ellen! It will all happen in time. I'm going to invite him to the party. Never know. That may trigger his mind to settle down and think about a relationship."

"Yeah right. All I want is to get to first base with him; one night of passion and then I'll be happy!"

"Calm down, Ellen. You will, sister. Knowing you as I do, you won't stop until you've conquered your prey. Men are hunters by nature; they like to be in control, take the lead, but when you reel him in, he won't even realize that the chase was on! He'll come after you like a wild, crazy man. Watch, you'll see, Ellen! You're a very attractive woman. Do you think Mr. T.D.H. is going to let you slip by him? Just keep your bait ready for the catching."

Ellen changed the subject back to Robin so as to not let on about hiring Kimble.

Florida

Weesee was on the airplane less than an hour from landing in Daytona. She was reflecting back on the day she first laid eyes on Sterling Powers; her mind was deep in thought.

"Excuse me, my lady. Would you be so kind as to pass me the business magazine in your front seat pocket?"

"Yes, I do mind sir, and I'm not your lady."

"Miss, I'm terribly sorry. I meant nothing by that gesture. In my country we often address beautiful women in this custom."

"Well, since you put it like that, I guess I can cut you a break. Where are you from anyway?" Weesee asked, now noticing his accent.

"Thank you very kindly," he said, taking the magazine from Weesee. "I'm from Somalia, Africa. My name is Malik," he smiled and extended his hand to greet her.

"Sorry, Malik, but I don't make a habit of shaking stranger's hands. I didn't know many Caucasians lived in Africa," Weesee admitted, thinking to herself, *For a white guy, he's quite attractive with his olive skin, deep brown eyes and jet-black hair, which was pulled back in a ponytail.*

"If I may call you my lady, because you haven't introduced yourself by name. There are many, many Caucasians, as you call them, in Africa. My country is plenty full of people of all walks of life, shapes and colors. Might I please inquire of your name?"

"Excuse me, Mr. Malik. But you've gotten what you asked for in that magazine. Now you're asking for too much," Weesee insisted.

"My lady, I'd like to address you by your full name, that is all. A woman as attractive as you must have a name to match."

Softening up with his compliments, she responded, "Elouise."

Reaching for her hand to hold he said, "Elouise is a very beautiful name. I like it. I like the beautiful face that fits the name. Just lovely, my lady!"

Taking a closer look at him, Weesee smiled. She felt a bit more comfortable with him.

"Do you live in Daytona, Ms. Elouise?"

"No, I'm here on business, visiting with friends."

"Me, too. I'll be in Daytona only a few days. I'm staying at the Ambassador Castle Hotel. Here's my business card, " he said, handing it to her. "I'd like to have a cocktail with you, if I may? I take great pleasure in being in the company of a beautiful woman. Please take my card."

"Listen up, Maleaky, Ma…whatever your name is. You don't know me like that. Besides, I don't date Caucasian African men—nothing personal!"

"Elouise, dear, but I know beauty when I see it! Please just take my card. You never know, we may never see one another again," Malik said while staring at Weesee's glossy lips.

Getting totally frustrated with this guy, Weesee grabbed his business card with a heavy sigh. She casually glanced at it. Hmmm. Oil connoisseur. Her eyes lit up when she saw the word oil. Malik must have it going on.

Weesee's sigh turned into a coy smile as the thought of Malik dripping in money reeled through her mind. Guess I can't judge a book by its cover. Why can't I date a Caucasian man from Africa? What do I have to lose?

"Thank you, Malik. Thank you very much. I just might take you up on your offer," Weesee's demeanor softened dramatically.

"I'm only in Daytona for a short stay as well. If we can't hook up for cocktails, I'll gladly phone you at the hotel," she flirted.

"I would be very honored, my lovely lady," Malik said dreamily.

"Okay then, Malik. It's a date."

"Thank you, beautiful queen. My driver will be waiting for me upon arrival. May I offer you a ride to where you are staying?" he asked, sizing her up from head to toe. He thought she was terribly sexy.

"That will be very kind of you, Malik."

"The pleasure is all mine. Thank you, Elouise."

His accent, sexy smile and business card had warmed through Weesee's suspicious heart.

Just then the flight attendant announced the plane's arrival in Daytona.

Malik was attracted to Black women, and he had been instantly drawn to Weesee. Something was different about her from the women he'd been used to. Malik had met scores of women since he was the King of Oil. From a well-to-do family in Africa, Malik had been sent to America by his parents to find a bride.

While Malik was here on legitimate oil business, he also had his mind on the finer things of life, and Weesee was one of his first catches of the day.

St. Michael's Hospital

AJ walked into the waiting room to find Diane sitting alone, staring blankly out the window.

"Baby girl, what are you doing here by yourself? How's OJ? Where's Samone?"

Diane smiled as she saw AJ approach and heard his comforting voice. "OJ is the same, AJ. Samone left to see the kids, I guess." Diane's disgust with Samone was evident by her facial expression.

"I can tell by the look on your face you and Samone were at it again, Diane. What happened?"

"She made me so damn mad, AJ. I slapped her before I realized what I had done. That woman is not good enough for our brother!"

"Baby girl, you promised me you'd try to get along for OJ's sake."

With puppy dog eyes, Diane replied, "You're right, AJ. I'm sorry, but as soon as she opens her damn mouth, she pisses me the hell off! Never mind the fact that she prances around here with Sterling Powers. The nerve of that bitch!"

AJ reached for Diane to hug her and held her close. "It's okay, sis. I understand. You're just looking out for OJ. I can't blame you." AJ felt the same as Diane, but he tried to cover up his feelings.

"Hey, Diane, why don't you take five and check on the kids; take a rest. I'll stay here for a while."

"I don't want to leave you all alone, AJ."

"I'm fine. I've rested, and I'll call you if there's any change in OJ's condition. I promise."

Diane knew she needed rest to recuperate from her rage and anguish. She hugged AJ goodbye and made him promise once again to call if anything changed whatsoever.

AJ stood at the window looking out at the dreary day. It was pouring rain. His mind drifted in three different directions—OJ, Robin and Dameon. It was as if the rain droplets mesmerized him, and his life became a movie as he reflected back on the day he met Dameon.

They both were in France on business and were standing on a bridge overlooking the scenic view, both hearts hurting, battered by the loss of a woman. Dameon approached AJ first, rambling on about his broken relationship to a fashion model who ran off with his best friend.

AJ, feeling the very same pain after his recent break up with his woman, listened to Dameon for hours. They bonded instantly like brothers, deeply sympathetic to what each other was feeling. They spent the next week together, sightseeing and having a blast. Their friendship flourished. Although miles stood between them, they stayed connected once back in the States. Before either realized it, they were lovers.

The more popular each became in the world of business, the deeper their affection for one another grew. It was as if they both thrived on the other's success. A competitive hunger drove them to the top of their industry. They wanted nothing but the best for each other, and by this time, they had fallen deeply in love. AJ thought about all their years and passion. Was he really in love with Dameon or was it the flamboyant lifestyle or his aggressive business sense that drew them together? They were so similar in their drive, determination and demeanor. Was Dameon a mere reflection of himself, AJ wondered? A man who had everything except someone to love?

AJ began to do some deep soul searching as the rain pounded against the window, breaking down the barriers of his mind. *Why did I fall in love with Robin, then? Was it because she was off limits,* he asked himself? *Sure she's attractive, but so are countless other women he'd encountered. Was it because she was someone my brother wanted? Am I that hard hearted and competitive? Is this love I feel or a deep jealousy of what OJ has?*

AJ's heart was wrenching with despair and turmoil. He felt sick to his stomach as he let his innermost thoughts wrestle about and come to the forefront of his mind to be dealt with. *What about OJ? God knows I love my brother, my flesh and blood. We've always been so close. I've always admired his low key, reserved personality—slow but sure OJ, carefully calculating every move. Am I jealous?*

A tear fell down his cheek as thoughts continued to race through his mind. He had to face his feelings. How could I have allowed another man to penetrate my heart? A woman I don't even know to tear down my stony heart to tell her I love her? How could I be jealous of my own flesh and blood? He finally reached within himself for the answers he didn't want to face. "Illusions! I've been such a fool! All illusions!" AJ said, while shaking his head in disbelief.

Ridgemont Hotel, Florida

"Malik, I appreciate having your limo driver give me a ride. You're so sweet. Thank you again," Weesee said with a wink as she departed the elegant black limousine.

"Beautiful Elouise, you are more than welcome. I look very much forward to our evening together for cocktails. Might I suggest tomorrow evening? I'll have my limo come for you," Malik said as he tenderly grabbed her hand to kiss it.

"I'll call you, Malik, to confirm," Weesee said as she casually blew him a kiss.

"I'll look forward to your call."

Weesee made her way into the hotel, plopped her luggage down and checked in. As soon as she was comfortably situated in her room, she phoned Sterling.

"Hello, Sterling Powers speaking."

"Hey, baby. I'm here!"

"Hey, sexy momma! Good to hear your voice! Where are you now?"

"I'm staying at the Ridgemont Hotel downtown in room #107—come on and bring it, hot man!"

"Give me about an hour, Weesee. Let me close this last account, and I'll be there in a hurry."

"Okay, big daddy. Don't make me wait forever. It's been a long exhausting flight. I need you to put Momma to sleep."

"Hold that thought. I'll be right there."

Sterling was tying up loose ends at the office when the phone rang again. He hesitated before picking it up, his mind picturing Weesee looking luscious and waiting for him in bed.

"Uh, hello. Sterling Powers speaking."

All Sterling could hear was intense sobs; he couldn't make out if it was a wrong number or what. Suddenly he recognized the voice. It was Samone.

"I need someone…someone to talk to…" Samone was hysterical.

"What's going on, Samone? What has something happened? Is it OJ?"

"It's everything. Help me. (sobbing) I'm falling apart. Heeellllpp…"

Sterling's heart plummeted as he heard her distress. He would do anything for Samone.

"Where are you, baby? I'm on my way."

Samone looked around, but was unable to recognize her location. "I don't know, Sterling. I'm a wreck. I'm on some side street. Oh please help me, Sterling."

"Samone, honey, listen to me. Can you drive to my house? Can you find your way there?"

"Yes. Yes. My head is spinning. Yes. Your beach house."

"Go there, Samone, to the beach house. I'll meet you right there. Be careful. I'm leaving right now."

"Please hurry, Sterling. I need help," Samone's voice trembled with fear and exhaustion.

Without giving second thought to Weesee, Sterling rushed out of the office as if he'd seen a ghost.

St. Michael's Hospital

AJ was still gazing out the window. He has two cell phones on his belt. When one rang, he assumed it was OJ's since he'd purposely kept OJ's on in case Robin called.

"Hello."

"Mr. O'Neil?"

"Yes, this is he, but I'm afraid I'm not taking any business calls at this time."

"Mr. O'Neil. My name is Fred Dukes. Did I happen to reach you at a bad time?"

"Yes, Mr. Ummm (forgetting his name)."

"Fred Dukes, sir."

"Well, I'm sorry Mr. Dukes, but I'm not taking any business calls right now. Please call my office on Monday and leave a message with my secretary."

"I'm sorry to hear your plight, Mr. O'Neil. I'm here in Daytona for just one more day, and I have an offer on some property I know you can't refuse. I was hoping to make a purchase in cash tomorrow."

"I apologize, and under normal circumstances we could make a deal, but I've had to put all business matters on hold due to a family crisis."

"Oh, I see. I'm sorry, Mr. O'Neil. A partner of mine referred me to you. I saw a piece of your property up for sale, and I've got to have it. Cash $120,000, on Camber Drive. When can we strike a deal?" (Fred was bluffing; he was actually calling from a phone booth in Westchester.)

AJ was getting short tempered. He wasn't thinking about money or property. "Look, Mr. Dukes, your timing is way off, man. The offer sounds okay, but I've got to pass on it right now. Call my office on Monday."

"Sure enough, man. You're a tough businessman. I'll give you $160k cash if you make a deal with me. C'mon, man."

AJ quickly put a few figures together in his mind and realized this Mr. Dukes was offering triple the value of the property. "Mr. Dukes, I'll tell you what. Since it means so much to you, I will meet you tomorrow for an hour, draw up the papers and close the deal. How's that?"

"That's what I'm talking about, man. See, I was raised on that property years ago. It's got sentimental value to me. Can you dig that?"

AJ, rushing to get off the phone said, "Yeah, Dukes. I understand. Give me a number where I can reach you. I'll call and set a time and place to meet."

Fred stalled a second. "Well, umm, I'm just getting in town, and I haven't checked into a hotel yet. How 'bout you giving me your numbers, and I'll check in about eleven tomorrow?"

"Sure enough then. Call me on this number, and if you don't reach me, take down my home number—889-0001."

"Thanks, man. I apologize for the timing, but I appreciate your willingness to meet tomorrow. Talk to you then."

Westchester—Dameon's Place

Mr. Kimble sat outside the gated mansion waiting to see if the beautiful woman in the silver Mustang would leave. He peeped at his watch; it was 9:00

p.m. and he was getting tired. Just as he got his mind settled on leaving, the Mustang came through the gate. Kimble trailed her to Club Lamarge. Waiting for her to enter the club, Kimble followed soon after. Inside, he saw Alexis seated at a table with a man. Immediately he took out his pocket zoom and snapped photos.

Who the heck was this, he wondered. Alexis was quite flirtatious with this gentleman, which confused Kimble all the more. *Could it be she was creeping around while Dameon was away?* Kimble's cell phone rang so he went to the restroom to take the call. It was his associate reporting in with regards to Seattle. Kimble learned Dameon did not fly into Seattle, and there was not any activity at the house.

More unanswered questions, Kimble thought. Trying to piece the puzzle together was getting a little more complicated than he had bargained for. But he was determined. Never once had a case beat him, and this one would be won.

Kimble hung out at the club until Alexis left with the mysterious man. He followed her to another hotel where she went in with him. More photos and playing the waiting game. Kimble hung out in his car another forty minutes and then called it a night. He was exhausted.

Meanwhile Ellen dropped Robin home. To her surprise, Robin discovered a box of long stemmed roses placed on her doorstep. Ellen smiled with happiness for Robin.

"Boy, I hope my man Dameon sends me some of those. I could get used to this kind of love expression real quick!"

As Robin put the gorgeous bouquet into a vase, she spotted the note, which read: "To my sweetheart with all my love; the only woman I ever will love always. Thinking of you." Robin smiled, thinking about how thoughtful OJ was. As soon as she had them perfectly arranged, she called to thank him but got his voicemail.

"Thank you, my darling. The flowers are lovely! I love you, OJ!"

The very first thing Fred had done upon being released as a free man was to search for Robin's address. He had found it, thanks to a little help from O'Dell's connections, and he had sent the flowers to her.

Ellen sped home, hoping to find a message from Dameon on her machine, but there were none. Walking to the cabinet to pull out a bottle of wine, Ellen figured she'd drown her sorrows. She and her bottle of wine had become good friends in recent months. It was the only friend she could count on; it was always there, ready to help her forget her woes.

Ridgemont Hotel

Weesee lay in bed watching the candles melt down. An hour had passed since she'd spoken to Sterling. She wondered what was keeping him, but she was too proud to try his cell. Trying not to get restless, she dialed room service and ordered a bottle of fine champagne. She hadn't seen Sterling in so long she felt a celebration was in order. Dressed in elegant deep pink lingerie, she sat waiting for her man to take full control. How her body hungered to be with him. His passion. Her passion. Where in the hell was he? She was starting to get annoyed.

Meanwhile Sterling was oblivious to Weesee's lustful telepathy. He was on his way to his beach house to rescue Samone from her pain. He phoned the beach house to see if she had arrived safely, but there was no answer.

The rain was pouring down in buckets, and he could barely see out the front windshield. Come hell or high water, he was going to Samone. He made his way to the beach house and saw Samone's car parked in the front. The house was pitch dark. Where was Samone? He barely made out her figure sitting on the porch. He ran to her. She was drenched, shivering and sobbing uncontrollably. Immediately he took off his jacket and wrapped it around her.

She sat in a daze; still unaware he was even there. Upon unlocking the door, Sterling picked Samone up and carried her inside. She was in shock.

He took her into the bathroom, gently undressed her and put on his bathrobe. Samone stared straight ahead without acknowledgment of his presence. Sterling continued to dry her off her trembling body and then carried her to his bed. He then went off to the kitchen to prepare something hot for her to drink. Sterling was concerned; he had never seen Samone in such a state.

Taking in a hot pot of tea, Sterling carefully sat down beside her and stroked her hand. "Samone, baby, it's going to be all right. I'm here; I'll take good care of you. Everything's going to be okay."

Samone had recovered years before from a nervous breakdown that only she and OJ were aware of. She was under the care of a psychiatrist and taking daily medication, but her state of mind was fragile. OJ's accident must have set her on the brink of another emotional storm. Unaware of who she was, where she was or what was going on, Sterling sat by her side throughout the night, trying to comfort her. He made no calls to her kids, to Weesee or anyone for that matter. He was deathly afraid for Samone.

Her weakened body tossed and turned endlessly for hours; no words were uttered. Finally she broke down and cried while Sterling held her in his arms like a baby. "Let it out, my baby," he tried to console her. For every tear she cried, he felt her pain. He adored her; he loved her. He could not bear to see her in so much anguish.

Samone looked deep into Sterling's eyes, searching for truth.

"You love me, Sterling?"

Caught totally off guard, Sterling sat speechless. Gazing into her eyes, he couldn't resist his love any longer. "Yes, my sweet Samone. I have always loved you."

It was as though a ton of bricks had been lifted off Sterling the minute those words came off his tongue. He leaned towards her, and their lips met in a passionate kiss. Samone savored his strength and security. She took him in her arms and their embrace grew in its intensity. They made passionate love. As Samone drifted off into a peaceful sleep, Sterling sat watching her in awe. She was his princess. His love for her was like none other he had ever experienced. He would be there for Samone. Whatever she needed. Forever.

As he continued to savor her sweetness, Sterling began to think back to the many women he had loved or was it lusted, he thought. None compared to Samone. His reminiscence ended abruptly when Weesee came to mind. I'm gonna be a dead man, Sterling realized. How the hell could I have forgotten her?

Still caught up in the moment, Sterling dismissed Weesee's impending tirade and continued to watch Samone sleep like a baby. "You'll never have to worry as long as I'm around. I love you, sweet Samone."

Westchester

Fred hung up the phone with AJ wearing a big smile across his face. *I got it,* he said to himself. AJ's personal home number. O'Dell will be pleased with my work. I'll put it in the mail to him tomorrow first class.

Fred's smile beamed brighter as his thoughts turned to Robin, wondering if she had received the flowers yet. He thought just maybe he'd drive by her house just to see if her light was on.

He parked his car on the street across from her house. With puppy dog eyes, Fred looked at the house and noticed the upstairs light was on. "Soon, my sweet Robin, very soon we'll be together again!" Fred's mind was full of fantasy as he hopped back into his car and drove away.

Robin, relaxing in a bubble bath, smiled at the thought of OJ's flowers. She closed her eyes and let her mind and body soak up the memories of their passionate lovemaking. "Hmmm. Robin O'Neil. That has a nice ring to it. Thank you, Lord, for blessing me!"

Florida

Dameon arrived at the airport in the pouring rain. He looked for his driver holding his name, and after five frustrating minutes, he tracked him down. Immediately they sped to AJ's home.

Hope he keeps the spare key in the same hiding place, Dameon smirked to himself. He couldn't wait to see AJ's expression. He needed to see him, be with him, talk with him, hold him, and love him. Dameon was on a mission. He had made the mistake of his life, and now he was speeding forth to reconcile it.

Ridgemont Hotel

Weesee had fire in her eyes she was so angry! She had never been stood up by any man in her life! She never expected in a million years the first would be Sterling Powers. *How dare that bastard stand me up! Who does he think he is?* She tried to keep her emotions intact, but before she knew it, a tear fell from her eye. She loved Sterling. Her tough exterior was crumbling, crying for a man.

Elouise, you just dry those tears right now. Stop this foolishness! You're better than this. Hell, you can get any man you want. Damn Sterling Powers! You can do much better. He's the one missing out on this good lovin'. Don't take it, girl. Don't get mad, get even! she said to herself, wiping the tears from her face.

She shot over to the phone. *One monkey don't stop nothing! There's bigger fish in the sea,* she said to herself as she picked up and dialed the number to the Ambassador Hotel.

"Malik, darling, how about that drink? Send your limo over for me, sweetie."

"Certainly, my beautiful queen. Happy to hear you're available tonight."

Instead of hanging up the phone as a queen would, Weesee threw it against the wall. Who was she fooling? She was so pissed off. It was Sterling she wanted. Now look what she'd done. She ran over and picked up the phone to try to stop Malik from sending his limo, but it was too late.

Weesee had never allowed any man to penetrate her heart as Sterling did. She tried to focus her mind on getting ready for Malik. *A new chapter in my memoirs,* she toasted to herself as she gulped down a glass of champagne. The more she fought the feelings, the more tears flowed. She poured herself another glass and toasted to the end of what could have been a committed relationship between she and Sterling.

Damn this love stuff hurts. Never again, Elouise, never again will any man hurt my heart. And with that, she finished off the last of the champagne, which helped her take Sterling completely out of her mind. She had successfully turned the switch. "Someone will pay for my hurt," she seethed.

AJ's Place

As the limo pulled around back, Dameon noticed the black Lamborghini was parked in the driveway and the Jaguar was gone. This meant AJ wasn't home. *Great,* Dameon thought, *my plan to surprise him will work.*

While the driver removed his bags, Dameon sat mesmerized by the Lamborghini. He vividly remembered the day they purchased it at the auction together. Dameon had made the first bid on the car, knowing AJ had always wanted one. The bidding got intense, but Dameon was determined to win. No matter the cost, he wanted AJ to be happy. Reflecting back to the good old days made Dameon realize just how much he loved him.

"Sir, excuse me. Will there be anything else?"

"Umm. No. Thank you," Dameon said, suddenly realizing he had been daydreaming. Quickly he jumped out of the limo, found the spare key just where he remembered it, and then let himself in.

He walked through the huge kitchen accented with shiny black and mauve ceramic flooring. Dameon stood for a second admiring the tasteful décor. Home away from home.

He made his way into the living room area and noticed the drapes were drawn closed, which blocked out the sunlight, so he opened them. Then he noticed on the table sat an empty glass AJ had drank from. Dameon removed his suit jacket and made himself comfortable. He took off his tie as he approached the built-in wall bar to make himself a drink. Off from the living room was the greenhouse. Dameon made his way through the glass doors and walked along the brick walkway until he reached a large swinging bench. He sat down, admiring the beautiful tropical plants. AJ loved his garden and took great pride in his expensive flowers. Dameon laid his head back on the swing, contemplating whether or not he should phone AJ to meet him for dinner or wait to surprise him when he came home.

He sipped on his glass of brandy, exhausted from the flight. He wanted to relax before he took his bags upstairs. He could hear the rain pattering on the glass ceiling and its rhythm helped him drift off to sleep.

Westchester

Ellen relaxed on the bed buzzed from her wine. Her mind wondered on Dameon. In her right night stand drawer she had a photo taken of she and Dameon at a luncheon given at the office. She removed the photo from the drawer and gazed at it. *What a handsome couple,* she thought to herself. She held the picture close to her chest, hugging it as if it had life. How much she wanted to lie in his arms. Had he taken the mystery woman along with him on his sudden trip, or maybe he was going to meet her there. Ellen couldn't wait to hear from Mr. Kimble so her mind could be put to ease. She placed Dameon's picture underneath her pillow and dozed off to sleep.

Robin's Place

Meanwhile, Robin was watching the late night news, hoping OJ would call after she left the message thanking him for the flowers. She looked on at the single rose she had placed in a vase beside her bed and smiled at the thought of loving this man so much. Soon they would wed and never have to worry about parting or distance again. Her eyes swelled with tears as she reflected on meeting OJ. She thought about how life can often throw someone a curve but when it's least expected, God turns around and blesses them. Robin felt after all the drama with Fred, she would never love or trust another man until she met OJ. She smiled, said her prayers and fell off to sleep.

Florida—St. Michael's Hospital

AJ looked on at his brother as he slept peacefully in a coma. He sat by his bedside, hoping for a change. He reached for OJ's hand to hold.

"OJ, man, I love you. If you can hear me, please come out of it. I need you, man. The kids need you. I'm right here for you, OJ. You're gonna make it. I prayed—believe that. God is gonna make it right! We're gonna get through this."

Unaware that a nurse had entered the room, she startled AJ when she said, "Please excuse me, Mr. O'Neil, but you have a call at the ICU desk."

"Thank you, ma'am," he said, wondering who in the world would be calling him at the hospital close to midnight. Samone or Diane? "Hello?"

OJ's son, Junior, spoke meekly into the receiver. "Uncle AJ, it's Junior. I'm sorry to call, but I wanted an update as to how dad was doing. Mom said she'd call, and Nichole and I have been waiting. I know mom is very upset, and it probably slipped her mind to call us, but we started to get worried."

"Junior, your dad is progressing. Don't you worry, son, he's going to be just fine. Is Nichole okay?"

"Yes, sir, Uncle AJ. Nichole is just fine. We're just getting sleepy waiting up for mom to get home. May I speak with her?"

"Your mother?" AJ repeated, trying not to show his emotional state and concern.

"Yes. That's why I called. I figured if we just said goodnight on the phone, we'd head off to bed now," Junior replied.

Gosh, Samone left the hospital hours ago. Damn. Where could she have gone? AJ worried, getting a bit frantic as to what to tell Junior.

"Well, your mother will be home very soon, son. You and Nichole lock the doors and hop into bed. Say your prayers because your dad needs them, okay?" AJ tried to sound positive and upbeat.

"Yes, sir. We'll lock up the house together right now."

"Good boy. When your mother gets home, have her call me on my cell right away, okay?"

"Sure enough, Uncle AJ. Thanks for seeing after my dad. He'd do the same for you."

"Yeah, I know, Junior. I love you! Now get your sister in bed, and I'll see you both tomorrow. Good night!"

"Good night."

AJ hung up the phone absolutely furious with Samone. *Where in the hell could she be?* He didn't want to get Diane all riled up, but he was concerned about the kids. Quickly he remembered he had OJ's cell phone and it had Samone's cell number stored on it. He immediately dialed her number, but was taken to her voicemail. "Sorry I can't take your call, please leave a message."

"Samone, this is AJ. It's after twelve in the morning, where in the hell are you? You damn sure aren't at the hospital with my brother. You do have kids at home who are worried sick! Call me immediately." He hung up the phone.

AJ didn't want to leave OJ alone, but he felt responsible for the kids. He had always looked after them while OJ was away. They were like his own, and he decided he must leave the hospital in order to check on them. He rushed to OJ's house in the pouring rain, totally disgusted with Samone.

AJ's Place

Dameon awoke as the clock struck midnight; the rain poured down outside. He'd been asleep for hours. AJ still hadn't made it home yet, and Dameon became worried. Heading to the kitchen to make something to eat before going upstairs, he phoned AJ's cell, but his voicemail picked up. He hung up without leaving a message. Dameon finished his sandwich and headed upstairs with his luggage. He wanted to relax in AJ's hot tub and keep himself awake until AJ came home. He placed his luggage in the master bedroom. As he reached for the lamp, he heard something fall. It was a photo. Dameon reached to put the picture back in place, and as he did, he noticed it was a picture of a woman, and it wasn't Diane, AJ's sister. He had seen pictures of both Diane and OJ. He was stunned to say the least. Who in the hell was this woman? Knowing AJ as well as he did, it had to be someone special for him to have it on his nightstand next to his bed.

All kinds of ideas were going through Dameon's mind. He knew AJ often dined with different women, but it was nothing he'd take seriously. The horns of jealousy began to rise. *Had he turned completely straight,* Dameon wondered. His mind sped in a million directions. He loved AJ so much, if it was a woman he wanted, then Dameon was willing to do whatever he had to do to keep him all to himself. Figuring AJ would be home momentarily; Dameon undressed, turned up the hot tub and got in amidst the bubbles.

Meanwhile, back at Sterling's beach house, Samone was sleeping soundly while Sterling looked on at her longingly. He was like a watchdog, watching her every breath. Not once had he thought to contact her family. He had waited for years for this very moment, and he practically had to pinch himself to believe it was actually happening! Sterling reflected back to the first day Samone had walked into his office. He interviewed her for a broadcasting position. Impressed with all her answers, he hired her right on the spot. In no time her expertise and beauty helped her to earn a promotion. Her tenacity and aggressiveness eventually helped to push her to the top, becoming a radio producer. Sterling admired her determination and fell in love with her strong will. He had never seen her in a vulnerable state, the way he had found her, sitting in the rain on the porch.

He knew she wasn't herself and that he was going to help her through whatever was causing her trauma. Little did he know the problem was way bigger than he ever had imagined. Samone was on antidepressants, which she took daily to deal with life. She suffered a breakdown in the beginning of her relationship with OJ when her mother was murdered. She buried her hurt in her work, and kept her problem a secret from all except OJ. After her breakdown she became very distant in her relationship with him. She loved him and her kids very much, but she was so afraid of getting close to anyone. She was petrified of having them taken away like her mother was murdered. Before her mother's death, Samone had been a very affectionate, loving person, but after her breakdown she became an outspoken, selfish witch, but with a capital "B" in front of the word.

Samone had two sides to her personality, and she played both roles very well. When she's sweet, she's loving, only if it benefits her, but when she's nasty, she's just that. Sterling had yet to see the cold side of her.

OJ knew the real Samone and why she was the way she was. He knew the reason for the strain on their relationship. There was no way he could leave his kids alone with Samone. Besides, emotionally she couldn't handle the responsibility alone.

Ambassador Hotel (Malik's Suite)

Malik sat in his penthouse suite waiting for Weesee to arrive. He ordered an assortment of delectable seafood, cheeses, fruits and wines to entertain her senses. He wanted nothing but the very best upon her arrival. He also ordered two dozen long stem red roses, which were lavishly displayed. Malik's dreamy eyes once again undressed her from head to toe in his mind. He had been instantly attracted to her, and all he could think about was her glossy full lips and the way she pronounced his name. He had to know this woman. He had the hotel staff arrange all the food and drink on the long dining room table set for a king, waiting for his queen to arrive. He asked the attendants to place candles throughout the penthouse and even sent out for fresh rose petals to be placed as a walkway just for her. The suite was magnificent, and Malik was ready for the opportunity to get to know Elouise.

AJ drove over to OJ's house to see if Samone's car was home yet. Nope. Not in the driveway, and by now it had been many hours since she'd left the hospital. The house was dark, and AJ didn't want to wake the kids so he sat and stewed inside his car. Pissed off was putting it mildly. The first thought that came to his mind was that Samone was with Powers. He was angry at the thought of Sterling taking advantage of his brother's woman. AJ didn't know what to do. He certainly didn't want Diane to get word of Samone's staying out half the night and leaving the kids alone, but he was absolutely exhausted. "I'll deal with Samone in the morning. All looks safe and sound here," he said to himself as he put his car in gear and began to drive home.

Upon arriving, he entered his house mad as hell and went straight to make himself a tall drink to quiet his nerves. Exhausted mentally and physically, AJ continued to run images of Samone through his mind. He couldn't believe her not being in contact with the kids. Had something happened to her? Did she have an accident? AJ shook off his exhaustion and decided to wait for her to call.

Suddenly he heard music coming from upstairs. He thought his mind was playing tricks on him. Hmmm. First the kitchen light had been left on (and he hadn't remembered even turning it on) and now—music. As AJ headed up the stairs, Dameon was coming down them, dressed in a deep hunter green silk bathrobe with high-heeled hunter green and cream slippers to match. Face beautifully made up with a bone straight auburn shoulder length wig, smelling delectable, Dameon said, "Surprise sweetness!"

"Why Dameon! When in the hell did you get here?" AJ looked like he was in shock and meant to say, "What are you doing here?"

Dameon tossed off his remark and continued his saunter down the stairs and kissed AJ smack dab on the lips. "I've been here all evening waiting for you to come home. I had to be here for you, AJ. You need me now. How could I not be with you at a time like this? I love you, AJ," Dameon said passionately while gazing into AJ's eyes.

Full of anger and ready to explode with the situation with Samone, AJ blurted, "Now is not the time, Dameon. I have to go through this alone. I appreciate your taking the time, and I know you care, but I have to deal with this alone."

Dameon's eyes were full of hurt as he turned away from AJ. *This is the last thing I need right now—to deal with Dameon. Crap!* AJ thought.

But Dameon had turned away only for a brief second, just long enough to collect his thoughts. Immediately he confronted AJ face-to-face. He was not going to be pushed aside and ignored. "Who the hell is she, AJ? I have a right to know."

"What are you talking about?" AJ yelled back defiantly.

"The woman's picture on your night stand. Who the hell is she and what does she mean to you?"

Caught off guard and speechless, AJ just stood there, his mouth ajar.

Before realizing his hot temper had gotten the best of him, Dameon found himself punching AJ in the face. AJ fell down like a limp wet noodle.

Dameon stormed up the stairs to gather his things. AJ's not answering him spoke volumes. He was outta there. Dameon now knew the woman in the photo definitely meant something to AJ.

As Dameon hurriedly threw his clothes in his suitcase, AJ woke up to find himself on the floor with blood all over his shirt. His lip was bloody. Suddenly Dameon heard AJ running up the stairs after him so he locked himself in the bathroom. Dameon sat crying on the floor, his makeup running on his silk robe. AJ was banging madly on the door "Open the door, damn it, Dameon! Open the door or I'll kick it in. Let me talk to you. I don't need this drama from you right now. Open the door NOW!" AJ said, yelling at the top of his lungs.

"Go away, AJ. There's nothing for us to talk about. Your silence said enough. I'll gather my things and be out of your house and your life for good. I've been a fool long enough."

Dameon had barely finished his statement when AJ kicked the bathroom door in. He grabbed Dameon, shook him endlessly until he shook his wig to the floor. "What the hell has gotten into you, Dameon? If you want out, then go, but before you do, let me tell you one thing. I do as I damn well please, and I don't need all this drama from you! Yes, I care for you, but I said now is not the time. Look what you did to me?" (Pointing at his bloody shirt)

Dameon, feeling sorry he had hit AJ said, "I'm sorry. I didn't mean it. Please forgive me. I'll gather my things and call a cab to the airport." Dameon began to walk away sullenly when all of a sudden AJ grabbed him, broke down and cried. Dameon held him close. They held each other for what seemed like eternity. They both hurt for different reasons. AJ broke away out of Dameon's arms and pleaded, "Please stay, Dameon. Don't leave me like this. Please, I have no one to talk to. My brother's dying in a coma. I need you, Dameon. Let's talk this out tomorrow."

"I'm here for you, AJ. I love you; that's why I came in the first place. Now let me take care of that lip…"

Westchester

Ellen lay in bed, still in her clothes from the night before. She'd fallen off to sleep after drinking half a bottle of wine. Awakened by the phone ringing, she knocked it over as she reached to answer it. Her head was pounding. In a faint voice she answered the call, "Hello."

"Ellen, my dear. I'm sorry to call you so early, but I have a few photos I need for you to look at. Can you meet me at the coffee shop at 8:00 am?"

Ellen sat straight up in her bed and glanced down to see that it was 7:00 a.m. She had less than an hour to pull herself together. "Yes, Mr. Kimble. Of course I'll meet you at eight. See you then."

Her heart was pounding and so was her head. She didn't know what to expect, but she wouldn't let anything stop her from getting to the coffee shop to see the pictures.

Florida AJ's Place

AJ and Dameon were having breakfast in the greenhouse.

"About last night, AJ, please forgive me. I lost my head. Now are you ready to talk about the woman in the photo?"

"Dameon, that's my brother's girl. I always keep the photo here for him out of Samone's sight. Really, it's nothing for you to be concerned about. Right now my concern is for my brother's complete recovery. I appreciate your support—you're being here for me—believe me, it means a great deal to me. Don't worry about the woman in the photo, Dameon, okay?"

"AJ love, when I heard your voice over the phone, I just had to come. Tell me, is OJ gonna pull through this? What can I do to help? Anything? Please let me do something. I feel so badly about how I reacted last night."

"You've done more than enough, Dameon. I'll be spending all my time at the hospital so I won't be very good company to you, that's all. I think we need to put our relationship on hold until this situation is better," AJ said as he reached out to hold Dameon's hand.

"Anything to make you feel better, AJ. I'm so very sorry for everything. I won't pressure you until you're ready, but please promise to stay in contact with me. I'm worried about you. I love you."

"I promise. Once everything is back to normal, we can talk about us. We both can decide our future. Right now I need to focus on my family…"

"I totally understand," Dameon said, looking longingly at AJ.

"I gotta get going, now come on now, Dameon!" AJ winked at him.

"Would you mind terribly dropping me to the airport on your way to the hospital? I've made arrangements for a charter flight back to Westchester this morning. Maybe it's best for me to leave. I just want you to know that I really care, AJ. More than you'll ever know…"

"I do know. I care for you too, but I need time, Dameon. Please understand."

"I do. I do now, AJ. Please try not to worry. OJ will pull through. It was 'us' I was worried about. I'm sorry I lost my cool."

"Let's give it a rest for now. I'll tell you what I'll do. Next weekend I'll fly to Westchester and we can talk things over when I come. I'll stay for a few days. How about that?"

"That's a great plan. Now let's shove off. I've got to stop in North Carolina for business on my way back to Westchester, so feel free to call me on my private line if you need me for anything, AJ. Absolutely anything. I can handle it, my love."

Westchester/Florida Airport

Running late for Mr. Kimble, the phone rang and Ellen wasn't going to answer it. Something gnawed at her gut so she did. "Yes?"

"Hello, Ellen?"

"Dameon?"

"Yes, Ellen, it's me. I apologize for such short notice. I meant to call you last night, but I was detained. Listen—I'm on my way to North Carolina. Johnson Matters called to arrange a dinner meeting with you and me tonight to discuss our proposal."

"That's fantastic, Dameon! That's a huge account, and I'm very excited!"

"Yes, dear, so am I. Listen. I've made all the arrangements for you to fly to North Carolina today. I apologize for such short notice. Your flight leaves at noon—four hours from now. It'll be a mini vacation for you as well. Matters insists on you being there."

"This is wonderful, Dameon! How I need to get away! I'll be there. Let me go and get busy. How long will we be staying?"

"We'll stay overnight and fly back tomorrow afternoon. Will this be a problem for you, Ellen?"

"No, not at all. I look forward to seeing you. Besides, we've both worked so very hard on this account."

"Very well then. Take down this information. You'll be staying at the Crystal Hotel, and the reservations have been made in my name. There will be a limo escort waiting for you upon arrival to the airport holding a sign with your name. Oh yes, there seems to be some sort of convention in town, so the only room I could get was a suite. I hope you don't mind sharing it."

Ellen couldn't believe her ears—the moment she'd been waiting for. She was both overcome by excitement and nerves, and completely forgot about her meeting with Mr. Kimble. After hanging up with Dameon and packing her suitcase with the nicest clothes in her wardrobe, Ellen remembered Mr. Kimble. "Oh no!" she said to herself, "I'd better call him and explain why I've missed our appointment."

Upon getting his voicemail Ellen replied, "Mr. Kimble, it's Ellen Berk. I'm sorry, something urgent has come up. I'll have to meet you later in the week. I have urgent business out of town, and I do apologize."

The Airport

AJ and Dameon said their goodbyes.

"I'm laying over in North Carolina for the night so be sure to call me when you get an update on OJ's condition, you hear?"

"I promise to call, Dameon. Thanks for caring."

With that, Dameon leaned over and kissed AJ on the cheek and whispered, "Remember, I love you very much."

"I know, Dameon. Now go catch your flight. I promise to call."

Dameon hopped out of AJ's Jaguar dressed to kill and smelling delicious. The heads of all the women turned to check him out as he walked through the airport. He was a very attractive man. AJ looked on as he made his way through the doors, thinking about his dilemma with Dameon. He cared for Dameon, but he was uncertain if he wanted to make a life with him; he also had feelings for Robin. He couldn't believe Dameon had acted so jealous. AJ realized what happened the night before meant that Dameon was very clear on what and who he wanted. AJ thought he'd put their relationship on the back burner and deal with it later. For now, he needed to focus on OJ, staying in contact with Robin and finding out what was up with Samone.

It was after eight so he took a turn to head over to OJ's to see if Samone had made it home. As he drove, he heard a slight beep. "Ahhh, OJ's cell," AJ said to himself. "Guess I'd better check for messages."

Sure enough there were several from Robin. He especially noticed the excitement in Robin's voice message about the flowers, even though he didn't remember sending her any flowers.

Westchester

"Hello?"

"Hi, honey."

"Hey, sweetheart. Thank you so very much for the gorgeous flowers. They're lovely!"

AJ played along with the game, still not knowing who in the world could've sent the flowers if he or OJ hadn't. Hmmm.

"You're welcome, Robin. How's your day starting out?"

"Just fine now that I've heard your voice. Are you feeling well, sweetie?"

"Yes, fine. Just keepin' long hours at work."

"Did you get the heart monitor results from the doctor yet, honey?"

"Yeah. Uh yeah. Everything was just fine."

"Thank God for good news! I was very worried about that. I love you so much—the thought of anything happening to you frightens me terribly."

"Baby, rest your mind. I'm going to be around for a very long time. I love you too, very much, Robin!"

Just as Robin was about to say something, another call beeped in.

"Honey, I've got another call coming in. Do you mind holding? It could be Larry."

"Go ahead, Robin. Take your call, and I'll call you back later tonight. Love you."

"Love you too, OJ. Have a great day!"

Robin took the call. It was Ellen, and she was out of breath from excitement.

"Are you sitting down or standing?" Ellen chided.

"I'm talkin' to you Ellen. What's up? Is everything all right? You sound all out of breath and very excited."

"Robin, Dameon just phoned and, girl, I'm on my way to North Carolina to meet him for a business engagement tonight. We're staying overnight in the same hotel suite! Oh baby!"

"You gotta be kidding me, girl. He called you at the spur of the moment early in the morning just like that?"

"Yeah. My flight leaves at noon! I'm so thrilled!"

"Did you pack yet, Ellen? Be sure to bring some sexy nightwear. You have to have the right bait to lure your fish, and I know how much this means to you. Let me come over and help you pack a few things," Robin said, hurrying to get off the phone so she could get to Ellen's.

"You're a life saver, Robin! I can't think straight, I'm so nervous!"

"Don't worry about a thing! I got your back, and I have the perfect nightwear for you, too. I bought extra stuff for my trip and never got around to wearing it. Get your suits in order and leave the night attire to me, my friend."

"Okay, Robin. I'm waiting on you, girl."

Ellen hung up the phone and went to her closet to pick out her attire. Dameon told her to look her best, and by all means, she was going to! She had a new black two-piece suit that she had been saving for the right moment to wear. The suit fit her perfectly—very conservative yet with a certain sex appeal. She wanted to look absolutely radiant for Dameon. Quickly she phoned her hair stylist to stop over for a fresh look before leaving. Ellen was on a mission preparing herself for the moment she had longed for: time alone with Dameon.

She was so excited about her rendezvous that she completely forgot she'd woken up terribly hung over.

Outside Robin's house sat Fred in the near distance. He longingly watched her get into her car and pull away, and he followed close behind. Robin had no idea whatsoever that Fred had come back into her life.

Florida
(Ambassador Hotel)

"Good morning my beautiful Elouise," Malik spoke with this enchanting accent.

"Morning, Malik. So ummm, so did we ummm (stuttering) you know? Get into anything last night? I mean I drank more than I should have. I can't hold too much of the alcohol. I wasn't myself last night, and I shouldn't have come."

"No, no sweet Elouise. We didn't indulge in any sexual activities if that's what you're talking about. I'm saving myself for my bride, and Elouise, I'm so very, very glad you came."

"What? You mean to tell me you've never been with a woman?"

"I have, my lady, but I've been celibate for years. I'm saving myself for someone special."

"Yeah, okay, Malik. Listen—you save yourself. Let me get ready; it's time for me to leave. I appreciate the invitation, but I should never have come."

"Lovely Elouise, please don't go. I enjoy your company so very much."

Looking at Malik in disbelief, "I enjoy your company, too, Malik. I thank you for the gorgeous evening—the delicious food and beautiful flowers, but both of us are in dangerous positions so I must be going."

"What do you mean?" Malik looked at Weesee with a funny smirk.

"I mean you're not being active in a while and me wanting to get busy. Man, you don't know the danger you're in! So I'd better get going before I make you do something you may regret."

"Beautiful Elouise, what's wrong with a man saving himself for that special lady? I gather you've never run across any such man."

"No, as a matter of fact I haven't in my entire lifetime, Malik. Not that there's anything wrong with it, but men hardly ever hold out waiting for that 'someone special' as you put it."

Malik reached for Weesee's hand to kiss. "Well, I'm one of a kind, Elouise, and I'm sure my bride will appreciate me and my abstinence."

"I'm sure she will, Malik," she said, raising her eyebrows. "Well, Malik, it's been nice, but I need to get back to my hotel now. I have work appointments later on today."

"I understand, my beautiful Elouise. May I please have dinner with you tonight? I'll be the perfect gentleman!" he smiled at her coyly.

"I'm sure you will, Malik. Thanks, but no thanks. Just keepin' it real with you."

"Keepin' it real? Is that a saying in your country?"

"Yes. Look, I don't have the time to translate my language—I really need to split."

"If you must, you must. Let me phone my driver. But before you leave, Elouise, I have something for you. A gift that I wanted to present to you over dinner. Will you please accept it now?"

Weesee didn't know what to make of this guy. He was quite the gentleman, but odd at the same time.

"I can't accept any gifts, Malik. Your hospitality has been more than gracious. I'm sorry if I fell asleep on you."

"That's rather fine, my lady. I took great joy in watching you sleep. You look so peaceful, so beautiful. Please, please Elouise, take my gift."

"Okay, but if I do, then will you let me go?"

"Excuse me for one moment while I phone for the gift—then I will call my driver to bring you to your hotel. I hope you will change your mind about dinner tonight, my Elouise."

"We'll see, Malik."

Malik went into the other room and made his phone call to the front desk to have the diamond ring he had locked away in the hotel's vault brought up. Malik traveled with the expensive diamond ring in hopes of finding his bride. After meeting Weesee, he felt no need to look any further. She was the woman he wanted to marry. He knew it the moment he laid eyes on her shiny, glossy lips. The way she talked to him aroused him like no other woman. She was the chosen one. She was his queen, his bride even though he had encountered a number of other women he thought were chosen ones in the past.

Weesee was in the bathroom fixing her makeup and hair. In the mirror she saw two uniformed security guards enter the living room. They gave Malik a beautifully wrapped box. *What the hell is going on*, Weesee thought to herself. *How did I get myself into this one?*

Malik escorted the guards out and he proceeded into the room where Weesee was. Malik solemnly knelt down on one knee in front of her. Weesee was almost exasperated by this point by his oddity. "What in the hell is going on around here?" Weesee demanded.

Still on his knee, Malik reached up for her hand to hold. "My lady, your beauty was breathtaking the minute I saw you. I knew in my heart I had to have you with all I have to offer. Here's a small token of what's in my heart. I know you don't love me yet, but I promise you, the love will come. Elouise my beautiful angel, will you be my bride?"

Weesee was taken aback. Shocked is more like it. "This is a joke. You're kidding me, right?" She almost went so far as to ask him if he'd lost his damn mind, but she stopped herself.

Malik had a very serious expression on his face. "No, sweet Elouise, this is no joke. Please open the box."

Weesee looked from Malik to the box and back and forth like a robot. Her hands were trembling as Malik placed the box inside her hand. When she opened it, inside was the biggest diamond ring she'd ever seen. The shine alone blinded her. And with that, Weesee's eyes rolled around in her head and she fell faint to the floor.

St. Michael's Hospital

"Diane, do you expect Samone to visit today?" Dr. Casey asked.

"Yes, Dr. Casey. I suspect she'll be in at some point."

"I'd like to meet with you all to update you on your brother's condition upon her arrival."

"Have things taken a turn for the worse, doctor? Please tell me what's going on. I need to contact my brother AJ."

"Please don't be alarmed, Diane. I will explain everything in detail when the rest of the family arrives. Have the nurse's desk page me when this occurs."

"Yes, doctor." Diane immediately got on the phone with AJ. Her expression was worried; her voice tense. "Hello, AJ, where are you?"

"I'm on my way to the hospital, sis. What's wrong?"

"Dr. Casey wants to meet with Samone, you and myself."

"I'm a few blocks away, baby girl. What about Samone? Is she there already?"

"Nope. Samone is nowhere to be found. I guess I'm in a panic because Dr. Casey wants to give us an update on OJ's condition. Oh Lord, please I pray there is some good news."

"Diane, please try to calm down. First things first. Try to reach Samone. Quit worrying because I'll be there momentarily."

AJ hung up the phone more furious than ever. He was right around the corner from OJ's house so he drove by to see if Samone's car was in the driveway. When it wasn't, he immediately dialed OJ's home phone. Junior answered.

"Uncle AJ? I think my mom left early this morning for the hospital. When Nicole and I woke up she was already gone."

Trying to cover for Samone so as not to worry the kids, AJ replied, "Yeah, Junior, she's probably at the hospital."

"Uncle AJ, my mom didn't leave a note or anything. That's not like her. What's going on? Is my dad gonna be all right?"

"Listen, son, don't you worry about a thing. Your dad is going to be just fine. Your mom just has a lot on her mind right now. Please don't worry."

"Okay, but please have my mom call us when you talk to her, okay?"

AJ couldn't believe Samone had stayed out all night, not thinking about the kids or OJ. Luckily AJ was able to get a hold of a sitter to be with the kids while Samone was missing in action.

Sterling's Beach House

Samone sat in the bed rocking back and forth, tears falling from her eyes. Sterling was in the kitchen making breakfast. Samone began to look around the room as if she was lost. Unfamiliar with her surroundings, she became frightened.

Entering the room with breakfast, Sterling said, "Samone, honey, why are you crying baby?"

He put the tray down on the dresser and sat down on the bed next to Samone.

"I need help, Sterling. Please. Please get me to a doctor!" she screamed, shaking uncontrollably.

"Anything you want, baby. Let me help you to get dressed. I'll take you to St. Michael's and then I'll contact the kids."

Samone was unable to answer. She had withdrawn into a shell; no words, only tears and her constant rocking back and forth made it difficult for Sterling to dress her. Her condition had worsened greatly and he knew he must hurry and get her to the emergency room quick.

Westchester
Ellen's Place

Ellen's busy packing her bags for her trip to Carolina.

"Robin, can you believe it? We're going to be staying in the same suite? Only thing that will be standing between us is a door! Whewee!"

"Girl, all you have to do is walk through that door with this negligee on and I promise you, you'll be staying in his room for the night!"

"I'm ready for him, too. Do you know how long I've waited for this moment?" Ellen giggled.

"You sure don't have to tell me, Ellen, I know. Look how long it took me to meet OJ. After all I went through with Fred, OJ was certainly worth the wait."

"I'm so happy for you guys! Getting married soon! I hope things turn out that good for me!"

"They will, girl, just be yourself. Make Dameon see what he's missing out on!"

"You're right, Robin, tonight is going to be our night. I'm going to wear my hair up the way he likes it, along with my perfume and the beautiful negligee. What man would resist?"

"That ought to hook him, all right. Your hair is lovely, Ellen. Once he gets a look at you in this slinky teddy, he's going to be like a wild man all over you! Like butter in your hand!"

"Girl, I hope so, and I won't be fighting him off or letting him go!" They both laugh.

Robin offered to drive Ellen to the airport once she was all packed. Little did she know Fred was still waiting and watching. His car was parked a bit down the street, and with nothing better to do, he followed them to the airport.

"Go get him, girl!" Robin yelled to Ellen as she headed into the terminal. Ellen put thumbs up and smiled broadly as she mouthed goodbye.

Dudley Correctional

O'Dell sat in his cell reading the letter he'd received from Fred with AJ's private number. The letter read:

O'Dell, man, I came through for you as promised. It was tough getting a phone number out of your son at first. Apparently I timed it just right. He kept saying he'd had a family crisis. What that is I have no idea, but his home number is 889-0001. Man, I kept my end of the bargain, now I hope you can find it in your heart to come clean with the truth. If you need to contact me for anything, call me at 222-1717. Take care of yourself, old man. Later, Fred Dukes.

O'Dell was happy that Fred had kept his word. He wanted to hear his son's voice and wondered what could have happened—what was the crisis Fred spoke of. If anything ever happened to one of his kids, he'd just die. O'Dell planned to make the call during recreation time out of his cell; he couldn't wait for the chance to hear his son's voice.

Dameon's Place

Alexis is on the phone with Dameon.
"Is everything okay, Alexis? Are you enjoying your stay at the house?" Dameon asked.
"Your maid, Hilda, has been very attentive. My stay has been absolutely wonderful."
"Very good. I'll be home tomorrow evening. I have a lay over in North Carolina for business tonight, but I did want to call and check in and see how you were doing."
"All is well, Dameon. I'll look forward to seeing you tomorrow."
"I can't wait to pick back up on the conversation we were going to have about transformation. I've decided to go through with it."
"Are you sure, Dameon? You've made up your mind completely? Already?"
"Yes, Alexis, it took this trip to give me all the answers I needed. Without a doubt I'm ready to make the change."

Ambassador Hotel

Malik bent down over Weesee and tried to rouse her from her fainting spell upon seeing the diamond ring.
"My lady. Please come back! Please come back!"
Weesee was out cold for a few minutes and Malik couldn't resuscitate her

so he carried her to the sofa and then placed a cool damp rag on her forehead. Weesee slowly came to.

"Malik, Malik. Was that rock real? Are you serious about wanting to marry me?"

"Beautiful Elouise. Thank goodness you are okay. Yes, I'm very serious about my intention to marry you. Are you feeling all right? You fainted on me! You've been out cold for a good five minutes."

Weesee sat up on the couch and looked Malik straight in the eye and said, "If you saw a diamond that big for the first time, you would've fainted, too! Let me see it again please? I may have to think about this marriage stuff."

Malik reached in his pocket and took out the diamond to show Weesee.

"Damn, look at the shine on that rock! That's got to be worth millions."

"Yes, it is, my lady."

"Can I at least try it on?"

"Please do, my beautiful lady."

Weesee looked at Malik, gazed at the diamond and back at Malik again. She put the ring on her finger and said, "Damn. Damn. Damn. This comes with a husband! Like in I do? Me and you for life—that sort of stuff?" Weesee was just thinking out loud. She was absolutely amazed by his offer, but after the shock wore off, she took the ring off her finger and handed it back to Malik.

"Look, Malik, that's the most beautiful expensive diamond I've ever seen in my entire life, but I can't accept your offer. I don't even know you! You don't know me, and I thought people marry because they love one another."

Malik looked Weesee in the eyes with a very serious look on his face. "My queen, love is a word but feelings are something that start in the heart as a seed planted in the earth. It roots and grows into something very strong, beautiful and lasting if it's nourished just right. I know you don't know me, or I you, but we can flourish together and grow to love each other and have something strong. My sweet lady, my heart spoke to me from the minute I saw you. I knew I wanted you to be my bride. Please, will you marry me?" His dark eyes pierced through her soul.

She stood up and said, "I need to think about all this, Malik. I've never had anyone ask me to marry them. I can't answer you this very minute; I have a lot to think over, do you understand me? Giving a sista a rock like that makes the decision awfully hard."

"My queen, my heart is set on you. Think all you have to, and when you're ready you know how to contact me. Now I will call my driver to bring you to your hotel."

Weesee stood there with her mouth open—she was absolutely speechless.

St. Michael's Hospital Emergency Room

Sterling carried Samone into the hospital. She was too weak to walk and completely out of it by this point. Samone was suffering from severe depression and had had another nervous breakdown.

Sterling answered all the questions he could for the nurses at the reception desk. He stayed with Samone until the doctor examined her. Upon completion, the doctor insisted Samone be admitted into the psych ward until she recovered from acute depression. Sterling explained to the doctor that he was her boss and that he needed to contact her immediate family. He was so worried. Did she remember they had made love? He also wondered whether it was a conscious decision on her part. The last thing he would ever want to do is to take advantage of her. He loved her too much. Sterling waited patiently until the doctor medicated her with a relaxer, and then he made his way to the fifth floor to find AJ.

As Sterling got off the elevator, he was worried sick about Samone; he felt so helpless. He always knew Samone to be a strong woman, and he had no idea all she'd suffered from. Within seconds of the elevator doors opening, Sterling practically ran into AJ.

"Powers, what in the hell are you doing here? Have you seen Samone?"

"AJ, man, look I didn't come here to fight with you. As a matter of fact I have seen Samone, and she's down in emergency. She's had a mental breakdown."

"Say what, Powers?"

"Samone came to me AJ, absolutely hysterical and helpless. I've never seen her so out of it. All the stress has taken a toll on her. Man, she scared me. She kept crying, saying she needed help so I brought her to the emergency room."

Before AJ realized it, he had grabbed Sterling and pushed him against the wall. She's been with you all right! If you've done anything to provoke this or took advantage of her in any way, I swear on my mother's grave that I will kill you."

Sterling pushed AJ back off him.

"Look, AJ, it's high time you and I set the record straight. I know you've never cared for me, and it's all good, but what Samone and I do is my damn business! She's not your woman. Now we can stand here and fight like two fools, but all I know is that Samone needs our help!"

215

"Powers, you're right. Let's set the record straight. Samone is my brother's woman and don't you forget it! Now get the hell out of my face!"

Sterling walked away. AJ went to the waiting room to tell Diane about Samone.

North Carolina

Ellen arrived at the Crystal Hotel. She looked around the lobby at the expensive décor. She admired Dameon for his taste in everything. He and everything he did or touched was elaborate. Look at this hotel; she had never stayed in such luxury in her life! Upon checking in, Ellen was escorted to her suite where Dameon was waiting. Ellen walked in confidently, she was dressed elegantly. She wore the expensive tweed sweater Dameon had given her accented by a short black mini skirt with black high heels. Ellen was getting the evil eye from women as their men looked on at her graceful walk and long luxurious legs. She could have been one of Dameon's models; she certainly had the height and body for it.

Up the elevator and escorted to suite 312, Ellen knocked to see if Dameon had already arrived. Ellen's knees began to knock when she heard Dameon call out, "Just a minute, sweet Ellen." Dameon appeared at the doorway as handsome as ever in a silk robe with his masculine hairy chest bursting to greet her. *Boy is he ever sexy*, Ellen thought to herself, hoping she was able to keep her lust under cover for now…

"You made it! Please come in, Ellen."

The bellboy carried her bags in, Dameon tipped him, and he went on his way.

"Ellen, dear, you look absolutely stunning in that sweater! It fits perfectly! Nice selection, my dear!"

"Thank you, Dameon." Ellen was all smiles.

"Hope your flight was okay. Would you like to get comfortable, rest up and relax a bit before our meeting tonight?"

"That sounds perfect, Dameon."

"Well, start, girl, by kicking off those high heels and rest your feet!" Ellen couldn't get over how outspoken Dameon was, and since her feet were hurting she figured, what the heck!

"I feel like a shower and chilling out a bit. Then we can go over the contracts one more time before meeting with Mr. Matters."

"That's an excellent idea. I must be honest, Ellen, I have so much on my mind right now I'm trusting you to take the lead on this account, okay? Besides, Matters has taken a special interest in you; he's single dear, and available, too!"

Ellen looked at Dameon with a frown on her face and said, "Is that right, Dameon, he's available? Trust me; I'll leave a good business impression with him. Don't worry I've got this account locked tight, and I'll have him eating out of the palm of my hands by the time he finishes dinner. I know how to represent. Don't you worry, leave it up to me," Ellen assured him, taking off her heels and strutting her stuff as she walked by Dameon. This was her way of flirting with him, but of course he didn't get it.

Dameon looked at Ellen with his dark piercing eyes. "That's what I admire about you, Ellen, your confidence. All right. You've got the floor tonight. Now let me show you to your room so you can freshen up and relax. Are you hungry? I can order something if you'd like."

"I could eat a little something, thank you, Dameon." She stared into his dark eyes and smiled profusely.

Dameon showed her to her bedroom, which was off from the living room area. His bedroom was next door to hers. They shared the bathroom, which separated the two bedrooms. Ellen couldn't believe he was that close. She knew she was going to pay him a visit that night in her sexy lingerie.

"You get relaxed, Ellen, and I'll phone for something to eat. Would you care for a drink while you're unpacking?"

Ellen thought she'd better take it easy on the drinks until after her meeting. Besides, she wanted to leave a good impression on Matters so Dameon could be proud. She thought the drink might come in handy later to boost her self-confidence to tell Dameon how she felt about him. Yes, later she'd need that drink. "No, thank you, I'll have one later, Dameon. Thanks for asking."

"That's another thing I admire about you, Ellen. The way you strive to make things happen. It's a great asset to have. I know what Matters sees in you, and I thank you for your excellent representation for my business."

"Why thank you, Dameon," Ellen said coyly, thinking all along she'd like to forget Matters—it's you I want! She bit her lip from telling him so right then and there.

Westchester

Robin stopped at the grocery store to pick up a few items. She was shopping down one aisle while Fred was in the next. She took her groceries to the check-out line and as she removed them from the cart, she suddenly remembered she'd forgotten something. Quickly she stepped out of line and headed down the aisle to retrieve the forgotten item. Suddenly she glanced up and saw Fred. She did a double take because she thought her eyes were playing tricks on her. When she looked the second time, nobody was there.

I must be tired; it's been a busy morning and I need to go home and relax, Robin figured. Little did she know it was Fred who had disappeared through the double doors before she could get a second glimpse of him. Robin paid for her groceries and walked out to her car to find two of her tires flattened. *Geez, this isn't my day,* Robin thought. She immediately phoned Roadside Assistance to help remedy the problem and then went back inside the store to wait for the service to arrive.

As she stood waiting, Fred watched her from the distance. He had let the air out of both tires just to have the opportunity to get a closer look at her. How Fred adored her, how he wanted so badly to talk to her. He watched her until the repairman came; he even waited for Robin to get into her car, start it up and leave the premises. Oh how he wanted to reach out and touch her, as he lurked in the background down one aisle where Robin couldn't see him.

He managed to exit the store unseen and followed Robin to her home. Again he sat in the distance, watching as she carried her groceries inside. "Soon, yes very soon, my love. We'll come face to face once again real soon," Fred said under his breath.

Fred remained transfixed on Robin's house until he no longer saw any lights on. He knew his princess must have retired for the night. "Until tomorrow, my love, sleep tight," he whispered as he drove off.

St. Michael's Hospital

"Did you get a hold of Samone yet, AJ? Is she on her way?" Diane asked.

"Baby girl, I'm afraid I've got some more bad news."

"What is it?" Diane was very concerned.

"Powers was just here at the hospital. Apparently he brought Samone into the emergency room. She's had a breakdown."

"I knew it, AJ! See, I told OJ not to get tied up with that crazy nut. I knew she wasn't wrapped too tight when OJ first introduced her to us, and she thinks my brother is going to marry her?"

"Baby girl, have a little compassion. She's been through an awful lot with OJ's accident, and it probably took her over the edge. I need to go and see her. You know, we're the only family she has now. OJ would want it this way. He'd want us to look after her, you know, Diane."

"You go right ahead, AJ. Do what you have to do. I'll check in on the kids. In fact, on my way home I'll pick them up and bring them to my house until things get better. I can at least do that much for my niece and nephew for OJ's sake."

"That'll be a big help. See if you can page Dr. Casey and see what's going on with OJ—you know, explain the situation to him about Samone and all that. Tell him she's not capable of making any decisions concerning OJ right now, and if he needs to consult with anyone, it should be either you or I."

"Okay, big brother. You go see what's going on, and I'll handle things here."

AJ made his way to the emergency department. Samone had been moved to the psychiatric ward. AJ knew of the trauma she'd dealt with witnessing her mother's murder. OJ had always confided in him and told him how he could never put Samone under any emotional strain. OJ had told AJ how he had always felt that leaving Samone alone with the children would cause more distress upon her. He remained in the relationship for the kids as well as keeping Samone stable and balanced.

AJ entered Samone's room and found her staring at the wall. She wasn't even blinking her eyes and didn't move as he approached her bed. Her face was expressionless when he said, "Samone, I'm here. Everything is going to be all right. We're going to get you better so you can go home and be with the kids. OJ needs you; you're gonna pull through this!"

Samone turned to face him, looking at him with a strange look on her face and said, "OJ, you came! I'm so glad you came. Take me home, OJ. Momma was killed, you know. I saw the man who killed my momma. He's a bad man, OJ. He killed Momma. Why did he kill Momma?!" Samone began to cry, rocking back and forth. "OJ, please help me. OJ, Momma has been killed."

AJ just held her close and began to cry. He had never seen Samone in this state before. He felt so sorry for her, OJ and the kids. He never realized how the trauma had affected her, and he had never realized the strain of OJ and Samone's relationship until this very moment. AJ held her and soothed her until she drifted off to sleep.

AJ exited the room. Standing outside the door, he put his head against the wall and let out a huge sigh. He couldn't believe all this was happening. "Please God, help us! I can't handle this alone! Why is this all happening?"

Dudley Correctional

O'Dell sat at the dining hall table, picking at his food. He couldn't wait until phone time so he could make his call in the hopes of AJ answering the phone. He wondered in his mind what the family crisis could have been, and if it was something serious had happened to one of his kids. He was very irritable, apprehensive and afraid. He put his plate up and quickly headed to the recreation room so he'd be first in line to use the phone.

Ridgemont Hotel

Weesee was very restless at the thought of Malik's proposal. She kept thinking about the diamond ring—gosh, she had never in her life seen anything that gorgeous. Weesee paced back and forth, contemplating marriage to a total stranger.

She had always set her standards high, wanting a man who was wealthy but never had run into anyone with Malik's credentials. She sat on the bed daydreaming of all the things she could spend his money on. But after adding up the cost against not knowing him, she reasoned in her mind that maybe she could get to know him better, spend some money and then maybe marry him.

Weesee had always said her ship was going to ride in, but now she was afraid to take the ride. She kept wondering why he was in such a rush to find a bride. All kinds of thoughts raced through her mind until she finally told herself, *I'm gonna get to know him better and then worry about being his bride later.*

Meanwhile, her mind took a detour on no-show Sterling. He hadn't left any messages as to what had happened to him or why he had stood her up. Thinking about his selfishness and inconsideration, she became angry with him all over again. Even though her body longed to be with him and she really did love him, she refused to call and ask him why he was a no-show. She had way too much pride to give any man that much control over her.

As bad as she hurt inside, she was determined not to give into calling him first. No way. She stood up, looked at herself in the mirror and said, "Elouise, don't sweat it. He'll come running back to you. Now pull yourself together and go pamper yourself." So she grabbed her purse, room key and headed for the salon, which was located on the third floor of the hotel.

She was greeted by a bright-eyed receptionist who asked, "Hello, how may we serve you today? Would you care to hear our specials?"

"No thank you. I'd like a pedicure and a full body massage, please."

"Certainly, miss. If you'll please have a seat, your technician will be out to assist you. Barbara will be your tech today."

Weesee sat glancing through the magazines perfectly arranged on the table. Her mind drifted back and forth between Sterling and Malik. Just then her thoughts were interrupted by Barbara who came to get her. Barbara escorted Weesee back to the room, which was accented with a few candles burning the smell of expensive aromas, soft jazz and a nice soft table to lie on.

"Please get comfortable. There's a variety of oils to choose from, and I'll be back in a few. Your towels are nice and warm…please relax."

"Thank you, I need it. It's been a hell of a morning!"

Weesee got undressed, laid on the table face down and waited for Barbara to come back. She felt every muscle in her body tighten up as she longed for Sterling. Barbara entered the room. With the softness of her hands and warm oils, she began to rub Weesee's back. Closing her eyes, Weesee allowed herself to be absorbed in every gentle stroke. Barbara began to make conversation.

"It's a lovely day today, ma'am, isn't it?"

By this point Weesee was half asleep, "Yes," she answered sleepily.

"Soon I'll be out enjoying our beautiful Florida weather. I won't have to work these long hours. In fact, I won't have to work again in life."

"Is that so? Girl, what did you do, hit the lottery or something—or did you hook a rich guy?" Weesee asked, intrigued.

"You guessed it right. I'm engaged to a very wealthy guy. We're going to be married soon. I have to work now and I do enjoy what I do, but my fiancé wants me to stop after the wedding. He says he can take care of me!"

"Then, girl, let him! What's wrong with you? I wouldn't be massaging nobody's back, getting my hands all greased up if my man had money and wanted to take care of me. See, it's sistas like you who make it hard for women like me."

"What do you mean?" Barbara asked with a bewildered look on her face.

"If a man wants to do for you, hell let him! It's not like you have to give into him first if you know what I mean. They always want something before they give something so if he wants to do it, let him!" Weesee said enthusiastically.

"Yeah, I know what you mean. No, my guy isn't like that—he's special. He says he can wait until we're married—he's been holding out for his bride."

Weesee sat up on the table and thought how strangely coincidental that two men in this world were saving themselves for their bride.

"Something's just doggone strange around here, Barbara. Your man sounds like someone I know. He wouldn't happen to be Caucasian?"

"Yes, he is, but what does that matter?"

"From Africa?"

"As a matter of fact, yes."

"Is he in the oil business?—and his name is Malik?" Weesee blurted.

"Why, yes! That's my boo!"

"That's your baby, huh? Tell me please, how did you meet this Mr. Malik, (the smooth operator)" she mumbled under her breath.

"I met him here at the hotel last month. I was called to his room to give him a massage, and he later asked me to join him for dinner that same night. That's when he broke out with the ring and told me he'd been searching for his bride. One look at me, he said, and his search was over. Then he asked me to marry him.

Weesee stared at Barbara in disbelief. *I don't believe the nerve of this guy,* she thought—*trying to play me and girlfriend. That diamond must've spoken to her like it did me.*

"Well, girlfriend, I hate to be the bearer of bad news, but your man Malik just asked me to marry him last night. He gave me the same line about the search being over, and I was to be his bride. Oh, and I saw the same diamond he flashed before your eyes."

Barbara looked at Weesee in a state of shock and then she began to cry.

"How could my boo do this to me? He wouldn't cheat on me; he wouldn't even sleep with me. He said I was the one."

Weesee felt sorry for Barbara to have shattered her dream, but she couldn't stand by and let her be betrayed by someone who meant neither of them any good. Weesee was furious with anger; she felt Barbara's pain. She tried to console her and show her that she deserved better than the scum that Malik was, but Barbara still continued to cry.

"I'm sorry to break it down to you like this, but he's a worthless piece of crap. You're a beautiful lady. Wouldn't you want to marry someone you can trust...someone worthy...someone you can truly love, unconditionally love?"

Barbara weeping said, "Yes, but he's been so good to me. He visits with me every chance he can, and he's always buying me lovely things and gifts."

Weesee put her hands on her hips and said, "But do you love him?"

"Yes, I think I do," Barbara answered in between her sobs.

"Come on, girl. You don't love that man. You just love what gifts he has to give. You can't buy love, and you certainly can't trust no man like him! So tell me, have you set a wedding date?"

"No, not yet." Barbara looked at the card with Weesee's name on it so she would remember who she was when she confronted Malik.

"Well, Elouise, I thank you for your opinion."

"Call me Weesee, but this ain't my opinion, Barbara. This is fact. Hard cold fact. Malik is a liar, a cheater and a no good schemer. Your life is better off without him."

"I know you're right, but I thought for once I had met the man of my dreams—someone to take me away from this life!" Barbara's eyes drifted off into the distance.

"I feel you, but don't you mean someone to take care of you so you don't have to work? Spend all his money, take nice vacations, kick your feet up and do nothing kinda life? Hey, girlfriend, we all have those same dreams. But catch my last word—dream. That's what it is. Face it, Barbara, it's gonna be all right. I can relate to what you're saying because I've been there myself. Let me give you some words of wisdom. Be your own money maker, use what the good Lord gave you as your ticket out of this life. If the men want to play then make them pay! Make him feel like it's a privilege to have you. Surround yourself with men who've got it going on in the mind. Learn the tricks of the trade, educate yourself and get into his mind! Learn his business strategies, read the Wall Street Journal, follow the stock market, broaden your horizons. Use your good looks and mind to get you above all this!" Weesee spoke with confidence.

"I hear you, Weesee, but..."

"No buts. See, I didn't always have money until I met a man who showed me how to invest my money to make more money. He taught me the strategy of good money marketing profits that benefitted me. You can and will rise above this, Barbara. I only need a man for a good lay, financially I'm doing all right, girlfriend! Now isn't that a role reversal?" Weesee said sarcastically.

"That sounds like a plan for future use, but I'm tired of rubbing backs, tired of working these long hours. Hell, if it weren't for the tips I make, I'd probably be holding down a second job," Barbara confided.

Weesee was feeling Barbara's pain because she had been there before she met Sterling. Working her factory job in Westchester and surviving from paycheck to paycheck, robbing Peter to pay Paul. How she related to what

Barbara was saying. Just then a light bulb went off in Weesee's head. She had an idea but needed Barbara's help to pull it off. Besides, she wasn't about to let Malik or any man play her for a fool. She thought it was time to get even. Make him feel sorry for the day he ever laid eyes on Elouise Prescott. (Weesee had devised a plan…)

"Hey, Barbara, sit down here a minute! This is your lucky day! Dry those tears and get yourself together, girlfriend. I've got a plan that both of us can benefit from, but I'll need your help pulling it off. See, it's time Mr. Malik comes face to face with his match! I'm gonna show him who the chosen one is all right! By the time I'm finished with him, we both will profit from his wealth, and you can leave this lifestyle behind."

They high fived each other. "I'm with you girlfriend!" Barbara said with a smile.

"Now you talkin'. When you get off work, come to room #107 and we'll talk more about it. Meanwhile, I'll give Mr. Malik a call and make him think I'm down with his offer to be his chosen bride."

"He's staying at the Ambassador Hotel."

"Oh, I know how to contact him!" They both glared at one another with revengeful looks in their eyes. Weesee wanted to kill two birds with one stone—Sterling and Malik.

Westchester

Robin had just gotten off the phone with whom she thought was OJ. She couldn't help but sense something wasn't right in the sound of his voice. She had been worried about him lately. He never mentioned visiting with her or the party plans. *I've got to call him after school,* Robin thought to herself, *and make sure he's okay with everything…*

Outside of Robin's house sat Fred. His fixation on Robin had turned into obsession. He had made a plan to get inside of her house. He figured he'd call a locksmith to say he was locked out. In the meantime he sat waiting for Robin to leave. Fred drove around the corner to make his call to the locksmith. He needed to get inside of the house to see how Robin lived.

"Please send someone to 1147 Kingston Drive. I've locked myself out of my own house, and I'm without a key," Fred lied to the locksmith.

"Someone will be there very soon. We'll need to see identification, sir."

"Not a problem. I'll be sitting in my car in the driveway—please hurry!"

"Yes, sir. We'll get there as soon as we can."

Fred had already had a fake identification card printed with Robin's address. He had thought of everything. Feeling very proud of his cunning ways, Fred sat in the car and waited.

Meanwhile, Robin just couldn't wait until after school to call OJ. She dialed his number on her cell phone, but all she got was a busy signal. This worried her even more.

The locksmith showed up, and Fred willingly presented his fake ID card. He played off his scam real good. "I can't believe how careless I was coming out of the house without my keys. Damn. By the way, thanks for getting here so quick."

"Not a problem, sir. It's happened to all of us. Just give me a few minutes, and I'll have you inside in no time."

"Thank you very much, sir. You've made me one happy man!"

Upon finishing his job and opening the door, Fred's smile grew even wider. "No need to change the lock or anything, I know exactly where I left my key in the bedroom. Now you probably got a bunch of other calls. I don't want to hold you up," Fred saying paying the guy and trying to nonchalantly hurry him along. After all, he couldn't wait to get inside and see his baby's house. He could smell Robin's scent the minute the door opened, and how he longed for her.

Fred entered the house and locked the door behind him. He walked as though he lived there. "Immaculate housekeeping. Yes, that's my Robin," Fred said out loud. He walked into the kitchen and made himself very comfortable in the fridge. He made a sandwich, drank a half liter of Coke and when his stomach was full, he searched the rest of the house for more clues. Next he meandered into Robin's bedroom. On her night stand he saw a picture of her son, Larry. How he remembered Larry being much smaller, but his face was still the same. He then noticed another picture on the side of Larry's. It was a picture of Robin and a man. Fred looked on, wondering who the man was and raging mad at how happy they looked together.

He removed the photo from the frame, took out his pocket knife and cut off the side of the photo with the man. Then he placed the half side picture of Robin back into the frame. His jealous rage was running rampant. *What the hell is she doing letting another man into her life?* Fred demanded. But there was no one to hear his cry.

After feeling sorry for himself and ranting and raving for a good twenty minutes, Fred took a look at his watch and realized he'd been in the house for more than two hours. He still needed to make an impression of the keyhole and have a key made so he knew he'd better get a move on.

He took a few items of clothing from Robin's closet—a silk scarf with the scent of her perfume and a purple sweater—the very sweater she wore when she was in the grocery store. How he loved the way it fitted her.

Gathering up his things, he put them in a bag and then placed them inside of his jacket pocket. He then made his way downstairs to the back door where he took out his clay to make the keyhole impression, a trick he had learned from an ex-con buddy. Upon letting himself out, Fred smiled broadly. "Now that was easy enough. I'm going to keep a close eye on Robin from now on," he said under his breath. "Maybe I'll even have to ask Joe about helping me plant a hidden camera. Yes, that's it. You're a genius, Fred!" he told himself as he walked out to his car.

St. Michael's Hospital

Sitting around the conference table Diane made Dr. Casey aware of Samone's condition, as he was just about to give AJ and Diane an update concerning OJ's condition.

"I'm so sorry Samone cannot be present; I trust that she will recover with the excellent care she will receive here."

"Thank you for your concern, Dr. Casey. Now please, let's get down to OJ," AJ demanded.

"Your brother has improved tremendously. His vitals are strong, and he's taken to the medications very well. We would like to remove the respirator and see if he can breathe on his own. This afternoon, he'll be moved out of the ICU to the third floor where he will be watched closely. It's truly a miracle how he is steadily improving. His brain is functioning very well, considering the fall he took. I think you all have a lot to be thankful for."

"Praise the Lord for the good report!" Diane practically screamed in happiness.

"Thank you, Lord! Yes, Dr. Casey that's wonderful news. We trust you to do what you think is best for him," AJ said.

"What about the coma, Dr. Casey? How long will he remain like that?"

"I can't give a time estimate on that, Diane, it all depends on Mr. O'Neil, but it's a miracle he's progressed this much so let's continue to hope and pray for the best," Dr. Casey said.

"Guess we'll be seeing each other on the third floor from now on! Gosh, I feel so relieved," Diane chirped.

"Will his kids be able to visit him now that he's out of ICU?" AJ asked.

"Sure enough, by all means," Dr. Casey answered as he stood to leave. AJ shook Dr. Casey's hand, and Diane gave him a hug. As soon as he left the room, Diane and AJ hugged one another tight. "Boy, we are certainly blessed," Diane whispered.

"Baby girl, I prayed for the first time in a long time, and it worked! God heard me!"

"Of course he heard you. Momma always told us to talk to God if we had no one else to talk to, remember her always telling us that? To keep our faith in God?"

"Yes, and it works!" AJ looked toward the sky and said, "Thank you, Lord! Thanks for hearing me!"

Carolina

Ellen was dressed in a two-piece navy suit with a sheer cream blouse. She looked very elegant yet professional for the dinner meeting. She wore her hair up the way Dameon liked it along with the perfume he admired. Dameon also dressed in a navy suit. They looked like the perfect couple dining together. As they sat at their table in the hotel restaurant waiting for Johnson Matters to arrive, Ellen exuded confidence. She knew she had the account. Dameon was a bit nervous it seemed. He continued to check his watch, as if he was expecting something other than Matters to arrive. He was waiting on a call from AJ. Meanwhile Ellen tried to make conversation.

"I'm so pleased Matters decided to consider our offer. He's got plenty of stores to market your sheer blouse collection. I'm wearing the cream colored one with this suit, do you like it, Dameon?"

"Yes, Ellen, it looks very lovely."

Ellen stared into Dameon's distant eyes. "Are you all right, Dameon? You look like you're worried about something. Is it the deal?"

"I'm fine, dear. Just wondering what's taking Matters so long. I'm tired. I'd like to close the deal and turn in early if you know what I mean."

Ellen raised her brow, "Yeah, I understand that. Don't worry. I've got Matters under control."

"I'm sure you do. You know he insisted you be here for the meeting; I think he's attracted to you, Ellen, so if you feel the need to stay in Carolina for a few days longer, that'll be fine with me. I can get someone to cover for you until you get back. Besides, you've done a fantastic job—that's the least I can do for you."

"Thanks, but no thanks, Dameon. I'm not interested in Matters like that. All I want to do is keep it on a professional level and do my job."

"Dear, he's available, and he's been asking a lot of questions about you. He's a good guy. Johnson and I go way back. Believe me, I wouldn't push it if I felt he wasn't right for you. I care for you, Ellen. I only want your best interest."

"Is that right, Dameon? Well, my interest is on someone else right now, and my main interest is getting this account right now."

"I understand that, Ellen. So tell me, who is the lucky guy?"

Just as Ellen was about to spill her guts to Dameon, Johnson Matters appeared out of nowhere at the table. Matters sat down at the table and proceeded to stare at Ellen. It was apparent he didn't have the account on his mind whatsoever. Dameon was picking up the vibe he was sending toward Ellen, and after they finished eating dinner, Dameon made an excuse to leave Matters and Ellen alone.

"Johnson, Ellen is my top notch marketing executive so I trust she can handle this account without me taking up more of your time. I need to excuse myself and go back to the room to make a few calls."

"I trust I'm in good hands, or shall I say she'll be in good hands with me?" Matters smiled at Ellen.

Ellen was so mad. How could Dameon leave her with this baldheaded freak? She had heard rumors about Johnson Matters, and they weren't things pleasing to the ear. She was furious!

"Maybe you can stay a little longer to go over the quality of materials with us?" Ellen hinted at Dameon.

"Ellen, dear, I've put together a listing of the various silk fabrics; it's inside the folder with the price listings. Dear, you've got everything you need. Now, will there be anything else before I leave?"

"No, Dameon. I've got everything I need!" Ellen blurted sarcastically.

"Very well then, if you both will excuse me. The tab is on me so feel free to indulge in dessert or an after dinner cocktail."

Matters stood up to shake Dameon's hand as he left. Ellen was so mad, the first thing she did was to call the hostess over to order the most expensive wine they had. She wondered what was wrong with Dameon—who did he need to call? She knew he trusted her to handle the account, but she didn't want to be left alone with Matters. How dare he! She wasn't at all attracted to Matters. Ellen had fire in her eyes she was so angry.

Matters sat back down, undressing Ellen with his eyes. She poured a big glass of wine and gulped it down. The more she drank, the more Matters looked like a big fat pig with glasses. She hurried up and explained the proposal to him in hopes of closing the deal and finishing their meeting. A half hour had passed since Dameon had left. She was trying to hurry to get to him before he fell off to sleep for the night. By this point, Ellen had drunk three glasses of wine.

"Mr. Matters, that concludes my presentation. Our fashion wear represents women of the millennium. She can dress it up or dress it down with a variety of colors to chose from. All the figures are as posted on the documents."

Matters looked at Ellen, not listening to her campaign, not looking at one document she had shown him. Instead, he lustfully stared at her as if he had more than business on his mind. He kept looking at her breasts through her sheer blouse. Ellen tried to ignore his advances, but her mind kept yelling "You pig!"

Reaching to touch Ellen's hand, Matters said, "You've sold me, Ellen, but before I sign, why don't you come up to my room for a nightcap?"

Ellen was about to tell him off, but she thought of Dameon, and how she wanted to land this account for him. She figured she'd better select a nice choice of words instead of saying what was really on her mind. She'd better act professional, put him in his place without blowing the deal or misrepresenting Dameon.

"Thank you, Mr. Matters, for the invitation, but I've had more than I should to drink. It's been a very long day, and I'd like to close this matter of business and call it a night. I'm sure you understand my position."

"Why, it's early, my lady. The night is young, and you're looking so beautiful, I thought we could…"

Before he could finish his sentence she interrupted him. "You thought you were going to be taking me back to your room to sleep with you? Well, let me tell you something, Mr. Matters. That's not my style! If that's what you're looking for, you've got the wrong woman! I carry myself like a lady, and if that's what it takes to land your business, I'm sorry, we aren't interested. Please excuse me!" She turned to walk away.

Matters felt two inches tall. Never had any woman in her position put him in his place before. All his other business clients always pre-arranged for the woman to spend the entire evening with him. He realized Dameon ran a respectable business, and Ellen displayed it by the way she'd cut him short.

"Ms. Berk, please! I apologize. I just thought you were like the rest. Please, I beg of you to excuse my forwardness. I'm sorry. Where should I sign?"

Ellen turned around, came back to the table and sat down. As she pulled out the contracts from her briefcase, she got a little lightheaded. *The wine*, she thought. "Apology accepted! Please forgive my loudness." (Everyone in the restaurant was all eyes and ears as Ellen had told him off.)

As Mr. Matters signed the contract, Ellen couldn't help but secretly smile at her accomplishment. Then they walked to the elevator.

"Thank you, Mr. Matters. I assure you, you will be very pleased."

"Ms. Berk. I'll be sure to tell Dameon what a great representative you are, and again I apologize for getting out of line back there."

Ellen got into the elevator and as soon as the door closed, she gave out an enthusiastic "HURRAH!" and then laughed at the whole episode. She glanced at her watch—10:00 p.m. She wondered if Dameon was still awake.

She arrived at the room, fumbled in her purse for her room key, but dropped it as she began to really feel the effects of the last glass of wine she had chugged before telling Mr. Matters off. *Guess I'm ready for Dameon now. As ready as I'll ever be*, Ellen giggled to herself.

Boldness was her friend. She was ready for a night of passion; she was going to open the door and charge in on her man as if she was a quarterback on a football team and show him what she was made of. She opened the door and found Dameon sitting in the living room waiting for AJ to call.

"I didn't expect you back so early, dear. How did it go?"

"We got the account; the documents are signed and in my briefcase."

Dameon stood up and walked towards Ellen and kissed her on the cheek. "I never doubted you for a minute. Congratulations! Another job well done, Ellen."

Ellen looked at him with his silk robe and hairy chest showing. She couldn't take another minute looking at him like that. Before she realized it, she boldly blurted, "Dameon, kiss me!" Her eyes were drunken, and she began to move closer to Dameon, putting her arms around his neck.

"Dameon, please, I said, 'Kiss me'! Kiss me like a man wanting his woman."

Dameon was shocked. Gently he took her arms from around his neck and put them down to her side. He couldn't believe what he was witnessing.

"Ellen, dear, I think maybe you've had one wine too many. Maybe you should retire for the night."

"No it's not the wine, Dameon. It's you! You made me love you! I want you to make love to me."

Ellen began to take her long shoulder length hair down. She removed her suit jacket and then unbuttoned her blouse all as if to say, "Take me, I'm yours!"

Dameon was getting aroused by her aggressiveness. She's gone mad; she's out and out ready to attack me! She doesn't need a drink if it makes her act like a wild woman. Dameon picked her up and carried her to her bedroom and laid her on the bed. They wrestled on the bed until Dameon got tired of fighting her off. Then he got angry!

"Damn it, Ellen! Get a hold of yourself. This is not like you. You need to take a shower, sleep off the alcohol, and we'll deal with this in the morning."

Dameon walked out of the room and slammed the door, his bathrobe was hanging off him thanks to Ellen's groping.

Ellen on the other hand was not about to take no for an answer. Yes, she'd had a few drinks, but it wasn't the alcohol talking, it was her heart. She wanted him the moment she'd laid eyes on him, and the time had finally come for her to tell him.

Ellen got up off the bed, tore open her suitcase and put on her sexy negligee. She went to Dameon's bedroom, but the door was shut. She reached for the doorknob, but the door was locked. Ellen didn't sweat it. She took her foot and kicked the door open.

Dameon was sleeping on the bed. He thought he'd heard someone fumble with the doorknob, but he didn't pay much attention. He turned back over in his sleep. As soon as Ellen saw him lying in bed, she charged into the room. Dameon woke up startled and sat up in bed, surprised to see Ellen standing there in a hot pink negligee with two wine glasses and a bottle of wine.

"Ellen, what is wrong with you? Please. Put on some clothes."

"You're what's wrong with me!"

Dameon jumped out of bed, grabbed his suit and backed up against the wall, trying to get dressed as fast as he could. Ellen was at a standstill, watching him like a wild animal getting ready to attack her prey. Her hair was wild; she stepped closer to him with lust in her eyes.

Dameon was dressed by this point, and he was mortified. "Ellen, this is too much. I'm out of here!" He ran past her out of the room and into the lobby bar. He was in a state of shock, having to run from Ellen—his trustworthy co-worker.

Once Dameon had charged out of the room, Ellen collapsed on the bed crying, wondering why he didn't want her. She began to get angry because she'd finally built up the nerve to tell him her feelings, and he acted like such a coward by taking off.

Three hours had passed. Ellen had cried herself to sleep in Dameon's bed. When Dameon tip-toed into his room, assuming Ellen would be sleeping, he was shocked to find her stretched out in his bed. He couldn't help but look at her beautifully shaped body and notice how sexy she was in her negligee.

"Lord give me the strength! This can't be happening!"

Ellen felt him in the room. She woke up, stood to her feet, put her hands on her hips and said, "Dameon Davenport, let me tell you something! You think I'm drunk, but I'm not! You're wondering why I'm acting like this? I'm acting like this because of what I feel for you. I'm desperately in love with you! I'm not sure you'll ever understand. It's the kind of love that's all-consuming and at the same time, it gives me the feeling that I have to have you!"

Ellen poured her heart out from the depths of her soul. It felt good to let it all out.

Dameon stood speechless, scared to make a move. After being hurt by a woman years ago, his interest towards women had changed drastically. He felt sorry for Ellen because he did understand the kind of love she spoke of. It was the same kind of feeling he had for AJ.

"Ellen, you're a beautiful woman. I'm sure you can have any man you go after. I'm sorry, but I'm very involved with someone who means a great deal to me. Maybe it will be best if I leave and go back to Westchester tonight. I'm very sorry."

Ellen stood, staring at him with tears falling from her eyes. How she wanted to be with him so desperately. Dameon turned to walk away. He went into the living room area and sat down, feeling just awful. He liked Ellen, but he couldn't return the love she needed. He didn't want to hurt her. Dameon sat with his head hung, trying to think what he might do to make her feel better. It was too deep for him. He called for her to come to him. Maybe if they talked it out, it might help.

"Ellen, please come and let's talk about this. I certainly don't want to ruin a good business relationship."

Ellen came out of the bedroom half naked in her negligee. She sat next to Dameon, and he looked her in the eyes.

"Please, Ellen, I can't take advantage of you—you mean too much to me. I'm not like your average man. I mean, I wouldn't do anything to hurt you. Do you understand what I'm saying?"

Her face was deeply grief stricken. "It's fine, Dameon, but I take back nothing I said to you because I do love you!"

Dameon took one long look at her, and before he realized it, he was passionately kissing her. He was giving into the temptation. She looked very sexy and innocent. The kiss aroused them both. Ellen pushed him on the couch, and Dameon was definitely caught up in the moment. He began to caress her body, but suddenly he realized he couldn't go any further. He gently pushed Ellen off of him.

"I can't do it! I'm sorry! I've got to get out of here." With that Dameon got up and left her sitting on the couch, her body trembling from his kiss, longing to be with him and wanting all of him.

Dudley Correctional

O'Dell was nervous; he made the call to AJ's house and the phone rang three times before the answering machine picked up.

"Hello, please don't hang up before leaving a message. This is the O'Neil residence. I'm unavailable to take your call. Please leave a message after the beep."

O'Dell hung onto the phone without saying a word. He desperately wanted to say something, but what? So he quickly hung up the phone. He stood with the receiver in his hand, not realizing others were in line waiting to make their calls. He'd finally got a chance to hear his son's voice. How he longed to see all of his kids. O'Dell stood daydreaming, but was soon interrupted by a guard.

"O'Neil, man, the warden needs to see you ASAP. Man, do you hear me?"

O'Dell snapped out of his daze, "Yeah, I hear you."

He was escorted by the guard to the warden's office. O'Dell thought it must be very important if the warden wanted to see him at this hour. What had he done wrong?

The guard knocked on the door. "Follow me, O'Neil."

"You can leave now, Stevens, this will only take a few minutes."

"Yes, sir. I'll be right outside the door."

"Have a seat, O'Neil."

O'Dell sat, anxiously wondering why he'd been called into the warden's office.

" I know you're wondering why you've been called in here this time of night, right?"

"Yes sir. What seems to be the problem?"

The warden stood up from his king-size leather chair and glanced out the window before looking at O'Dell. Then he walked around in front of his desk and sat on the edge of his desk, directly in front of O'Dell. Looking him in the face with a very serious expression he said, "The last member of the Carilini gang died today in prison. There were written statements found in his cell addressed to the governor of New York claiming your innocence along with detailed descriptions of how they framed you for the bust that went down twenty years ago. By word of the governor of New York, we have to let you go. Carilini wanted to redeem himself before he died; he wanted the truth to be told. In his full explanation to the governor, he explained that because he was dying, he felt no need for an innocent man to die in jail. He confessed on a dated document that O'Dell O'Neil had nothing to do with the gang. He gave full details, concrete evidence which proves your innocence, and he mailed out copies of the documents to the Governor to ensure your freedom. You're a free man!"

"Praise the Lord!" O'Dell said in a state of shock. He couldn't believe what he was hearing after all these years. He sat there dumbfounded without saying a word. He didn't know what to think. His emotions were spiraling. He was numb.

"O'Neil, I'm sorry for all the years taken away from you."

O'Dell's eyes were filled with tears as he looked at the warden and said, "Thank you, Lord, you heard my prayers!" Tears streamed down his face. The warden was teary-eyed as well. It was a very emotional moment. The warden then excused himself and gave O'Dell some time alone. O'Dell wept like a baby when the warden left the room. He just kept giving God the praises for his miracle. All kinds of things were going through his mind. His first thought was his kids. Twenty years of his life had been taken away from him; how was he to begin to live a civil life outside of these prison walls? He was happy, but he was also afraid.

Reentering the room the warden said, "O'Dell, man, are you all right?"

That was the first time the warden had ever addressed O'Dell by his first name. O'Dell had never seen this emotional side of the warden. He always thought he didn't have a heart; he was so cold and very unfriendly to the inmates.

"I'm cool, sir. Just in a state of shock!" O'Dell smiled.

"That's understandable. I know this is good news to your ears, but there are a few more things I need to explain."

"Yes, go ahead, sir. Nothing can be as surprising as this news."

"O'Dell, because of the seriousness of the crime and all the people who were involved, the Governor wants to put you in a witness protection program until you gradually get your life back. Although the last member of the Carilini family is dead, there's no telling what enemies they have on the outside who can identify you as once being associated with them. This is for your own protection. Do you understand that?"

"Sir, you mean to tell me twenty years of my life have been taken away from me, and you just told me I'm a free man, but you still want to keep me in lock down? No way! Warden, I have kids I haven't seen in years. You go home to your family every night don't you?"

"Well, yes, I do, but…"

"There ain't no buts! I haven't seen my babies in twenty years. It's time to make it right!"

"O'Dell, I understand what you're saying but this is for your own protection. Once you've become a part of the program your kids can slowly be brought into your life. It's your call, but remember, it's for your own safety."

"Am I free on all charges?"

"Yes, you've been cleared and will be released soon."

"Then when can I get the hell out of here? I don't want no part of your program. I just want to walk through these doors a free man as you put it. I can take care of myself."

"It's going to take at least two days to clear all the records, and then you can go free."

"That's all I want, sir. No witness protection program. Just do the paperwork so I can get out of here."

"If that's the way you want it, O'Dell. I need you to keep this to yourself. Don't mention a word to the other inmates, okay?"

"Do you think I'm crazy, sir?"

"No. It's for your safety. I'll be calling you back in a few days to sign release papers. When that time comes, you will be released and free to go!"

"Okay. Great."

The warden called the guard, and as O'Dell turned to walk out the door, he said, "Thank you, warden."

"Thank Leo Carilini. Oh yeah, one more thing. It may be in the late hour of the night when you get called back to see me."

"I've had nothing but time to deal with these past twenty years—a few more days won't kill me. Will that be all, sir?"

"Yes, O'Dell O'Neil."

For the first time in twenty years, O'Dell O'Neil smiled because he had something to smile about.

Ridgemont Hotel

Weesee was back in her hotel room and had checked the answering machine to see if Sterling had called. No messages. Weesee was now more than ever determined to get even with Sterling and Malik. She was not about to be played by no man. As much as she loved Sterling, she wanted him to come crawling to her. She wanted to teach Malik a lesson as well as to stop playing with women's hearts.

Weesee prepared a hot bubble bath to soak in and think while she came up with a scheme to get Malik right where she wanted him. Figuring she'd play along with Malik's plan to marry her, she'd make him buy the radio station before she would accept his offer. She wanted control over both men. This way they'd both be eating right out of her hands. Once Malik agreed to her plan, then she was going to bust him by letting on that she knows Barbara. Weesee had it all planned out. Once she got Malik to buy the station, she was going to kick Sterling out of his position and give Barbara his job. Weesee felt so sorry for Barbara. She knew the struggle of feeling boxed in a life you want to change but couldn't.

She lazily soaked in her bath and planned her strategy. Upon dressing, Weesee picked up the phone and dialed Malik's room. "Malik, darling, I've been thinking about you all afternoon. About that dinner invitation. Have your driver pick me up around 8:00 p.m., baby, and you won't regret it. I'd very much like to see you."

"My beautiful Elouise, I'm so glad you've changed your mind. I look ever so forward to seeing your elegance this evening."

Yeah, I bet you do, Weesee thought to herself. "So do I, Malik. Oh before we go, I have a small favor to ask of you sweetness."

"Anything you want, my queen," Malik's syrupy voice sickened her.

"I saw a tennis bracelet I really admired today at Macy's. I really want it, honey. Do you know what I mean?"

"Say no more. Anything your heart desires, my love. Have you given thought to becoming my bride, Elouise?"

"Yes, I have Malik. Now, did I hear you say 'Anything my heart desires'?"

"Yes. Those are my words. Money means nothing to me, my lady, if I have no one to spend my life with."

"Well, since you put it like that. I want you to buy me a radio station."

"Anything for you my beauty queen. Tell me, Elouise, where is this station?"

"Sterling Powers will tell you all about it. His number is 227-0000 ext 271. He's the head of the station. Tell him you're interested in buying the station for investment purposes. You know, Malik, better yet, skip the middle man. Don't call Sterling. Call Wayne Jones at the same number."

"Whatever you say, Elouise. I'll make the call and have my driver pick you up at eight. I can't wait!"

"Malik, sweetheart, why don't you come along for the ride and come to my room and get me yourself?"

"Okay then. I'll be there, my queen. See you this evening. I'm counting the minutes."

Weesee hung up the phone, laughing to herself and thinking, *Let's see how you get out of seeing me and Barbara at the same time, smart aleck Malik.* Just then, the phone rang.

"Hello?"

"Elouise," a familiar voice blurted. "Don't hang up on me. I know you're upset, and you have every right to be, but please hear what I have to say. A friend was in dire need of help last night. I apologize for standing you up. It was a horrendous thing to do. Please forgive me."

"A friend needed help, huh? What do you think I needed, Sterling?"

"I know, I know, but it was a real emergency, Elouise."

"Who's emergency—yours or your so-called friend?"

"A friend really did need my help. Let me make this up to you. Let me see you tonight. I do apologize profusely."

"All right, Sterling. If you insist. Let's make it 8:00 p.m. sharp and be ready!"

"Sounds perfect. Thank you, Wees."

Weesee hung up, smiling to herself. As much as she loved Sterling, she had no intention of seeing him. She wanted him to feel what he'd put her through. Her plan was to make him come begging to her. *Hmmm,* Elouise thought to herself. *Barbara must be on her way over soon. I can't wait to tell her the plan!*

St. Michael's Hospital

"Baby sis, why don't you go check on the kids. OJ is settled in his room, and if anything changes, I'll phone you."

"The kids need to know what happened to Samone, AJ. I think we should both tell them. Why don't I pick the kids up, bring them to my house and you can stop by on your way home? That way we can talk to them together."

"Okay, baby girl. I just want to spend some alone time with OJ and then check on Samone, and then I'll be over."

Diane left the hospital to care for the kids. AJ wanted to be sure OJ was comfortable in his room before he left. He walked into the room to find fewer machines hooked up to OJ. He laid there as though he were sleeping. AJ sat beside him on the bed and looked down at his face to see himself. The resemblance was unreal—they looked so much alike. AJ said a silent prayer and then left. He made his way to see Samone where he found her resting quietly. As he turned to exit the room, she awoke.

"OJ, please don't leave me. Stay with me, please. I need you!"

AJ didn't say a word, he just hugged her until she fell back to sleep.

Westchester

Robin came home after a long day of work and school. She checked her phone messages, and there was only one from Larry. She was disappointed OJ hadn't phoned. It had been an entire day since they'd spoken, and it struck her as odd.

Before calling him, Robin got comfortable. She went to the fridge to get something to drink and there she noticed half a bottle of soda was gone. *I must be losing it; I don't remember drinking the soda. It was here this morning.* Perplexed, Robin tried to figure it out. She poured herself a glass of soda and made her way upstairs to shower. Robin entered her bedroom, got undressed and put on her bathrobe. She sat on the bed, reached for the phone and then noticed the cut photo in the frame. She picked up the photo, screamed and dropped it to the floor. Something strange was going on. Robin was terrified. Grabbing the phone in a panic, she called OJ.

"I'm unavailable to take your call, please leave a message," said OJ's voicemail.

"OJ, please call me. Something has happened. I'm so afraid! Please, I need you!" Robin cried.

Robin panicked. Ellen was out of town, and she was afraid to stay alone. She thought if she called the police they'd think she was losing her mind. She jumped in the shower and waited to see if OJ would call and tell her what to do. When he didn't, she figured since she had a key to Ellen's place, she'd spend the night there. Packing her bags in a hurry, she headed over to Ellen's.

Meanwhile Dameon phoned Alexis at his place to alert her he was coming home early.

"Hello, Alexis?"

"Oh hi, Dameon, what's up?"

"I need to talk to you about something very serious. Please hear me out before you say a word. I know we were going to discuss the surgery once I returned home, but I can't wait until then. My mind is made up to have the surgery. I've given a lot of thought to this while I've been away, and I've had two experiences in the past few days that convinced me to make it happen. I need your help!"

"Anything, Dameon. What do you want me to do?"

"Okay, Alexis, listen to me close. First thing I need you to do is contact Mark and his team of surgeons. Tell him I've decided on the surgery, and I want it done as soon as possible. Secondly, I need for you to check back into your hotel room. I've decided to fake my own death and come back as Dominique who'll be my sister. She'll inherit everything I own. In truth, I have no living relatives. Dominique will be me."

"Have you lost your mind, Dameon? How are you gonna pull that off?"

"My plane will crash, but I won't be on it. This is why I need your help. Trust me, Alexis, it will be worth every penny if you help me to pull this off. I'll compensate you for your efforts."

"Are you serious about all this, Dameon?"

"Serious as ever. I have to do it this way; there's no other way possible. I've thought about it very hard. See Dominique will actually be me, and I won't lose a thing—not to mention I'll be happy being who I know I am on the inside. If anyone could understand, I'd think it'd be you."

"Yes, I understand, but to fake your own death—that's so morbid and scary. What if it all backfires on you? What if someone finds out?"

"No one will know but you, Alexis, and I'm going to pay you very well for your silence; a very handsome price indeed, my dear."

"All right, Dameon. Mum's the word. When is all of this going to happen?"

"Very soon. Within the next few days. I'm leaving Carolina tonight. I have to get a driver for the plane, someone I can pay off as well. Someone's who's not afraid to jump from the plane using a parachute. Someone who will say they saw the crash coming and jumped but didn't have the time to save me."

"I can help you with that as well, Dameon. A good friend of mine has his pilot's license and is a very good sky jumper. I'm sure if the price is right, he'd be willing to help, even lie, if he has to."

"Very good, very good. Tomorrow I'll phone you back to see if you can contact this friend as well as set up my appointment with Mark. Meanwhile I have to make a few good-bye calls from my end, tie up all business matters and transfer some money around."

"The more I think about it, Dameon, the more I believe you're onto something. At least this way no one will know the real truth about you. I mean, with you being so well known and all. All of your secrets will remain just that. You never have to worry about me saying a word to a soul."

"Part of the reason I came up with this plan is because I don't want to destroy my reputation, but instead I want to bring out what's inside of me."

"I understand totally, Dameon, say no more. I'll pack my things and tomorrow go back to the Grand Hotel, and you can reach me there."

"Very well, Alexis. I can't thank you enough. I will contact you tomorrow after I've left Carolina and moved to my next city. I'll phone you with the details of exactly where I am for you to give your friend instructions. I will have to phone the airline he works for to request his plane and then the fun begins. Once the plane goes down, I will have already made it to Westchester. Once I make it to Westchester, I'll have to lie low for a few days until things blow over, and it's time for my surgery."

"Yes, Dameon, as soon as I hang up from you, I'll phone Mark. He may want you to fly to Brazil since that's where my surgery was performed."

"Great, that will be even better to get out of the states altogether. I'll have to disguise myself so that no one will know me. You talk to Mark before I leave here, then I'll know which direction I should go. Talk to you later."

Carolina

Ellen laid on the couch where Dameon had left her. She was lifeless, depressed and worried about Dameon. She'd cried so much there were no more tears left. She loved him so very much, and she wasn't ashamed of anything she'd said to him. It felt like weights lifted off her. She wondered who this person was he said he was involved with. At that moment, she thought about her meeting with Kimble. Ellen couldn't wait to get back to Westchester to set an appointment with Kimble. She needed someone to talk to so she phoned Robin.

Robin answered the phone on the first ring, thinking it was OJ calling back.

"Robin, oh Robin, I'm so glad you're home," Ellen said crying.

"What's wrong, Ellen? Why are you crying? Talk to me girlfriend, what's up?"

"He ran off on me, Robin. I thought we were going to have a perfect evening, and he ran away from me."

"What? Ran away from you! Calm down, Ellen, and tell me exactly what happened."

"Well, I sort of had too much to drink, and I was very aggressive. I told Dameon how I felt—I was buck wild! But Robin, he couldn't handle it. He ran off on me, left his bags and everything. He says he's involved with someone, but it didn't feel like that when we kissed. I told him I was in love with him."

"You're kidding me, right? He really ran off on you?"

"Yes, and I don't think he'll be returning any time soon. What's wrong with me, Robin?" Ellen began crying uncontrollably.

"There's nothing wrong with you. Get yourself together girl. It's him, not you. I don't ever want to hear you talk like that. It's his loss. Besides, tell me of any man you know running from a woman or resisting the moment? Something's not right with your Mr. T.D.H. Dameon. Now try to relax, Ellen. When will you be home?"

"I'm taking an early flight tomorrow morning. Maybe he'll be back before then."

"Stop worrying about him, Ellen. He's a man; he's fine. I'm worried about you. Are you gonna be all right?"

"Yeah," Ellen sobbed uncontrollably. "I'll be okay. It just hurts so badly, Robin."

"If you need me to come, I'll take the next flight out. I know it hurts. It's his loss. Believe that, Ellen!"

"No flying for you, Robin. I'll be just fine. I'll see you tomorrow around ten in the morning, okay?"

"I'll be happy to get you from the airport. Is it all right if I stay at your place tonight?"

"Sure, no problem. Is everything okay there?"

"Yeah. Just fine. I figure you're closest to the airport, that's all."

"Okay then. Hey, girl, I'm sorry I called you like this."

"Don't you ever be sorry, Ellen. I'm always here for you! Try not to worry. Dameon will come around, and if he doesn't, the Lord has someone better for you Ellen. You deserve the best!"

"Thanks, Robin."

Ellen hung up the phone not feeling any better. She'd wrecked her brain wondering what Mr. Kimble had to show her; she couldn't wait to get home.

Florida

AJ left the hospital very burdened by Samone's condition. How was he going to tell the kids their mom had been hospitalized for a nervous breakdown? He listened to OJ's phone message and figured Robin had called. He heard the devastation in her voice and called her immediately.

"Robin, honey, what's going on? I just got your message."

"I'm so glad to hear from you, OJ. Something terrible has happened and I'm so frightened."

"What is it, Robin? What's going on?"

"I came in from a long day and went to the fridge to pour myself a glass of soda. Well, half the bottle had been drunk, and then on my night stand where our picture sits of the two of us together—well half the photo is there, but someone cut your side of the picture off. I'm so scared!"

"Have you called the police, Robin?"

"No. They'll think I'm crazy or something. Think about it; it doesn't sound normal, but believe me it's the truth!"

"I want you to go to your girlfriend's house, Ellen's, and stay there. I'm going to get the first flight out to be there with you for a few days until I know you're safe."

"Thank you, baby. I need you. I'm so scared. What if someone broke in? All kinds of things have been going through my mind."

"Baby, stop that. Don't let your imagination fool you like that. Who would want to harm you? I won't rest until I know you are safe. I'll be there as soon as I can. I can only stay a day, Robin though, because I've had an emergency here."

"What's wrong, OJ? I knew something wasn't right when I didn't hear from you all day."

"My brother has been in an accident. He's critical, Robin."

"I'm so sorry, OJ. Gosh. I don't want you worrying about me then. You stay there with your brother; he needs you now. I'll be just fine."

"But baby, I'm worried about you."

Robin cut him off in mid-sentence. "No, OJ, I mean it. You stay with your brother. I'm going to Ellen's, and I'll stay there and be safe."

"Do you promise you'll go right now?"

"I promise. You stay with AJ. I'll phone you when I get there."

"Once I find out AJ is out of the danger zone, I'll be there for you; do you understand me?"

"Yes. Gosh, I'm so sorry about AJ."

"I love you, Robin."

"I believe you, and I love you, too!"

AJ hung up the phone with a feeling of overwhelming anxiety, now worried about Robin. He sat in his car for a few seconds before driving off, wondering why all this tragedy was happening. He felt like his love for OJ and Robin were at war with one another. He couldn't decide if he should go to Robin's rescue or remain by his brother's side. Just hearing her voice brought back all the feelings he had for her.

AJ felt very defeated by all the chaos. He desperately wanted to be there for Robin, but he couldn't bear to leave OJ alone since he felt responsible for what had happened. He put his head down to pray for Robin. "Dear Lord, please keep Robin safe. Please keep her from all danger. Amen." AJ had to believe God could hear him because there was no earthly person who could help him through his crisis. Just as he started the car, his cell phone rang.

"Hello?"

"AJ, I waited for your call. Is everything all right?"

"Yes, Dameon. Things are the same. I've been very occupied at the hospital. OJ's woman, Samone, has been hospitalized, and the kids don't have a clue about their mom. It's just been one helluva day. Please understand I haven't forgotten about you."

"Man, you've got a lot on your plate. I just called to say not to worry about me, I mean us. I have always loved you and always will. I thought it'd be best if I gave you your space to get through this difficult time. I don't want to be a burden on top of all you've got going. I really wanted to be there for you, but I guess my absence is better for you right now, and I understand."

"No, Dameon, what are you saying? I appreciated you coming, and I know how you feel. There's no need for you to feel you're in the way. I definitely felt better talking to you about OJ's situation. If it's the disagreement we had, we can work through that later when everything's back to normal."

"Sometimes I think you're better off without me in your life. I know now is not the time for a goodbye speech, but you've made yourself obviously clear. If it's a woman you want in your life, I have no choice but to step back and let you have your space. I've thought this over long enough, and you can't take love from someone who's not ready and willing to give it freely. Please don't try to defend yourself. My mind is made up. This is goodbye for good, AJ, and I pray that you find the woman who can give you all the love I couldn't."

"Dameon, please. My world is crumbling before me! Please don't do this now! You're the only one I can talk to. I need you as a friend."

No further words were spoken. Dameon had hung up the phone. AJ just sat there listening to the dial tone; he couldn't believe Dameon had just hung up on him and shut him out of his life. He felt heartbroken, torn and scared about what was going to happen next. He'd always had better control of his life, but suddenly everything was falling apart. A part of him did very deeply need and love Dameon. He sat in his car for what seemed like eternity asking God why. Why can't things be like they were?

Ridgemont Hotel

Weesee heard a knock at the door. She peeped through the door hole and saw it was Barbara so she opened the door and welcomed her inside.

"I made it, Elouise! I'm not sure why I came, but I'm here!" Barbara exclaimed as she made her way into the suite.

"First, let's get one thing straight. Please call me Weesee; everyone else does. Secondly, you came because you want to get even with that no good excuse for a man, Malik. Last, but not least, you want something better for yourself. Sit down, girlfriend, take a load off your feet. Let me tell you what I have in mind…"

Weesee began to explain her plan to Barbara about getting Malik to buy the radio station that she'd later put Barbara in charge of running. She told Barbara she planned on faking Malik out by becoming his fiancé, then after he purchased the station in her name, she'd drop all plans of marriage and call him on his lies and deception with Barbara. Weesee would then tell him she felt betrayed and no longer trusted him.

What Weesee didn't bother to tell Barbara was that she was a woman scorned by love, wanting to get even with her man, Sterling Powers. Weesee could care less about Malik. Her revenge with him was his trying to be a player; no man was ever going to play on her intelligence and make a fool out of her without paying the cost. Barbara fell for the whole thing; she loved the idea of her running a radio station by herself. For once in her life she would have power and be in control. She loved Weesee's plan.

"Weesee, you're something else! And smart as a whip! I've never met anyone quite like you before."

"Girlfriend, you never will! Elouise Prescott is one of a kind. Now are you with me? You down with the plan?"

"I'm down, Weesee, but when will you bust Malik and tell him about me?"

"After his purchase of the station, and I suck him into my web. I'll make him fall head over heels for me. Girlfriend, by the time I'm finished with him, he will have forgotten all about you. No offense to you, but I have that kind of effect on men. You just leave Malik up to me. What I need for you to do is to continue to be available when he calls. You can't act any differently toward him or let on to him that you know about me. You got that, Barbara? We're in this together, girl!"

"Yeah, Weesee, act normal. I got it!"

"Okay, then let's shake on it and roll with it. He'll be arriving here within the next hour to pick me up for dinner. What I'd like for you to do is to stay in the bedroom with the door slightly cracked so you can hear us talking. I want you to see me in action and see the man you think you're in love with. See two players in action, Barbara."

"I can do that, but it'll be hard. I do care for him; he's been so nice to me. How can someone so nice be so rotten?"

"You thought your ship had rolled in, right? In you I see myself years back when I'd do just about anything to gain a better life for myself. I know Malik don't mean no more to you than a zebra having stripes, a baby knowing its momma, and those are the facts! So come off that 'I love him' bit and stop frontin' with me."

"All right then. You called me out. Maybe it ain't love, but the man is rich!"

"I'm feelin' you on that, Barbara. I can relate. The money's awfully tempting. Go along with the plan and trust me, you won't regret it! You'll have plenty of your own money in the end."

"We're on!"

Westchester

Fred was parked down the street from Robin's house spying as if he could see through the walls. He pulled out of his coat pocket the half picture of the man he had taken from Robin's nightstand photo. He was tormented at the thought of her being involved with someone. Although many years had passed, in his mind, she would always be his wife and the only woman for him. He felt betrayed and cheated on.

As his mind raced with evil thoughts, he began to crumble the picture in his hand. He made a tight fist and punched his hand into the dashboard of the car. He was enraged with jealousy. Sweat began to run from his brow, and when he looked up, he saw Robin getting into her car. He waited until she was a block down the road before he started up his car to follow her.

As he drove, his jealousy became more intense. What if she was going to meet the man in the photo? His anger escalated without him realizing how fast he was driving or how close up on the rear of her car he was. Fred began to run Robin off the road.

Before she could identify him, he drove off at a high rate of speed. She was forced to the side of the road and panting terribly; she was shaking like a leaf, and her entire body was trembling. Afraid to move, she reached for her cell phone to call the police. She had no information to give except that a car had tried to run her off the road, and that the car was going so fast, she couldn't identify the make or model of the car or the driver. Robin sat in her locked car, waiting for the police to arrive.

Meanwhile Mr. Kimble sat patiently outside of Dameon's house. He had been parked in front of the house for hours, hoping to capture any activity that looked unusual. Suddenly the tall attractive woman came out of the house loading luggage into the Mustang that was parked at the front door. Kimble took close range photos of the woman. He then followed her as she drove to the Grand Hotel.

He waited until she had checked herself in and then he went into the hotel to see if he could get any information from the desk clerk as to what her full name was.

To no avail, the desk clerk was tight lipped and wouldn't give any information even after Mr. Kimble had offered him a fifty. *Why had she gone to the hotel?* Kimble wondered.

St. Michael's Hospital

"Psych ward. How may I direct your call?" a nurse answered the ringing phone.

"I'd like to inquire about the condition of Samone Henderson please?" Sterling asked politely.

"Sir, she's in satisfactory condition."

"Is that all the information you can give? That's what you said yesterday."

"I'm sorry, sir, that's all the information I have. If you are a family member, please consult with her doctor."

"Thank you very much, I'll do just that."

Sterling was very worried about Samone. He kept thinking back on how he had found her in the pouring rain sitting on the porch. He needed to see her, but he was expecting a visit from Weesee. He felt really bad about standing her up, but Samone had desperately needed him; he loved Samone and had to be there for her. Sterling kept thinking back to their lovemaking and how sensual Samone was; how sexy she looked even in her confused state. He couldn't get her out of his mind.

Looking at the clock, he noticed it was 7:00 p.m.; he knew Weesee would be over in less than an hour, but he had a longing to see Samone. His heart called for her. He just had to see her so he put his plans with Weesee once again on hold because he had to go and see the woman who mattered most—— Samone. Sterling left for a quick visit to the hospital.

Carolina

Dameon phoned Ellen back at the hotel.

"Hello," Ellen answered in a very low, depressed voice.

"Ellen, it's Dameon. Please don't speak, just listen to me. I don't understand what happened between us, but it's got my head all messed up! You're a very beautiful woman, and I think the world of you, but I can't be the one you love nor can I give that love back in return. Please don't make me say any more than I have. I would never do anything to hurt you, please know that dear. I just called to say I won't be returning back to the hotel so you don't need to worry. I care for you, Ellen, please believe that."

Without giving Ellen a chance to respond, Dameon hung up the phone.

"Dameon! Dameon!" Ellen yelled into the receiver. A dial tone was all she heard.

Ellen dropped to the floor with the phone gripped in her hand as the man she loved worried about saying goodbye. She held the phone to her chest, and on her knees, she rocked back and forth crying hysterically. "Doesn't he know how much I love him? Doesn't he care how much I hurt?" Her heart ached like it never had before in her life.

On the other end, Dameon hurt, too. It hurt him to be honest with Ellen and know how devastated she was, but he had to do what he had to do. He never had any indication that Ellen felt something for him before this point. In his mind, all they had was a deep respect for one another in a strictly business relationship. Dameon reflected back on conversations they'd had and how naïve he was not to have recognized Ellen's feelings before this. How could he have been so blind? He felt absolutely awful about her loving him. He didn't want her to feel those feelings towards him; he figured if he said goodbye for good, that way she could go on with life and find someone else to love. Dameon admired Ellen's tenacity, and he thought she was very attractive. If he had to have a woman in his life, he'd want someone like Ellen. *What a mess,* he thought to himself as he hung his head down and wept.

Dudley Correctional

"O'Dell, I've got the release papers for you to sign right here. Once your signatures are on these papers, you're free to go."

O'Dell stood looking at the warden with a blank look on his face, as if to say, "Where am I gonna go?"

"It's the moment I've been waiting for, sir. Where do I sign?"

"Sign all the highlighted lines so I can stamp them. For the record, O'Dell, you were one of my better inmates. Never gave me a problem, kept your nose clean throughout the years. I'm gonna do something that's against all the rules. I'm gonna personally drive you into town, if you don't mind the company of someone who's not as bad as everyone makes me out to be…"

O'Dell looked at the warden with amazement; he couldn't believe he had a soft spot in his heart.

"I'd surely appreciate it, sir."

"Okay then, let's get these papers signed, get you into some civil clothing and be on our way."

O'Dell looked at him as if to say, "I don't have no clothing" so he just signed the forms.

"In this envelope you'll find all the contents you had in your possession the day you were arrested. I've managed to get you a change of clothing to wear out. Your clothes are outdated and way too small."

O'Dell took the envelope with tears in his eyes as he opened it. Inside contained a wallet with pictures of his kids and wife. He stared at the photo as tears rolled down his cheeks. Then he removed his wedding ring along with $200 in cash. He held on tight to his wedding band and cried all the harder as he looked up to Heaven and said to his belated wife, "Baby, I'll never stop loving you. Thank you, Lord, now it's time to see my babies."

"Let's do this, O'Dell. Here are some pants, a shirt and shoes for you to change into. I'll be back in a few."

"Thank you very much, sir."

He quickly changed into the clothing and immediately felt like a different person. He was both elated and scared at the same time because everything was happening so fast. He knew his destination was Florida. *I'll ask the warden to take me to the train station,* he said to himself.

The warden walked back into the room and smiled at O'Dell. He couldn't get over how different he looked without his numbered uniform. He cleared his throat and instructed O'Dell on the details. "We'll be going out the back door, and once we're in the car, I'll need you to lie down in the back seat. No one is to know you're being released. As I stated before, it's for your protection. Once we're outside of the prison, you can sit up front with me. Is there anywhere special I can take you?"

"Yes, sir. I'd like to go to the train station. My kids are in Florida."

"Not a problem. You ready to do this?"

"Ready as ever! Let's go!"

They made their way out the back door into the dark night.

Westchester

"Miss, can you give us a description of the car or a license plate number?" the police asked Robin.

"No, officer, it all happened too fast! All I know is someone tried to run me off the road."

"Miss, I'm afraid we can't file a report if we have nothing to go on. But what we can do is escort you to your destination safely. Ma'am, are you all right to drive?" "Yes, officer. I think I'm okay now. It shook me up a bit, but I'm fine now."

"Very well. I'll follow you to where you're going to make sure you get there safely. If you can remember anything at all about the car, you can always make a report at a later time."

"Thank you, officer. I appreciate your escort."

"Not a problem, Ms. Jacobs."

The police followed Robin to Ellen's place where she felt safe. She went inside, locked the doors and put on the alarm. Then she dialed OJ's number.

Meanwhile, across town, Dameon phoned the Grand Hotel to speak to Alexis to see if she had any new information.

"Grand Hotel, how may I direct your call?"

"Please connect me to Alexis Colton's room, please."

"Yes, sir. Please hold while I direct your call."

"Hello, Alexis. Dameon calling. Were you able to speak with Mark?"

"Why yes, Dameon, as a matter of fact I did. Don't be alarmed by what he told me, but he said there's no way possible to do any kind of surgery so soon without first going through all the proper procedures. I'm sorry, Dameon, he told me to pass this along to you."

"Damn, Alexis! You call him back and tell him my mind is made up. I want this done ASAP, no matter what the cost."

"Dameon, dear, slow down. Don't you realize these things take time and extensive testing? I should know, I've been there. Look, you need to relax and think more rationally about things. Believe me, you'll be glad you did. I don't know what happened while you were away, and it's none of my business, but whatever it was, there's no reason for you to rush into anything. Besides, I've got a back up plan for you so all is not lost yet if you're serious about going through with this."

"Why of course I am, Alexis. What's your plan?"

"Okay, Dameon, then chill, okay? I'm on your side. You follow through as you planned, faking your death and coming back as Dominique. You can come back to Westchester as your sister a day or so shy of the supposed crash. Be Dominique for as long as it takes for you to have your testing done and then the surgery. No one will suspect anything. You've got the clothes and everything you need. It's really very simple, Dameon. You just play Dominique up until the surgery. Mark will be performing the surgery in Brazil because that's where his top surgeons are. You can have all the time you need for the extensive testing, surgery and recovery this way. Besides, becoming Dominique will give you a new feel for your new life ahead. The good news to all of this is my pilot friend is willing to work with us."

"Alexis, maybe you're right. Maybe I am rushing it. Thanks for setting me straight. You've got a point that will give me more time to get my personal affairs in order. Thanks. And I'm glad your pilot friend is willing to help."

"See, Dameon, I wouldn't leave you in a lurch."

"Now, how am I supposed to come back to Westchester as Dominique when I don't have the right attire? I left my luggage and everything back at the hotel. It's a long story, and don't bother asking why. If I were to go shopping to buy clothes to dress the role, it could be traced back and would be very suspicious."

"You're right, Dameon. How about I contact Birdman and tell him to pick you up the proper attire. Once you get to Westchester you can change into your own things. Let me just say I peeped in your closet while at the house, and I tell you, you've got some expensive taste in clothes! I'd love to dress like that!"

"What the hell kind of name is Birdman? Can this guy really be trusted?"

"Yes, Dameon. You can trust him for sure. Birdman is his slang name. His real name is Mike Simmons, and he's very trustworthy given the money he's going to make."

"All right then. I'll take your word on this, Alexis. When am I supposed to meet with this Birdman?"

"When we're done talking, I'll call him and give him a contact number so you two can hook up and go over the plan. He's a very good pilot, Dameon. You have nothing to worry about. He did tell me that once the plane goes down, he'd have to stick around long enough until the media dies down, but he'd arrange for a friend of his to fly you wherever you needed to go without anyone knowing."

"Can his friend be trusted? Will he know what's going on? I don't want too many people involved here."

"Don't worry about it, Dameon. Birdman knows what he's doing; he won't pass up an opportunity to make big money without any slip ups. Now tell me what you need so I can have Birdman pick it up."

"I really don't like anyone picking my clothes for me, Alexis."

"Do you really have a choice, Dameon? Come on!"

"Guess I don't. Okay. I'll need a wig, a nice pants suit with a pair of shoes size 11, a 36 C cup bra and makeup. Please tell Birdman I'll reimburse him for everything."

"I've got everything, don't worry. Now give me a contact number for you."

"It's 317-222-0777. When should I expect his call?"

"No later than tomorrow morning. Why don't you relax, get your head together and know everything will work out just fine."

"Okay, Alexis. Maybe you're right. It's been a very emotional two days, and I'm totally drained."

"I can hear it in your voice, Dameon. Get some rest, and I'll phone you back later after I've talked to Birdman."

"Thanks, Alexis. For everything."

Florida

AJ was on his way home after leaving Diane's place and telling the kids the bad news about their mom. AJ had become teary eyed over their reaction; he'd had enough for one day. He wanted to go home and relax for a while before returning to the hospital. Just as he pulled into his driveway, OJ's phone rang.

"Hello, baby, I'm here at Ellen's place. You're not going to believe what happened on my way over here."

"Honey, calm down. You're talking a mile a minute. Are you all right?"

"Someone tried to run me off the road. I called the police, but the car was going so fast I didn't get a description of the car or the driver. Baby, I'm so frightened."

"Say no more, Robin. I'm gonna get the first flight out in the morning. You shouldn't be alone right now. Are all the doors locked? Do you feel safe at Ellen's?"

"Yes, OJ, but I want you to stay with your brother. I'll be fine. Ellen's due back in town tomorrow so there's no need for you to worry. Besides, you've got your hands full there. How's he doing?"

"He's progressing. He's in a coma, but we're praying for a miracle. My sister Diane is with me."

"Honey, I'm so sorry. I'll be praying that he comes out of that coma just fine. Please don't worry about me. It'll pass, soon I hope. Maybe it was just some young kid road raging just to see how fast he could go. Now you hear me, right? You need to stay right there."

"But honey…"

"But nothing. That's my final word. I love you, and I'm worried about you. Have you had much rest yourself? You sound exhausted."

"I'm fine, baby. Now don't you go worrying about me. Soon as my brother is out of the woods I'm there with you, okay?"

"I can't wait, OJ."

"Now you're sure you're safe, Robin? I'm on my way home to rest a bit before I head back to the hospital. You call me if anything happens, okay?"

"Yes, sweetie. I'm fine now that I've talked to you. You get some rest, and I'll phone you later before I go to bed."

"Double check the doors just as soon as you hang up, okay Robin? As a matter of fact, why don't you do it right now while I'm on the line."

"Okay Mr. O'Neil, the doors are secure. Is there anything else?"

"Yes. One more little thing. You know I love you, don't you?"

"Without a doubt. I love you, too, OJ."

AJ sat in the car torturing himself at how badly he wanted to be there for Robin. His body went numb with pain for his entire situation.

St. Michael's Hospital

Sterling arrived at the hospital just in time to meet up with Samone's doctor who was examining her. Samone was awake, looking straight ahead at the wall. Sterling approached her bedside.

"Hi darling, I'm here. Are you feeling any better?"

Samone just continued to stare at the wall with no response at all.

"Excuse me, sir. I'm Dr. Thompson."

"I'm sorry. I'm Sterling Powers, a family member. What's her diagnosis, doctor?"

"Well, she's in a state of shock. Apparently she's experienced a very traumatic setback. Her blood levels indicate she has not been taking her medication regularly so this along with the stress contributed to the breakdown."

"Will she recover from this setback? I mean—get back to normal?"

"Yes, of course she will with time. Once this new medication takes effect, she'll be back to her normal self, but she'll still need guidance—someone to make sure she takes her meds regularly and all."

"Of course, doctor, that's not a problem. I can do that myself. Does she recognize anyone?"

"Yes, she does. Sometimes it takes awhile for the patient to comprehend words right away. I'll leave you alone to visit. If you have any more questions, please feel free to consult the nurse at the front desk. Samone will recover in due time, Mr. Powers."

"Thank you, Dr. Thompson."

Once the doctor left the room, Sterling took Samone's hand and held it tightly. "Samone, baby, you're going to pull through this. I'm here for you, and I love you so very much. I promise to take care of you."

Samone stared at him, as if she was taking in every word but unable to speak. Sterling sat by her side until she fell off to sleep.

Ridgemont Hotel

Malik knocked on the door to Weesee's room.

"Just a second, Malik sweetie," Weesee answered while whispering to Barbara to hide in the bedroom but keep the door cracked so she could hear them. "I'm coming, Malik."

"My beautiful, Elouise. You look absolutely radiant this evening."

"Thank you."

As Malik walked into the room, he said, "My beautiful lady, I have a gift for you."

"Malik, darling, you didn't! Well, what is it? Bring it on!"

Malik removed a nicely wrapped box from his suit jacket and gave it to Weesee.

"Open it my lady, I picked it out myself just for you."

Weesee unwrapped the box and opened it. To her dismay, it was an expensive tennis bracelet with a $10,000 tag still on it. Weesee's eyes almost popped out of her head when she saw the price and the sparkle of diamonds. Her immediate response was to hug Malik. She hugged him so tight, he began coughing from her choke hold!

"My lady, you're strong! Can you please let me go?" he coughed and laughed at the same time.

"I'm sorry, baby! I'm just so excited! I love it! It's gorgeous!" She let go of him and began to do a little dance around him in a circle. Malik was smiling from ear to ear; he had never seen any woman react like this over a gift presented to her. Barbara, in the bedroom listening to every word, was getting jealous and angry. He'd never spent that much money on her.

"I can see you're elated, my queen."

"You got that right, sweetie. Can I make you a drink or get you anything, Malik?"

"Just say you'll be my bride. That is all I want of you, my beautiful Elouise."

"Daddy, whatever you want! You mean to tell me you paid that kind of money for a bracelet just for me, and I ain't gave up nothin' yet? Damn where were you all these years of my life?"

Malik looked at her strangely, trying to figure out what she was saying.

"You will be my wife! Nothing is too costly for the woman who'll become one with me."

"Okay then. That's what I like to hear. When are we gonna go get the radio station?"

"My queen, I will phone Mr. Wayne Jones tomorrow and have him name his price for the station and it's yours."

"Just like that?"

"Just like that. That's what you want, is it not?"

"Yeah, of course I do!"

"Then you shall have it. My lady, are you happy?"

"You'd better believe it! Don't you see me cheesin'?" she smiled really big, showing all her teeth.

"What is cheesin' my lady?"

"Don't you see this big smile on my face with all of my teeth showing? That's cheesin'. I guess I've gotta teach you a few things!"

"Well, I'm very happy you're cheesin' my lady. You're beautiful."

"Thank you, Malik. Thank you very much. Now are you sure I can't get you a drink or something? What are our plans, my sir?"

"Well, I've had the Orchard Restaurant shut down just for us."

Weesee stopped in her tracks on her way to the bar to make them both a drink.

"You did what?! Shut down the most expensive restaurant in the state of Florida just for us?"

"Yes, that's what I said, my queen. Nothing but the best for you."

"Damn! You've got that kind of loot?"

"Loot. What do you mean by that?"

"Never mind, sweetie. We're dining in style tonight. Let me change into something more elegant."

"My queen you look exquisite right now. There won't be anyone there except us and the attendants."

"Umm, baby. I've got to savor this moment. I need to look sophisticated. That place is the bomb! So excuse me for just a few minutes while I get changed."

"Yes, Elouise. Anything you say. Whatever makes you cheese. The bomb you say?"

Weesee just looked and him and shook her head, smiling at his naiveté. When she entered the bedroom, Barbara was sitting on the bed pouting like a little kid who'd lost her best friend.

"I don't know about your plan, you seem to be the one benefiting from all this, Weesee. First a ten-thousand dollar bracelet and now an expensive restaurant. What am I gaining?" Barbara demanded.

"Stop your crying. You're gonna be the head of a radio station when he buys it tomorrow, Barbara."

"Yeah, but you'll own it. I've been thinking about that."

"Girlfriend, let me tell you something. I've waited a long time for my ship to roll in. Do you think I'm gonna let this ride on by me? Besides, he's interested in me. I don't care if he was seeing you. It's obvious to me, it's me he wants. Now you can walk through these doors and expose yourself or work with me on this. And by the way, Barbara, if you're thinking about going out there and blowing it, that won't be a problem because all I've got to say is, may the best woman win! I hate to tell you, but this man is crazy about me."

"Okay, Weesee, I don't want to fight with you. As long as I get something out of the deal."

"You will, I promise. Now help me get dressed! I'll even be nice and bring you back something from the restaurant. I ain't no selfish bitch."

Two days later

NEWS FLASH on just about every television station in the nation. There's been a fatal plane crash in Philadelphia. Entrepreneur and world renown fashion expert Dameon Davenport was on board, and he was pronounced dead at the scene.

Neither Ellen nor AJ had gotten word of the news yet. Dameon, meanwhile, was lying low at his house, looking on at the news as the media covered details of the crash and his life. Multimillionaire killed in charter plane crash. Dameon sat sipping on a glass of scotch, shaking his head at the media. *Boy, I guess I was a bigger deal than I ever realized with this type of coverage,* Dameon thought to himself. *I guess it's time for Dominique to make an appearance…*

Florida

Meanwhile O'Dell had taken the train and made it to Florida. He was staying in a downtown hotel deciding when the time would be right to approach his kids. He sat looking at their picture, staring at the phone number he had for AJ. He had also found Diane's number listed in the phone book. He reached for the phone to call Diane's house, hoping she'd answer so he could hear her voice.

"Hello. This is the O'Neil residence. Trevor speaking."

O'Dell held onto the phone for a minute and stuttered, "May I please speak to Diane?"

"I'm sorry, my mom isn't in. She's at the hospital visiting with my Uncle OJ. Who may I say is calling?"

Wondering if this was his grandson O'Dell said, "Hello, Trevor, I'm so sorry I missed your mom. Tell me, how is your Uncle OJ doing? This is your Uncle OJ's good friend Mr. Jones."

"Mr. Jones, Uncle OJ is bad off. Mom's been crying ever since it happened."

"I'm so sorry your mom is sad, Trevor. Your uncle is a fighter; he'll get better. You're a big boy, you understand that your mommy just loves her brother right? She just wants him to get better. How old are you, by the way?"

"I'm nine years old, Mr. Jones," Trevor informed him.

"You gotta be the man of the house and watch over your mom, okay?"

"Yes, sir. I do, but I don't like it when she cries."

"I know, Trevor. It's going to be all right. Now what hospital was that again? I'm gonna go see your Uncle OJ just as soon as I hang up."

"St. Michael's Hospital, Mr. Jones."

"Thank you, Trevor. Now you be a good boy and take care of your mom."

"Yes, sir."

O'Dell hung up the phone excited about having a grandson but worried about what was wrong with OJ. He decided not to wait a minute longer, and he headed to the hospital to see if he could get any information.

Westchester

Mr. Kimble sat outside of Dameon's house. He'd kept a watch on it since he'd been unsuccessful getting information about the attractive woman from the hotel desk clerk. Kimble sat waiting for Dameon to arrive, little did he know Dameon had snuck inside in the middle of the night. All of a sudden the radio had a newsflash. It was something about an accident and Dameon Davenport, so Kimble turned it up.

"Well I'll be damned!" he said out loud. Shocked by the sudden news, he phoned Ellen immediately from his cell phone but got no answer. Kimble couldn't believe his ears. The beautiful woman had gone to a hotel and then a sudden death. Wow! *Something didn't seem to add up, however,* Kimble thought. He put his car into gear and headed to the hotel to find the attractive woman to get some answers. He needed to know what her relationship with Dameon was before he presented his pictures to Ellen.

Ellen had been shut up in her apartment since she'd arrived back from Carolina. She was so depressed, she didn't go to work, answer the phone or talk to anyone. She sat in her apartment with the shades drawn, not knowing if it was night or day. Her answering machine steadily blinked with calls from Robin who'd she'd kicked out in anger the night before. Mr. Kimble had left a few calls as well, hoping to meet with her to present her the photos of the mystery woman. By this point, Ellen could care less. Nothing seemed to matter anymore. Ellen lay on the sofa lifeless.

Meanwhile Robin found a note on her car windshield when she went out during lunch break. "I'm closer than you think. Don't worry your pretty head; we'll be together soon!" The note was attached to a single white rose. Robin panicked and took the note to the police. She didn't dare worry OJ or Ellen; instead she kept it to herself even though she was frightened out of her mind. She didn't want to worry her son Larry either. By this point she was convinced someone was stalking her and who that someone was worried her more than anything. On her way home her phone rang.

"Hello, Robin? Girl, what's been going on? Why haven't you returned any of my calls? Is everything all right with you?"

"Yeah, Raine. Everything's fine. I've been so busy with class; I've been meaning to phone you."

"I know you, girlfriend, and that's not like you now. You wanna stop frontin' with me and tell me what the hell's wrong?"

"All right, Raine. You know me too well. Someone is stalking me, girl!"

"You say what? Stalking you as in following you like a crazy person?"

"Yep. Some weird stuff's been going on these past few days."

"I knew it. I felt something wasn't right. The boys and I are coming to be with you for a few days. You should go and stay with Ellen. I called her, too, but there was no answer. Is she out of town?"

"No. But she's going through a difficult time right now."

"What in the heck is happening? I leave Westchester and all kinds of crazy stuff starts going on. Somethin' with you and Ellen. She's your home girl, she wouldn't leave you alone like that, now."

"I know Raine. I haven't told her everything so don't you dare say a word. I'll be fine. The police are on it."

"You're not fine. I can hear it in your voice. I'm hanging up and checking on flights right now."

"No, Raine, that's not necessary. Really, I'm okay."

"I'm not gonna rest until I get there so don't be tellin' me everything's fine. You're my girl, and I gotta come. I'll call you with my arrival time once I make the reservation——besides the boys miss you."

"Okay, Raine. You win. I never could argue with you! Thanks, girlfriend."

"I love you, Robin. You'd do the same for me."

"Yes, and without thinking twice. I feel so much better already. I can't wait to see you all."

"Well, let me go and check on the reservations; I call you back in a bit."

"Thanks, Raine. Later."

Raine hung up the phone worried sick. She phoned Weesee and left her a message to call her back ASAP. They were all like sisters, always have been and always will be there for one another.

Robin felt relieved to know Raine was coming to visit. Raine tried phoning Ellen again but got the answering machine. As Robin drove to Ellen's, all of a sudden a newsflash came across the radio, and that's when she heard about Dameon's death. Robin hoped Ellen hadn't heard the news yet. This whole thing with Dameon took Robin's mind off her own problems. She hated to be the bearer of bad news, especially when she knew how much Ellen loved Dameon.

St. Michael's Hospital

"May I help you sir?"

"Yes. My son Oscar O'Neil is a patient here. How might I find out about his condition? I'm from out of town."

"I can try paging the attending physician for you. Please give me a moment to look up the information, and I'll page the doctor. Have a seat in the waiting room, please, and I'll be right with you."

"Thank you."

Over the intercom, the receptionist paged Dr. Casey to the front desk. Within minutes, Dr. Casey arrived.

"Dr. Casey, there's a family member requesting information about a patient of yours." She pointed to O'Dell in the waiting room.

"Hello, sir. I'm Dr. Casey. How may I help you?"

"Hello, Dr. Casey. My son, Oscar O'Neil, is in your care. Please tell me his condition. I've traveled far to see him, and I haven't contacted his brother or sister yet. I wanted firsthand information."

"Please, Mr. O'Neil, have a seat and I'll gladly explain your son's condition."

They both sat down in the closed waiting room.

"Your son had a terrible fall from a building, Mr. O'Neil. He's a blessed man and very lucky to be alive. He's been in a coma for weeks but he's not in any serious pain. We've kept him very comfortable with meds. He's suffered internal bleeding and lost a lot of blood. The first week his body rejected the initial medications, but we've finally stabilized him. He was on a respirator for a while, but now it's been removed, and he's breathing on his own. He's still not out of the woods. In fact, I was just about to contact your children to give them the results of his last test. I explained to your kids that this medication can have both positive effects but negative repercussions as well. The medication has fought off all infections, but it has weakened his kidneys. I'm afraid he'll have to undergo dialysis treatment for the rest of his life."

O'Dell sat speechless. Dr. Casey sensed his emotion.

"Are you all right, Mr. O'Neil?"

O'Dell sat crying like a baby. The news was overwhelming, and he felt so helpless.

"I'm so sorry, Mr. O'Neil. This is a difficult time."

"My baby boy!" he moaned. "See, I haven't been able to be there as a father should and now I feel so helpless. I've got some personal issues I need to settle with my children. In fact, Aaron and Diane don't even know I'm in town. Please can we keep our conversation confidential until I've had a chance to meet with them?"

Dr. Casey felt sorry for O'Dell. He didn't know the reason for the strain on the relationship with his kids, but he saw a man who was very concerned about his son. A very broken man.

"Yes, of course, Mr. O'Neil. We can keep this conversation between the two of us. Do you have any more questions, sir?"

"Yes. How long will he remain in the coma, doctor?"

"I'm sorry to say it's very unpredictable. I'm unable to put a time limit on it. His brain is functioning well; he can hear everything that's said to him. A coma is a prolonged unconscious state, and it all depends on the individual."

"Are there any alternatives to dialysis treatment, doctor?"

"Mr. O'Neil, I'm sorry there are no medications to alter what his body needs. He needs a new kidney. A transplant donor would help his situation. I was going to give the family this option to see if anyone was a match donor, if not then he could be placed on the national donor's list. He still will have to undergo dialysis until he's gotten a kidney which will function with his body."

"Then he's got my kidney! If that will make my son better, take mine."

"Mr. O'Neil, it's not that simple. We have to perform tests to see if yours is compatible with OJ's."

"Well, let's do it. When can we get started?"

"Sir, I can see your determination, and I appreciate your enthusiasm, but I have to consult the kids about this first. Your son Aaron wants to be notified of any changes."

"Please, Dr. Casey, before you say anything to my kids about his kidney problem, please perform a test on me first to see if I'm a match. I'm begging you, doctor. I don't want to get personal about my business, but I owe all of them this much. Please, sir, I beg of you to at least do the test to see if I'm a possible match for him."

"Very well then, Mr. O'Neil, we'll get to work with blood work and the needed tests."

"I'm ready, willing and able."

"Let's get started with blood work, and then tomorrow I'll schedule the other tests for you."

"Thank you very much, Dr. Casey. This means a great deal to me. One more thing, doctor?"

"Yes."

"Please don't mention any of this to my kids right yet. If I happen to be a perfect match, I'd like them to be told it was from an anonymous donor. I'd like to be the one to tell them."

"Not a problem. I understand. Now let's get to the lab and run some blood work on you."

As Dr. Casey escorted O'Dell to the lab, O'Dell asked determinedly, "May I just stop by to see my boy for just a second please, doctor?"

"Yes, of course, Mr. O'Neil."

Dr. Casey escorted O'Dell to the room where OJ remained in a coma. Luckily Diane had gone home for some sleep, and AJ hadn't arrived yet. O'Dell stood over his son nervously shaking. He couldn't believe his little boy had grown into a man. He stood mesmerized by how much OJ resembled him in his younger days. He reached for his hand and in a low, faint voice he whispered, "I love you, son. Oscar John, you were my first born, and this is your dad speaking to you. I know you don't remember me, but I never went a day without you. I love you, son. "

O'Dell rubbed his forehead with his hand as he prayed. "God, please help my son, help us all Lord. I know what you can do, what you have done. Please let us be a family once more." O'Dell prayed from the depths of his soul. A single tear fell on OJ's body, and at that very moment OJ's body moved ever so slightly. Dr. Casey witnessed this miraculous movement.

"I believe your son is responding to you. He just flinched. Did you see him?"

"Yes, doctor!" O'Dell's face was brimming with pride.

"I hate to break up this very special moment, but we must get to the lab—I have to make my rounds."

O'Dell leaned over to kiss OJ goodbye. "I'll be back later, OJ. I love you."

Psych Ward

The medication had finally settled in, and Samone had been getting better as each day passed.

"You look lovely today, Samone, with your makeup on and hair all dolled up. You're very pretty."

"Thank you, nurse. My honey is visiting me today. I mean, my husband is coming for me, and I've got to look my best!"

"Yes, you look lovely indeed, Samone, but you can't go home just yet. Not until the doctor says it's okay."

"We're going to Jamaica to celebrate our honeymoon. We just got married!"

"No wonder you're glowing! You look pretty as a new bride!"

Samone just smiled. A few minutes later Sterling walked in with flowers.

"How's my favorite girl doing today?"

"Just fine, my sweet husband. You came to take me home?"

"No, baby, not today, but real soon. My, my you look gorgeous today! Simply radiant!"

"Oh, Sterling, I want to go home!" Samone started yelling and screaming. "Take me home! Where is OJ? I gotta go home, OJ is waiting!"

She became hysterical to the point that the nurses rushed in to sedate her. Sterling never left her side; he sat with her until she drifted off to sleep. He gazed at her lovingly. She looked like a princess sleeping.

O'Dell finished giving blood and wanted to see OJ one last time before heading back to the hotel. As he got into the elevator, he stood in the doorway to keep the elevator from closing. Instantly he knew the woman in the elevator he saw before him was his baby girl. She looked exactly like his wife did years ago.

"Excuse me, but are you getting on or off?"

Stuttering O'Dell answered, "I-I-I'mm sorry Miss, I'm getting on. He couldn't help but stare at Diane. She was the spitting image of his wife. Same height, weight, hair color and beautiful light brown eyes.

"Excuse me, Miss. I'm visiting this hospital for the first time, would you happen to know where the chapel is?"

"Yes. I'm getting off at the very same floor so I can show you where it is."

"Thank you, kind lady. Thank you so very much."

Diane was feeling a bit uncomfortable with the way he looked at her. As they got off the elevator, they stood standing face-to-face, and Diane got a good look at O'Dell's face.

"Follow the yellow arrows around, and the chapel will be on your right."

"Thank you."

O'Dell couldn't take his eyes off Diane and didn't move from his spot once he got off the elevator. He stood staring at Diane as she walked away.

Diane could feel his eyes piercing her from behind. "Sir, excuse me, but have we met somewhere before?"

"I don't believe so, young lady; I'm a stranger in town." His heart was racing.

"I'm sorry; it's just that I feel like I know you from somewhere."

"I know the feeling. People say we all have a look alike in this world of ours." He smiled.

"Are you visiting a relative or friend?"

"A very dear relative," he answered.

"I pray they get better. I've spent a lot of time in the chapel myself."

"Have you been praying for a relative as well?"

"My dearest brother. He's been hospitalized for some time, and thank the Lord, he seems to be doing a little better."

"That's reassuring to know. What's your brother's name and I can include him in my prayers when I go to the chapel?"

"His name is Oscar, but we call him OJ. Thank you for your prayers; that's very kind."

O'Dell's heart just about fell to the floor. This was indeed his baby girl!

"Well, I'll keep OJ in my prayers. Don't worry your pretty self too much. God has got this under control!"

"Thank you, sir. Well, I'd better be going. Don't forget, follow the yellow arrows to your right."

O'Dell walked straight ahead following the yellow arrows as Diane had directed him to. He went into the chapel, laid down on the floor before God and first prayed for a divine miracle of healing for OJ and then he lifted up a prayer of thanks for allowing him to see two of his kids in one day.

Ridgemont Hotel

Weesee had been dating Malik strong over the past few days. He had even put in an offer for the radio station so Barbara was happy. Weesee was definitely starting to feel something for this man. She looked forward to their dates, especially since Malik was always full of surprises, dining Weesee in style first class. She loved it! She sat in a bubble bath contemplating what he had on the agenda for tonight. Suddenly the phone rang.

"What's up? This is Weesee speaking."

"Weesee, baby, how you doin'?"

"Raine, girlfriend. How the hell are you? The boys?"

"I'm fine; the boys are good. You're a hard woman to track down, you know. I thought you were in San Francisco the last we spoke."

"That was damn near three weeks ago. You know I'm on a roll, Raine. Gotta keep it movin' What's up girlfriend? I hear a tightness in your throat. Is everything all right?"

"Wees, our girls need us. I don't know what the hell Ellen has gotten herself into. Robin's not saying much about her, but Robin's in deep trouble with some weirdo stalking her."

Weesee sat straight up in the tub. "Raine, hold on, let me get my ass out of the tub." She got out and dried off.

"Now, Raine, tell me this again. Somebody is after Robin? Damn she must've laid some serious lovin' on somebody and drove him crazy."

"Stop clowning! I'm serious. She's scared to death."

"No shit! Well, where is Ellen? What's up with her? Why isn't she there for my girl? She must have got her some dick finally and can't think straight. I knew it would happen to her one day."

"Weesee, get serious. All I know is Robin hasn't said anything to Ellen and she needs us. I'm flying out in the morning to be with her for a few days."

"Damn, Raine, I just hit a gold mine. The jack pot. He's romancing me and everything, but I guess if my girls need me, I'm there, too. Should I phone Robin?"

"No, Wees! I promised her I wouldn't tell anybody."

"All right, Raine, let me see if I can get a flight for tomorrow. I'm gonna have to go all the way to Westchester and kick this stalker's ass because he's interrupting MY program now."

Raine laughed. "See you soon."

AJ's Place

AJ awakened from a long nap. He wanted to catch the news before going to the hospital. He sat in the living room area, flicked on the remote in time for the news. Across the bottom of the screen he caught sight of a newsflash: "Man killed in plane crash. Details ahead."

AJ sat back sipping on his cognac while the commercials played. The news came back on detailing the specifics of the crash.

"Multimillionaire Dameon Davenport, traveling by charter plane was killed when his plane went down outside Philadelphia. Despite the plane going up in flames, the pilot survived. The accident is under investigation."

AJ stood to his feet! He couldn't believe what he was hearing. He flipped the channel to another station to get the news to be sure he heard what he thought he was hearing. The news flashed the same report. AJ fell to his knees. "NO! NO! Dameon you can't be dead!" AJ was hysterical.

Westchester

Meanwhile, Robin was speeding in her car to get to Ellen's and suddenly she heard a police siren behind her; she looked into her rearview mirror to find the siren blaring so she pulled over to the side of the road.

"Miss do you realize you were driving sixty in a thirty mph zone?"

"Officer, I'm so sorry. This is an emergency."

"I'm sorry, but I'm going to have to ticket you. May I have your registration and license please?"

"Yes, of course, officer." Robin reached into the back seat of her car for her purse. As she did, she was startled to find scattered pieces of OJ's picture on the floor of her car. It was the picture from her night stand. Her hands began to shake uncontrollably.

Noticing her hands shaking, the officer asked, "Are you all right? Why are you trembling? It's only a ticket."

"You don't understand, officer. Someone is after me. Someone is watching me—they've been in my house, in my car and ran me off the road!"

The officer was confused. "I'm terribly sorry, I still need to issue you a citation" he said, writing out the ticket.

"I'm not giving some lame excuse to get out of a speeding ticket, officer. This is the real deal."

"Sure enough then. Here's your ticket and slow down."

Some help the police are, Robin thought to herself. *This guy doesn't even believe me.* She took the ticket and drove off to Ellen's; she was only minutes away. As she got out of the car, Robin looked around to make sure she hadn't been followed. Damn! She was dreading to see Ellen to tell her the news.

Robin was still trembling as she took out her keys and walked toward the main building. Taking a deep breath before entering, she unlocked the door to Ellen's darkened apartment. "Ellen. I know you're here. It's me, Robin! Ellen?"

Robin reached for the light. She saw Ellen stretched out on the sofa, a complete wreck with empty wine bottles scattered all around her. She went over to awaken her.

"Ellen. Ellen, are you okay? Wake up, Ellen!"

She didn't move a muscle. She was out cold.

"Let's get some coffee in you and get you cleaned up. I'm here, Ellen. I'm going to take care of you."

Ellen's voice slurred. "You came, Robin. I'm soooo sorr-rry. I just love him, Robin and he don't want me. Why Robin? Why don't he want me?"

Robin just hugged Ellen and cried. "It's going to be just fine, Ellen. Calm down now, girl."

Robin knew she had to get Ellen in the right frame of mind before she could tell her about Dameon's death. She had to be strong for her. Ellen laid back down while Robin went to the kitchen to put on some coffee.

She's so vulnerable, Robin thought to herself while she worked in the kitchen. Tears filled her eyes as she watched her desperate friend. It hurt to see Ellen like this. Ellen had always been the strong one who took in everyone else's problems, always giving advice, always the pillar of strength holding Weesee, Raine and her together whenever a crisis happened. Now it was Robin's turn. She had to be strong for Ellen.

Just then the phone rang.

"Hello?"

"Robin? What the hell is going on? What's happening?" Robin couldn't answer, she just broke down in tears.

"Listen to me, Robin. Hold the shit together until I get there. Just hold tight, girlfriend. Raine and I are on our way. I love you, girl. We'll be there soon."

Robin couldn't speak; she just burst into tears.

As she hung up the phone, Robin realized she'd better get it together if she was gonna be of any help to Ellen. Wiping her tears away and fixing her face a bit, she made her way back to the living room with the coffee. She went over and sat Ellen up like a baby and then forced coffee into her.

It took a few hours, but eventually Ellen began to come around. Robin even got her into the shower to clean up. As she did, Robin cleared up all the empty wine bottles.

How in the world am I going to tell Ellen, Lord? When is the right time? Please give me the words to speak, Heavenly Father.

Ellen came out of the bathroom dragging and lifeless. She and Robin locked eyes before saying a word; they hugged.

"I can make you something to eat, Ellen. You should eat a little something."

"No, I'm not hungry. I'm just ashamed of myself, Robin. I'm sorry to put you through this."

"Girl, we're in this together. I'm sorry I left you alone, Ellen. I really should have insisted on staying with you even though you kicked me out! I'm here for you now, and I'm not leaving! Guess what? I have some good news."

"What?"

"Weesee and Raine will be here tomorrow!" Robin couldn't get a reaction out of her; she was so sad in spirit. They both sat silently for a while until Ellen finally said, "Robin, I'm dealing with this my way, and I really want you to know I'll be fine if you wanna go home."

"What? You're kickin' me out again?! Well, I'm not going! You're not fine."

"What's that supposed to mean?"

"Well, since when did you pick up your drinking habit? I've never known you to drink anything alcoholic, and I found three bottles of empty wine. Do we need to get you some help?"

"Help?! Robin, I got this. I don't need no help! Why don't you go on home and wait by the phone for OJ to call."

After saying that, Ellen felt bad. She was obviously taking her anger out on Robin.

"I'm sorry, I didn't mean anything by that. Please forgive me, Robin."

"It's okay, Ellen, I understand."

Robin moved closer to Ellen to talk. "I care about you. You've been like a sister to me."

"I know, Robin. So now what's this again? Raine and Weesee will both be in town tomorrow?"

"Yep! It's time we all got together like old times. We'll have a ball!"

"Yeah, lots of fun! What day of the week is it, Robin? I sort of lost track of time."

"Today is Wednesday. You've been shut up in the apartment since I picked you up from the airport. I've called so many times. I tried to give you space, but I just got so damn worried about you."

"Please don't worry. This will pass. Dameon is just a man! Like you said, there's more fish in the sea, right?"

"Yeah, but I understand how you feel."

"You don't know how I feel, Robin. You got your man. You're about to plan a wedding and you gonna sit there and tell me you know how I feel!"

Ellen was very defensive and bitter.

"I know what it feels like to love someone—that's all I meant to say, Ellen." Robin tried to keep her voice calm and not get agitated.

"You know, Ellen, there is something very important I must tell you."

"Do me a favor and tell me some other time. I don't feel much like talking any more. In fact, Robin, I'd rather be alone right now."

"Okay then, Ellen. Have it your way. Dameon is dead."

"What? What nonsense are you saying?"

"I just heard on the news, that's why I rushed over. Dameon Davenport was killed in a charter plane accident."

Ellen started screaming. "NO! NO! NO! He can't be dead. It's all my fault. If I hadn't come onto him, he never would have left. Robin it's all my fault! I killed him!"

Robin slapped her face to bring her out of shock. "No, Ellen, it's not your fault. I'm so sorry!"

They both hugged and cried together.

Dameon's Place

Dameon was on the phone with Alexis.

"Have you seen the news?"

"Yes, Dameon, it's on every station. I guess you're officially dead."

"Yeah, I am. You hear all the nice tributes given to me? I had no idea I had impacted so many people. It's humbling."

"You're a rich man and have contributed money throughout the community and even to different colleges. I can't believe all the charitable contributions you made. It's very inspiring to hear the tributes of your life on the news."

"My mother always said, 'When you give, you get back.' I believe that one-hundred percent."

"So what's your plan now, Dameon?"

"I need to make an appearance as Dominique to make the funeral arrangements."

"I can help you with that, Dameon. Maybe we should meet somewhere later."

"Let me first make an appearance to the media as Dominique. Let the media get the news of me and then we'll hook up. I see Birdman has got his alibi together. The media is all over him! He's good!"

"Money means nothing to you, but to the Birdman it's everything. To make the kind of money you're paying him, he'd lie on his own momma."

"Well, he's earned his pay and then some. Yes, Alexis, I will need your help with the arrangements. Remember, I'm from out of town so I won't know much. You'll be my secretary for the time being, okay? We'll go to my office and clear out my personal belongings."

"When?"

"Tomorrow I'll step in there dressed to kill as the grieving sister. Look for me on the news tomorrow front and center. I've picked out the perfect outfit. Dominique will be drop dead gorgeous!"

"Knock 'em dead, Dameon—I mean Dominique!"

"I will! It will be a stellar performance. I'll phone you tomorrow then, Alexis. Thanks for everything."

Florida

AJ was in a daze; he couldn't believe Dameon was dead. His companion, his friend, his lover. He was shattered. He sat staring at the television set as the news seemed to re-play his entire life over and over. He never made it back over to the hospital that day. He just couldn't take his eyes off the television screen out of disbelief. How could his life get any worse? What else could happen? If this wasn't living hell, he had no idea what was. First OJ, then Samone then Robin and now Dameon. Damn it.

How was he going to leave town in the midst of all the crisis and go to the funeral? As he replayed the last few days in his mind, he became overwrought with emotion. It was all starting to add up in his mind, the goodbye call from Dameon. He didn't understand when they last spoke.

"If it's a woman you want, I'll give you your space to be happy…" those were Dameon's last words to AJ.

AJ loved Dameon; somehow he felt Dameon knew something was about to happen. After what seemed like days, AJ pulled himself together to phone Diane to tell her he must leave town for a few days. Then he decided to call Robin to tell her he'd be in Westchester. He couldn't remember Dameon speaking of any family. He just had to be there.

Picking up the phone, he decided to call Robin first.

"Hello?"

"Are you all right, Robin?"

"No. Not at all, OJ, I'm a wreck. My close friend Ellen lost a dear friend today, and it was so hard breaking the news to her. I'm so worried about her. I just gave her a sleeping pill to relax her. She's out of her mind grieving."

"It wouldn't happen to be Dameon Davenport would it?"

"Yes! Do you know him, OJ? Yes! He was killed in a plane accident."

"I know him very well. He's a good friend of mine. I'm going to be coming to Westchester to see you and attend his funeral. It's such a terrible tragedy."

"What a small world! Dameon was Ellen's boss. I never met him, but by the news accounts, he sounds like he was an amazing, giving and powerful man. It's a terrible accident. I'm sorry for you as well, but I'm so glad you'll be coming into town after all. I really need you, OJ."

"Has something happened more with that nut?"

"I had a bit of a scare, but I'll tell you all about it when you get here, sweetie. I feel so much better knowing you will be holding me in your arms soon."

"Are you staying with Ellen then?"

"Yes. She's taken the news very, very hard."

"There has been so much horrible news this past week. It's almost overwhelming."

"I agree. But we will both feel better once we see one another. I just know it."

"Robin, I can't wait until I see you. What is the news you will share with me?"

"You have too much on your plate right now, OJ. I will be just fine taking care of Ellen. Trust me. We can talk when you get here."

"Okay then. I have to talk to you about something very important, face-to-face as well, Robin."

"Is it us OJ? Your brother?"

"Don't you go worrying on me wondering. We'll talk all about everything when I get there."

"Well, listen, OJ, my other two close friends are flying in tomorrow. All us girls wanted to get together to be there for Ellen."

"Baby, that's wonderful."

"Yeah. I guess we all really need each other like old times. I'm happy because with you coming up now, they'll get to meet you!"

"Well, don't plan on me for much entertaining, Robin. My spirits are not the best right now. I wanna pay my respects to Dameon, spend some time with you and that's about it. Not that I don't wanna meet your friends and all, but it might not be best to count on me for any special get-togethers on this trip. Do you mind?"

"Okay, OJ, I understand."

"Since your girls are coming, I'll check into a hotel."

"But OJ…"

"No, I insist. I can only stay up for a day to see you and attend the funeral, but then I have to get back for my brother."

"We'll work out all the details later. When is your flight?"

"I don't know yet. I haven't heard anything about the funeral arrangements. Have you?"

"No, I haven't. The news has been blasting all kinds of tributes about him, but nothing about the funeral. Did Dameon have a lot of family?"

"I've never heard him speak of his family. I really don't know."

"It's so sad. Ellen is beside herself. She was in love with Dameon."

"Is that a fact? She loved him, huh?"

"Yes, love to die for. She's a real mess. It's gonna take some time for her to get over this."

"I imagine it will. Well, let me go and try to find out something about the funeral. I love you, Robin, and I'll call you tomorrow with my flight details and everything."

"I love you, too, OJ. How is your brother doing today?"

"No change, but we're praying for the best, one day at a time."

Ridgemont Hotel

Weesee was on the phone with Sterling.

"What's up, Weesee? I thought we were cool? I guess you're my new boss, am I understanding this right?" Sterling was furious! His ego was crushed, and the tone of his voice was angry.

"You got it right, baby! I'm in charge. I run the show now at WBLK. I'm your boss! Funny how things come full circle sometimes, isn't it?"

"Weesee, really now, let's be fair. Just because I missed our date, you can't be serious about taking over my station and becoming my boss. Besides, where did you come up with that kind of money anyhow?"

"I'm very serious, Sterling. I'm the owner of WBLK, and as far as my money is concerned, that's none of your business. For the record, this has nothing to do with your standing me up for a date."

"Yeah, Wees, I bet. I know how you feel about me. You love me; can't do without me. You're just upset right now. We can work through this. Why don't you let me come over there and let's talk about it—work it out our way. Let me make this up to you."

"Sterling Powers, let's get one thing straight and this is for the record. Yeah I HAD a thang for you but don't swell up your head so big to think I, Elouise Prescott, can't live without you! Yeah, I appreciate all your help—maybe I could have loved you just a tiny bit, but your arrogant ass thinks a woman has to run behind you and lick your butt, well, you got that wrong. You're fired! How's that for loving you!" She hung up the phone.

Weesee was so mad she began to cry. She hurt too because he was right—she was in love with him. She cried for a little while, but then she caught a glimpse of her lovely tennis bracelet Malik had bought for her, and her tears dried up real quick. She began to smile as she thought about all the nice things Malik had done for her. She was really starting to feel for him. She realized she would miss him these next few days while she was gone up to Westchester.

"Hi, Malik baby, I've missed you today."

"My queen, Elouise. Good to hear your lovely voice. I've missed you as well. I'm cheesin', as you would say!"

Malik made her laugh. "I'm cheesin' too, Malik! Listen, sweetie, a friend of mine needs my help and I must make a short trip to visit her. I'll be leaving in the morning. Can I see you tonight?"

"What do you mean you'll be leaving?"

"I have to go to Westchester, New York, Malik. When I leave there you and I can hook up in Cancun or anywhere you'd like."

"Yes, Mexico. We can get married there."

"Malik, now listen. I have something I need to talk to you about. I need to thank you from the bottom of my heart for buying me the radio station. It was too kind, and it means the world to me."

"You are most welcome! For my bride-to-be, anything you want!"

"Damn, Malik! You're making me feel bad. You're too good of a guy for me!"

"Don't you feel bad, my queen. There is no reason. Anything you want is yours if I can buy it!"

Weesee started to cry, apologizing to Malik.

"I'm so sorry; I never meant to…" she couldn't bring herself to tell him how she'd used him so she hung up the phone. Malik was left stunned, holding the phone.

273

"My queen, are you crying? Talk to me. Please, are you there?" Malik got a dial tone.

Weesee took the phone off the hook so as not to receive his calls back. She was so hurt and ashamed of what she'd done. Malik was so good to her, but her heart ached for Sterling. How was she to tell Malik the truth after he'd been so generous to her? She felt horrible.

Meanwhile Malik was so confused he didn't know what to think. He was pacing back and forth—wondering what he could've done to make Weesee cry. He loved her so much. He kept phoning her room, but all he got was a busy signal so he cancelled all of his meetings for the rest of the day and asked his secretary to have seventeen dozen roses delivered to her hotel room in an assortment of colors. He chose the number seventeen because that was her seat number on the plane.

Malik slicked his hair back into his long ponytail, got dressed and had his chauffeur take him to Macy's to buy the earrings that matched the tennis bracelet. Then he planned to pay Weesee an unannounced visit. Whatever was bothering her, he wanted to know. Malik wanted his queen cheesin'. He loved it when she smiled, and it turned him on when she wore her glossy lipstick. Weesee had a beautiful smile, and he'd do anything to make it return to her face. No crying for his queen. No way. He was on a serious mission to take away all of her tears.

St. Michael's Hospital

"Yes, Mr. O'Neil all the tests have been completed. Congratulations, sir, you're a perfect match! Your son can live a normal life with your kidney."

"Thank God for miracles, Dr. Casey! How soon can we do the surgery?"

"I'd like to perform the surgery within the next few days. I'm meeting with your kids this afternoon to tell them of his kidney failure and of course the good news that he has a matched donor."

"You mean a matched anonymous donor, right? Please, doctor, don't reveal to them that I'm the one giving him the kidney. I have to be the one to tell them—I beg of you."

"Yes, of course, Mr. O'Neil. I can keep the donor information confidential. Should they ask, which they probably will, I will tell them the truth—that the donor wanted the information to be kept anonymous."

"I can't thank you enough, Dr. Casey. Believe me, in time they will know.

The main concern is my son's health. I pray that I can make a difference."

"Believe me, what a difference it will make. Your son will be able to lead a normal life, and he's fortunate to have a donor match. Patients have waited years to find a match. He's a lucky man, and you're a good father."

"Correction, doctor! He's a blessed man, and I love him! He's my boy!"

"Very well, Mr. O'Neil, can you come to the hospital tomorrow to sign all the necessary papers?"

"Yes, of course. Thank you again, doctor."

"You're very welcome. I'm sure your kids will be very proud of you when you decide the time is right to tell them."

O'Dell was ecstatic! He wanted nothing more than for OJ to get better and to do something to make up for not being there for him. He was beside himself with happiness. Fearing to be seen inside OJ's room, O'Dell passed by his door and said a prayer of thanks. He went back to his hotel room a very happy father.

Florida

"Mr. Malik, sir, there's a Barbara Jenkins on the line. Will you take her call?"

"Yes, please put her through." Malik picked up the phone as he rode in the back of the stretch limo on his way to Weesee's hotel.

"Yes, Ms. Jenkins, state the nature of your call, please."

"What? Malik you want to get business sounding on me all of a sudden? Why haven't you returned any of my calls?"

"Ms. Jenkins, I'm sorry I've been terribly busy. I do apologize. Is there anything I can do for you?"

"Yeah. You can tell that gold diggin' Weesee to step off! Malik, she's using you. She used you to get the radio station, and now she's gonna dump you and leave you hangin'. You don't need her. Besides, I was here before her. She planned this whole charade. She's gonna drop you like a hot potato—using an excuse to tell you that she found out about us having an affair. She never had any intentions of marrying you. She scammed you into buying the radio station only to later dump you."

Malik couldn't believe what he was hearing. He thought Barbara was just telling him this out of jealousy and to come in between him and Weesee. He cut her short—not wanting to hear anything further negative about the woman he had fallen in love with. He spoke boldly in Weesee's defense.

"Ms. Barbara Jenkins, my lady, there's no need to falsely make accusations about another woman's interest in me. Your opinion of Ms. Prescott's interest in me is of no concern of mine. Your worry should be my interest in her! She is to be my bride no matter what you or anyone else has to say of her. Do I make myself clear?"

"You gotta listen to me, Malik. Just hear me…" Barbara was yelling into the phone hysterically.

"Good day, Ms. Jenkins. This conversation is finished." Malik quickly hung up the phone.

Malik had his chauffeur drive him along the ocean shore before going to the hotel to see Weesee. He needed to think. He didn't want to believe there was any truth in what Barbara had told him. The limo was piled so high with gifts for Weesee that the driver could barely see out of the rearview mirror! He just couldn't be a fool for her.

Malik got out of the limo and walked along the water thinking about the past few days of how and when he'd met Weesee. The more he thought about her, the more he began to smile. He loved her no matter what, he decided. And with that, he walked back to the limo; his decision made.

"Let's be on our way to the Ridgemont Hotel. Take me to my woman, my queen."

Malik rode with hopes of Weesee telling him the truth. He wanted to give her a chance to be honest with him. "Pick up the pace, sir. My lady awaits!"

Westchester

Mr. Kimble arrived at Dameon's mansion early the next morning. He saw media cameramen taking pictures of the brick mansion. The media was everywhere covering the story of the multi-millionaire. Kimble looked on to see all the chaos. Soon a black stretch limo pulled up to the front door. Kimble sat straight up. He had no idea anyone was in the house. As the front door of the mansion opened, a tall, gorgeously dressed woman came through the door. She was dressed in a bright red suit with diamonds that glittered so bright, they reflected on the sun, which almost blinded Kimble. The woman was simply glamorous, elegant beyond words.

Kimble had never seen such beauty. The media crowded around her as she made her way out to the limo. Immediately Kimble got out of his car to hear what the woman was saying to the news media.

He got as close as he could to listen and heard the beautiful woman tell the reporters that she was the sister of the late Dameon Davenport. She said her name was Dominique Davenport, and she had arrived in from France after hearing of the tragic death of her brother. She spoke with a very sophisticated accent. She told one reporter that her brother wouldn't have wanted people to mourn his death but to celebrate his life. She also said red was his favorite color so that's why she was wearing it—in honor of him. Reporters swarmed the beautiful woman as she got into the limo and rode off. Kimble hurriedly took as many pictures of her as he could.

Kimble was amazed; shocked to know Dameon had a sister. He was even more shocked how she had gotten into the house without him seeing her, seeing that he'd been sitting in his spy post for the past few days. Hurriedly Kimble got back into his car and followed the limo to the Grand Hotel. He parked within distance of the stretch limo to take pictures of whomever this Dominique was meeting.

To Kimble's surprise, it was the woman who was at Dameon's house with the Mustang. Kimble zoomed in with his camera. As Alexis got into the limo, also dressed in red, she spotted Kimble in the distance with his camera. Kimble couldn't figure out what the relation was between the woman driving the Mustang, Dameon and now the sister who had appeared out of nowhere. Once again determined to put the missing pieces together, Kimble got back into his car, ready to follow the limo. He had them in eyeshot but lost them in traffic a few minutes later. *Something just wasn't right*, Kimble thought to himself. He couldn't quite put his finger on it, but he knew something very strange was happening before his very eyes.

Meanwhile, inside the limo, Alexis was praising Dominique on how gorgeous she looked.

"Dominique darling, you look fabulous! All dressed in your red! I love that suit, it's tight!"

"Thank you, Alexis. Later I'll have one made for you. I'm still a fashion designer, remember?!" They both laughed.

"Yes, of course you are. Did you take notice of the man standing across from the hotel taking pictures of us?"

"Actually I didn't dear; I was too busy fixing my makeup. The media has been flashing the cameras all morning. I gotta look fresh! Maybe it was one of those reporters from the tabloids trying to get a cover story."

"I don't think so, Dominique. I saw that man twice a few weeks back in the lobby of the hotel. I also found out he made an inquiry about me at the receptionist's desk—asking all sorts of questions. Who could he be and why is he on my trail?" Alexis was paranoid.

"I haven't a clue, dear. Maybe the man just likes what he sees."

"I don't think it's just that. There's something about him that gives me the willies. I just don't have a good feeling about him."

"Now stop thinking negative. I'm sure it's nothing. Fix your hair, dear, we'll be at my office soon. It'll probably be swamped with reporters. Remember, we have to represent in Dameon's honor. You're my personal secretary if asked any questions by the media. We just flew in from France after the tragic news. You got all that Alexis?"

"Yes, I've got it."

"Very well then, look pretty! We're here! Show time!"

Dameon and Alexis got out of the limo and were surrounded by cameras. Dominique was loving all the attention. Dominique shed a few tears as she spoke to the reporters about her brother's tragic accident, and then they went inside to collect all of Dameon's personal items. Once inside the office, they toasted on champagne.

Ellen's place

Ellen was still asleep. Robin looked on at the news coverage that was centered around Dameon. She couldn't believe how successful he was, how handsome, rich and giving. No wonder Ellen was in love with him—he had so much going for him. Robin flipped through the channels and finally came across a story that highlighted his sister. *It must be nice to have money*, Robin thought to herself. Dameon's sister, Dominique was dressed exquisitely and handled herself like a movie star with reporters. She cried as she continued to watch the tributes and think about poor Ellen. They would've made a gorgeous couple.

Just then the phone rang. "Hello."

"May I please speak to Ms. Berk? It's of an urgent matter."

"I'm very sorry, but she's resting right now. May I ask who's calling please?"

"Yes. This is Drake Kimble. Please have Ms. Berk contact me as soon as possible."

"Yes, sir, Mr. Kimble. I'll be sure to relay the message."

"Thank you kindly."

Robin took down the message so as not to forget. She didn't want to disturb

Ellen since she had been through so much and was now resting peacefully. The sun had finally come out and was streaming in the living room so Robin went over to draw the drapes. She looked out the window to see a man standing in the shadows looking up at Ellen's apartment. Hurriedly she closed the drapes. Her hands began to tremble, knowing the man was watching for her. Just as she picked up the phone to call the police, Robin's cell phone rang.

"Hello?"

"Hello, Robin? What's wrong? You sound like you just saw a ghost," OJ asked.

"Yeah, I'm okay, just a bit of the jitters, that's all. I'm sorry to say but this sudden death of Dameon has overtaken Ellen in a big way. I'm scared for her. I've never seen her this out of it."

"Relax, baby. You need to be strong for Ellen's sake. She needs you now and so do I."

"I will, OJ. I'm here for the both of you."

"I wanted to give you my flight information. I'm getting into Westchester at 6:00 p.m. From all the information I've gathered, the funeral will be the day after tomorrow."

"According to the news reports his sister wants to get it done and over with."

"Pardon me? Dameon has a sister? I haven't heard anything to this nature on the news here."

"Yes, OJ. Her name is Dominique. She's very beautiful, and she's been on our news here all day."

"Thanks, honey. Maybe she's staying at Dameon's house. The least I can do is call to give my condolences. We were good friends."

"Yes, you should. Sweetheart, you never mentioned Dameon Davenport's name before. How were the two of you friends? He was filthy rich I can see by the news reports. I had no idea what kind of life and influence this man had."

"We were college roommates and never lost contact over the years. Yes, Dameon was a very wealthy and powerful man."

"If you were so close, how come you didn't know anything about his family?"

"Honey, he was very private like that. You had to know Dameon to understand."

"Oh, I see. Well, his sister is a real knockout. She definitely knows how to play up to the media hype."

"Is she? Tell me, did Dameon and Ellen ever get together? You mentioned that she was in love with him."

"Yes, she adored him. She loved him so much he was all she dreamed of. They casually dated on a business level, but that's all I know other than her loving him deeply."

"I see. Poor Ellen. Dameon was a good person, easy for anyone to love—so giving and caring."

"Ellen spoke very highly of him, and by the news media accounts, I can see why. It's just one glowing praise after another."

"He was a wonderful person." AJ choked up and tried to hold back his tears. "I'll miss him terribly. He was one of my best friends, Robin."

"I'm so sorry for your loss. You must be really hurting right now." Robin begins to cry softly.

"I'll be okay, Robin. It's just an awful lot of pressure right now. Please forgive me for breaking down. I never meant to make you cry. That's twice I've said those words to you. Please forgive me, I'm so sorry."

"When you hurt, I hurt. I cry when you cry. I'm so sorry for you and for Ellen. My heart is aching for both of you."

"Sweetheart, I know I love you for being you. You stay close to Ellen, and we'll see each other tomorrow."

"Yes, I can't wait!"

Robin hung up the phone just as Ellen came out of the bedroom walking slumped over, holding onto her stomach as if she was sick. Robin rushed to her side.

"Ellen, please let me help you. You're weak. Lie here on the couch while I make you something to eat. You've got to get some food in you."

"He's dead. Dameon is dead! What am I gonna do?"

"You're going to take it one day at a time. For now you're gonna get your strength back before you get sick. Dameon cared for you, Ellen, and he wouldn't want that."

"Yes, you're right. I believe he did care for me."

Ridgemont Hotel

Malik was at Weesee's door knocking.

"My lady, please open the door! I know you're in there."

"Malik, please go! Go away. I can't talk to you right now."

"My queen, I will not leave this hotel until we are face to face. Why are you crying? Please let me see your face."

Weesee very slowly opened the door. Her eyes were blood red from her tears. Malik held her close and whispered in her ear. "I love you, Elouise Prescott. Why do you cry? I'm here for you. Let me in. Let me take away your sadness. Talk to me, my queen."

Weesee was so ashamed she couldn't look Malik in the face. She broke from his arms and turned to walk away. Malik pulled her back and looked deep into her eyes.

"Is there something you want to say to me, my queen? I am a man, and I can take more than you should bear."

"Malik, I haven't been up front with you about some things. I'm not the woman you think I am. I treated you like I have other men in my past, and I'm so ashamed of myself. You're such a generous, nice person, and I've taken advantage of you. I feel you don't deserve someone like me. I never had intentions of being your bride. These past days being with you I realized that there was someone in this world who can love me just for me. You never asked anything of me except my company. You've been like the perfect gentleman, and I like you a lot, but I can't go on letting you believe I'll be your bride. You deserve so much more."

"My beautiful Elouise, I know nothing of your past, nor do I care to know of the way you treated other men. One thing I'm sure of is how you make me feel, how I feel for you and most importantly, your being honest with me. I know everything, and I must apologize for the error of my ways as well. You see, I'd met Barbara Jenkins before you, but never meant to lead her on. Barbara phoned me and told me about your charade. I was hurt by her news, but I wanted to give you a chance to be honest with me. Thank you for speaking the truth. I cannot lie to you or my heart. My love for you is real. I'm going to ask you again. My lady, will you be my bride?"

"I can't marry you, Malik. I mean, I like you a whole lot, but..."

"But you're not in love with me, is that what you're saying?"

"Oh, Malik, I can love you—there's no doubt about it. It's just that I'm not ready. I mean I need more time. We just met, and marriage is supposed to be forever. I don't know if I'm ready for that or not. I'm sorry, I'm not the one for you. Please forgive me. I'm so sorry for what I did, and if you want the station back, I'll understand."

"My queen, I cannot force my love on you nor can I make you want me, but my heart tells me you are mine. As for the station, I gave that to you and it is yours to keep. My love for you runs very deep. Never in my life have I been so sure of anything. Yes, I forgive you. Love does hide a multitude of faults. If given the chance, I will be all that you want in a man. I will love you beyond what you can imagine, but I cannot make you want me. My queen, I'm sorry we are on separate pages. Please forgive me for wanting what I cannot have. I will leave you now."

As Malik turned and walked towards the door, Weesee called out, "Please don't go, Malik! Maybe we can work something out. Maybe we can grow into a committed relationship, but please don't go! I can't stand the thought of losing you altogether."

Malik turned to kiss Weesee. For both of them, it was a new beginning.

St. Michael's Hospital

Samone was dialing Sterling's number from her hospital bed.

"Sterling, I need to see you right away. We need to talk."

"Is everything okay, Samone? How are you feeling?"

"I'm feeling much better. I want to thank you, Sterling, for being there for me. You've always been very, very supportive. I guess it took this happening to see a lot I've failed to see up to now."

"Yes, of course, Samone. You know you mean a great deal to me. I'll always be there for you."

"You mean a lot to me, too, Sterling. Listen, about what happened between us. I want you to know I was in complete control of myself. I realize we made love, and I don't regret being with you nor do I want you to feel bad about it or my problem."

"It's good we're getting this out in the open. Please know I would never take advantage of you. You mean too much to me, Samone. I love you. Always have, always will."

Samone took a deep breath before answering. "I've felt for you for some time, and I've come to the realization I've only been fooling myself. I've been going through the motions with OJ in hopes of our relationship getting better. We've only been co-existing. Neither of us are happy. Everything built up on the inside of me, which caused this setback. Being as I am has made me face a lot of real feelings I've kept bottled up on the inside. OJ and I have to free each other from our pain. We've held each other prisoner to a love that died years ago. Sterling, I can't live a lie any longer. I have to confront the truth and free myself. It's you I care about, and I can't hide it any longer."

"Am I hearing you right, Samone? Do you know how happy I am to hear you say those words?! I promise you that I will and can be everything you want in a man if you will let me show you. Hell, why am I telling you this over the phone?! Woman, I'm on my way over there right now! I LOVE YOU!"

Meanwhile, in OJ's room Diane and Dr. Casey were meeting regarding his scheduled surgery. "Dr. Casey, I'll have to sign for OJ's surgery since my brother AJ had to go out of town on sudden business. I'll be sure to tell him how fortunate we were to get a donor for our brother. I believe our prayers have been answered. I'm believing OJ will come out of the coma soon. Thank the Lord for this kidney. I'm sure I speak for my entire family when I say we will want to personally thank the donor."

"Ms. O'Neil, I'm sure you'll have the opportunity to thank the donor in due time. For now, I'll need you to sign the release form for the surgery."

"You stated, doctor, that OJ will be able to function normally once the surgery is complete, correct?"

"Yes. With all success, your brother will function as if it were his own kidney. He's come a long way."

"I do see progress, Dr. Casey. I'm just believing God for him to wake up any time. Thank you, doctor, for everything."

"Tomorrow will be the big day. Surgery is scheduled for nine in the morning."

"I'll be here. Thank you for everything."

AJ was on his way to Westchester. Weesee had promised to return quickly to Malik's side, and she and Raine were on their way to Westchester as well.

While on a layover in Pittsburgh, AJ began to think about the day he had met Dameon on the bridge in France. The more he thought of him, the sadder he became. AJ kept thinking about Dameon's sister. How come he never made mention to him of a sister or any family for that matter? He wondered how much Dameon's sister knew of her brother's lifestyle or if she knew of him. AJ thought he'd take his chances of phoning her in hopes of expressing his sympathy before the ceremony.

"Good day, this is the Davenport residence. How may I help you?"

"Hello, is this Hilda the maid?"

"Yes, sir. This is she. How may I direct your call?"

"Hilda, hello, this is Aaron O'Neil. AJ. I was a good friend of Dameon's, and I was wondering if his sister was staying there at the house?"

"Yes, Mr. O'Neil, I remember you. Yes, sir, Ms. Davenport is residing here. Shall I call for her?"

"Please, Hilda. Thank you very much."

"You're very welcome, Mr. O'Neil. Please hold while I see if Ms. Davenport is available."

Hilda excused herself from the phone and knocked on the door of the den where Dominique was.

"Ms. Davenport, there's a gentleman by the name of Aaron O'Neil on the phone waiting to speak to you. He stated that he was a good friend of Mr. Davenport."

Dameon became very nervous when he heard Hilda telling him it was AJ. He wasn't ready to speak with AJ just yet.

"Hilda, please tell Mr. O'Neil that I'm resting at the moment, thank you."

"Yes, Ms. Davenport. I'll pass on the message."

Hilda went back to the phone to relay the message.

"I'm very sorry, Mr. O'Neil, but Ms. Davenport is resting at the moment. Such a tragedy for us all. Mr. Davenport was the kindest man to work for. Such a terribly sad loss…"

"Yes, of course, Hilda. My condolences completely. Please express my sympathy to Ms. Davenport as well, and let her know I'll be attending the funeral. I shall speak with her there."

"Yes, sir. I will give her the message."

Hilda gave Dominique the message. Dameon knew AJ would attend, and he was prepared to meet AJ as Dominique without him recognizing that it was him.

AJ's cell phone rang just as he hung up from the Davenport's. It was Diane. AJ's voice cracked as he answered.

"AJ, is that you? Are you all right? You sound terrible."

"Yeah, baby girl. I'm just fine. A little jet lag, I guess. What's wrong? Is everything all right?"

"Yes. Everything's fine. In fact, I've got great news! OJ has a matched kidney donor, and his surgery will be done first thing in the morning!"

"Thank God! Baby girl, that's fantastic! It didn't take very long to find a match. It's unbelievable! From what Dr. Casey explained, these things can sometimes take years. Thank the Lord for miracles! I want to personally thank the donor when I return. Maybe we can arrange something special for him or her. Do you know who it is?"

"No. I haven't met them yet. We can do something nice when you return. I'm happy this news cheered you up a bit. I'm sure you're going through some tough times with the loss of your friend and all."

"I'm dealing with an awful lot, but I'll be fine, Diane. My stay in

Westchester will be short. Right after the funeral I'll return home. Can you hold it together?"

"Yes, big brother, I've got everything under control. Don't worry about us. I'm still believing God for a miracle for OJ to wake up any minute. He's got a new kidney coming so that's a start."

"Don't worry, baby girl. He's a fighter. I'll be home as soon as I can. Hey, if you don't hear from me, call me after the surgery tomorrow to make sure everything went well, okay?"

"Talk to you soon, AJ. Love You."

Ellen's Place

Weesee and Raine had arrived. They were busy catching up.

"Robin, what the hell is going on? Girl, who's after you? You must have put some serious lovin' on somebody to make him crazy actin', stalkin' you like a fool," Weesee sounded worried.

"I haven't a clue who it is nor have I done such a thing. OJ is the first guy I dated since my divorce. I wished I could put an end to this madness."

"Robin wouldn't do anything to a soul so whoever it is must have some serious issues," Raine added.

"Yeah, you're right Raine. Robin, how long is Ellen gonna sleep for? That's too bad about her man. I really feel for her. She got lucky with him, he was loaded," said Weesee.

"Ellen's been out of it since the accident. She really loved Dameon. I had no idea he was that fine. I gave her a pill to relax her so she'll be out for a while," Robin said while pouring some lemonade for Weesee and Raine.

"Good looks and plenty of money all wrapped in one package! No wonder she's out of it. That would make me lose my damn mind!" Weesee continued.

"Is the funeral tomorrow then, Robin?" Raine asked.

"Yes, and I know Ellen won't stay away. She'll want to attend and pay her last respects for sure," Robin answered.

"Well, girls, we're there too then. We gotta back my girl on this. She needs all our support. Besides, I don't mind a good rich funeral! Never know who you might meet!" Weesee smiled.

"For sure," Raine replied. "What time is OJ arriving, Robin?"

"I pick OJ up from the airport at six tonight. You guys won't mind keeping an eye on Ellen would you?"

"Go handle your business, girl. We know you gotta make up for lost time with OJ. It's cool. We understand, don't we, Raine?" Weesee replied.

"Yeah. Go and be with your man, Robin. We'll look after Ellen."

"Thanks you two. I appreciate you both coming."

"Robin, you know you and Ellen are my girls! Raine and I had to come. Now go and get yourself pretty. It's already four o'clock, and you wanna make him lusting for you when he sees you. I hear he's quite a sight. Is he related to that real estate tycoon Aaron O'Neil by any chance?"

"I forgot to tell you, Weesee, that's OJ's brother," Robin said.

"I knew the name sounded familiar. When you said your man lived in Florida, I put the last names together. I met Aaron years ago at a party. The man is rich and fine as they come. I'll never forget him because he was running away from me! I was trying to hook him with my charm. Maybe it was a bit too much for him," Weesee giggled.

"I bet it was, Wees. When you go after a man, you go full force. You probably scared the poor guy!"

"Believe me, ain't nothing poor about this man with his fine self. I'd know him if he walked through that door this very minute 'cause he looks like money. Robin, is his brother loaded too?"

"No, Weesee. I just plain love him so much, money doesn't make a difference."

"Say no more," Weesee said.

"What, you goin' soft on us, Weesee?"

"No, Raine. I like sweet, but I like sweet with money better. Just like my Malik."

"Malik? Someone new, Weesee?"

"Yes, my new man. Maybe my only man. He wants to marry me, and I may accept."

"What? Marry you? Are you serious?"

Robin and Raine looked at Weesee's facial expression and saw that she was very serious about possibly marrying this man. They both were very surprised but ecstatic for her.

"Well, it's time someone stole your heart, Weesee!" Robin said.

"Congratulations Wees! This calls for a celebration!"

"Yeah, I'll toast to that!"

They opened up a bottle of wine Ellen had in the refrigerator and each drank a glass while Ellen remained asleep. Soon after Robin excused herself to go to the airport to pick up OJ. She couldn't wait for her friends to finally meet him.

St. Michael's Hospital

Samone is sitting up in the rocking chair in front of the window rocking. Sterling entered the room with a dozen of the most beautiful roses he could find. Their eyes met, and without a word, Sterling knelt down to kiss Samone. She stood to her feet, and they embraced in one another's arms. Neither could hold back the love they felt for one another. Sterling began to caress her hair as he gently moved his hands along her face.

Samone began to speak, but Sterling covered her mouth before she could utter a word.

"Baby, don't say a word. Marry me! Be my wife, Samone. I've loved you for way too long to let you get away from me now. Please say yes."

"Yes, Sterling, yes. I'm so happy! I can no longer hide from you, OJ or myself. I want to live, love and break these chains that have held me for too long. How can I do that—let go while OJ lay in a coma? I can't turn my back on him now, he needs me. Sterling, he has been good to me over the years. The love has faded, but I still care about what happens to him. I can't rush into anything until he's better. Do you understand that?"

"Yes, of course I understand, Samone. I'll wait for you no matter how long it takes. We're in this together. I want you happy, well and to be my wife. I can't tell you how long I've waited for this moment."

"Thank you, Sterling. Oh, thank you for staying with me while OJ recovers. There are still issues I need to deal with regarding my own health. The medication is working fine now, but what about later on down the road? Are you willing to go through setbacks with me, can you handle me in such a fragile state?"

Sterling reached for Samone's hand to hold, and then he looked straight into her eyes.

"Baby, did you not hear me say that I love you? You'll never have to worry about me leaving you alone. Setbacks or no setbacks. I'm in this for the long haul. Do you understand me?"

"Yes, honey. I love you, Sterling, more than you know."

"I love you with all I have to give. Now it's time for you to rest. You lie down, rest yourself and don't worry about a thing. I'm here to care for you, for now and forever."

Samone made her way over to her bed to lie down. Sterling stood right by her side, holding her hand and caressing her arm until she drifted off to sleep.

Westchester

Mr. Kimble sat in the tiny booth in back of the coffee shop where he normally met his clients. He had waited for several days for Ellen to return his calls. As he sat there waiting, he reflected back on the day he first met Ellen and how deeply she'd expressed her love for Dameon. He knew she must have been devastated by the tragic accident. He felt sorry for her. What a shame a nice looking woman like her got hooked on someone who'd never give her the time of day because of his celebrity status. *This could be my daughter*, he thought to himself. Desperately in love with someone who's not worth her time. He felt like he had to do something to ease Ellen's worries. He had to figure out what the connection was between Dameon, the woman in the Mustang and Dominique the sister.

His gut feelings were telling him something wasn't right. The only lead he had to go on was the photos he had taken of Dameon and the woman at his house getting into the car together, along with the photos of Dominique and the woman together. Kimble sat contemplating what the connection could be. He was puzzled, thrown off by the woman in the Mustang as she dated several other men he saw visiting with her at the Grand Hotel. All he could do was base his assumptions on what he saw. He figured the gorgeous woman in the Mustang must have had an affair with Dameon which didn't last very long because she'd been with other men while Dameon was out of town. The only thing he couldn't piece together was the connection between the woman and the sister. *Could it be the sister, Dominique, knew of the affair? Of course she had to know*, he thought. She wouldn't if the woman was her personal secretary. He sat sipping on his coffee trying to piece the puzzle together. Still clueless, he felt obligated to Ellen. He took out his notebook to write Ellen a letter of explanation with his findings and possible answers as to who he thought Dameon's mystery woman was.

He thought maybe she was no mystery at all. Maybe he was aware of her affairs with other men. Kimble wrote the letter with explanations of contacting her several times but was unable to reach her. He expressed his deepest sympathy of her loss along with the photos he took. He placed everything in the envelope addressed to Ellen. As he walked out of the coffee shop and placed the envelope into a mailbox, something in his gut told him to stop by the Grand Hotel one more time out of curiosity to see if he could get any information on the woman.

The Airport

Robin sat anxiously awaiting AJ's arrive his plane would land within the next thirty minutes. Robin was both excited and nervous.

Meanwhile AJ sat on the plane nervous about seeing Robin as well. How was he to react? Was he going to feel the same towards her? Did he really love Robin? All kinds of emotions were eating at him. He had been through so much, not to mention the loss of Dameon.

AJ thought about his brother lying in a coma, with kidney surgery scheduled for the next morning. He felt so responsible for everything that had happened. Despite his remorse at having to lie to Robin, he felt deep down if he didn't love her, he'd better continue to play the game at least for OJ's sake. *It's the game that caused all this trouble*, he thought. *If only I hadn't insisted it could be done; the switch between the two of us. I gotta be strong enough to eat my own words; I've got to play the role for both me and OJ.*

The plane was circling the area to land. Robin was waiting at the gate with a huge smile on her face. As AJ drew closer, AJ's heart was beating rapidly. The moment they saw each other face to face, AJ realized that he still loved her. They greeted with a kiss and embrace with a hug.

"Hi, baby. I'm so glad you came! It's great to see you!"

"And it's so good to see you, too, sweetheart!" AJ cuddled in close as they walked together to baggage claim.

Little did Robin know she had two men to contend with. AJ wasn't OJ, and Fred was sitting outside in his car, waiting for her. It seems he had followed Robin to the airport and was deeply troubled as to who she could be meeting. Fred had camped outside of Ellen's place for hours looking in from the outside, watching Robin like a hawk.

Parked just a few rows over from Robin's car, Fred was furious when he saw Robin and the same man who was in the picture walk from the elevator holding hands. He was so angry he picked up the knife he carried and began stabbing the seat with repeated thrusts over and over again. Fred was blind with anger. He looked on in rage as AJ opened the car door for Robin, got in on the driver's side and then started the car.

Slowly Fred followed behind them. He was right on their trail. The more AJ sped up, the closer he followed, and the angrier he became. AJ realized the person behind him was road raging so he sped up. Fred kept up with the speed and bumped him from behind. Robin was petrified.

She started screaming at AJ to slow down, but he kept speeding as they rapidly approached a railroad track. The railings were coming down, and the train was drawing near. AJ made it across the tracks before the rails were down, but Fred, who was traveling at an equally high rate of speed, didn't have enough time to stop. He was struck by the train and instantly killed. Robin and AJ looked on in horror.

St. Michael's Hospital

Samone went to visit with OJ. She realized she couldn't dismiss their entire life together and the family they shared. As she entered his room, she found him sleeping peacefully and her mind drifted off to the day they met and how much they had once loved one another. She stood beside his bed, tears falling from her eyes, and she began to talk to him.

"OJ darling, what happened between us? How did our love slip away? We've had a great life together. Two beautiful children, and you've been a wonderful provider for all of us. You're a great father, and you've always done your part. I've appreciated everything from my heart, but it's time we stop fooling ourselves. We can no longer hold each other in bondage like this. I know that you love me, but you're not in love with me nor I with you. It's so hard for me to say this, but it's very true. I want to be free; you need to be free. Our pretending days are over. We have to let go and live. I'm willing if you are…"

Just then OJ motioned and moved his eyes. He had heard every word she'd said, and in his mind, the angels in Heaven were singing "Hallelujah! Hallelujah!" This was music to his ears. Words he had been wanting to say for a long time, but had held back because he didn't want to hurt Samone. His eyes opened slowly, and he looked up at her as if to say, "Thank you! Thank you!"

Immediately startled, Samone yelled for the nurse. "He's awake! He's awake!"

She leaned over to kiss him.

At the Grand Hotel, Westchester

Kimble 's intuition led him to the lobby at the Grand Hotel. He drove up to the entrance, and through the huge glass doors he saw Alexis cuddled up close with a man. Kimble parked his car in front of the door and went inside to inquire about a room.

Alexis noticed Kimble immediately as he walked through the door and in her gut she knew something was up. As Kimble continued to talk to the receptionist about a room, Alexis slipped out the front door and into Kimble's parked car. She hid in the backseat, out of sight. Alexis had a shady past when she was Alex, and she knew it would one day re-surface. She thought Kimble was onto her for a crime she had committed years ago. Her nose could sniff out a P.I. anywhere.

Kimble abruptly ended his conversation with the front desk gal when he noticed Alexis had once again evaded him. *Darn that lady is a quick one,* Kimble thought to himself. *I must be getting old. It's all these hours I've been working, and I haven't listened to my doctor since my heart condition has worsened. Detective business was his life, and he sure wasn't going to give it up just yet.*

As Kimble pulled into his driveway and parked the car, many thoughts continued to swirl in his head. He still couldn't seem to shake his gut that something was definitely up with this Alexis. Just then, Alexis sat up in the back seat and scared the ever-living crap out of Kimble. She touched his shoulder and asked, "Hi, cutie, are you looking for me?" And with that sudden scare, Kimble's heart stopped. He died from a heart attack on the spot. Kimble was slumped over the wheel, so Alexis got out, flagged down a cab and headed back to the hotel as though nothing had ever happened.

The Funeral

Dominique, dressed to kill with a long black veil covering her face, sat in the front pew of the church as guests paid their last respects to Dameon. She couldn't believe the vast amount of people and media coverage. She was saddened by all the emotion expressed by the people who walked by the closed casket with Dameon's picture on top. The only person she looked for was AJ as she held onto a long white stem rose clutched in her hand, covered by black gloves.

As Dameon continued to watch the passers by, he was amazed at many who stood in line who never even liked him. *Look at all those sorry phony tears,* he said to himself. *How could they front like that?* He was amused by some of their actions.

Suddenly AJ appeared with a very attractive woman on his arm. Dameon's hands became sweaty in his gloves. This was the first time he'd seen AJ since his Florida trip. He knew he was going to come over to him to say something.

Sure enough, after viewing the casket, AJ made his way over to Dominique. Dameon made sure his veil was in place so that AJ couldn't see his face. How Dameon wanted to reach for him and take away his sadness. AJ approached Dominique.

"Hello, Dominique. I'm Oscar O'Neil. My deepest condolences. Dameon was a dear close friend. Please know if there is anything I can do, please call me. Here is my card. Please take it and call me should you need absolutely anything. And please meet my fiancée Robin." Dameon's hand trembled as he reached to greet AJ and Robin. He wondered why AJ would introduce himself as his brother. Then it dawned on him. It was the woman he was with. She was the one in the photo on his night stand. His heart was crushed. Apparently this woman was someone he loved. Dameon's heart ached. How could he have been such a fool? He felt sick to his stomach. At that moment he hurriedly excused himself.

"Please, excuse me, Mr. O'Neil. I'm suddenly feeling terribly ill. It's nice to have met you. Please excuse me," Dameon said as he hurriedly got up from the pew.

"Certainly, Dominique. Is there anything we can get for you?"

"No, thank you. I just need a few minutes alone and a breath of fresh air."

"Yes, of course. I'm terribly sorry."

Robin stood by AJ's side holding his arm. Dameon went to the restroom to get himself together. He was extremely taken aback.

Meanwhile Ellen, Weesee and Raine appeared. They stood in the receiving line to view the casket. Weesee and Raine held Ellen up since she was faint with emotion. Robin noticed her girls from across the room and went up to them. AJ stood waiting for Dominique to return. He thought Dominique was very attractive, what little he could see with the veil she wore to cover her grief. Just then Weesee called from across the room.

"Robin, over here! We made it!"

"Hi, everybody. Thank you for bringing Ellen. Are you feeling any better, Ellen?"

"I'm okay, Robin. I want to meet Dameon's sister. I have to say something to her."

"She just left for the restroom because she wasn't feeling well, Ellen. You don't look so steady on your feet either, my friend."

Ellen was shaking as the line moved closer to the casket. Dameon had composed himself and returned to his front row seat in time to greet Ellen.

"Robin, my baby is dead!" Ellen cried something terrible. Reality had set in when she saw the silk white expensive casket.

"Where's your man OJ?" Weesee asked Robin. Pointing across the room, Robin answered, "OJ's over there. I'm gonna introduce you to him when we go around."

For the next few minutes Weesee studied OJ like a hawk. Then she blurted, "Robin, you're kidding me, right? That's Aaron O'Neil. Girl, I'd know that face anywhere! Money! Money! Money! I remember Aaron like I'd met him yesterday, and to prove my point, he's got a birthmark on his hand in the shape of a dollar bill. I checked every inch of his body that my eye could see. That's Aaron O'Neil I tell you!"

"Weesee, now's not the time or place, but you've got my honey mistaken for someone else."

"Are you sure, Robin? Weesee ain't never missed a beat, girl," Raine interjected.

"I'm positive. I'll prove my point when I introduce him to ya'll," Robin replied calmly.

"Yeah, and I'll prove mine to you girlfriend. Check his hand, Robin. I'm positively sure. Look at him! He's gorgeous! You got yourself a real dime! If I wasn't your girl, I'd have to lay my charm on him!" Weesee teased.

"That's what ran him off if that's who you say he is, Weesee!" Robin chided.

"I'm sure that's him. Besides, those days are over for me. My man Malik is more than enough."

They all made their way over to the casket. Robin, Weesee and Raine all supported Ellen, who took one look at Dameon's picture and burst out crying uncontrollably.

Dameon looked on through his veil. He had to go to comfort her. He took Ellen in his arms and hugged her as she continued to cry like a baby.

"Now, dear, please stop crying. My brother wouldn't want you to be upset like this," Dominique said while patting Ellen on the back.

"I'm sorry. I loved him so very much. He was my boss, and he never knew how much I cared. I'm terribly sorry for you and your family's loss. My name is Ellen."

"I'm sure my brother knew in his own way, Ellen. Dear, if you need to talk or want anything, please call me. I'm staying at my brother's place."

"Thank you, Dominique. I'm so sorry. I should have better control over myself, but I can't help it."

"Don't apologize. I'm here for you, Ellen. I'm sure Dameon would want that if you worked closely with him."

"Thank you. Thank you very much Dominique, but what can I do for you? You're hurting as well."

"Be my friend, Ellen. I think we can comfort one another."

"Yes then, Dominique. I'll call you. Please excuse me for right now," Ellen said as she made her way out of the chapel with Raine. Weesee walked over with Robin to meet OJ.

"OJ, honey, I'd like for you to meet my dearest close friend Elouise. We call her Weesee."

AJ had his back turned, and as he turned to face Robin and Weesee, he was shocked to see Weesee again. He'd never forget that woman as long as he'd live. She'd literally tried to rape him a few years back. But AJ played it off, he was cool.

"Hello, Weesee, nice to meet you."

Weesee was whispering to Robin to look at the birthmark on his hand.

"See I told you, Robin!" Weesee interjected.

"Nice to meet you, too. Somehow I feel as though we've met somewhere before."

"No, I'm sorry. You may have confused me with my brother. The other O'Neil. We look very much alike."

Weesee looked at him very suspiciously. What were the chances of two brothers having the exact same birthmark on their hand? Weesee stared Robin down with her eyebrows raised.

"Yeah, OJ, maybe you're right as to say I don't believe you."

Weesee looked at Robin as if to say, girlfriend, you'd better do your homework.

"I'm going to check on Ellen and Raine. It's been my pleasure to meet you, OJ."

Happy she was gone from the picture, AJ asked Robin, "What did she mean by her comment that you'd better be doing your homework?"

"Nothing, OJ. It's just girl talk. That's Weesee for you. She likes you, I can tell."

Despite her feelings of overwhelming love for OJ, something inside of her snapped. She suddenly felt suspicious of him. After all, he had the mark exactly where Weesee said it would be.

AJ wanted to say goodbye to Dominique before leaving, but she purposely ignored him and busied herself with other guests. After waiting another ten minutes, AJ and Robin finally left. On the drive to the hotel AJ noticed Robin was strangely quiet.

"Robin, honey, is something wrong?"

"No, I'm fine, OJ."

"Well, my flight leaves in three hours, and I'm all packed. How about something to eat?"

"No thank you, OJ. You just got here, and we haven't had any real time alone to talk about us…the wedding…"

"I know it's hard, honey, but my brother just had surgery this morning. I told you I had to make this a quick trip, and I'd have to go back right away. I thought you were okay with that."

"I am, OJ. It's really not a problem…but…do you love me?"

"Yes, of course I do! Where is that coming from, Robin?"

"I need to hear you say it, that's all."

"I love you, my sweet Robin. Yes, I do really and truly love you."

St. Michael's Hospital

OJ and O'Dell both lay in recovery from their respective surgeries, which were both a success. Diane was waiting patiently to see her brother as Dr. Casey entered the waiting room.

"Ms. O'Neil, your brother is recovering just fine. Everything went very well."

"Thank the Lord! And he's out of the coma, too, I hear! It's a true miracle!"

"Yes indeed! Can you believe it? It must have been something Ms. O'Neil said to him because he came right out of it."

"And how is the donor, doctor?"

"He is recovering nicely."

"I'm so pleased! God is good!"

"Yes, he is—all the time! Good day to you, Ms. O'Neil. If you need anything, please don't hesitate to reach me on my pager, okay?"

As Dr. Casey left the room, Samone walked in.

"Samone, thank you for coming," Diane said while giving her the once over.

"You know I had to be here, Diane. I care for your brother."

Just then Diane reached for Samone's hand. "Do what you have to do, Samone. I'll always be your friend. I know I made it hard for you at times, and I'm sorry. Please forgive me and be my friend."

"I do forgive you, Diane. I'm sorry, too. Life is way too short." They hugged and both felt better about the future because they had made amends with one another. It was a new beginning for them both.

The nurse called them back to recovery, and as OJ slept peacefully, they both said a silent prayer. Diane asked the nurse if she could peek in on the donor. The nurse, not knowing it was a secret, allowed her to visit his room. Samone stayed with OJ while Diane walked into the next room. To her surprise, lying in bed was the man on the elevator a few weeks back who had asked her directions to the chapel. Diane gazed at the stranger as he slept. The more she looked at him, the more he reminded her of someone. But she couldn't quite place who it was. Diane said a silent prayer of thanks and as she turned to leave, she noticed his chart at the foot of his bed. She picked up the chart to make a note of his name so she could personally thank him.

She scanned the top of the forms for a name, and when she saw O'Dell O'Neil boldly written, she instantly dropped the chart to the floor and screamed, "It can't be. You're dead! You cannot be my father!"

As kids they had been told he had died, and as Diane took a closer look at him, it instantly came to her. This man lying before her resembled her brothers. Yes, indeed this was their father. Crying tears of joy, Diane couldn't wait to share the news with both AJ and OJ. She had so many unanswered questions. She knew in her gut that this man was indeed her father. She was frozen in place just staring at him. Again she thanked the Lord for his mighty blessings! Her brother was out of the coma, and her dad was alive after all these years!

Meanwhile a few miles away, Malik was busy with business, but he couldn't seem to get Weesee off his mind. He picked up the phone and dialed her cell.

"My queen. I miss you something fierce. I haven't cheesed since you left me, my love."

"I miss you, too. Once we're married, Malik, we'll always be together."

"Is that a 'Yes' my lady?"

"You're damn right it is, Malik. Distance makes the heart grow fonder, and once I left you, I realized how much I really do love you after all."

"You should see me cheesin', my queen! I'm coming for you!"

"Malik, now slow your roll, honey. My girls need me. We'll get together soon. I'll be back in just a few more days, I promise you."

"Oh, my sweet Elouise. You make me so very, very happy. You are my queen, my lady, my bride, my soon-to-be wife."

"I'm cheesin', too, Malik! I love you, too!"

Westchester

Dameon sat at home devastated when he finally came to terms with what he had done by faking his own death. He also realized that having the transformation wasn't a good idea after all. Apparently AJ had gone on with his life and had met the woman he wanted to be with. Somehow he was happy for him, but he couldn't tell him the truth, not after faking his own death. He figured he'd just remain being Dominique. Right now as he contemplated his life, he was mostly worried about Ellen. He had never seen her so depressed. He decided to give her a call.

Meanwhile, Ellen had just received Kimble's package upon arriving back to her apartment. She was furious as she looked at the pictures of Dameon with the beautiful woman. Her heart was aching because there had been someone else in Dameon's life. She didn't want to accept it until now. Kimble's pictures forced her to come to terms with it. She had gone from feeling sorry for Dameon and loving him to feelings of despise and loathing in a matter of minutes. In the midst of this, the phone rang.

"Hello."

"Hello, Ellen. This is Dominique, Dameon's sister. How are you, dear?"

"Not very well at the moment, Dominique. I just received some shocking news."

"I'm sorry to hear that. I thought maybe you'd like to come to the house for lunch tomorrow. I can have my limo pick you up."

"Thank you for the invitation, Dominique, but I'm not at all ready to come back into the house if you can understand where I'm coming from. It's just too fresh for me right now."

"Yes, I understand perfectly. We can eat somewhere out, then. I thought you might need to talk, and I can use the company."

"Yes. Yes. As a matter of fact I do. I need to ask you something about your brother if it's not a problem."

"I don't mind one bit. Shall I have my car come for you then?"

"How's tomorrow at eleven?"

"That's great. We'll dine at Lamarge. I hear the food there is excellent."

"That was one of Dameon's favorite places to dine."

"Like brother, like sister. I'll see you tomorrow, my dear."

The Airport

AJ's flight was scheduled to leave within the hour. He and Robin sat talking in the lounge. Robin had received a call from the police to verify what had happened at the train accident. It was at that time that the police informed her that the driver of the vehicle who had perished was Fred Dukes. Robin's face went pale in shock when she heard the news.

"Robin, what is it? You look like you've seen a ghost."

"The man driving that car who was killed by the train was my ex-husband, Fred. I can't believe it. He must've gotten out of jail and was stalking me. In a weird way, it totally makes sense all the stuff that's been going on."

"How could you have kept this from me, Robin?"

"OJ, I told you, I had no idea. I'm as freaked out about this as you are. First to find out he was the one stalking me, and now to find out he was probably going to kill us! He was a deranged man. Please let me put this out of my mind right now so we can concentrate on our future—not my past."

"Well, some day I want to hear all about it..." AJ replied while grabbing Robin's hand. She couldn't help but stare at the birthmark.

Trying to focus her attention on the here and now she interjected, "You know, OJ, with everything that has happened—you losing your dear friend, the drama with Fred, having to leave because of your brother's surgery and all, we haven't had one single moment to be alone. Not one time to slip between the covers and make love. Had the thought even crossed your mind?"

AJ turned to face her and looked her straight in the eyes when he expressed from his heart how he truly felt. "Robin, I wanted you the day I laid eyes on you. Of course the thought has crossed my mind about a million times, girl! Everything will be back to normal soon, and we'll spend the rest of our lives together making love, okay? Thank you for being so understanding."

"You're right, baby. I just need reassurance to know that we're okay. I mean that nothing has changed between us. You did say you wanted to talk to me about something earlier, didn't you?"

"Why would you think such a thing? There's nothing in this world that I need to say to you right now other than that I can't wait to spend the rest of my life with you. You are my soul mate, the love of my life. I love you, Robin. Nothing at all will ever change that. Now, stop worrying your pretty self about nothing. We're totally cool. You're stuck with me, baby!"

Just then they called for AJ's flight to begin boarding. They both stood up and walked towards the gate. Robin was teary-eyed as they kissed goodbye.

"No tears now, baby. Don't make this any harder for us. I promise we'll be together very soon." He held her close and kissed her passionately. Then they parted. AJ, remembering what OJ shared with him about not looking back as they said their goodbyes at the airport previously, continued to walk straight towards his plane. He had successfully played the game once more.

Ellen's Place

It was the next morning and Raine and Weesee were coming in from shopping. Ellen was coming out of the bedroom dressed to meet Dominique.

"That's my girl!" Weesee called out happily. "She's back, Raine! Ellen, girlfriend, I was so worried about you. Now you're back to looking like your gorgeous self. Where are you off to?"

"I'm meeting Dameon's sister Dominique for lunch."

"Great idea. Get in good with the family. I know you're still grieving over the loss of your man, but you never know, the sister might hook you up!"

"Have a heart, Weesee!" Raine chimed in. "You know how she felt about Dameon."

"Well, yeah, but he's gone now, and she has to live. Gloss those lips up, Ellen, put a smile on your face and work your stuff. Ain't nothin dead around here!"

Ellen gave Weesee a big sigh. Just then the doorbell rang. It was the limo driver for Ellen.

"My ride is here, girls. I'll be seeing you in a little bit."

"Have fun, and remember what I said. Work your stuff. You never know who's watching. Shake that bootie girl!" Weesee called after her.

On the ride to Lamarge, Ellen kept thinking about her last encounter with Dameon. She could hear him telling her in her mind how he was involved with someone. She wanted to find out from Dominique who the woman was in the photograph and ask why this mystery woman wasn't at the funeral service. Deep down Ellen felt responsible for his death. After all, she reasoned, if she hadn't come onto him, he wouldn't have left right away. She just couldn't seem to let go of her guilt.

Ellen was nervous as the limo pulled up to the curb outside of Lamarge. She could see Dominique sitting at a table as she walked up to the entrance. Dominique was dressed to kill in her tangerine suit with matching purse and shoes.

"Ellen, dear, please have a seat."

"Thank you for inviting me, Dominique. I haven't been myself since the accident. I miss your brother tremendously."

"Yes, I understand. Dameon and I kept in contact weekly by phone. He was a special man. Are you hungry, dear?"

"I think I'll have something light. My appetite hasn't been very good either."

"Come now, dear. I know you can't be counting calories with a figure like yours."

"No, it's not that at all. I just haven't felt much like eating. Somehow I feel as though my world has been crushed by the loss of your brother. He meant so much to me. I don't feel like eating, visiting with friends, working or doing much of anything."

"Well, you need food in your system to give you energy to get better and get out of this funk. How about if I order the Chicken French? It's delicious."

"Okay, Dominique, if you insist. You remind me of your brother. He had a take-charge personality and would always order for me, too. That's one of the traits I grew to love about him."

"Is that right?" Dominique smiled, trying desperately to change the subject. "Ellen, tell me what your plans are for work. You still have your position with the firm, and I understand you were one of the best marketing executives on the team. I'd like to keep you on."

"Thank you, Dominique. I hadn't realized you would be taking over in Dameon's footsteps. Dameon was such a motivator; he always helped me to do my best."

"Yes. Yes he did. Now, before we order, would you like a glass of wine, Ellen?"

"No, thank you. I'm on medication for my nerves right now."

Dameon looked at her and a sudden rush of guilt and sadness overwhelmed him. How he desperately wanted to comfort her. He tried so hard to get her off the subject about talking about him, but she kept going on and on. Dameon was thankful when lunch arrived. They sat in silence and ate. Then Dominique said, "Ellen, would you like to go shopping after lunch? Maybe that will relax you."

"No, I don't think so Dominique. Please forgive me."

"Not a problem, I understand. Would you care to ride with me to pick out my brother's tombstone?"

Ellen's face lit up.

"Sure! I'd love to go along. I'll help you pick something really nice. That's the least I can do."

"Ellen dear, what do you mean by that? You paid your respects; you've been a damn faithful employee. Why do you feel like you owe Dameon more?"

Ellen broke down and started to cry.

"It's because, Dominique, I'm the reason why your brother is dead!"

Dameon couldn't believe what he was hearing. He needed to know why she felt this way. Why she was feeling guilty for something she didn't do. He grabbed Ellen by the hand and took her to the limo to calm her down. Trying to console her Dominique said, "Dear, Dameon wouldn't want you carrying on like this. I know my brother well enough to know he wouldn't want any one grieving over him like this. Dameon had a great life; he'd want you to be happy. Now stop those tears, please Ellen, and smile in his honor!"

"I'm sorry, Dominique. You just don't know. You just don't understand."

"Help me, dear, so I can help you. We're gonna go to a quiet spot so we can talk. Here, drink this club soda. But please, no more tears!"

By this point Dameon was getting nervous. He had the limo driver take him to his private apartment downtown that no one was aware of. They arrived at the apartment and both went inside.

"Ellen dear, make yourself comfortable. How about some tea? This was my brother's hideaway place when he needed solitude."

Ellen's voiced trembled, "No thank you, Dominique." Her eyes were blood red from crying so much.

"Why don't you go into the restroom and freshen up a bit, my dear. Your mascara is running from your tears. You're way too pretty for such a sad face. Come! Come! Let me show you the powder room." Dameon literally pushed Ellen into the little room because her non-stop crying was about to drive him insane. He listened to her crying through the closed door and after ten minutes he pounded on the door and yelled, "Stop this crying right now, Ellen. You're gonna make yourself crazy. Dameon would be terribly upset with your actions!"

Ellen opened up the door furious at Dominique's insensitivity. She was getting sick and tired of everyone telling her to get over this and stop crying. No one understood what she was going through.

"Dominique, I loved your brother. You don't seem to understand. I was with him the night before he died in the crash. Had I not pushed him away he would still be alive. I killed him! I caused all this to happen. It's my fault he's dead! I'm the one to blame for all this. Why won't anyone listen to me!" she screamed.

Dameon, feeling both sorry and angry with Ellen, had had enough of her guilt. Before he realized what he was doing, he grabbed her by the arm and pulled her close to him.

"Ellen, look at me! Look into my eyes!"

Ellen stared into Dominique's penetrating eyes. Eyes she'd know from a mile away. Eyes of a man she loved. She saw Dameon's eyes.

"NO! NO! NO! It can't be you. You're dead!" Ellen screamed and backed up into a corner at the shock of seeing Dameon's eyes. Ellen flailed her arms at Dominique who had a firm grip on her, despite the fact that Ellen was totally flipping out.

"Listen to me, Ellen! It's not your fault. It's really me, Dameon. I had to do this. I could never love you or any other woman. I'm who you see before you. Don't you see I left the hotel because I didn't want to hurt you? I did what I had to do to save you. I care about you, Ellen. Please know that! You're a beautiful, talented woman and if I were a straight man, you'd be mine. You didn't kill me. I killed me to be who I am right now!"

"Let me go! Let me out of here!" Ellen screamed in terror. "How could you? You monster! How could you be so heartless! Do you realize what you put me through? How much I loved you? I loved you so much I hired a private investigator to find out who the woman was in your life. Lies. Lies. All lies!"

"Calm down, Ellen. You loved me that much? All you had to do was ask me, and it would've saved both of us a lot of grief. There was no woman in my life. Listen to me. I want what you want! It's a man I'm in love with. I'm sorry, but it's the truth."

"NO! NO! I'm not listening to you. I have the pictures in my bag. Why would you fake your own death, hurt people for your own selfish motive? How dare you be so cold?" She broke away from his grip and slapped him as hard as she could across the face. Dameon grabbed her and kissed her. She broke away from him yelling, "You're crazy! You're sick!" Ellen ran wildly out of the apartment, leaving her purse and the photos. Dameon took off after her, knowing that he had to catch her and talk to her. She must keep his secret…

St. Michael's Hospital

OJ was awake and recovering nicely from his surgery. Diane was sitting beside his bed, in complete awe of all the miracles that were happening—OJ's coming out of the coma, and their father being alive. She couldn't wait to tell

AJ the news. She looked at her watch. AJ's plane was due in any time. Just then the nurse walked in to tell Diane she had a phone call at the front desk. Diane guessed it was AJ. She couldn't wait to tell him the news.

"Hello?"

"Hey, sis, it's me. I made it back. How's OJ doing? How did the surgery go?"

"Big brother I'm so glad you're home. I have great news! OJ is out of the coma and he's talking! The surgery was a success. Hurry here! You're not going to believe it!"

AJ was ecstatic! How he desperately needed to make amends to OJ.

"I'm on my way right now, Diane! I can't wait!"

"Drive safely, AJ. And just so you know, I have another surprise when you get here! Hurry!"

Diane hung up the phone and went into O'Dell's room to see if he was awake. He was sitting in a chair when Diane walked into the room.

"Excuse me," Diane said.

O'Dell turned to look in her direction. Shocked to see her he said, "Hello."

"Hello. My name is Diane O'Neil and I know you are my brother's donor. I wanted to personally thank you."

O'Dell had a surprised look on his face, wondering how she had found out. He couldn't lie to her. "Yes, I am. How is your brother doing?"

"He's fine thanks to you. Why did you keep this a secret, Dad? Where have you been all these years?"

When he looked up at her, tears filled his eyes. "Diane, my baby girl, I'm very much alive and have been for years. You all were too young to know the details of my lifestyle. I was an FBI agent undercover. I got busted for a crime years ago when you all were way too young to know. I've been in prison all these years. It was a case of wrongdoing, a setup. Everything that happened, including my leaving you all, was just for protection. A day never passed without me thinking of all you. Look at you, girl, you're all grown up and lookin' just like your mom!"

Diane just stood there in disbelief. It was her father after all. She walked over to him and put her arms around him to give him a big hug. "I've missed you so much, Dad." She began to cry.

O'Dell held onto her as he kept repeating, "My baby, my baby. It's all right now. I'm here…"

Diane wept in O'Dell's arms like a baby. Meanwhile in the room next door, AJ rushed into OJ's room, anxious to make peace.

"OJ man, you gave us some scare. Man, I'm so sorry all this happened.

Please forgive me. I'm so sorry. I never meant to hurt you. I love you. You're the closest person to me. I prayed for this moment. Thank God for miracles." AJ shed a tear.

OJ's frail hand extended for his brother's hand to hold. His faint voice whispered, "I love you, too, AJ. You're my brother, and I forgive you. Please do something for me, AJ I beg you."

AJ leaned closer to OJ so he could hear him better.

"Anything, OJ, anything you want."

"Go to Robin and tell her the truth. Please, can you do that for me? She deserves the truth. God dealt with me, AJ, about my life. I have to make the wrong right. I need you to do this for me, okay?"

"Of course, OJ. I'm sorry for letting Robin come in between us. I'll tell her the truth. The whole truth."

"Thank you, my brother. I'm pleased. Now show me some love."

They hugged and held onto each other very close. As tears rolled down both of their faces, Diane walked in. She greeted AJ with a hug.

"Hey big brother! Look who's back!"

"Yes, God is good! I'd like to thank the donor for OJ's kidney."

"Me, too," OJ replied.

"Well," Diane started. "There's no time like the present. But first, I have a surprise for you both. Remember when we were kids how we'd always said we wished and prayed that Dad hadn't died? How we would never tell the other kids our daddy wasn't with us?" Diane started to cry. "How we loved Dad so, missed him and…" her voice choked up.

"Yes, Diane. Where is all of this going baby girl? Why the tears? What does our so-called father have to do with any of this?" AJ interjected.

"I know how you feel, AJ. You've always been angry for Dad's absence, but you have to get over that. He loved us more than we ever knew; more than we realized. Aaron and Oscar, our dad was the donor of this kidney, and he's just outside in a wheelchair waiting to come inside. Will you both open up your hearts and receive him?"

OJ and AJ looked at Diane in complete shock. OJ slowly sat up in the bed. "Hell yeah! Let my dad in here!" OJ called in a strong voice.

O'Dell was pushed into the room by the nurse, and they all embraced before a word was even said. No eye was dry in the house.

In the coming days, O'Dell made it straight with his two boys and daughter. Life was beginning anew for them all. God had answered their prayers and brought them together as a happy, healthy family.

Westchester

Dameon caught up with Ellen who was totally devastated and wanted nothing to do with him. She vowed never to tell anyone of his secret. Even though he'd crushed her heart, she never stopped loving who she knew the real Dameon to be. Within days Dameon left town with Alexis to live in France. He started a new life, putting the past and all the hurt behind him.

Ellen, left behind with the shattered memories of a man she never really knew, took a leave of absence from her job to get her life in order. The whole ordeal put her into shock, and she needed intensive counseling and time to get over both Dominique and Dameon.

AJ arrived in Westchester without Robin even knowing he was coming. Somehow he felt telling her the truth would be a weight lifted off of him. Yes, he loved her, but he loved his brother and wanted to keep his promise. God had blessed him, spared his brother's life and had given them back their father.

During the limo ride to Robin's house, AJ thought about Dameon and how he couldn't return the love he sought. He looked out of the window as the limo pulled into Robin's driveway.

As he exited the car, AJ took a deep breath. He was ready to make his wrong right. He walked to the door and rang the bell. Robin opened the door and was so happy to see him; she smiled from ear to ear. She hugged him tight. AJ kept his hands to his side and didn't return the hug.

"Baby, let's go inside. We need to talk."

They went inside and closed the door.

"What a fantastic surprise! What's going on? Why didn't you tell me you were coming?"

"Robin, honey, sit down. We need to discuss something very important."

"Talk to me, OJ. Tell me, what is it?"

"Please know that I do love you first and foremost. From my heart, I really do. I fell in love with you the first day I laid eyes on you. Please believe that. You made me realize what true love really is."

"Of course I believe you," Robin comforted him. She looked deep into his eyes and was aware he was deeply troubled. "Are you all right? Is it your heart? Please tell me, OJ."

"Listen to me Robin, before you say anything else. I'm not the person you think I am."

"What do you mean by that? What are you saying to me, OJ?"

AJ stood up and walked in front of the fireplace. Dressed in a gray Italian suit of expensive taste, he paced back and forth.

"Robin, I'm a twin. My brother and I are identical twins. You fell in love with my brother OJ. He was the one you met at first. You both fell in love. I'm Aaron, my brother's identical twin. OJ couldn't bring himself to tell you the truth that he lived with a woman for years. She was the mother of his two children. Their relationship had died long before you came into the picture. He met you and fell in love and by then, he was in too deep to tell you the truth. That's when you came to Florida. He didn't want to disappoint you by calling the trip off, but the woman he lived with had planned a trip for the two of them that he couldn't back out of so he and I schemed a plan. I took his place to be with you in Florida while he took his trip with Samone. He did this because he loved you, Robin. He's never, ever been in a situation like this nor did he want to let you go. In the process of all this game playing, I fell for you too. I'm so sorry. We never meant to cause you any pain. OJ has been the one in the hospital for the past month. He's out of his coma and his kidney transplant surgery was a huge success. He loves you more than life, Robin. He asked me to come up here to tell you personally and to set the record straight. Please forgive us both. We were wrong."

Robin was numb; she couldn't say a word. All she could think about at the time was Weesee. Weesee had been right all along. Suddenly Robin became frantic. She slapped AJ in the face and told him to get out. "Get out of my house, you bastard! How could you? Get out of here before I call the police!"

AJ tried to reason with her. "But Robin, I care for you. OJ did this for you. Please understand."

"'Get out,' I said. Out of my house right this minute!"

AJ was devastated. With his head hung low, he got into the limo and asked the driver to drive. He needed time to think.

Robin laid on the couch crying endlessly. She was terribly confused and angry on top of it. She felt betrayed. There were so many emotions rolling around in her head. She wanted to die. *How could he do this to me? How could they do me like this?* She realized at that moment how Ellen must've felt. She cried and cried. Who did she love? She couldn't tell the two of them apart since they looked so much alike. She felt so stupid.

Meanwhile AJ rode for miles in the limo. By this point he was out of the city limits and riding through the country. He was broken hearted. Although he had done the right thing, it still hurt in the pit of his heart. AJ spotted a bridge where he asked the driver to stop. He figured he'd get out and clear his head for a bit. He had plenty of time to spare since his plane wasn't due to leave until later that night.

As he slowly walked across the bridge, he picked up stones from the walkway and shot them into the water. He continued to walk; it felt good in his soul to be out in nature. As he neared the end of the long bridge he saw a woman standing close to the edge, as if she was going to jump. AJ ran to her. It was Ellen.

"Hold on! Please don't do it! It's not worth it," he called out to her, running frantically to stop her. "Don't jump!" he gasped, out of breath from running and pulling her into his arms.

"I beg your pardon? Please let me go! It's none of your business what I do."

"But nothing is worth throwing your life away for…" AJ looked deep into her eyes.

"Don't I know you from some place?" Ellen asked AJ, thinking his face looked mighty familiar.

"Aren't you Robin's girlfriend Ellen from the funeral?"

"OJ? Is that you?"

"Well not exactly. I'm OJ's twin brother Aaron. I'm AJ. That's what everyone calls me." AJ stared at her. She was beautiful as her hair blew in the wind.

"Well, AJ, I wasn't going to jump even though I damn well felt like it. Life is such a bummer. I'm so tired right now…"

"You're a beautiful woman, Ellen. Life can't be that bad."

Ellen looked at him; she thought he was very handsome. She smiled.

"Look at that smile. It's worth more than all the sour lemons ever dealt your way. I'd be honored if you'd have dinner with me, Ellen. I can use the company and you look like you could use a friend. Please say you will."

"Why not. I sure could use a friend about now."

There wasn't a moment of silence between them from that moment on. They hit it off just right, as if they were destined to meet.

Meanwhile, Weesee was busy talking some sense into Robin. "So what they played you. It's obvious the man did it because he loves you. You mean to tell me there's two of those fine brothers walking this earth?"

"Wees, come on now. It's not about looks or money. I've been abused."

"Abused my ass! Do I have to come back to Westchester to hit you over the head for a light bulb to come on in that brain of yours? Girl, that man loves the hell out of you. Stevie Wonder can see that. Now, are you gonna sit there mourning in your own pity or are you going for your man?"

"I can't, Weesee! I feel so betrayed...so used..."

"So be it then, your loss. Tell me. Is the brother loaded like Aaron? Does he have money, too?"

"What does it matter? It's over. I never want to see either of them again."

"Yeah, I guess it doesn't matter if he does as long as you're in the family. If they are twins and close like you said, if one has loot the other does too, but you're right. That don't matter to you anymore. You stay by yourself, Robin, if that's what makes you happy. But if I were you, I'd be on the first plane flying to get my man. I got mine. Me and my baby Malik are getting married! I'm here for you, girlfriend, when you need to talk."

It took a few days, but Weesee's advice sank in. Robin realized she did love OJ so she booked the next flight to Florida.

OJ rested comfortably in the room all alone. All his family had visited with him and gone home for the evening, and he laid with his back turned away from the door thinking about Robin. AJ had explained to him how she had taken the news. OJ felt broken hearted. The last thing he ever wanted to do was to hurt her. He prayed endlessly for her pain, asking God to touch her heart and for her not to hurt or feel bitter towards him or any other man. Somehow he felt she'd get over it and go on with life, but he'd never see her again. He was all alone. He and Samone had agreed to let go. As he continued in his prayers, he heard a soft voice calling his name.

"OJ....OJ...I just had to come. I'm here, OJ."

OJ turned around to find Robin standing in the doorway. He couldn't believe his eyes. As she walked towards him, she looked deep into his dark brown eyes as tears filled hers.

"Why couldn't you be honest with me, OJ?"

"Robin, baby, had I told you the truth about Samone, you never would've given me the chance to know you. The day I laid eyes on you when I serviced your furnace, my heart spoke to me. I had to know you. Please forgive my stupidity. I never meant to hurt you or make you cry. I love you, Robin. Always have and always will until my dying day you'll be planted in my heart."

Robin was speechless. Her love for him was what made her go to him. It was too strong to let it go. She walked towards OJ, climbed on top of his bed, snuggled close to him and whispered in his ear, "I've loved you with an everlasting love. I forgive you."

They cried together and then they kissed for what seemed like eternity. They held onto one another in silence for hours, just embracing a love that was meant to be. OJ held her tight, never to let her go. He looked toward Heaven, thanking God for everything. Robin snuggled in his arms like his sweet baby as he whispered in her ear, "Marry me, Robin and be my wife!"

"Yes! Yes!" she answered.

Months later they were all married together in the same church. OJ to Robin, Weesee to Malik, Samone to Sterling and believe it or not, AJ to Ellen. It was the biggest wedding ever. As they all said, "I do" in unison the church bells rang and rang. Robin looked up at the bells with a smile. The sound became louder and louder. That's when she reached over to shut off her alarm clock. It was the sound of the alarm ringing in her ear.

She sat up in the bed, shook her head and then reached over for her husband. She shook OJ awake. "Honey, wake up. I gotta tell you about my dream. You were there; almost everyone I care about was in it. It was so real..."

It was all an illusion of the heart...

The Illusion

Felt so bad I forgot how to cry…
Couldn't think straight, it was like I was high…
Laid down to dream, saw me looking in the mirror…
Images and feelings never seemed clearer.
Looked in the mirror, started thinking on the past…
Memories going by they were going real fast.
Saw just about everything that I ever went through…
Saw everything I did and what I do.
Saw interrogation, saw determination
Saw sensation and saw what was the cause of separation.
Started to get mad, started to get sad.
Saw stuff that was bad, and some stuff made me glad.
I saw that dreams come true.
I saw dreams are not made by one but with two.
Saw people who in my heart they had their own place…
But they seemed strange; I hardly recognized their face.
I still fail to realize why did we have to depart?
Why did you have to leave me with this broken spirit and broken heart?
Heard everything that I ever said…
Saw when I woke up and slept in bed.
Saw that my love was like an injection…
Saw everything from my reflection.
Thought of something special and I saw I was crying.
Thought of losing something and I saw I was dying.
Thought I was crying for somebody who I care…
But when I wiped my eyes, nothing was there.
Started to worry and be full of fears…
I never knew I could cry so many tears.
Sometimes I searched for a love I'll never meet.
I failed to realize that love was always at my feet.
So why, why did you leave me?
Why did we have to depart?
Why am I feeling as if it were all an "Illusion Of My Heart?

Loretta Heard and Alexis Wilson

Printed in the United States
57889LVS00008B/26

9 781424 117093